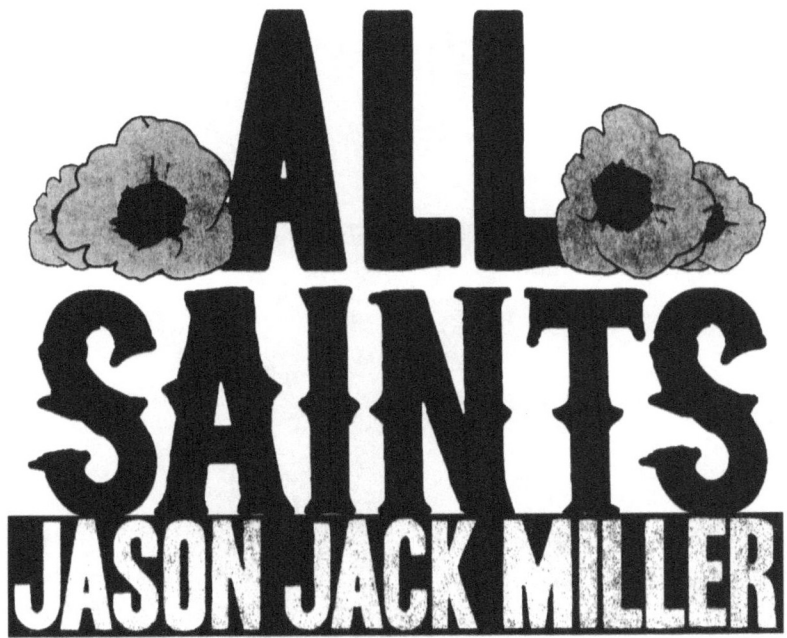

ALL SAINTS

JASON JACK MILLER

RAW DOG
SCREAMING
PRESS

Published by Raw Dog Screaming Press
Bowie, MD

First Edition

Cover: Jason Jack Miller www.jasonjackmiller.com
Book Design: Jennifer Barnes

Printed in the United States of America

ISBN: 978-1-935738-99-2
Library of Congress Control Number: 2017953618

www.RawDogScreaming.com

*Back in the summer of 1998, I got to know
some newlyweds who lived in an apartment off Westwood Boulevard
in Orlando. Having just arrived in Florida, they were a little scared, kind of
idealistic, and very much in love. The rest of the details are a little fuzzy, but I do
remember that they craved a life filled with adventure and magic above all else.*

And that they both wanted to write.

This novel is dedicated to them.

*This book is also dedicated to the memory of the little panther that slept in our
bed for the last thirteen years. Puddahs, you will always be in our stars.*

ALL SAINTS

Nobody made a sound. Even the wind that whistled out of the mountains west of Kandahar dwindled to a whisper. SPC Xavier Green pushed onto his elbows and scanned the trees next to the school.

The snap of an AK sent X scrambling into a drainage ditch that ran between the bright red poppies and the road. "Too fucking close. There are twenty eyes back there, and I just need two of them to get on that sniper."

"Indirect fire incoming. Get down. Get—" SGT Eric Yama kept his mouth open as an 82mm mortar round exploded in the field twenty-five yards out.

Xavier shook his head to clear his ears.

"Came from the left of the school." Yama slipped behind the wall and raised his rifle. "X—get the rest of those fucking kids back here and suppress."

X said, "I can't see shit from down here, and if I can't see, I can't move."

More gunfire ripped through the dry air. Three of the children who'd fallen to the ground when the mortar hit broke for the compound. The smallest—a young Pashtun girl wearing a rose-colored scarf—stopped to pick up books the others dropped.

PFC Zack Jackson strayed from cover to round up the kids, but an older boy and girl who had been cut off by the field of fire refused to move. Zack pointed at the compound and shouted, "Zmaa sara raaza," but they remained hidden in the poppies.

Yama turned to the men in the other fireteam. "We need to suppress all the way up this west side until the air support gets here."

Another mortar exploded in the field, much closer this time. Zack dove for cover.

Yama spit the dirt out of his mouth and wiped his eyes. "Really motherfucker?"

"They're hitting us from two angles, sir," X said. "Twelve o'clock and...fuck if I know. Nine? From these fucking scrubby trees all along the left."

"Well, something's hitting the fucking corner," Yama said. He turkey-peeked to get a visual, but a volley of return fire hit just inches from his face. He dropped to his knees.

X said, "Sir, you tell me where it's coming from and I'll light 'em up. I got three hundred left."

Before Yama could reply, Zack yelled, "Get down. They're hitting that fucking corner again."

Dogs barked from the back of the house. A woman screamed out her little girl's name. "Uzhmakai...."

Then a moment of silence.

Another round of fire came from the trees. Clumps of clay exploded out of the wall behind Zack's head. "They're moving southwest, sir."

"Yeah, well this shit's making my ass sweat." X cocked his head, put his eye up to the scope, and released four short bursts. He waited, then released another. "I see them. They're stretched out in those trees. Trying to flank us. But I need eyes."

Zack kicked a hole in the western-facing wall with his boot and fired into the scrub. "It's because there are at least two clumps of those fuckers. Maybe three. Got eyes on the second but not the first. Looks like they're trying to spread out our fire."

X stood and sprinted down the trench to get a better angle on the lead group.

Yama said, "Stay close, man. What the fuck are you doing?"

He hit the dirt with a thud when a small burst from an AK clacked in the thicket. "Yeah, yeah. I'll be down in this jawn if y'all need me."

Yama said, "Zack—get out there with your fucking man and suppress."

Zack ran a few yards, knelt and fired. The insurgents in the first group disappeared into a ditch which ran west between the poppies and a cornfield. X could only see the tops of their heads through the rows of bright young plants. He fired again then returned to cover.

Yama said, "X—you and Zack fall back. We got air support in two."

Zack responded immediately, backpedaling as he watched for movement in the brush. X ran farther into the poppies.

Yama said, "What the fuck is he doing?"

But X never hesitated. He just plowed through those bright red flowers, probably wondering how much each stem would be worth in real cash money on Woodrow back in Chester, figuring just a few pounds of that shit in his A bag would fill his closet with old school Jordans and New Era Strap Backs to match for a year.

That's what's up, he probably thought.

Yama opened his mouth to yell again, but quickly shut it when X took a knee to help the last two kids to their feet. The boy oriented himself and ran toward the wall. Uzhmakai wouldn't budge, though, and remained curled within a furrow. When X picked her up, she clasped her hands behind his neck and cried into his Kevlar.

Zack said, "Covering," as X dropped his head and ran.

Someone from the other fireteam said, "Hustle up, now," and laughed.

Yama slapped X's shoulder when he came past and said, "Take cover. We got birds in sixty."

The girl's father collected her without a word. But instead of retreating indoors, they all went southeast, toward the center of the village. Men, women, and children looked back over their shoulders as they scurried through the poppies. X watched them carefully navigate the plants, knowing damn well they'd never see more than a few dollars for all their efforts. Just like on Woodrow, back in Chester.

"Thirty seconds." The distant whoosh of inbound planes made Yama pause. "On your feet, kids."

X smiled when the Warthogs fell into the valley. Their shadows raced over the green fields and dusty wadis. "Got eyes on 'em."

"Listen," Yama said. "We absolutely have to hit these fuckers as soon as they scatter. I want to break east real fast and I don't want to give them a chance to regroup—"

But the rest of what he said got lost in the rip of the A-10's rotary cannons. Clouds of smoke and dirt flew from the trees to the left of the school, followed by a flurry of red flower petals that hung in the air forever. The planes quickly completed their run and circled against a backdrop of snow-covered mountains.

Before Yama could give the order to move out, the compound erupted in a spasm of smoke and noise. The explosion knocked Yama and Zack to the ground. Daylight turned into dusk as fist-sized pieces of clay rained down. Small arms fire poured through the burning gap in the northwest corner of the wall.

The squad responded with a heavy barrage of their own. An unwavering torrent of lead. Spent brass casings piled up like drifting snow.

"Reloading."

The insurgents were so close X could hear them shouting to each other, but really they were just shadows at the edge of the smoke. Like ghosts manifesting in a dream. As soon as Yama gave the order to fall back, the Warthogs lined up for another run.

"Reloading here."

When Yama saw that their new flight path came at an angle nearly perpendicular to their first pass, he yelled, "Take cover. Take cover," and pushed Zack to the ground.

The planes spit lava right into the heart of the old school. The 30-mm rounds bisected the poppies along a trajectory that ended at the squad's position. The clay walls crumbled like a sandcastle in the rain.

Yama yelled, "Check fire. Check fire," into his radio, but couldn't do a fucking thing to keep his guys from being hit. He shouted because it was something he could control. The insurgents from the trees to the left of the school capitalized on the error and charged through the poppies. Yama took aim and released a controlled series of shots. "ETAC. We need those Hogs to check fire."

"Medic."

From within the smoke, somebody else repeated the call. "Medic."

"Fuck." Yama shook his head. "Let's fall back to the LZ for a medical evac."

"I need some hands here." Zack said, "Medic."

Yama said, "X—I'm going to need you to lay down some cover so we can bug out to....what's that LZ?"

Zack shook his head. "X is down, sir."

"Down?"

"Down." Zack stared at the blood on is sleeves. "I fucking hate this place."

"Then what?"

"I don't know. I couldn't read anymore of that government bullshit. But just because it's the official report doesn't mean it's the official truth. Only they know what happened that day, right?" My temples throbbed. "And none of them are alive to talk about it."

"There's nothing you could've done, Ben. It's difficult to accept, but—"

"I could've fucking been there and tipped the scales. I could've taken my vitamin C and drank my cough syrup and got my ass out of bed and been there."

"You had pneumonia."

"Did I? Or maybe I just had a really bad sinus infection?" I made a fist and pressed it into my head. "I always figured I'd be able to rise to the occasion and I should've been there, Dani. Instead I was recovering in a bed with a fucking IV in my arm."

"It's not your fault."

"Maybe it isn't. But it sure feels like the universe is shitting all over me."

"The universe doesn't make mistakes, Ben. You know that."

Even though she said it too low for me to hear, I saw her mouth the words, "And I know that too."

ONE

Ben slept while I couldn't. He hadn't yet learned that sleep couldn't free him from his cage.

Whereas I had.

A very long time ago.

And I haven't slept since.

The wet horizon swung from the empty north of our pasts to places too remote to appear on maps. Just over the bow, high clouds reddened as the sun set beyond the Americas.

Behind us, dusk turned into night and starlight grew like grass on the water. Our course ran southwest, first to Mexico for supplies, then on to Costa Rica. We'd convinced ourselves that as long as we kept the road beneath our feet and possibility ahead of us, we still had a chance to find happiness with each other. But now that we were at sea, with the scent of the Tropic of Cancer in the breeze, memories of the life we left behind hung in the air like drunken fireflies, as if the concrete itself were solely responsible for our contentment.

As a girl, I saw the universe no matter where I looked. The glassy stars that floated above the jagged border of beech and birch that embraced my father's fields found me no matter where I slept. How I yearned for the stories they told, and dreamed about the day I'd finally be able to rearrange the stars to tell the stories of my own. They were simple desires, immature and full of innocence. An escape from the darkness that poverty and famine had created for my family. But instead of endless possibility, the heavens seemingly offered only loss, heartache, and war for me, and I resolved to do more than just listen to their chatter. The absolute sky refused to hear my ideas about the way my story should be told, so when I left home I'd turned my back on it for good. The time for passivity had passed.

I had to learn to write my own stories.

None of them ever ended happily though. Conflicts went unresolved. The antagonists always emerged victorious. Supporting characters never made it through to the epilogue. I soon learned that trying to write my own fate made me feel as helpless as trying to rearrange the stars had.

But tonight I just wanted to see Sagittarius and the Milky Way reflected in the sea. A reminder of the things I used to believe in. Bread just out of the oven, or the smell of Père Tanguy's shop. Instead, I could see only cold lights in the water.

Anymore, whenever I wrote *Once upon a time...* the story slipped away from me after a few chapters. This one felt no different.

It began with a woman nursing a broken heart, and clinging to the damaged soldier she thought could repair it. She never denied that she'd hurt people. She'd only just admitted that after a very long time. But the pain she'd inflicted over the years returned to her tenfold. She learned to eat alone. Stopped savoring the taste of food. The sound of music and laughter. The soldier didn't know what that meant, but wanted to help because it seemed like a way for him to live externally, outside himself.

And for the longest time, their story was about simply surviving together.

Living on wine and whatever they could pull from the ocean way down on Hatteras Island where nobody could find them.

Always far from his family and anybody else they didn't want to see hurt by the collateral damage of their collaboration. But the avoidance had taken its toll. Worn them out. Food wasn't a pleasure for them anymore—just calories and energy. Music became a sad reminder of everything they'd left behind.

They'd tried cities, mountains, deserts. Small towns and ghost towns. Soon enough, they'd run out of places to run.

And that was how they ended up on Reynard Bertrand's boat, Remedios the Beauty, *bound for Cozumel.*

She thought she could rewrite her story by starting a new one. As she always had.

He thought he'd finally found the woman who could save him from himself.

And for the moment, at sea, they felt safe.

"Tell me about the good wars?"

A nightmare had taken Ben's breath. For a long time, he spoke to reassure himself. To remind himself that he still lived.

He said, "Hemingway and all that? People romanticize the past, right?"

"There is no such thing as a good war." I ran my fingers through his hair and said, "There's only war."

"The diesel reminds me of Kuwait. We sat around for days wondering what waited for us on the other side of that line in the sand. Never would've guessed in a thousand years I'd be more worried about homemade bombs than the Republican Guard."

"You can't change the past, Ben, but changing a memory is easy. Biographers could write a version of your life that even you wouldn't recognize. We are in a new world, with new rules. From now on your story will include an entirely unique point of view, and this is why you can't trust your memory." I leaned forward and kissed his forehead. "We are on a boat, a thousand miles from land, five thousand miles from that desert and your past."

He said, "I need something to help me get back to sleep," and reached for his Klonopin.

"It's not time yet." I guided his head back to my lap and pushed my bag beyond his reach. "I will help you get back to sleep."

He watched the stars as I sang the lullaby that my mother sang to my little brother. Ben closed his eyes and began to cry.

I whispered, "You need the kind of help that the world cannot give you."

Ben Collins belonged in another era. He believed in rules, and order, and reacted violently to injustice. In the short time we'd been together, I learned that he couldn't process the changes that had taken place in the world while he wore that uniform. He had yet to realize that anger and volatility would only pull him deeper into a hole he'd so desperately tried to claw his way out of. Or he'd forgotten.

I, on the other hand, belonged to no particular time. No nation would have me. Nor would any lover or family. My attempts to get closer to the world only left me cursing the very people who flinched whenever they heard my voice. As if the syllables themselves carried the malevolence of my dealings with vile men. Attempts to change identities, clothes, ideologies, and mother tongues could not dampen the notion that I possessed an infinite evil because I'd once made a very unholy deal.

If there was one thing Ben Collins understood, it was that a person needed to be given the chance to be redeemed.

He knew me by reputation before he'd ever met me. Through melodramatic warnings and indirect admonitions that never revealed my whole story. A mysterious woman with a very long, dark past. He'd heard my name as a curse. A cautionary tale.

In the simplest of terms, he'd heard I was despicable. Foul.

Villainous.

Vile.

Yet he'd perceived something in me the others hadn't. A dim light, perhaps, where he saw none of his own.

But in him I sensed more than just a spark. A smoldering cinder. My love and a little oxygen, I figured, could be the kindling that ignited an inferno.

But she'd forgotten about the unresolved conflicts from all those unfinished stories. The ones she began telling herself after turning her back on the sky so many years ago.

That was how the sudden appearance of a forgotten antagonist demanding revenge for her role in one of those tales could so easily surprise her. This man wanted her blood—now that she bled—for his own pain and suffering.

And she didn't want to tell her lover that Hanno Krupp-Toussant had been following them since nautical twilight broke. The running lights on his boat looked like stars low on the horizon. She watched them for hours, in silence. Waiting for them to rise as the night wore on. But they remained fixed in the distance off the stern.

Steady and unmoving.

She knew that if she wanted this story to end on her terms, she would have to rearrange the heavens once and for all. People would cry. There'd be harsh words spoken. There would even be blood if she wasn't careful, but she'd exhausted almost every other possibility.

To truly end this—to rewrite her tale in her own voice—she'd have to start with those stars hanging low on the horizon.

In the distance off the stern.

Steady and unmoving.

TWO

September 13, 2001

Mom and Dad,

When nobody showed up for my 9:00 COMP II on Tuesday, I went downstairs instead of heading back to my office. Nobody—I mean nobody—lingered in the halls. I made it to the student union in time to see the second plane hit. They told us to cancel classes and be available if anyone needed to talk, but the new TAs were never trained for this, so I just told everyone who asked to go home and be with their families.

Cora wanted to be with her parents too, so I drove her up to Cranberry last night. NPR broadcasted the names of the missing and dead instead of their usual stuff, and we kind of felt like we had an obligation to listen. But in the time it took to get there they didn't even get through the entire list. I couldn't listen to anything else though. Music made me feel guilty and the silence felt worse. As we got closer to Pittsburgh I wanted to see planes circling the airport because I still couldn't believe it was true. I hated feeling powerless.

This isn't easy for me to write, but I hope you understand why I'm doing it. I want to make you guys proud, and know that dropping out of school isn't the way to go. But I can't sleep thinking that you and mom, or Katy, or grandma are so vulnerable. I refuse to live in a version of the world where we are powerless to control our own destinies. I just can't sit back and take it. I won't.

I'll finish grad school when this is over, I promise. I'm not sure the world needs another writer at the moment anyhow. Enlisting doesn't change the wedding plans—it just pushes the dates around a bit.

Hope you can find peace in all this. Whatever it takes, just find a way.

Thinking of you,

Ben

Danicka and Reynard argued. Her cheeks were red, her arms crossed. Reynard rubbed his eyes. They flanked a Mexican blanket covered with all sorts of breads and cheeses and jars of olives and preserves. I could smell the Camembert before I even sat down. Dani saw my reaction, and smiled. Reynard did not. When I joined them in the shade of the Bimini top, she handed me my meds and a bottle of water. I couldn't separate seasickness from the Klonopin's side-effects.

"Look at this pow-wow," I said, scanning the flat horizon with my hand above my eyes to block the sun. It should've been to our left, not trailing behind us. "Ain't you all just a sight?"

"Ah. Set the little plates on top of the big ones." Reynard poured himself a glass of Beaujolais. When we'd met him in Florida, he wore a white Oxford with khakis and a simple leather cap-toe shoe. Today he looked a bit more seaworthy, but barely. Barefoot and sweating, he'd traded his khakis for boardshorts. "Just like that, one speaks of the wolf and now we can see its tail."

"What's going on here?" I kissed the top of Dani's head and sat where I could see the open water behind the boat. The Klonopin made everything look like it floated in a dark haze. "Everybody good?"

Reynard watched as I swallowed my pills, then shoved a bit of bread my way. His long mustache rose and fell violently as he chewed. He tipped his glass, and said, "With sunlight and patience the soil gives you grapes and wheat, no? Life's simple treats?"

"Eat it with this this." Danicka handed me a jar of strawberry preserves.

I crossed my legs and scooped the jam onto my bread. The scent of the fruit lingered on my lips. Heaven compared to the scent of vomit on my shirt. A side effect of the meds.

They ate in silence, a direct contrast to the hubbub that had pulled me from below deck. I tried to see if he'd said something to hurt Dani, but she seemed to be holding her own. The air remained still except for the crackle of hot sunlight hitting the green gulf. The engine's steady rumble was easy enough to ignore, and the sea birds had abandoned us during the night.

"You must be dumber than a coal bucket if you don't think I know what's going on here." I took a big bite of bread. "Something had you two all riled up."

Before Reynard could swallow and respond, Dani said, "We must go west. There is a strong low pressure system over the Cayman Islands. It is drifting this way."

14

She put her hand on my knee and added, "Don't be mad."

"Weather's weather, right? Why would I be mad, baby?" I stared into our wake. Not being able to see the other boat felt worse than watching it bob in the distance all night. I only hoped she hadn't seen it. I clenched my fists and said, "Sky looks pretty clear to me."

Dani forced her fingers into mine. "I saw the radar myself."

"Doesn't matter. We paid him to go south—not west. It's thunder and lightning and not a hurricane." I shoved the rest of the bread into my mouth and reached for more. "We knew we might get wet on this ride."

"Let's call a cat a cat—you should be happy I don't make you swim." Reynard pulled a pair of binoculars out of a pouch next to the windscreen. He dropped them in my lap and said, "You think we can outrun that boat if we just keep heading south? It's on us like scales on a fish."

I smiled, then turned to see if Dani looked surprised. She didn't.

"*Oui*, I saw it. As soon as we entered international water, in fact. Bad news, Mademoiselle?" Reynard sat and yanked the cork out of his wine. "But those are not my onions. Any person who would force a young couple like you out to sea is bad news. So it pains me to see we are being followed perhaps only slightly less than it does you."

I said, "Well, there's more than one way to chase the Devil around a stump." I reached for the wine and Dani pushed her water bottle my way. *Thirst beats pride every time.*

She said, "Not with the Klonopin," and smiled.

I clenched my jaw, then took her water and drank. "Running is all we know anymore."

"The running does not hurt. Running is just motion." Before I could chime in Reynard cut me off with a flick of his wrist. "For thirty years, I fished from Miami to Havana to Gustavia and La Ceiba. I miss my home, but I liked being in motion very much. On the sea I didn't feel pressure to be a better man or an angry man. I felt like I could just live. Running, yes. But also living."

"I don't smell bait," I said. "It's been a long time since you dropped a line in the water."

Reynard flinched, then tipped his head and drank. "I liked fishing because I enjoy life's simple treats. Then the reefs dried up like an ocean desert. Then the Gulf spit up a billion gallons of oil and nothing can be done. Life makes choices for you when you can't make your own. Remember that."

"Don't make like I don't know anything about tough choices." A gust of wind blew over the stern, cooling the perspiration on my neck.

Danicka said, "I don't believe he was being judgmental."

Reynard tilted his head, an exaggerated gesture to show he expected me to object. When I didn't, he said, "See? Even the wind is trying to warn us. Now you know that the storm preventing us from arriving safely in Isla Mujeres is very real." Reynard raised his hand to the sky as if he created the breeze with some secret command. "Perhaps you only have the illusion of choice. A glimpse, just to keep you running. If that's true, then I am like a fortune teller, no? Showing possibility only where possibility already exists."

"Please don't be unkind." Dani intervened with a stern whisper. "We've been more than generous with you."

"We will see about that, won't we?" Reynard said.

"I told you we shouldn't trust him." I avoided Dani's stare because I knew she'd win. I bit my lower lip to stifle the adrenaline surging through me. Then I said, "If we had our own boat we could go wherever we wanted. Part of me wants to just drop him into the ocean and be done with it."

"Don't let the drugs get the best of you." She kissed my forehead. "Figure out how much of this is the medicine and how much of this is you."

I tried to smile. My hand trembled and an inferno raged in my brain. "Maybe it is the Klonopin."

When I turned my back to Reynard, he said, "Tell Monsieur Ben that you know."

Dani whipped around and responded in French. Something angry and forceful. She stepped toward him, grinding her fist into her palm as she shouted.

I stood. "We're not going to play this game all the way to Costa Rica."

"Maybe that is for the best, Monsieur Ben." Reynard shrugged and held up his palms. "But ask her. She knows who is on the boat."

I put my hand on her shoulder and turned her toward me. Her skin smelled like cloves and roses.

"I didn't lie," she said, backing away, glaring at Reynard. "I never once lied to you."

"So you know who it is?" Electricity flowed through my arms. The dark haze over the ocean thickened. *Fucking Klonopin.*

"Possibly."

Lightning flashed on the horizon behind us. It made no sound. "Then you did lie, Dani. You lied to me."

"Ben, when I told you I didn't want to discuss my past you assumed—"

"Bullshit, Dani. Whatever you're going to say is bullshit. I *assumed*? Is that what you're going with? *Assumed*?" I grabbed the wine from Reynard and chugged until my air ran out. Dani tried to take it from me and I backed her away with my elbow.

"Stop, Ben. Please. Let me explain."

But I couldn't look at her. I threw the empty bottle into the sea. Composing myself, I turned and said, "Let's talk about this when we're alone."

She turned her shoulder to me.

Now that the power had shifted, Reynard sat back in his captain's chair and crossed his arms behind his head. He said, "Now I will create the illusion of a choice for you, Monsieur. Tell your fortune."

"Hanno Krupp-Toussant is the worst devil of them all. One of the few men on Earth able to truly yearn for the era of meaningless titles and slave labor in the colonies. His father supposedly made a deal with the devil at the beginning of the Great War." He leaned forward and laced his fingers together. "I'd seen his boat in Miami the day before you hired me. I knew I could never outrun those Caterpillar twin v-12s. He can do 65 knots easily. Why do you think I was so willing to take your money? Toussant is everywhere the sun sets, running drugs, people, and weapons. He has his hands in the *Federales*, the cartels, and the DEA. In La Ceiba he is more revered than Jesus Malverde because he answers prayers with fear and money. So whatever this one…" he said, pointing at Dani. "Whatever she did to upset him—when we hit the beach in Mexico, Toussant's men will be waiting for us. I think it's better for you to find another way south."

"Dani," I said. "How do you know him?"

"I know a lot of people." She folded her arms and stared into the water. "He's the worst kind of dog. He bites before barking."

"Stop fucking around. Respect me enough to be straight with me."

She backed over to the other rail. Her delivery fell flat, like she'd been reading from a book. Her eyes never left the sea. "Born in East Berlin, a child of privilege in a city with none to give. Like most of his peers, he became active in the Free German Youth, a student branch of the Worker's Party. But so much equal opportunity bored Hanno. He instigated feuds—school yard bullying, but with his family's money. He believed that ideology without action was dead thought and sought a way to act. He fled to West Berlin to join The Red Army Faction as a freelance *advisor* at some point after the German Autumn. In reality he just sold weapons—plundering family warehouses to fill his pockets. Some say he helped design the explosive device used to detonate the car bomb at the Rhein-Main Air Base, but I think that's giving him too much credit."

17

Reynard watched, waiting for her to finish the story. He tapped his knee, a Morse code of anticipatory nervousness. "And?"

She clenched a fist. "If there's something you'd like to add just say it."

Reynard held his palms up to the sky and shrugged as if we'd given him no other choice.

"Toussant is not simply an ideologue." He sprang from his chair and stepped behind it, using it as a podium. He jabbed the cushion with his finger, and said, "It was business. Defense contracts."

He took too much pleasure in his denouement. I couldn't look at him when he spoke.

He spun the chair twice and said, "Mademoiselle, now tell us something that the newspapers didn't report."

Danicka planted her fist onto her hip, then inhaled deeply. Ignoring Reynard, she took my hand, and said, "Toussant spent the nineties in the Balkans with Serb militias. You knew I lived there, right?"

I nodded.

"See, Ben? This is not a lie. Just so many things I've tried to forget. Toussant traded Chechen oil for weapons and cash to fund his operations in Bosnia. That's how I came to know him. I worked for an aid group that smuggled children out of Sarajevo, and he sniped in the hills—the worst kind of monster. That was in the nineties. A different time. I'm not sure what else Monsieur Reynard would like to know." She shrugged dismissively. "Time is a black hole that destroys the past."

"Yeah, a long time ago. Things change." My mouth got dry and I couldn't look at her. The revelation left me with a sense of lonely dread, like the last few threads that connected me to all that I knew had been snipped one-by-one. I needed certainty. No more blank spaces. "But you know what you're withholding. I don't. Reynard seems to think he does."

"I'm sorry?" She glared at Reynard, jaw clenched to keep her from saying more than she had to.

"The details. It feels like you're holding back—"

"May 1995." She held up her hand like a cop halting traffic. When she spoke her shoulders slumped, and she crossed her arms. "The NATO airstrikes had begun and I'd negotiated a ride with the Red Cross to check on an orphanage in Tuzla. Toussant and his men had just taken Vrbanja Bridge from the French peacekeepers in Sarajevo, trapping us on the south side of the river. I provided information that lead to his capture. When the siege ended, he was tried and received three life sentences for war crimes. That's the last I heard of him until today."

Now satisfied, Reynard nodded.

"I'll tell you exactly what happened after you parted ways." He paced the deck and fiddled with the buttons on his shirt like Atticus Finch before cross-examining Mayella. But unlike Finch, who remained stoic in the courtroom, Reynard struggled to suppress a smile. "The inmates in Tartu attacked Toussant mercilessly for weeks on end. Then a U.N. tribunal determined that the guards had failed to protect him, Toussant sued. Those bastards awarded him fifty-thousand dollars for his suffering and transferred him to Sremska Mitrovica in Serbia. He bought an army there—mercenaries and assassins handpicked from the inmates in the Fruška Gora cellblock. Hell's doorstep. They raped and beat the women. Tortured the men with mock trials and executions. When the war in Kosovo began, Toussant fled the Balkans. My brother heard he'd settled in Chechnya to instigate tensions with Russia. Some say Toussant is responsible for the bombing of Pushkin Square in 2000."

Dani rubbed her little amber amulet with her thumb as she calculated. Then she put her hands on her hips and approached Reynard. "If you already knew so much, why did you ask?"

He raised an eyebrow and faked a smile.

Being lied to burned. Even though I could almost still taste the Klonopin—a little like mint, a little like banana—the drugs couldn't push that sting away. A sensation that felt both emotional and physical. But I didn't want to be alone either, and in the end, it came down to which hurt less. I had to pick a side. "Why don't you answer her fucking question?"

Dani seemed surprised, and put her hand on my arm.

Reynard backed up to the consol. "Maybe what she doesn't say reveals more than what she does? I don't know. But I was going to tell you your fortune, so allow me to finish. Hanno Krupp-Toussant will not stop until she is suffering. If he wanted her dead, he would have destroyed us once we reached the twelve-mile limit. He wants to put her on trial and find her guilty. He wants her to beg for death like those men in Sremska Mitrovica. He wants her to thank him with her last breath for ending her pain and suffering. He will stop at nothing less."

"So what's your plan? Let him catch up and hand us over?"

"And suffer for having assisted you? That's idiotic. And pointless. We have to sink him. That is the only way out of this. Once the sun sets we will turn back into the storm and charge. He's faster, but the *Remedios* is unsinkable. You will board his boat and kill him."

19

I began to object, but Dani cut me off. "There has to be another way. Ben can't kill him." Her voice trailed off and she lowered her head in thought. "Reynard, you must do it. We can pay you."

"Your sense of right and wrong is no different than a child's. Is your version of morality truly so black and white? Make it look like an accident. Call it self-defense if that helps. Or make him swim. Let the sea decide." He sat and swiveled back toward the windscreen. He'd made up his mind. "Either way, I'm not the one he wants. It doesn't matter to me."

"I am trying to change, to be a new woman, but the circumstances are making it very difficult." She held my face and kissed my chin and cheek. She searched for validation in my expression. "Ben, whatever it takes, we will find a way, okay?"

I flinched a bit, thinking about the words she used. I wanted to believe her even though it hurt to do so. I wanted to trust her even if I had to lie to myself. After thinking about it I chalked her word choice up to coincidence and said, "I'll do whatever you think is best. I promise."

Her head fell onto my shoulder, and she held me tightly.

Suddenly I felt like I'd made a big mistake.

We sat at the stern for a long time just waiting for whatever came next. The sky darkened and the wind stiffened, blowing the scent of the ocean and of animals living far below to our noses. When I closed my eyes, I could smell land and the things we left behind. Notes of red spruce and Blackwater from mountains I'd never see again. I knew that sand from Africa and the Middle East drifted much higher in the atmosphere. The Trade Winds that blew past the Canary Islands and over the blue Atlantic carried dust from Tikrit and Fallujah. A bit of my past returning to me from on high. In that wind I could almost taste blood.

She said, "For you, there is blood everywhere though, right?"

"My head hurts." I closed my eyes. "I want to take something. Is it time?"

"Not yet, my love. You have to remember that the pain is not physical. You don't carry the dead with you like loose change. You can leave the hurt where and whenever you decide. It doesn't mean forgetting. It means that you try to live again."

So I pushed it out of my mind and tried to focus on the miles. And while Dani rested her head on my lap I squinted into the distance to try to get a bearing on Toussant. But the flat sky proved to be my undoing. With too much grey I could only see bad things. And when I thought of the way Toussant would die by my hand, the way his silky warm blood would coat my fingertips, the way his muscles would collapse beneath the weight of his bones, the way I'd no longer be able to hear the air wheeze in his lungs, or see the way his pupils stopped responding to changes in brightness, I felt complete.

"Why are you so patient with me?" I said.

"It's because I've been where you are now." She didn't look at me when she spoke. I could barely hear her voice. "Many, many times. I know that it doesn't go away, and I think if I can help you, then I will be able to see how it's done."

"I'm sorry to hear that." I leaned forward and kissed her head. "Now I feel weak for wearing so much on my sleeve."

"Don't feel that way. If I hide mine well, it's only because I've tried all the other ways." She wrote strange little letters on my knee with her fingernail. "Do you know how many times I've tried to kill myself? How many times I've cut away at my wrists only to bleed and bleed until I passed out? That's why I am patient. And I hope when the time comes again, you can be as patient with me."

I hoped so too.

Dark clouds formed above the foamy sea, creating an arena for tonight's showdown. A mass of fluttering debris approached. From this distance, it could've easily been mistaken for a flock of swallows. Toussant's boat waited just on the other side of all that wind and lightning. And the dark mass that flickered toward me could've been a mile or ten miles away. I said, "It's like a blizzard. But with leaves instead of snowflakes. Or paper."

Dani rolled onto her side and tried to focus on what I saw. "No, my love. I think they are birds, maybe. We are too far from land for it to be anything else.

"It's not moving like a flock of birds though." The mass rose and fell on the updrafts, obeying meteorological, rather than biological, rhythms.

"It will be dark soon, so we should prepare," she said, ignoring me.

"Dani, if I get a chance to finish this tonight...."

"The universe has a plan for him, Ben, just as it does for us. Don't believe for a second those plans are mutually exclusive."

"What about my plans?"

"Ben, you can be any kind of man you want to be." She stood, placed her hand on my shoulder, then bent over and kissed my head. "The greatest thing about the universe is that it recreates itself constantly."

"And all cats are grey in the dark."

"Tapping into the river of anger that flows all around us will only drown you. I know. That's what I've done. And I am trying to make my way back to land. I need a lifeline, so you need to stay on land. Don't give in to that anger." When she finished she paused to make sure I understood. And before giving me a chance to respond, she went below deck.

Waves that broke beneath the bow sent up sprays of warm water that coated my skin. I finally stood only as the first bands of rain splattered the deck. The sky swirled with grey and green light. The mass of birds spun ever closer. Rising and falling on the undulating edge of the front. I kept a hand on the rail. "Those aren't birds."

When the first of the red flower petals fell onto the deck, I wanted to call Danicka. Not to prove that I was right, but just to share the experience. To prove that I hadn't lost my mind. I picked up a handful of poppies—I'd expected roses—and let them blow back out to sea, but they stuck to my skin. I held one between my fingers, then rubbed it against my cheek. For a moment, I was back *over there*.

Bleeding in the dirt.

Crying where nobody could see.

Rain lashed the deck. Lightning clawed at the sky. Waves slammed the hull and *Remedios* rolled over peaks that felt like mountains. Reynard worked all evening to keep her headed into them straight on. He assured us that washing into them sideways would be bad. "Maybe we all swim," he said with a shrug.

And when Hanno Krupp-Toussant finally pulled to within a mile of us, Reynard never even said a word. He didn't flinch or change the tone of his voice or give any indication that he'd sold us out.

Wind hit us from all sides now that Reynard no longer manned the wheel. Water poured over the deck in a never-ending stream. Dani and I knelt, facing the sea, holding hands. Reynard jammed a .22 into my neck. Every so often I lifted my face to the sky to let the rain rinse the sting of salt out of my eyes. In the collapsing horizon I saw a white flash break through the weather. Toussant flicking his running lights as he approached. Staccato splatters that penetrated the rain in an unsteady cadence.

Morse code.

"Was this his proposal? Or did you offer us up to him, you fucking asshole?" I shouted into the horizontal rain. I did my best to read the dashes, but Danicka had already figured it out.

She said, "Monsieur Reynard, we have money. We could've paid you much more than Toussant will."

I turned as much as I dared. Figured Reynard should at least have to look me in the eye.

"He isn't paying for you." Reynard's face looked like a mask. He hid his real emotion behind a forced scowl. He hesitated, then said, "I offered you to him. An even trade. The Krupps love to barter."

The meds made me woozy. I had a headache and had to puke. Seasickness. Not a side-effect. But the adrenaline only compounded my discomfort. But I looked at Dani and immediately knew my role. I had to be strong. I needed to keep her safe. My little rose. Mostly thorns, but so sweet once you got close enough. And I had already gotten way too close.

"Yeah? And what are we worth?" Without showing my hand, I tried to sense the rhythm of the storm. Tried to anticipate the meter of the sea. The chop. The drop into another trough. At the moment, Reynard remained the only variable. The only barrier between us and the relative safety of a continuing pursuit. And in a few minutes, all of that would change for the worse. I calculated my odds of getting that revolver away from him without taking a bullet. *Not good. Not yet, at least.*

"I gain an ally, and once you are off my boat I intend to stay as far away from Monsieur Toussant as possible." Reynard used his pistol to punctuate his words. "I get respect. You don't respect anyone or anything. That's why you are on your knees now. You didn't respect me enough to perceive me as a threat."

"No offense, man. But I'm not sure I can respect anyone who's never thrown a hay bale or pounded a nail."

"What you respect doesn't matter now. With this trade I get sanctuary, Monsieur Ben. A big brother looking over my shoulder in every port from Tampico to Maracaibo."

"Bullshit. You're nothing. Powerless." I rocked back, pushing my weight from my knees to my toes. "This makes you think you're a player. Like you got some kind of legacy building. So when you go back to confront your papa on his deathbed you got something to show for yourself."

"Ben, stop—" Dani said.

Reynard flinched, then crossed his arms as he recovered.

"All your talk about *life's simple treats* makes you a fucking hypocrite—" I released Dani's hand and settled into a subtle three-point stance. "Lobster and wine and bullshit."

She grabbed my wrist, a sure sign of her disapproval. But this wasn't survival by committee.

Reynard stammered, "Because I like living well?" He needed to form a more substantial rebuttal, and retreated into his thoughts.

When his eyes drifted back to the incoming boat I leapt to my feet. I rammed the top of my head into his jaw and reached for his wrists. Dani spun and helped me push him to the deck.

Reynard yelped and twisted away from me. When I clamped down on the gun he fired a shot into the Bimini top. Another round went into the cockpit instrument panel. Dani climbed over me and gripped Reynard's jaw. When he twisted from her stare, she pushed her nails into his cheeks.

She said, "Do we not deserve the same freedom as you? Why, Reynard? We wanted to escape. We just wanted to run away together and you took that from us." Her voice crackled with pain and anger. Rain diluted the blood that dripped down his cheeks, and I swore it sizzled like oil on a hot skillet when it hit the deck. "And we were so close, but you took that from us."

Once I got both of my hands around his wrist he could only pull the trigger. I turned away from each shot. The noise still rattled me in a way that thunder and loud music couldn't. Those gunshots lit a fire in me. I pushed Dani back and raised my fist. Reynard shielded his face. When I connected, it felt solid. It shook me. His eyes rolled back, and I raised my fist again.

Dani steadied my hand, putting herself between my rage and my target. "I need to know that you have control." She pried the gun out of his hand, passed it to me, and pushed me back onto my knees. "Take a moment. I need you."

When I stood and regained my composure, she bent over and spoke into Reynard's ear. Her lips moved, but I couldn't hear the words over the storm.

But Reynard did. He tried to turn away.

Danicka closed her eyes and stroked his cheek with the back of her hand while she whispered a long, rambling passage. A warm wind fell down from the sky. Pushing the rain aside. Steam rose from the teak.

He clenched his eyes then rubbed them with the palms of his hands. Dani's stoicism remained a steady contrast to Reynard's drift toward some darker emotion. He sniffled and wiped away tears. She only released him after he nodded and said, "Oui, mademoiselle."

She reached for my hand and I helped her to her feet. Reynard remained on the deck. He couldn't look at me.

"What did you say to him?" I pulled the cylinder pin out of the .22 and used it to pop out the spent rounds.

"Nothing that I can tell you." She put her hand on my arm, but the gesture did not reassure me. "Help him to his feet."

I replaced the cylinder pin and did as she said.

Reynard averted his eyes as he passed me on his way to the cockpit. After a moment the old diesel coughed to life with a cloud of black smoke. The engine's high pitch meant we were back at full speed, even if it was already too late. Once he turned the *Remedios* back into the waves the sea became a bit more tolerable.

But bringing the boat about let Toussant know we were running. A multitude of spotlights cut through the murk now that surprise wasn't a factor. He came at us with everything he had.

"What did you say to Reynard?"

"You understand that there will always be things I won't share with you. Not things that I *can't* share. Things I *won't*, because they change the way you see me. My history with Hanno is something I didn't want to share with you, but was willing to so that we could move forward. What I said to Reynard is one of the things I won't tell you. So you shouldn't ask me to discuss it, okay?"

"Like I shouldn't ask you about walking on water? Or changing the weather, or whatever the fuck it is you do?" I bit my lip and tried to think of a different way to approach the subject. After a moment, I came up with, "You said you'd never lie to me."

"And I haven't." She kissed me and ran her hand through my hair. "I love you, Ben. I will never hurt you. And I will protect you as long as I am able to."

"You know Toussant's going to start shooting as soon as he gets in range, right? And we're running out of time." I backed toward the cockpit and Reynard. "Where are we headed, asshole?"

Reynard said, "Rio Lagartos, monsieur."

"How can I believe you?"

Dani said, "You have my word. You don't need his."

"You have more rounds for this thing?"

Reynard rooted in an ammo can mounted beneath the wheel and found a box. As he set it in his chair's cup holder, bright light engulfed us. The blowing rain ate most of it, but still we had to shield our eyes from Toussant's spots. Our shadows disappeared into the empty sea behind us. I took six cartridges from the box and reloaded.

With the first round of muzzle flash, I gently pushed Dani down to the deck. The fiberglass hull splintered in erratic clusters. I said, "I promise I won't let anything hurt you."

Reynard shouted, "Cover me," but from this far away his little Saturday Night special was about as useless as tits on a bull.

"Just stay low." I aimed, but the sea kept my field of view in constant motion. "He's still too far away."

Reynard said, "Shoot him. How can I steer—"

"This pistol is shit. I'm going to have to be right on top of him to hit him. What do you even use this for?"

Reynard said, "Sharks."

"And you must think I'm a toddler. Where's the flare gun?"

"There, in that locker."

"Reynard—you need to make this thing go faster." I knelt in front of the locker and dug through the PFDs and old tackle. His flare gun hid in the bottom, snugged away safely in its plastic clamshell. "What are you going to do in an emergency, man? I need a knife."

Reynard said, "In the locker."

"Fuck. You got more flares?" I cut the rest of the plastic away and popped the first one into the chamber.

Reynard said, "What do you need more for? There are four there."

"Because this ain't a four-fucking-flare job. That's why."

"Everything I have is in the locker. There should be more."

So I dug, tossing out the junk that got in the way onto the deck. "Road flares? You expected a flat?"

"You asked, monsieur."

"Hit your spots. Shine them right in his face." I aimed the flare gun at Toussant and handed Dani the extras. I held my breath. Then exhaled. Then fired.

It seared the air with a hiss and a cloud of sharp, pungent smoke. The flare stayed true, hitting the windscreen and bouncing over their heads. The oncoming boat swerved and the gunfire stopped temporarily. "That's why I need a few more flares." I shoved another one into the chamber. "You don't have anything else? I could really use something with a little more kick. RPG?"

He didn't reply.

"Fuck it anyhow."

In the light cast by our spots I could see the go-fast boat—probably a modified race hull with extra fuel tanks below deck. As far as I was concerned, that was good news. Bigger tanks meant fewer passengers.

I fired another flare.

The boat maintained its course this time. Toussant pulled to within a hundred yards. "Keep it straight," I yelled. *Two left.*

Toussant appeared in our spots now. He leaned over the rail and fired his AK, aiming high, possibly for the lights. I pushed Dani back onto the deck and shielded her with my body. "Give me one of those."

I knocked the cap off a road flare and prepared to strike it. The hail of bullets stopped when we'd pulled to within twenty yards of each other. Reynard had cut the engines and disappeared below deck. With nobody at the wheel the boat lurched in the waves. Each successive crest rolled the boat more deeply into the sea. I nudged Dani toward the relative safety of the cockpit.

"I am looking for the whore of the devil," Toussant shouted into the PA. His accent sounded thick and uneven. The worst parts of English and German and whatever else he carried in his inbred DNA. He wasn't a big man, and I supposed that surprised me somehow. Wiry, like a wrestler, his scalp was bare except for a large red scar above his ear. A birthmark or a burn. "Everybody pays a price, Daniella. I learned that when my father died. Instead of using those last moments to say goodbye, he cursed you and the way you destroyed everything his grandfather had worked for. I could've forgiven you for Bosnia. You did what you had to in order to save yourself—so what? I would've done the same. But you stole a moment from me. You were in my father's head when only I should've been. You took something very precious from my family. From me. You stole my birthright and my name and dragged them through the filth with your trite machinations. That is something I can't forgive."

Toussant's pilot idled toward us, keeping fifteen yards between the boats. A man with a Russian AK-12 covered Toussant from a hatch near the bow. He wore a black flak vest and a White Sox cap. *An American.* The sound of the wind and rain drowned out the noise from their engine.

Toussant fired a few rounds below the *Remedios's* waterline, then the PA crackled to life again. "But to be certain, you'll pay for all of it. If it takes the rest of my life and every drop of blood in me, you'll pay."

Trying to figure out where the shooting would come from was like trying to nail the stars to the sky. I got to my knees and turkey-peeked over the rail. Before Toussant could react I released another round from the flare gun. While they took cover, I struck the road flare and tossed it into their cockpit.

Shouts of alarm and confusion came from the open hatch near their bow. The American pushed himself out of the deck and the pilot disappeared below. I popped up and fired Reynard's shitty little .22, hitting just wide of where I'd aimed. The pilot stood—I saw the flash of his chrome-plated semi-automatic handgun. I fired another round at the shine.

The road flare flew over the rail and disappeared upon hitting the water. I unscrewed the cap on another, struck it, and tossed it into the cockpit.

The American reset himself in the hatch near the bow and released a spray of gunfire. Toussant shouted fierce screams, war cries that would've split the sea in two had he been shouting at it instead. White spider webs spread through the *Remedios's* windscreen. Wood surrounding the cockpit splintered. I pulled on the door that lead below deck, but Reynard had locked it. I shielded Dani with my body. "Reynard," I yelled just to yell.

Toussant said, "That woman is bad, bad luck. Maybe she doesn't die but I know you do. I'll bleed you white if I have to."

I heard a *thunk* against the fiberglass at the bow. I stood to look, but Dani pulled me back down. She yelled, "And you know there's no such thing as luck. Just a runt born into a litter with no other pups, thinking that makes him a very big dog."

"Maybe, Daniella, but I am very much alive and you are very much outnumbered. Maybe tonight you will find out what this runt can do."

I heard the thud again. When I dared a peek, I saw that the American had managed to snag a rail with a grappling hook and pulled the boats together. I stood and fired two shots, hitting him at least once in the chest. The impact knocked the wind out of him and he fell forward, hitting his head. He recovered, stuck his hand beneath his flak vest to feel for blood, and then took cover below deck. Toussant returned fire from the cockpit.

I took a knee and shot a flare at Toussant—the last one. The pilot paid it no mind, and picked up the rope the American had dropped. The flare smoldered in the rain. Grey smoke drifted up through the spotlights. For a moment I could smell burning plastic.

I fired another shot from the .22 then scampered past the cockpit, paying special attention to where my hands and feet were going. Before the pilot could recover and return fire, I dove toward the grappling hook and flipped it into the water. I turned and shot again, hitting him in the shoulder, high and to the right of where I'd aimed. He clenched his trapezius and disappeared into the hull.

I took cover behind an old steel bait cooler and reloaded. The *Remedios* heaved and fell down a massive wave that turned us perpendicular to Toussant's boat. The .22's cylinder pin skittered toward the sea. I swatted at it twice before finally getting it with the tip of my middle finger. I quickly pushed out the rest of the spent brass, then put the pin between my lips and shoved more rounds into the cylinder. The taste of gunpowder on my tongue sharpened my focus.

The sea pushed the two boats together with a squealing crash. When I had a clear shot I took it. But from this angle I could only see the legs of the pilot. He writhed in pain. Dani screamed from the stern.

I said, "Reynard—could really use you here."

I scrambled back around the cockpit in time to see Toussant shoving Dani below deck. She pounded him with her fists and thrashed, but the American had her by the feet, rendering her helpless. A second rope from a winch on the go-fast boat's bow had been secured to an old shallow water anchor bracket on the *Remedios's* stern with a carabiner. I pulled on the rope to bring the boats back together, and the American let off a few rounds. White flashes penetrated the rain. I knelt and shot back.

The American started the engines and frantically spun the wheel. Blood dripped from his scalp. I knew the boats weren't going to get any closer once Toussant cut the line, but wanted there to be another way. Deep down, I knew the truth. But knowing didn't make the widening gap any smaller.

I backed away from the rail, mentally calculating how much speed I'd need to hit my target. In my head I knew it didn't matter. I'd never have enough room. And I'd never have more time to think about it.

"On three…"

I tucked the revolver into my waistband and jumped, hitting the stern with a thud that knocked the wind out of me. Maybe even cracked a rib. My foot slipped on the swim deck's wet fiberglass and I wrapped both hands around a stanchion to steady myself. The smaller boat teetered more wildly in the chop than the *Remedios* had, and I had a harder time keeping my legs beneath me. As I tried to push myself back into standing position, the American caught my jaw with his elbow.

I set my feet and startled him with two quick lefts as I came into the cockpit. He watched me, feigning a bob, but I could see that his eyes hadn't found me. I connected with a solid right. Blood dripped from his nose. He raised his hands to defend, but I worked him to his knees and locked my arm around his neck. He tried biting, and punching me weakly. Then he gasped.

I needed this.

The world came at me faster now. I shrugged off the rain and the waves. My arms grew stronger with the aggression—I became part of the machine again. The video game scrolling in my head never stopped. Insurgents popped out of holes and I hit 'em every time. I picked up ammo wherever I landed. Cherries and peaches. Gold coins meant extra lives, and I needed them a whole hell of a lot more than Super Mario ever did.

God mode. Save your quarters, kids. I'm going to be here a while.

Before he blacked out completely I released him, stood over him, and kicked his ribs with my heel. Once. Twice. I clenched my fists and shoved them into my temples. All I had to do was rip out the memories to set myself free.

Time slowed down. Shadows made sense to me. My breathing stopped. Deliberate action made me a better man. Just liked they'd trained me to be. My head was the full moon floating in a sea of ink. Heaven sent this rain to keep me cool while I worked. All the fragments came together to make me whole again. Ecstasy and horror, together at last.

His terror made me unstoppable.

The creator and the destroyer.

Fuck my college loans and fuck my ex-wife and fuck you too, Uncle Sam. I got a stack of quarters but don't need them. Not in god mode, motherfucker.

Except the shadows changed. I slowed and looked over my shoulder. Reynard brought the *Remedios* about.

"You fucking coward."

The boat turned slowly, pulling the smaller boat along with it—he didn't know he towed us. For a second, the dark sea glowed in his spotlights. A crystalline jade that went on forever.

"Reynard."

I fired a warning shot. A tiny hole in his windscreen.

He turned and raised a shotgun. Birdshot peppered the cockpit to my right.

"Ben," Dani screamed from below deck.

The *Remedios* completed her spin. Reynard pushed her full throttle. I fired another shot. Reynard killed his spots, then his running lights. Then just like that, he'd disappeared into the murk.

I steadied myself against the wheel, waiting for the rope from the winch to pull taut. When the boat jerked forward, I fell backward and scrambled to recover.

"Fucking Reynard." I shook my head. Anger poured through me. Adrenaline made me bigger. A hundred fucking feet, at least. I turned and kicked the hatch that lead down into the hold, but the lock held. As I reared up for another go, the door erupted in splinters. Wood fragments blew out as Toussant fired the AK.

I fell to the deck and rolled to my right. I heard the click of the empty clip being released.

I stepped onto the captain's chair and went over the windscreen. The slippery fiberglass made it difficult to get any traction. As I slid toward the deck hatch the smooth silver surface behind me burst apart in a hail of gunfire. I reached for the latch as it flipped open.

Toussant popped up, but had to pull the AK close to his chest to get it through the tight opening. While he retreated to aim again, I got my feet around to kick him. He ducked before I could make contact, then fired another burst at me from below. White light filled the constellation of holes he'd created. I rolled toward the rail and caught myself before slipping into the sea. Another cluster of fiberglass splinters exploded out of the far side of the deck. I scrambled toward the stern and tried to flip myself back into the cockpit.

"Ben." Dani's voice sounded distant, and faint. "Stay with Reynard. It's too dangerous."

She didn't know that option no longer remained.

The shots came randomly now with strobing white flashes. A grouping near the bow. Another nearer the cockpit. Toussant's circles grew wider each time. When the hull splintered just inches from my head I knew I'd run out of room. I'd backed myself into a corner.

Unless you want to swim.

I hung off the port rail and tried to compose myself.

The sea nipped at my heels, and before I could swing myself back on board, we settled into a trough. The water came up to my waist. As we rose to the top of the next wave I struggled to hang on. My hands slipped on the stainless. Adrenaline made me jittery. Made my head hurt. The water and rain made me weak. I shouted for help, but nobody heard.

I didn't want to die. Not out here. We crashed down the backside of a wave and the sea covered my face. Salt burned my eyes and sinuses. Water dripped into the back of my throat, choking me. My hands slipped. I wanted to see Dani again. Which meant I had something to live for.

The shots came from the cockpit now, off to my right. I turned and caught my breath. Toussant stood on the deck and laughed. I slid hand over hand around the curve of the bow. Always inches away from his line of sight. My left hand found the stanchion the grappling hook had been tied to. Toussant fired again, and I'd evaded his shot by sliding down the cord into the dark sea.

At once, silence surrounded me. The pressure changed. My sinuses burned. An empty chill penetrated my muscles and bones. If I let go now, nobody would ever know. But I clung to my lifeline, always looking up to the bright spotlights as strange shadows passed overhead. The bubbles created by the thrashing surface looked like a million gold stars smeared across a blue sky. An impressionist's version of the sea and storm. Movement implied rather than experienced, as if the entire universe shifted and only I remained still. In a fleeting moment my memories and fantasies became tangled in ghost images and I couldn't distinguish between what existed in the world and what I saw in my head.

All I had to do was let go and fall into the blackness beneath me. Fall past the fish and coral. Fall into the universe I'd create as I descended. To a depth where the rules of physics didn't matter unless I made them matter. Becoming smaller as the sea crushed me into nothing. And all I had to do to be reborn was let go.

Time was a black hole.

Everything in the past disappeared.

And that was the only way to create a future.

I wrapped my wrist around the rope two, then three times. The abrupt appearance of sky over my head instead of sea let me take a deep breath. Then it disappeared.

The blackness felt very final—I may as well have been dangling from the moon. All of a sudden, I regretted drawing more hats than boa constrictors in my short time on earth.

I never should've left my little planet.

And I wondered how she knew. I wondered if she were an angel and how so many people could've been so wrong about her for so long. I wondered why I could fall asleep with my head in her lap when I couldn't fall asleep in a bed. When we left Mississippi I thought that my objective had been to save and protect her. But if she were an angel, and not the other thing, then I knew she had to save me.

In the darkness, everything became clear. Yellow light over my head sorted itself into a million layers of blue all around me. But below my feet only depth remained. Like the blackest night sky I'd ever seen. Layers of shifting darkness.

Something materialized in the void.

The mountains. My mom and dad. My cousins and aunts and uncles. For a moment I thought I'd been meant to see my cousin, Jane, again. Which would've meant I'd died. But I didn't, which meant this all took place in a very real future that unraveled before my eyes. It occurred to me that it had been a very long time since I'd had a tomorrow. It'd had been a very long time since I'd seen light emerging from darkness.

My lungs burned for air, but the sea wouldn't let me go.

At that moment I knew why Danicka had pushed so strongly for me to shed the anger and violence. She wanted to show me what she had been able to see all along. That I wasn't disposable, like old beer cans. And that she'd seen a future too.

Don't let me die down here.

She knew that I needed her to save me. But in order to do that, I had to save her first.

I had to find a way.

Up on the surface, the engine sparked to life. I unwrapped the cord from my wrist and pushed myself toward the stern. I ran my fingers along the hull with my free hand and let the line trail out from the other.

When I found the swim step I let go of the rope so both hands were free to grab hold. The boat rose and fell violently in the cold sea. Inches from my face, the go-fast boat's triple engine line-up sputtered water and fumes. I pulled myself up the ladder slowly. Toussant leaned against the dash as he shouted into the radio. He scanned the sea near the bow for my body. The American watched the dim glow of the GPS as he pushed the throttle forward. The engine grew louder. The vibrations made my hands tingle. But when he saw how we were still tethered to the *Remedios*, he pulled a knife from a sheath on his belt and ducked below deck to get to the hatch.

As soon as Toussant slid the radio back into its cradle, I jumped, aiming for the AK slung over his shoulder. And once I got a hold of it I pulled it like a fucking bow string. The strap caught his clavicle but didn't choke him. He clawed at it and twisted, but I wouldn't let go. Not for anything. I could smell the sandalwood in his cologne.

The American yelled, "Hanno," and burst back into the cockpit, pistol raised. I swung the AK around, got my finger to the trigger, and released a quick burst.

He dropped to get out of the line of fire, then lunged at my knees.

I fell onto the deck beneath Toussant and the American. The AK shifted, almost allowing me to choke Toussant with the strap. He gasped and spit, and the American struggled to get his fingers beneath the nylon to keep his boss's windpipe from getting crushed. And when he found himself unable to break my determined grip, he went for my eyes. I turned away as Dani shouted, "Stop. All of you."

She fired a shot into the water. The pilot's chrome-plated pistol flashed in the light.

I shoved Toussant onto the American, loosened the strap from his neck, and pushed myself onto my feet. My heart thudded in my ears. "I wasn't going to kill him."

Toussant rolled onto his side, wiped blood off his chin, and spit onto the deck. "See? She still loves me I think."

I kicked his throat. His eyes rolled back. He clutched his neck and gasped for air. She shouted, "Ben."

"Why?" I held onto the words I wanted to say for as long I could. I knew once they were out I could never take them back. But anger and fear always found the surface. "Because you still love him?"

Dani retreated a step, like I'd raised my hand to slap her.

Toussant laughed and rolled onto his side. He wiped blood from his lip and rubbed it between his fingers. It disintegrated in the rain.

"Fuck, Dani. I'm sorry. Baby, listen to me."

She crossed her arms and stared into the darkness. "It happened twenty years ago. Revenge. After so much time it's no different than an old girlfriend or ex-wife."

"This is very different." I said it to save face, but in my heart, I knew I'd made a mistake. "He's trying to abduct and kill you."

"You don't know a fucking thing about what I want." Toussant smiled. His teeth were pink with blood. "I want her to live for a very long time."

"Fuck you." I pushed the AK to his temple.

Dani held up her hand. "You need to make sure he lives. Not for me, but for you. The universe has a plan for him, and when he dies, he will die alone. But you can not kill him. For a murderer, there is no home. No respite. You will never be able to face you mother and father with so much blood on your hands. Ben, if I let you kill him, we will both be lost to this world forever."

"And if you're lying…." I had no threat, because I hadn't ever imagined a situation where I'd leave her. "I turned my back on my family to be with you. And I don't even know when your birthday is."

"Don't you see? If I could show you...." She put her arms around my waist and pressed her face to my chest. I could feel the warmth of her breath on my shirt. She said, "What do I have to do to prove it? Cut myself? Burn myself? Tell me and I will do it."

"Let me take care of this."

"If I let you do that then I may as well cut or burn myself. Is that what you want? Proof? Then I will prove it to you." She shoved the pistol into Toussant's mouth, breaking off the tip of an incisor. But instead of pulling the trigger, she screamed at him. She pulled the gun out and beat it against her palm.

I tried to stop her, but she twisted away and continued to yell. Spit flew from her lips. The rain washed her hair into her face and she didn't push it away. I swore the sea bubbled, like a pot left to boil. And the air got hot. Sweat formed at my temples. Steam drifted just above the ocean's surface before being beaten down again by the rain. Seeing how she'd lost herself so suddenly made me hate myself for not believing her.

Danicka embodied passion. Fire. Love. Raw emotion unhindered by flesh and bone. I felt myself being pulled into her heat.

Toussant's expression changed. At last, he seemed afraid.

I took the gun from her and tried to take her hand.

"You are the man that I love. What more must I do? Tell me, Ben, because I'll do it. I promise." She made a fist and beat her chest.

"Just stop. Please." I suppressed the tears that I felt. Grabbing her wrist, I said, "I'm sorry, Dani. I've been lied to before."

"Not by me, you haven't." When she rested her head against my chest, Toussant slipped below deck. I raised the AK and aimed into the cabin. Dani gently pushed the barrel skyward. "That's not very smart," she said.

The hatch flipped open and Toussant dove toward the bow, knife out. As I steadied myself on the pilot's chair to aim, he wrapped the rope around his wrist, cut it from the winch, and disappeared into the sea.

"Shit."

"It's okay," she said.

"It isn't. Because it's not over."

She ran her fingers through my hair, down my neck.

"You can't control that, Ben." She kissed me, then calmly whispered, "I'll find a way for us to be together. A new beginning is tough to come by, but it starts with a clear conscious. Not blood."

And there she stood. A calming glow in this dark little universe I'd created.

She said, "Your innocence is your freedom."

"What if it's too late for me?"

"It's not too late," she said. "I couldn't love you if you couldn't be redeemed."

I stared into the murk and looked for something from the *Remedios*. A light. A glow. At the moment, it could've been travelling on one of a thousand possible headings. A thousand ways this could go.

For now, I deferred to Dani's.

I pushed a strand of wet hair out of her eyes. Then I kissed her forehead and said, "I love you too."

Glassy stars rose from the water like sparks from a fire. The parting storm left high pressure in its wake. In the early dawn, we found clear skies and a following sea. But the stars....

"Ben, you need to sleep."

"I told you I can't. Not without my meds. Now that I'm up, I'm up." I shined a light into the cabin. We'd bound the hands and legs of the pilot and the American with the other rope. The American sat up, watching me, studying my face. One of them had gotten sick during the storm. It floated in the rain water that had collected below deck. The scent clung to my skin.

I unzipped Toussant's duffel. Stacks of cash and baggies of weed and pills. A chrome-plated 9mm. The pistol had been carried for a long time. Its edges were smooth, like the ridges on an old quarter. When Dani wasn't looking I placed it against my temple. I said, "Somehow getting found is still a whole hell of a lot easier than getting lost."

"Another reason to stop leaving so many bloody fingerprints upon this world."

I stood behind her, let my hand slide along her cheek, and leaned in close enough to smell her hair—roses, even after so much rain. "I just want to wake up from this dream. Try to figure out if we can really have something together. I'm sick of this, Dani. I can't do this forever."

"All of life is a dream, Ben." She took my hand in hers and kissed it. "Sometimes waking up from it is the same as dying."

Something in the distance caught my eye. I rubbed an AK clip as if it were going to grant me three wishes. My shoulders fell. "And sometimes we climb mountains just to climb more mountains. It scares me that he's not dead. And I hate to admit that."

"If we had killed him, you would have always wondered if it were an act of passion. Truth depends on point of view, no? That doubt in your head would've driven us apart." Dani looked up from the heading she kept, as if waiting for me to process it. And when she saw that I couldn't, she turned her shoulder to me. "Just because there are many possibilities doesn't mean the others are lies. Don't forget that. We are playing a very complicated game. We've lived complicated lives and have made tremendous mistakes. We move on together by not making more because there is no salvation for the guilty."

"That's what scares me."

"Love redeems us, Ben. Don't you see that? It places a value on who we are. Without you, I drift for all eternity." She gestured to the horizon, as if he were right there. "When the end comes, Toussant will scream for forgiveness. The world may hear his cries, but it will be helpless to respond."

"Well, we all die alone, Dani. I don't think there's a way around it."

"Ben—don't tell me. I've been dying for a hundred years. Begging God to take me. Believing a grey hair meant my prayers had been answered. Everybody I love ends up bloody and begging for the very life I'd grown tired of. So please, do not tell me about dying."

I pulled away from her touch. I really hadn't meant to. It was just a flinch. "I fucking love you too much, Dani. I can't control the emotions coming out of me. Killing Toussant would've been a way to let me prove it to you."

My mouth got dry. I wanted a fight. But there was no room to run, no space to get away and think for a few minutes. I went to stern and looked for a sign that the sun would rise again. Once I made sure she wasn't looking, I put the AK clip up to my nose and inhaled deeply.

"Ben—something's ahead. It's a ship, I think."

I returned to her side and looked for movement against a backdrop of razor sharp stars. "I don't see it."

"There." She covered the instrument panel to block the LEDs and GPS. "South. Maybe more south-south west."

"It's too big to be a ship." I threw the clip into the sea. "Those are streetlights. Land."

THREE

"No weather be ill if the wind is still." Ben sat on the deck next to me and stared into the churning wake.

After so much silence, he said it as a way to assess my disposition. A prodding to make sure I'd forgiven him for the things he'd said earlier, so I played along. "One swallow does not make a summer."

He smiled, as if I'd bested him, then stood and rested his elbows on the windscreen. "Yeah, well summer's in the rearview mirror now. We got no idea what's coming next."

That statement meant he was trying to rebound from last night's violence. As far as Ben was concerned, a man couldn't distinguish the illusion of control from control itself.

"It means one shouldn't put much faith into proverbs." I rested my head on his shoulder and stroked his arm. A genuine expression of the way I felt about him. In a much more assuring tone, I said, "Especially those pertaining to weather. The winds rarely blow the way we'd like them to."

His shoulders dropped and he exhaled slowly.

Somewhere behind us, an orange fireball cracked the lip of the slaty sea as the Pleiades coughed to life. I'd grown used to the Milky Way trailing us like a fishing line since the storm dissipated in our wake. As if that faint, glowing thread connected us to something much greater. We moved southwest deliberately, engines simmering in the loose chop. Every mile mattered now that Mexico filled our view. Even though it looked harmless enough from this far out, it signaled the start of something new and unpredictable.

"So, you think I'll be able to get my meds?" He rubbed his eye with the heel of his palm, talking mostly because he believed talking could make everything better. A result of too much group therapy and too much time alone.

"There will be a pharmacy in Mérida, I'm certain." I said it as a placeholder, a chance to gather my thoughts. The doctor at the VA prescribed dosages that allowed him to taper off the Klonopin, and I'd hoped our new circumstances would make a clean break easier for him.

"Because I'm going to need to take something first chance I get." He rapped the wind screen with his knuckles. A beat that craved a cadence. Something to occupy his mind.

Standing, I said, "Take over so I can stretch."

He kissed the top of my head before sitting.

Through the binoculars I could make out a long concrete structure hovering over the Gulf like a man-made island. Cranes and cargo containers rested on a rock foundation illuminated by streetlights. "There it is. The Progreso *muelle*."

Near the mid-point of the three or four mile-long pier rose a large building, maybe three or four stories high. Ben reduced the throttle. The rhythm of the engine and waves changed. Ben shut off all the boat's running lights. He said, "What do you think?"

"Customs and immigration, no doubt."

Ben took the binoculars from me. "They'll be waiting. I'd imagine Toussant gave them plenty of warning. Even if we passed Reynard during the night Toussant would've radioed the feds."

"Or the narcos," I said. "Depending on how Hanno wants this to play out."

He handed the binoculars back to me. "I see headlights. Three black pickups to the left of the dogleg. Just a few guys standing around."

"Narcos," I said.

"So..." He held the chart under a flashlight to get a bearing. "Progresso is off limits."

"I think so."

He shoved the chart back into the pocket next to the compass. "We don't have a lot of fuel. Not enough for Cancun. But there's a long stretch east of here with no roads. Looked like lagoons and reefs on the map." He eased the throttle up.

"We'll disappear into the jungle, no? That's our best option. We have a head start and will go as far as we can by road. We can get to the west coast and make our way to Costa Rica on the Pan-American." I tried to reassure him. "And you will no longer have to worry about student loans."

"Or sharks."

"That is true."

"But now we have all new sets of variables." Over the engine noise, he shouted, "Toussant probably has his hands in deep down here. If what Reynard said is true, Toussant could have his own army."

The boat skipped over the waves. My knees and back shook. Our prisoners in the hold tumbled as we dropped into choppy troughs. As the sun rose and the water shallowed, the deep water gave way to a lighter hue, like diluted Curaçao. The muelle shrank off our stern.

In the growing dawn, the silhouette of a small village bloomed from the horizon. Scrubby trees and concrete block buildings with flat roofs. A beach resort from a much different era. I could smell the grass, the leaves on the trees. Ahead of us, small sailboats and motorized skiffs drifted toward the Gulf like jellyfish in a current. Fishermen rising with the sun to fill their nets. Taking advantage of the only cover available, Ben steered toward them. "A little farther?"

"Maybe." I dug through Toussant's charts and found an old AAA road map for Yucatán tucked in the back. I quickly located Progresso, and ran my finger along the coast to the east. "There is a road south here. Chicxulub Puerto. There's not another way south for another twenty kilometers. There's an old wharf on the map, but I don't see it."

Ben tapped the gas gauge. "Miles?"

"About twelve."

"We're going to need a ride."

"We have money now." I picked Toussant's bag up. "A little bit will go a long way here."

"Yeah, we'll see about that." He cut the wheel toward a ruined pier, but maintained a low angle to take advantage of the shallowing water. "We need to scuttle this shit. Even if it's just symbolic."

Fishermen watched from shore, dropping their nets and tackle as they stood. In the shallows, old concrete pylons broke the surface.

"Hang on." He eased the throttle down, grabbed my hand, and steadied himself on the rail.

We lurched forward as a thud rocked the hull. Fiberglass groaned, then splintered. The sand amplified the impact of the boat settling on its side. I fell into Ben.

"We sure as hell ain't in Kansas anymore," he said. "You good?"

"I am."

He lowered himself over the rail and into the waist-deep water. "Drop the bag."

As I followed, the American kicked the fiberglass with his heel and shouted muffled curses. My face grew hot with rage and I stopped. Ben grabbed my hand and tried to pull me up the beach. "Wait," I said, stepping back into the sea.

I turned and pounded the hull with my fist. "You tell Hanno that his father couldn't kill me, and neither will he. Tell him that I'll dig my own grave and let the birds pick away all of my skin before I let him lay a hand on me ever again. You tell him that I said that."

"You are fire. You know that?" Smiling, Ben kissed my cheek and took my hand.

I had more that I wanted to say—I'd rehearsed this speech for a very long time. But the words felt wasted on his proxy. Saying them didn't liberate me from the weight of my anger. And I couldn't help but think I'd ruined a moment I'd spent years rehearsing because I couldn't control my emotions. "I don't think I burn like I once did," I said, walking up the beach. "Waiting for old plans to unravel is not always easy, but I need a fire to keep these demons at bay a little longer."

He said, "Well, if it's any consolation, I think this is far from over."

"I know that, Ben." *I decide when it's over.* I said, "The universe will decide when it ends."

Dogs barked from the village's dark corners. We took cover behind a low block wall. Little clouds of dust rose into the pale sky from a road to the south. Ben dropped into a three-point stance and turned toward the town. *Forever storming beaches.*

He gave my hand a squeeze. "You ready?"

Once we left the old wharf, the fishermen drifted toward the boat to investigate the shouting. We navigated the rubble and broken walls of an old bodega that had half-fallen into the soft white sand. He kissed me. "Stay close."

Low, sun-bleached buildings lined the street. Concrete hotels and shuttered bars. Some had thatched roofs that had been blown apart by last year's hurricanes—cheap construction begat cheap entertainment. Dogs stretched in the sunlight or followed us at a safe distance, perhaps hoping our presence meant they'd not have to beg for a bite to eat. Plastic grocery bags that had been blown into chain-link fences fluttered in the sea breeze like prayer flags. This could've been Albania, Azerbaijan, or Algeria. The only thing missing were the children playing soccer and the drone of scooters so early in the day.

Ben scanned the rooftops. He clenched his jaw and chewed on his back teeth.

"Snipers?" I asked.

"Old habit," he said. "It feels like…."

"It feels like a lot of places," I said. "And a lot of times."

The colors I'd seen on the buildings from afar faded as we got closer. The sun bleached everything to a shade of grey, and the flecks of lime green, turquoise and lemon yellow only provided context at a distance, like the individual spots of paint on a Signac canvas. The bright traffic signs at the ends of each block stood out starkly in this monochrome landscape, and I felt like Dorothy going back to Kansas after so much time in Oz. We moved on.

"Hear that?" Ben cocked his head around a corner. At some point he'd produced the pistol from Toussant's bag. He'd squared his shoulders, widened his stance, and grasped the weapon with both hands. "Sirens."

I gently pushed my fingers into his, loosening his grip on the gun. "I don't hear them."

"Let me make sure it's clear." He pulled away and jogged across the street. A small grey dog followed at a safe distance.

"Lookie here," he said, tucking the pistol into his belt and approaching a small motorcycle chained to an iron gate. "Don't tell me the gods aren't smiling down on us. We had one of these at the FOB in Zabul. X bought it in a bazaar for two hundred bucks. Honda Scrambler."

He unscrewed the gas cap and took a look in its tank. "So far so good. Can you get my knife out of my bag for me, please?"

A knot formed in my stomach. "You're not stealing this, I hope."

Half-listening to me, he said, "I'm going to strip these wires. The ignition barrel's in decent condition. Not great, but good. Somebody definitely babied it."

"We have to find out who owns it, and offer to pay him."

"No time, Dani. We've got to roll." He pointed at the sky. "Planes. Do you hear them? Toussant told them exactly what to look for. Once they find his boat it won't take them very long to find us."

"You don't have a knife," I said, cautiously. "It was in your bag."

"Fuck."

It hit him all at once.

"Fuck." He raised his fist like he wanted to punch a wall. "Fucking Reynard. I'm going to fucking kill him."

The grey dog stood, its ears at alert. In the upstairs apartment, a baby cried.

Ben clenched his jaw and jammed his fists into his eyes. A small part of me believed it would've been better to have allowed him blow off the stream. Even a raging inferno can only burn for so long.

But he'd only hurt himself. A broken hand from punching concrete. A broken nose from a fight he couldn't win. Or worse yet, he'd hurt somebody else.

A man leaned out of the window above us.

I asked if the bike belonged to him, and if we could buy it. He lifted a finger.

"What are you doing?" Ben ran his hands over his scalp and shook his head.

"Fixing this. So you don't have to leave so many bloody fingerprints."

I reached into Toussant's bag and pulled out a band of bills. A hundred hundreds. I counted out fifteen and zipped the bag.

"Dani." He spun around like a madman. His eyes were wide.

"Take a breath, okay?" I put the money into his hand. "It will be better if you do it."

The click of a lock preceded the sleepy young man's appearance at the door. Upstairs, a mother cooed to her child. He showed me a key ring.

I asked, "How much?"

He responded with a number far smaller than what I would've paid.

"Give him the money," I said.

"Dani, this is a lot."

"It is. But it is not our money."

Ben nodded and handed it over.

The man counted it, maintaining his stoicism throughout the transaction. A kid, no more than seventeen or eighteen, but with enough life experience to know when not to ask questions.

He handed Ben the keys and went back inside. The lock clicked again.

I said, "You must remember that we are alone now. We need each other out here. We can't rely on anybody else." I gently thumped my chest with my fist. "I am your team."

"I know." He handed me the bag and unlocked the bike. "It won't happen again."

The engine seemed too loud. Where leaving Florida hadn't felt like running, this did. When we got into Reynard's boat, we felt like we still had choices. I hung on as Ben aimed us south.

The grey dog barked as we rode off, then followed us to the end of the block. Ben stopped and stamped his foot at him, but the animal only retreated a few feet.

"Leave it, Ben." I turned. The man who'd sold us the bike stood in the window, singing to his baby. Watching, to make sure we were gone forever.

Ben said, "I don't want it to follow us onto the highway and get hurt."

"Well, obviously you're not able to outsmart it." I patted his shoulder. "Just try to outrun it, okay?"

He laughed and turned onto Calle 19. I watched the Coke, or Sol, or Tecate ads plastered to the cantina walls and storefronts zip past. Cinder blocks and sand for cement sat on pallets on side streets. The raw ingredients of progress. Passing through intersections let bright sunlight flood the east-west streets.

Birds sang from power lines instead of scrubby trees. At a small shrine to the Virgin Mary, Ben made a slow right turn beneath strands of orange, blue, and red flags. When we neared the highway, I finally heard a plane approaching from Progreso, flying low along the coast. The sound of sirens grew from the west. The noise did little to convince me that Ben hadn't imagined them earlier. At the roundabout on the south edge of town, Ben slowed.

I said, "We can do this. We just have to be there for each other."

He released the brake and took my hand, then drove on. Past lagoons filled with water that looked like tea, across a wide open plain with no place to hide. Here the earth spread out flat as a tortilla, and suddenly, it felt as if we had a lot to hide.

Iguanas broke for shrubs and clumps of grasses when we passed. Overhead, birds chased flies. Cumulonimbus clouds towered in the distance. Without trees to shelter the road, the asphalt soaked up the heat, magnified it, and sent it back up to us a hundred-fold.

I tried to keep an eye on the airplane, but lost it in the sun. I hadn't expected Federales to come racing down the road behind us until Ben suggested it. Now I only heard sirens. But we were alone again. It felt as if our watery horizon had been replaced with sand and scrub. Then finally, a sign—*Mérida 30 km.*

We could never run far enough to make the people we loved forget about the things we'd done. The guilt stuck with me like a shadow. Deep down I feared there'd never be enough miles to put my life behind me.

Miles had to work, because years didn't. The universe didn't forget a thing. Ever. It had to be miles because the time I'd spent working against the flow of the heavens only buried my innocence beneath a thousand heavy blankets. If I ever hoped to catch a glimpse of the person I'd been, I needed to leave the shadows. Needed to abandon the dark spaces that kept me from seeing the passage of so many more days. I needed to build my life on the bright stones that remembered the birth of the planet. Remembered the creation of all of this.

I laid my cheek on Ben's back and held him tight. He lifted my hand to his lips and kissed it. I said, "Maybe this is freedom. Maybe we were meant to run forever," even though he couldn't hear me.

Then the miles turned back into time.

Patches of dry grass gradually overtook the sand. In between the splashes of green, large swaths of brown and grey remained, as if locusts had swarmed. We passed a lonely homemade shrine, adorned with bright red roses, then at once, low limestone walls guarding snags of dead silver trees appeared along both sides of the road, a return to civilization, whatever that meant down here. A group of men in a pickup truck slowed as they got nearer. Their faces and clothes were covered in white dust. Ben looked away as we passed, then hit the gas. He'd seen enough ghosts in his life.

People did foolish things when they were afraid, and most were always afraid of something. This one's heart had been beating wildly since the day we met. Like a rabbit in a box trap. Some people never figured out that the only way to truly be free was to live without fear, as if dying meant nothing. The rest imitated the fearless, as if the appearance of a bravery somehow led to true bravery. A rare few were liberated by love, which felt like dying in a way, for the feeling allowed them to live without worry for their own well-being. Dreading a lovers' death more than their own became a temporary respite from the eternal plague of dread. A way to cheat their destinies.

But not a path to true freedom.

A cheat was not a victory.

Within moments we were in the midst of a small village—Chicxulub Pueblo. Ads for Bimbo bread and Cristal littered the low stone walls. A young man pedaled his pregnant wife and child on a bicycle with two front wheels instead of just one. We made a right at the town square and passed a cinder block church held together with pale violet paint. Trees with bright yellow flowers shaded the road at the edge of the village. A small pack of dogs gave chase at the end of the last wall, but the morning had grown too hot for them to make a day of it. Over the next few miles there were more farms and walls, and eventually one village became indistinguishable from the next.

The road doubled to two lanes, then four, just outside of a little place called Dzibilchaltún. Four lanes felt like an invitation for trouble.

We'd returned to the village of Chablekal, a few miles back from the main highway to Mérida. We met Doña Cathalina Chale Euan while buying soda at a little *tienda*, and inquired about a place to get out of the sun for a bit. I'd stumbled over the decision to use *esconder* over *ocultar*, but she didn't hesitate to correctly interpret our need to hide.

The old woman corralled us away from the street and onto a smooth path through the trees as if we were little more than a pair of wayward ducklings. For twenty dollars she fed us warm tortillas covered with beans and a fried egg topped with tomato sauce, peas, and cheese, and gave us the use of a *palapa* near the eastern edge of the ruins.

Ben wanted to sleep off his lunch while I talked to Doña Cathalina, and settled into one of the hammocks that hung limply beneath the dry thatch. But there no breeze blew to guide it, and half-formed dreams and a lot of mumbling punctuated his restless nap. The old woman watched him as we talked. She filled the gaps in her broken Spanish with words and phrases from Yucatec—a throaty, guttural language that sounded like a cat scratching the end of a sofa. Vibrant flowers embroidered around the neckline of her white dress danced when she spoke.

"He's a little weary." I made his apologies for him. For a moment I thought I would say more, but a rooster crowed and I felt as if I'd already said too much.

"From a recent fight or an old one, daughter?" Doña Cathalina poured a bit of mezcal into a small, cloudy glass with a splash of Coca-Cola. "He is still bleeding I think. Perhaps the body has healed, but not the soul?"

Beyond where Ben slept lay a clearing with several more small huts topped with thatched roofs built over high wooden frames. Ancient structures with oval limestone bases and small rectangular doorways. The air smelled like dry grass. Evading her question, I said, "This land feels very old. Like there are many secrets here."

Doña Cathalina laughed. "No more than what you brought with you."

I smiled and sipped the mezcal. Tiny swallows swooped down into the cool air that had settled above the well to catch flies.

"Daughter, why have you sought me out? There are easier ways to find the answers you are looking for?"

I flinched, and she took my hand. She said, "It's okay."

"I don't know." I closed my eyes and finished my drink. "I just want to be free. Is that too much to ask for? For a hundred years, I tried and tried and tried. Now I'm tired and just want to go home."

"You don't have a home, I think. Or you wouldn't be here."

"It's been a very long time."

"So long that you've forgotten how to be part of this world, I think."

Doña Cathalina refilled my glass.

We both sat quietly for a moment while Ben mumbled in his sleep. He had this dream often.

"I've tried to redeem myself." I said, "But I've made mistakes, and that's why I'm alone. I've punished myself, but can't create enough pain to feel anything anymore. I tried saving souls. Hundreds, over the years. It always ends the same way. I want to be a new woman, but the circumstances won't let me. So I go on the same as I always have been."

"A very sad story, daughter. And you think you can save that one there? You think he is so broken he won't know if you've failed with him?"

The open doorway let me see into her home. A kitten napped in a hammock woven from blue and gold fibers. A red chair was the only furniture I saw. The paint on the seat and back had almost worn through.

But her patience outlasted my attempt to deflect. When I saw she'd been waiting for an answer, I asked her to repeat the last part of her question, but in Yucatec rather than Spanish.

My mouth got dry when I finally responded. "He believes he can save me, I think. I have to let him try."

A garland of dried peppers hung from the rafters. Beneath them, a small quarter sawn board played hearth to three stones that formed a triangle around a small pile of old wood ash. A bowl sat on the board, along with a plastic milk jug filled with water and a set of fine china from the Gran Hotel Ciudad de Mérida.

"Daughter…" *Hija.*

I wanted the voice to be my mother's. I said, "I've wasted too many tears on hope. I've failed too many times. When I look back I can see the only thing those failed efforts had in common was me. The man before Ben? I loved him too much. I loved all of them too much. And it's always the same in the end."

Ben sat up in the hammock and tried to get his bearings. I smiled to assure him he was okay, and his expression softened a bit. He stretched, brushed the dust off Hanno's bag, and set it on his lap.

"Maybe this one is different, right?" Doña Cathalina *tsked.* "Still you hope."

"I suppose that's true." I responded in as much Yucatec as I could muster.

"His pain gives you purpose."

He unzipped the bag slowly, trying to appear casual in order to show us the contents of the bag didn't excite him on some subconscious level. Like the child left to mind the patisserie because he knew enough to hide his love of palmiers and macarons from his father.

My face got warm. I stood and placed a gentle hand on Doña Cathalina's shoulder. "I have to check on him."

"You need to sleep."

"Ben," I said, ignoring her request.

Doña Cathalina grabbed my wrist, using me for balance as she pulled herself to her feet. "Hija, you need to sleep if you're ever going to dream again."

Words I couldn't hear, not now anyway. With reluctance, I chose his needs over my own. Shuffling through the dust and grit. Stuck somewhere between Doña Cathalina's truths and Ben's wounds.

"I need my meds." He gripped the ends of the hammock with fists held tight. Before I even saw his face, he said, "What do you think about when you don't sleep?"

"Soon, okay? We may be able to find a pharmacy this evening." I cast a quick glance at Doña Cathalina. She pulled apart a tortilla to feed to her chickens.

"You want to know what I think about?" Ben paused as a pair of helicopters passed overhead. They were so low to the ground I could feel the pulses from their rotors in my bones. As they disappeared toward the north the sound of barking dogs could be heard.

"Tell me."

"X and Zack Jackson on my high school football team. I couldn't remember the play call. X kept telling me to break the huddle and I couldn't do it." Ben opened Toussant's bag and carefully sorted the banded cash. At the bottom of the bag he found what he searched for, and held it up for me to see. "Look at all this sticky bud."

His way of asking permission. "Yes, I can smell it from here."

"Just a little to tide me over until I get my prescriptions?"

"Ben…" I couldn't know if he lied. If he needed his medicine, or if he wanted to ease the pain. I'd prepared myself to deal with a wounded soldier. An addict was something altogether different.

"Fuck it. I knew you'd object. Reynard sailed off with my meds—it wasn't my fault."

"I am not your doctor, Ben." I looked at Doña Cathalina to make sure she wasn't watching. "This is not medicine."

"Maybe it is." He turned ever so slightly to keep the bag's contents hidden from me. From a side pocket he produced a small cloth pouch containing several balls of a black licorice-like substance. He didn't know what it was, but he revered it. His lips parted, and he tapped his thigh with his thumb as he set it aside.

"Please, Ben. Once we get to the city…."

"All this shit and it's off limits?" He poked at a greenish powder in a waterproof plastic container. "I don't even know what this is."

Even from here I could smell the honey. "You don't need that."

"What the hell is it?" His hands were shaking. "And how do you know?"

"*Kief.* From Morocco. The Berbers in the Rif Mountains produce it." I chose to answer the first question. I picked up a bit and rolled it back and forth between my fingers. The crumbles fell back into the container. "They pour honey on boys, who then run through the plants. The pollen sticks to the honey, which is then scraped off."

"You live at the edge of a whole other universe, don't you? No wonder I never know what the fuck you're talking about." He put everything back into the bag then wiped his hand on his shorts. With a tight-lipped smile, he said, "Well, I wasn't going to smoke any if that's what you were thinking."

I crossed my arms and stared into the distance.

He would've preferred a reprimand to the silence. Silence gave him room to think. Finally, he said, "I wasn't."

He threw the bag. It hit the gravel with a thud.

"How can I know, Ben? I'm just trying to be cautious."

"I know all about it, so don't tell me," he said, cutting me off. "But I also know that all these people coming after you—they're just people. Not the fucking devil. And it's nothing we can't handle back home. Toussant, the guys from New Jersey, Hicks—they are all just people. A round to the head is all it'd take to end this. I'm thinking the best place to protect you is back at the farm."

"With your family in West Virginia?"

"Yeah. It'd be real easy to defend ourselves there. Toussant wouldn't have made it into Tucker County without twenty pairs of eyes on him. And Rachael and Katy can help with—"

"Charms and hexes? Kitchen magic?" The incredulity in my voice stemmed from his selective faith, which he'd based more on sentimentality than logic. Or perhaps he'd just bruised my ego.

He turned his back to me. "If we stay here too long one of these dirt farmers is going to figure out who we are and try to cash in. Imagine what having a friend like Toussant could do for someone down here. A friend like Toussant would make you a king. Like the kid we bought the bike from. Bet you he talks. Look at the guys on that pier in Progreso. Strutting around on that government property like they owned it. That's what having a friend like Toussant does for you."

"So your plan is to one day return home? I thought we were running away."

"That was always my plan. The timetable's just changed."

49

"I see." My time to be hurt had arrived. "So South America—"

"We'll take it all one step at a time." Bolstered by his minor victory, he stood and stretched. "We need to get to Mérida so I can get my meds and some new clothes and shoes. We'll move once it gets dark. Maybe find a hotel and figure out our next move. Bet you a hundred bucks we'll be able to get home from Cancun or Cozumel. A private plane or another boat. We got cash and a little firepower. Just have to stay off the road."

He flew on auto-pilot now. Ticking boxes on his little checklist—check, check, check—like it would just be that easy. It made more sense for me to let him think he had control. I said, "How do we do that?"

"We'll ask around. Kill some time until it gets dark. Buy a few rounds. Maybe one of these guys will even show us a back way to the highway and a hotel for a little cash. Either way, I need to put gas in the bike." He stopped abruptly, as if waiting for his thoughts to catch up with his mouth. "Yeah. Put gas in the bike."

"The best way to kill time is to forget it exists at all. Maybe you shouldn't drink anything?" I put my hand into his to soften the suggestion and leaned in to smell his skin.

"God loves idiots and drunks, and since I was born smart I have no choice but to drink my way into his favor." He tried to pull me to my feet, but I refused to stand. He sat back down, and said, "Splitting up is a bad idea you know."

"I'll be right here with the bag. You'll know exactly where to find me."

"I figured—"

"Absolutely not. You can't take it with you."

"Well, I sure as hell wasn't going to bust in there waving hundreds if that's what you're worried about."

"It wasn't the money that concerned me."

"Well, I'm keeping the gun. You can have it when I'm back home eating a slice of Sirianni's. Henry and Levon can cover me and we'll have no more of this Toussant bullshit. If we were back home, he'd be at the bottom of a deep hole turning into mud." He rocked the hammock twice, then used the momentum to get back onto his feet. "Forget it. Keep the gun. Shoot anything that gets within ten yards of you. I just need some pocket change to play with anyway."

"Ben, I am trying to become a new woman. I want to shed my past. But the universe is making it very difficult."

He picked the duffel up, brushed the dust off, unzipped it, and checked the gun's safety. He slid three fifties out of their band, fanned them with his thumb and forefinger, and said, "Drinks on me tonight."

"Ben, don't draw a lot of attention."

"They'll be swimming in mezcal. Nobody'll even notice me." He set the bag into the hammock. "Give me an hour."

"Then what?" I stood and followed him onto the path. "You could do a lot of damage in far less time."

He laughed. "Don't I know it? Come and get me in forty-five if it makes you feel better. I don't care. If I can't work something out by then I ain't going to." He kissed me on the cheek then strolled toward the gap in the stone wall that surrounded the village.

On some nearby road, sirens passed and faded into the distance. A sign that the real world existed not so far away. *A bad omen.* I tried one more time. "Ben...."

"Mija, let him go," Doña Cathalina called from the front door of her home. She sat cross-legged in the grey dust, shucking ears of dry corn. "Come here. Sit with me."

Her deep brown eyes watched something in the distance while her hands pulled at the corn. Blisters on her thumb had callused, and turned to stone long ago. Her hens had mostly moved on.

I asked if she felt okay, and without hesitating, she said, "You need to find *x'men.* A real healer. That man needs help, but I am too old. Too weak. To find a real priest, you must go south. Farther from the city and beaches and hotels. It's difficult to be certain where though. Perhaps one of the villages near Cobá."

The Yucatec came a little easier to my ears now. I said, "What should I look for?"

"This land is so different today. Sometimes I don't recognize it. But I don't think I've changed so much...." She looked up at the sky. Patches of light crossed her face. "When I turned twenty my husband took me to Progreso for the first time, and it made me sad because I lived so long without knowing the sea existed so close. When we returned to this village, it felt at once too large and too small. But I think those feelings are true of everyone as we get older. Don't you?"

I nodded.

"Maybe the universe is the same—at once too large and too small." She placed a hand on my knee. "A priest will find you, but you must be patient. Trying to control your own destiny has failed you. In the end, the universe decides, and you must allow it to do so."

"I don't think I can." I suppressed the urge to argue with her. Even I knew better than to repay her kindness with strife.

"Mija, your inability to let people see their own destinies overwhelms you. Perhaps this is why you are blind to your own?"

"I gave up on my own long ago." For the first time in many years, I feared saying the words I'd kept locked away for so long. And for just a moment, I feared not saying them even more. "There is no hope for me. No redemption."

"No, mija."

I wanted to curl up next to her, and nap here in the sun. *It had been a very long time since I'd been mothered.*

"If you can't find hope for yourself, how can you expect to find any for him?" She took my hand. "Destiny exists whether or not we want it to. As long as you try to control your fate by controlling the people around you, you will fail to...."

She paused to allow another siren to pass, but never finished her sentence. In the silence that followed I thought about the things she'd said, but fought to keep them out of my long-term memory. By then, enough time had gone by to let me realize I didn't need to hear the rest. She handed me a corn cob and hummed while we stripped kernels into a steel pail, as if she'd forgotten our discussion altogether. In the silence I listened for commotion, or some sign that Ben needed me, but heard only birds and insects.

For the briefest of moments, the work allowed me to forget. To create space for memories to find their way into the confusion I'd created for myself. The dry chaff that hung in the air and the clean mineral taste of the limestone dust unlocked something so deep inside me that I trembled. My mother and sister carrying water to the barley and sugar beets from the stream at the bottom of the hill. My brother and I on a blanket, pulling weeds and watching.

As if sensing discord in my wandering mind, Doña Cathalina broke the silence. "There will be trouble. You have to collect him and move on."

I paused, hoping to get the memory back, but heard only the same insects and birds.

"You can flee through the ruins. They won't follow, but you shouldn't linger there once the sun sets. Past that mound, farther down the wall, there is another path." She flicked her fingers to the southwest. Through the trees toward the village I saw streetlights humming back to life. "But before you can return home, you will have to figure out whether or not the rules of this universe will work for you. And if not, how to go about creating a universe of your own."

I stood and kissed the top of her head. From town, across the square in front of the church, I heard the squelch of a police radio.

Doña Cathalina said, "*Bey ti' ka'an, bey ti' lu'um.*"

"As above, so below?"

"Yes, mija."

I said, "Thank you." Then I stopped just beyond her yard because I wanted to remember what it felt like to be alone, if only for a moment.

Walking along the shaded path toward the old stone wall pulled me back into the present. I smelled food, like baking bread, but sweeter. Then I heard voices. Laughter. Brakes squealing near the main part of town. The tinny chatter of Tejano coming out of a cracked speaker cone.

Dark women wearing brilliant white *huipils* like Doña Cathalina's lingered in the shadow of the bell tower of the old church. Dogs stretched in the fading daylight and yawned. An interest of convenience. They couldn't eat me, and I was not entertaining.

From the highway, I heard more sirens. Anticipating a change in pace, the dogs stood and stretched. As the sound of heavy footfalls neared, they came to attention.

"Ben."

He spotted me, turned, then looked over his shoulder. "Time to go."

"Through here. There is a path through the ruins."

"What about the bike?"

"We're walking now." I took his hand and pulled him back through the trees. "What happened?"

"They're looking for us. You see the cops?"

"Yes."

"It's bad. Worse than I thought."

When he took the bag from me, he made it seem as if it were to unburden me, but then he took out the gun and chambered a round. I stifled my reaction.

A large wooden cross draped in strips of cloth and broken bits of mirror marked the path Doña Cathalina had mentioned. It glowed in the orange light of one of the dusk to dawn lamps I'd seen from her door. Fire without heat. Giant Yucatecan moths eclipsed it periodically, like planets circling a star.

The setting sun cast long shadows through the spindly trees. Iguanas and lizards scurrying over the dry leaves made it seem as if we were being pursued on all sides. Mounds of rubble and white limestone stacked in unnatural heaps lay scattered about the forest floor. Trees and weeds sprouted from the tops of some. The roots could've stretched straight down to Hell for all I knew.

We pushed ahead steadily for a long time. Perhaps only seven or eight minutes passed, but that can feel like a very long time when somebody wants you dead. No other movement arose in the forest. I felt certain we were alone.

"I'm sorry." The alcohol made Ben unsteady. He gasped for breath, and said, "I should've stayed sharp but I don't know what happened. I didn't even have a chance to talk to anybody before I saw the cops pull in. I never wanted you to feel like you weren't safe and sound around me, but Dani, I swear I didn't do anything."

I ignored him. The memory of my family in the presence of Doña Cathalina haunted me, and I wanted rid of it as much as I wanted more. It felt like the first crack in a stone wall I'd been building since the day I left home.

But my response didn't matter. As long as the medicine controlled him, anything I said would be insignificant. I listened for footsteps. Men from the village or Toussant's hired guns chasing us. But only the crow of Doña Cathalina's rooster could be heard.

Still looking over his shoulder, he tried to take my hand. "You mad?"

"Security is an illusion." I crossed my arms behind my back. "Otherwise, we'd never sleep at night. Some people fumble through the darkness their whole life chasing dreams. Clinging to snippets of imagined conversations. Trying to pull names and faces out of the void. They exhaust themselves, then only a feeling remains. That is how time forgets, Ben."

"I'll kill myself before I forget X and Zack. And Yama."

"Forgetting is the universe letting you go on." I stopped in a clearing.

Bats dipped and swooped against the fading hues of a salmon sky. Venus hovered to the west just above the trees.

The dark silhouette of a large blocky building rose before us. Its bottom terrace, little more than a rocky nest of jagged angles rising straight out of the ground. Empty doorways took shape in the dusky light to stare down at us as we passed.

"A church?"

"Ruins." I tapped a placard on the ground with my toe. The description had been written in English, Spanish, and Yucatec. A virtual Rosetta Stone for the conversation I had with Doña Cathalina. The script reinforced her phonetics. "Called *The Dollhouse*."

"Dollhouse? What does that mean?"

"That's what I'm trying to read now. I'm looking for all the verbs."

"Do you know that language?"

"Not yet," I said with a laugh. "That's why I'm looking for conjugations. I can pick the vocabulary up as I go once I understand the verbs."

Ben kicked at a clump of grass. "I thought the Maya were wiped out by the Spanish?"

"They are very much alive, Ben," I said, then for a moment remained quiet. Thinking. Going back and forth between the Yucatec and English and Spanish.

Whispering and muttering to myself. Finally, I said, "The people at the cantina and in the villages are Yucatec. Their ancestors built these cities."

"How do you know?"

I tapped the placard with my toe.

He watched the trees, struggling to breathe in the thick air. If he had his way, a squad of Hanno's men would burst into the clearing and open fire and he'd be given an opportunity to redeem himself the only way he knew how.

A raised limestone path ran ahead, past square platforms adorned with cracks and rubble and struggling weeds. Desiccated flowers filled several old soda bottles on one. Sweet incense had been burned. Offerings from a recent ceremony. Ben drifted west, jumping at noises in the dark with pistol drawn and fist clenched. His eyes scanned the ground, always looking for a sign of the explosives hidden just inches below the surface.

I couldn't begrudge him his struggle.

Every so often he'd glance back to make sure I was okay. But his legs carried him always ahead, as if stopping for any reason just invited more strife. At each turn, the buildings that rose from the dry earth were even more asymmetrical and disjointed. A surrealist landscape that lived and died beyond any canvas. Disorienting and otherworldly, it existed in four dimensions. Ben didn't know how to respond to it. He said, "Dani—where are we headed? You have a plan, or what?"

He looked scared.

I'd stopped to read again, and didn't respond. The light died, and I needed the words.

"You hear that? It's one of those fuckers from town. Following us. I don't think we should be out in the open."

"It could be an animal." I turned and stared into the forest just to be sure. Highly refracted reds, golds, and yellows painted the trees. The rising night pushed stark black shadows out of the woods behind us. They'd eventually overtake us, bathing us in total darkness. Hiding everything but the stars. I stared for a long, quiet moment, and saw no movement. "You're just tired, Ben."

"Bullshit, Dani." He spun, looking for something to shoot. "If you aren't with me you're against me."

I weighed any possible response against the nature of his instability. Silence felt like the only right answer, so I bit my tongue and walked ahead.

"Don't act like you don't hear them."

"Ben, soon we will find a place to rest. Tomorrow we will visit a pharmacy first thing. It has been a challenging day, and I'm trying to be patient with you." I took his hand and lead him deeper into the ruins. Making the choice so he didn't have to.

The white limestone delivered us into a wide plaza. No wind blew. No insects stirred. Off in the distance swallows bedded down in dark crevasses, cooing themselves to sleep. As we walked, Ben stiffened and stared at the empty doorways that rested atop the ruined terraces.

"Hear that? Somebody's here." He pulled me up the nearest set of stone stairs.

I held my breath to listen. "No, Ben. We are alone."

"Right at the edge of the trees."

The sun seemed to fall faster now. Shadows snaked through the dry grass.

"Maybe even a sniper."

"No, Ben. Stop this," I said, pulling him back down the steps.

"Shut up, okay? I'm trying to fucking listen."

"You need to rest, Ben." I let go of his hand and retreated down to the plaza. "And you are withdrawing from your meds. You have to cooperate."

He wiped the sweat off his forehead with the sleeve of his t-shirt. "Look around you. There's at least three of them, maybe four. They've been following us since we left the village."

"There's nobody..." I lied. I knew what rested in the ground beneath our feet. Beneath all of these rocks. Doña Cathalina told me the Maya buried their dead in the floors of their homes. I could feel them in my stomach like a pound of stone. I could taste them even when I pinched my lips shut. I could hear their last words, they were so close. It felt as if they were all down there waiting, ears pressed against the bottom of the limestone path, listening.

Clinging to the ceiling of the Maya underworld.

Xibalba.

"Believing you is how I end up with a fucking bullet in my skull."

"Stop it. Give me the gun."

"You going to pull the trigger when the time comes?"

"Ben...." I grabbed the barrel and twisted it ever so slowly away. He would never know that since that night at the crossroads, restraint had become my only salvation. That I felt like the cat watching over the fledglings after having just killed their mother. His blue eyes stared down into mine the whole time. I whispered, "Tonight you need to dream sweet dreams. It's time to forgive yourself. It's time to unburden yourself."

He hunched his shoulders and rested his chin on his hand.

I said, "It's fine, Ben. I will help you."

"There's nobody there, right?" He inhaled deeply. "You swear?"

"I swear." At the edge of my vision I saw ghosts withdrawing into the darkness, and ignored them. "There's nothing there."

"So what am I going to do when I accidentally shoot a kid or an old man?" He sat and lowered his head to his hands. His shoulders shook.

When I joined him on the step, he leaned against me, and I could feel his warm tears on my skin. I kissed the top of his head, and he wrapped his arms around me.

"It's okay, Ben," I said. "It's okay if you did see something. Maybe this dead land still has a little breath in it yet."

"You saw something too, didn't you?"

"Shhh. None of that matters."

"You would tell me if you saw something, right? I can't be crazy, because if I'm crazy and a danger to other people, I can never go home. I can never see my mom again, right? What if I hurt her?"

"This is a very old place. Perhaps the dead still have much to say. Día de los Muertos is approaching...." I saw suffering and violence because I'd been trained to see it. The words inscribed on the ancient stairs and stelae verified it. But I couldn't tell him that I saw the past no matter where I looked in a place like this. As if it bled its own history.

I stood, gently pulling him to his feet. "We should try to find the hotel." I started down the steps. "Tomorrow this will all make more sense. You'll see that this has been a very difficult day."

"Dani." He wiped the tears out of his eyes. "I love you."

"I know, Ben. I love you too."

"I'd kill somebody for you. Do you know that?"

Exasperated, I could do little more than shake my head. "Please, Ben. Not tonight. Not now."

"I'm serious. I love you." He put the gun back into the bag and joined me. "And I'd fucking bury somebody for you."

FOUR

March 01, 2003

Mom and Dad,

Next time you hear from me, I'll be in Kuwait. That's the starting line. The finish line is one of Saddam's palaces. I'll call from one of his gold-plated phones.

You can probably imagine what it's like around here tonight—a bunch of soldiers drunk off their asses. Someone heard there's no booze over there so the MGD is flowing and my guys are screwing anything that moves. (Sorry mom.) They keep asking me if I'm scared and I tell them that I'm not because I honestly don't know. If any of them asks me if it feels like I made a mistake by enlisting, I lie.

We keep hearing that our mission is about WMDs, not oil. I'd hate to think I signed up just to be a puppet, but between the news and what they tell us in our briefings I don't know what to believe. There are always at least three or four versions of truth around here. I know our official role, and I'm 110% committed, but deep down I have questions I know better than to ask. Needless to say, I'm hoping the president's right on this one.

I really wanted to thank you both for all the help with the wedding. It wasn't easy to run up to Pittsburgh all the time, but Cora said her parents really appreciated it, and I thought it went really well considering how rushed it felt. You guys looked great. It felt a little like a send-off with everybody there, but I would never say that out loud.

There's not a day that goes by when I don't think getting married was a huge mistake. I don't know if leaving behind a fiancée would've been any easier than leaving behind a wife, but at least a spouse gets survivor benefits if something happens to me. School is keeping her busy and I know she'll make a fantastic doctor. It gives me piece of mind to know her life has meaning. Hopefully she won't have a lot of spare time to worry about me.

Love,

Ben

We checked-in to the hotel late last night. A newly-renovated hacienda that had been decked out with antiques and *hydrotherapy* tubs. Nothing like sleeping where the blood of slaves had been spilled to heal the spirit.

Stumbling through the trees toward the golf resort was the easy part. Once we spotted the glow of civilization it was a straight shot. Diving into the brush along the side of the road every time a pair of headlights came at us made the last mile feel like a hundred. Everything looked like a black F150 once the sun went down. Now that Hanno Krupp-Toussant lived in my head, Hanno Krupp-Toussant lived everywhere.

The front desk clerk turned her nose up at our sweat-stained clothes and Dani's shoeless feet. But once I put that cash onto the counter she smiled like a blue jay in a blackberry bush. We were in a master suite that smelled like lavender by 8:30 and the hydrotherapy tub by 8:35. Knowing that self-medication really was the best kind, I got into the mini-bar at 8:40, 8:50 and again at 8:55 to requisition a little nightcap. Room service arrived at 9:05, and I helped myself to the mini-bar again at 9:10 and 9:15. By 9:50 we were nestled into the king size bed. By 10:30, I was elbow-deep into my first nightmare.

We woke up and ate breakfast at the ass-crack of dawn. Cheesy *chilaquiles* with green salsa and fresh pineapple juice. As I settled the bill, I had the front desk call a cab to get me to the closest pharmacy. Walking into that joint felt a little like Christmas morning. Even with Dani's language skills it took a while to muddle through the generic names of all the drugs. The Klonopin translated the easiest—clonazepam. Didn't matter though. He didn't have it. The pharmacist said the cartels were trying to push it as a Rohypnol substitute, and kids north of the border used it as an alternative to weed. I said, "And now you know why I need it."

But once that pharmacist saw Toussant's fat stacks of cash he became more than happy to recommend substitutions. Like a drug concierge. He gave me escitalopram and quetiapine, then threw in some propranolol in case the others didn't do the trick. He bagged it all up with the rest of the meds on my list.

"The quetiapine is Seroquel, Ben," Dani protested. "An antipsychotic. The VA doctor wanted you tapering off it. It's to keep you from dreaming—do you understand?

Just give me a moment to ask the pharmacist if being overmedicated is worse than being undermedicated."

I grabbed the bag and said, "There's only one way to find out."

She said, "You're not even trying," and followed me over to the cashier. But before we could check-out, she spotted the morning paper in a wire rack. On the cover, a building engulfed in flames. Firefighters worked to keep it contained. The headline read *GUERRA DE DROGAS*.

"*Drug war*," Dani said. "Recognize the building?"

I didn't.

"It's where we bought the bike yesterday. When we came ashore."

I didn't say anything and she continued reading.

"Toussant burned the entire block." She dropped the paper and turned away from me. "The American in Toussant's boat was DEA. He told the feds we did it. Right after we kidnapped him and tried to kill Toussant. Needless to say, the Federales are looking for us."

I cracked open a bottle of water and took a pill without checking to see what it was. The angry static rushed into my head like flies at a pig roast. I shooed them out and tried to put together a few coherent thoughts. Best I could come up with was, "Doesn't change a thing."

"How so?"

I stared at the floor, because I really didn't have anything. My stomach cramped and I knew I'd just throw the pill right back up. So I chugged to make sure it stayed down.

And then I let the molten glass seep into my head. The heat burned through the fluid and grey matter. Through the corpuscles and neurons. Liquid mineral ooze glowing like a falling star. Suffocating folds and lobes. The man's face as he counted the money for his Honda Scrambler—like the one X bought in Zabul—burned away in a flash. The sight of him in the open window, holding his daughter and singing, up in smoke too.

As the molten glass solidified, I clung to the image of the grey dog. Chasing the bike as we rode south. When that glass hardened, it would be the only image left from that morning.

I collected these scenes like trading cards any time I lost something. They were a way to revisit the scene without seeing it again. The bridge over the Euphrates as we left Nasiriyah. An old soccer ball and a boy's jacket in an empty room in a house we were clearing in Fallujah. The half-finished bottle of blue Powerade on the floor next to the bed when I heard X and Yama weren't coming back.

And a man standing in a window, singing to his baby girl, as I stomped my foot at a little grey dog.

I tested the glass, to make sure nothing could get in or out. There were no bubbles. No cracks. No way I'd ever let it get to me. I said, "We stay alive and get home."

We hit the sidewalk like a couple of Morgantown winos—pills rattling, Dani in a pair of shiny new red flip-flops we pulled off a rack of beach stuff. I dipped into the rest of my meds as soon as that glass door slid shut. Even as I counted the dosages out we argued about whether or not I should double on them to make up for the ones I missed yesterday. When Dani stormed back in to ask the pharmacist, I went ahead and swallowed them anyway.

She returned and said the pharmacist didn't advise it. Her smile seemed pleasant, not gloating. So I smiled and kissed her. Then we trotted off to the shopping mall on the other side of the highway, hand in hand, looking both ways for the *hombres* in blue. Letting her think she'd won felt like a victory for me too.

Dani found solace in the familiarity of the mall. She mentioned how the *Galeries Lafayette* in Paris were the only source of consistency in her life for many lonely years, as if she needed a reason to replace the things she'd lost. I'd been in uniform for so long, I didn't know what to buy myself. And for every dollar I saved on Dickies and white V-necks at Sears she spent five. Shoes, skirts, tops and a dress. I reminded myself it wasn't my money and fell asleep while she bought moisturizers and other things at the cosmetics counter in the big department store. The air smelled like oranges and grapefruit and roses and jasmine.

At least I didn't dream. I credited the meds.

As we got ready to go, I transferred everything from Toussant's duffel into a pair of canvas weekend bags with padded shoulder straps Dani had picked up. Then, just before heading back into the wilds of Mexico, I ate fast food until my jaw ached. Burgers. Fries. Egg rolls. Lo mein. Pizza. Fried chicken. Tacos. And I didn't feel the least bit guilty. When Dani went to the ladies room I took another round of meds and just before we left I went back to Sears and requisitioned myself a nice knife with a four and a half inch blade and a multi-tool with all the bells and whistles. She bought a journal and pens at a stationary store. Different tools for different jobs.

But the shiny didn't last long. The mall made me homesick. The smells and the food were a cruel tease and it suddenly felt like I'd self-deployed without giving myself a chance of ever returning home. On the ride into Mérida I told Dani how I felt.

"What about Costa Rica? You'd agreed to that plan."

"I had. But I can't run anymore." I got hot and rolled the window down.

"It's not so easy to just go home like that. Not without passports. Besides, you'd be putting your family in danger."

"I don't care. I can protect them and they can protect me. I'll pay my student fucking loans like everyone else." I put my hand on her leg. I wanted to hold her. I wanted to be in a cool, dark room with nothing to worry about but whether we'd eat steak or lobster for dinner.

Or I just needed a fucking Klonopin real bad. These generics weren't cutting it.

Dani told the driver to take us to the bus station. She said, "It's twelve hours to San Cristóbal de las Casas. From there it's two hundred kilometers to Guatemala. That will give you time to clear your head. Help you see that it's okay to have hope."

"The quickest way to ruin a kid is to give him hope." The heat made it hard to take a breath. My mouth got dry. "I don't want to clear my head, Dani."

"I will get you home, I promise." She turned her back to me and stared out the window. "But first, we need to disappear."

The driver kept his eyes locked on the highway ahead, as if it took great effort to not look back at us. He weaved and jammed on the gas and brake almost simultaneously. Then without much fanfare, Highway 261 became a wide city street. Four lanes choked on a roundabout as strip malls and soccer fields replaced suburban factories and warehouses. Traffic thickened and we couldn't quite keep the same frantic pace anymore.

Dani poked my leg. "Listen."

The word *narco* trickled out of the cab's shitty speakers. I couldn't catch anything else.

"It's us," she whispered. "They said our names, called us fugitives."

"Doesn't mean a thing," I said. The meds kicked in. Brought me down a peg or two. For a second, I thought maybe I had heard our names, but that didn't mean I needed her to confirm it.

"It means they are looking for us," she said. "A manhunt."

I cracked open another liter of water.

City blocks fell by at a casual pace now. Too slow. I scanned rooftops for snipers. The road's surface for fresh concrete or asphalt. Old habits.

Women in white dresses with extensive flower embroidery at the neck and hem flowed toward the center of town carrying baskets and plastic shopping bags. Doña Cathalina had worn a similar dress, but not identical. Her flowers were different colors and patterns. More purple and yellow. Theirs were redder. Oranger. Watching them made me mad because it reminded me of the people I saw in Afghanistan. Just trying to live their lives.

The idea of such simplicity made me angry for all the complications in my own life and then immediately regretful. I knew people like me made it difficult for people like these women to keep living simply. We complicated things with our need to conquer and control because it took too much pain and blood for us to see conquest never worked. Not really, anyway. The women reminded me of my grandma back home and I wondered what she'd make of me now. She had my picture from basic training on the mantle, but I doubted she had any idea what the last ten years meant for me. I felt afraid that if she knew the truth, she'd prefer the idea of me more than the reality.

The drugs made me nauseous. I needed to get out of the car. Suddenly, I could only see our situation here as a problem rather than a solution. Like I always somehow appeared on the wrong side of the glass. We drifted southward with these women, beneath arches of green foliage, past banks and hotels and a massive monument adorned with a stone Maya warrior.

These statues don't represent their heroes. I thought about the kid who sold us the bike. *They live and die without heroes.*

"Ben, how much did you take?"

I tried to focus on her words, but had a hard time hearing.

"You're sweating and shaking." Dani slid her hand into mine and squeezed it gently.

The driver swerved left around a delivery truck, swerved right, then hit the brakes rather abruptly. I had to put my hand on the front seat to keep from sliding into it. The adrenaline cleared me up like a double shot of whiskey and espresso. "Hey, man—"

"Amigos," the driver said, drifting into a parking space behind another taxi. He panicked and began to stutter.

"It's fine."

He relaxed as soon as I saw the reason we'd stopped. A pair of *policía* searching all traffic entering the square. They peered into windows then waved cars on, one at a time. They let the old women in the white dresses pass right by.

"Shit. Bet they're looking for a pair of gringos. Approximately our age and height. Carrying a bag of money and drugs." My heart raced. My eyes itched. I looked for escape routes. "Amigo—Cancun? Give you a thousand bucks. American."

"*No, señor.*" He wiped sweat from his head with a white washcloth. His hands shook. "*Por favor.*" He went on and on, but it sounded like gibberish to me. I could smell the coffee on his breath.

Dani said, "He begs you not to ask him again."

"Okay, I won't." I got the pistol out of my bag and tucked into my waistband. "Just tell him to shut it."

Now that traffic had stalled, the cops made their way toward us even faster. They stopped about seven or eight cars ahead of us, checking IDs. They both carried M4s.

"What are you so afraid of? They ain't going to shoot you."

The driver turned. His eyes were red and he held his rosary in his hand. He stuttered and took shallow breaths. Like my pharmacological symptoms were contagious. In little more than a whisper, he said, "Hanno Toussant."

"Fuck Hanno Toussant. Should've fucking cut him up and fed him to the barracuda when I had the chance. All this fucking money and we're stuck inching through this shithole…should've just gotten my own fucking car." I looked through the rear window. "I can't buy a miracle. Tell him it's fine. Shut the fuck up, man."

Dani tried to console him. "*Dios bo'otik.*"

"What's that?" I said. Paranoia made me a little jittery. "Not Spanish."

"Yucatec Maya. Roughly translated, it means *God has already paid*. The closest thing to *thank you* in their language."

"And you're really just picking it up as we go?" I pulled the slide back to make sure there was a round in the chamber and swore to myself if those cops started any shit I'd be the last fucking man either of them ever saw.

"Something like that."

"Well, it ain't going to change the fact that things could get shitty quicker than a cat can lick its ass. Ready to walk? I can't protect you in this cab." I grabbed a fifty from the bag, folded it between my fingers and passed it up to the driver. "Here."

He got out and opened the door for Dani.

I hopped onto the curb, put the bag over my shoulder, and grabbed her hand, doing my best to keep my body between her and the cops. And before either of those Mérida pigs could say *alto*, I'd pulled her to cover between a pair of large concrete buildings.

To our south sat the town square. Sunlight streamed out of the crisp, blue sky. The narrow alley continued straight for ten yards then disappeared around a slight bend to the left. The hot air smelled like shit and garbage. After twenty feet, the buildings suddenly pushed together. The bright blue sky narrowed to a sliver.

The pale walls forced us through another passage that ran at a disjointed right angle to the main streets. Like Pac-Man. I slowed, taking more deliberate steps. I knew that blundering into bad guys would end this little sojourn real quick. I backed up to the wall, slid to the edge of the building, and turkey-peeked around. The coast looked clear, so we sprinted across the street to the next narrow passage.

I couldn't distinguish echoes from footsteps, which kind of slowed things down. Made me paranoid. I kept stopping, trying to change the rhythm of the game. Deep down I doubted myself—hated myself—and I knew I'd blame myself if anything went wrong.

As soon as the mosque with the blue minaret drifted out of sight I lost my bearings altogether. My first mistake. Our mission was to head through a wide corridor east of the city—a neighborhood called Askari—then make a big sweep to the south through the industrial districts and warehouses. When all was said and done, we were supposed to be headed west to rendezvous with another platoon. Problem was, I had no idea where west was.

Overhead, a Harrier screamed. Behind me, way in the distance, a Mark 19 let loose a burst of grenades. The successive *booms* echoed off the concrete walls. I wanted to cover my ears, but knew deep down my hearing was already fucked.

I held up my fist. "Keep an eye on those rooftops. Bet you a hundred bucks that's where they fucking hit us from."

"No shit, Collins. Tell us all something we don't know." The passage grew so tight that X had to pull his SAW up to his chest to turn around. "Just ragging on you, dog."

"We got to stay out of that fucking market. That's where they hit those British contractors last month. No way I'm fucking going home in plastic. Where's Zack?"

"Right here, sir?" He went down on one knee and caught his breath.

X said, "Well, check this chumpy out," and slapped Zack's helmet. "Snacks Jackson reporting for duty, sir."

"We got anybody else with us?"

"No, sir," Zack said quietly, intently watching the passage behind us just to make sure. "It's just us. When that roof collapsed Laird and his guys were on the other side of the hole. Sounded like they were headed this way though."

"You bring us something to eat?" X put the back of his hand up to his mouth and laughed. "Snickers? Don't tell me your mama ain't sending Snickers."

"All right, man. Keep it down." I put my forefinger up to my lips. "Let's see that map. Last time we saw Laird was where? 3320, 4345? Does that sound right? What'd you hear, Zack?"

"Just a whole lot of shouting. But I couldn't see a path through that rubble. Looked like we passed an empty house back there. We could check that out. Maybe cross over there?"

"Let me think on that." I rubbed my eyebrows. My temples throbbed. "If that doesn't pan out we'll try to get north and work back a few blocks. Maybe we can hook up with them from behind."

"Check it." X bumped me with his elbow. "They're taking fire again."

"Okay. Let's move. Worst case scenario, we have to push all the way back to the Brads and start over. They shouldn't be too hard to find from there."

"Shhh." Zack put his fingers to his lips. "Sounds like a lot of spraying and praying."

An AC-130 circled overhead. The low roar of its cannon echoed through the city blocks. I couldn't hear much beyond that.

X said, "You best BOLO them snipers, Collins."

"I know." I rubbed the sweat out of my eyes. "Let's try that house Zack spotted."

X slapped my shoulder twice, then followed Zack.

The family that lived there had scrawled verses from the Quran on the walls in white and black house paint. Not a lot of protection to be found in those scribbles anymore. Someone knocked over a kerosene heater on the way out. I coughed on the fumes. A few cans of baby formula had been stacked in a corner below a painting of Mecca.

Less than a block away a building exploded. The ground quaked. The stairs shook and I had second thoughts about heading up to the roof. *Probably a thousand pound JDAM.*

"That's what's up." X steadied himself on a door jamb and ripped open one of Zack's Snickers. "Soften those fucking targets."

"Well, shit's always going to smell like shit and Fallujah don't look much different from up here." To the north I saw the smoke and flames of the firefight. Ash from burning buildings fell like snowflakes. While Zack took a piss in a corner, X and I watched the glow of multiple fires illuminate the sides of the buildings farther down the street. X gave me one of his newly-acquired Fun Size Snickers.

"Thanks, Snacks," I said. "Thank your mama for me, too."

"Yep."

"Back off the fucking Kool-Aid," X said. "I know you ain't drinking that much water."

"Hydrate, X. Rule number one."

As soon as Zack said it, I got thirsty and had to drink too.

"Rule number one is don't pull your dick out on a rooftop in Iraq." X made a pistol with his finger and shot at Zack's crotch. "You're lucky some haji ain't shot that shit right off. Or maybe he need a bigger scope."

"It's funny how you finally get up high enough to see something and you can't see shit. Not another living thing." I squinted into the smoke and flames, trying to get a bearing on our guys. "Then as soon as you hit the ground they're shooting at you from everywhere."

The bright red sun sat low on the western horizon. Dust and smoke crossed its ruddy surface in waves that made no attempt to block its dense warm light. In the glare I saw the mosque. "Well, there's our landmark. The Brads should just be to the left. To the southwest, I guess."

In his best Ton Lōc voice, X said, "Let's do it."

We broke into a sprint as soon as we hit the street. The first building we passed was the one we'd gotten blown out of. A massive wall of rubble separated us from the firefight on the other side. The air smelled like sewage and burning rubber. When we heard small arms fire, I realized Laird and his guys were heading in pretty much the same direction as we were, just one or two blocks over. The only difference was they were surrounded by insurgents.

I said, "Should be up on the right here. Take it slow." I edged to the corner and watched the empty storefronts across the street. A carpenter's workshop and a garage. At my feet, a tin cigarette stand pocked with bullet holes sat in a pool of old blood.

A low shuffle came from the south. I dropped to my knee and flipped the fire selector switch from *SAFE* to *SEMI*.

"Shit, Collins." X peeked over my shoulder. "You going to bust a cap in Nana's ass? Told you white people were fucking crazy, didn't I Snacks?"

I flipped the selector back to *SAFE* and stood up.

They all wore stark white dresses, with flowers embroidered at the neck and hem. Like dust and dirt couldn't stick to them. Each carried a basket. Each patted my chest as they passed.

The threads reflected light at weird angles. The flowers grew with each step they took. My pulse throbbed in my ears. Red and gold buds expanded into a vibrant bouquet that went to seed in the space of just a few feet. Greens and blues turned brown then grey before crumbling to dust that fell to the hot Iraqi soil. The grey dissolved onto a velvety blackness exploding with pinpoints of white light that condensed like water droplets on glass.

The women crossed the heavily-cratered street in a shuffle. On the other side, they disappeared into a narrow passage between shops, toward the sound of church bells.

X said, "Got yourself a honey?" and pointed to the bright orange marigold one of the women had tucked into my Kevlar. "What's that sweetie back home going to think?"

"All right," I said, blowing him off. "Let's move out. Zack, we're right behind you."

Zack crept ahead, M4 raised. Before X fell in, he turned and said, "Collins, how close were we? Those fucking mortars…."

"I don't think Zack saw what we saw." I shook my head. "When I heard our artillery on the other side of town, I thought they'd get haji before haji got us. Then the fucking roof exploded. Last thing I heard before tumbling ass over teakettle into the street was *danger close*."

X said, "So fucking right on top of us, huh?"

"Yeah. We got lucky."

The moving air provided little relief from the heat. Sweat rolled off me and it felt like I'd throw up again. It didn't help that Dani insisted on leaning against me with her head on my shoulder. I needed moving air and a little space. But I'd grown more afraid of being alone.

It's a cycle… Dani had once said. But I didn't know what that meant. I didn't know where the anger came from, I only ever got scalded after it had boiled over. I didn't know if this felt normal or not. I didn't know if I could change, or if I'd eventually push Dani away because I couldn't. These thoughts made me angry, so I didn't say anything at all. If at one time I'd known how to handle these feelings, it meant I had reason to hope I could find it once again.

If I didn't push her away first.

She'd arranged the ride out of Mérida after we lost the cops in the market. Somewhere beyond the shark heads and lobsters and bananas and cages filled with brightly colored songbirds we stumbled into some kind of alternate reality pre-Columbian market. This only added to my disorientation because of the time I'd lost during my serotonin hangover. Dani found a place for me to rest and lay low. I remembered waking up to some very kind women. They kept watch and fed us *chimole*—a stew made out of roasted chili paste and turkey served with warm tortillas. I could've eaten that for days. Dani jabbered with them while I filled up.

Before splitting, I wadded up a few fifties and paid them. *Buying my way back into the human race, one soul at a time.*

But they were the ones that got us onto this *colectivo,* Mexico's version of a Pakistani *jingle truck.* Somebody's nephew needed to head east and it was just a matter of waiting for the truck to come around and collect us. Like glass bottles on Thursday. None of it mattered though, because we were on the move. Movement felt like action. Like a means to an end.

Toussant's money bought us six square feet in the back of a flatbed with several bales of hay, a case of Coke and eight farmers who eyeballed us like a pack of coyotes caught on the wrong side of the bull's fence. None of them wore deodorant. Dani tried starting a dialogue, but they wanted no part of her sorcery, or what-the-fuck ever. She seemed mildly hurt by this, which I found odd.

None of it mattered though. After a good hour we left the main, four-lane highway in a cloud of white dust and eased onto a heavily potholed road at a village called Kantunil. There we slid to a stop at the edge of an old, tired farm. Each of the men took a bale of hay with them as they slid out of the truck bed. The driver came around, grabbed the case of Coke and disappeared into the village.

I took Dani's hand and eased her onto the rocky ground. She kissed me and I felt really shitty about wanting some space earlier. I knew that moments like those didn't last long and hated myself for letting that one get away. Her skin smelled like clove and citrus and roses, even after that long ride. So I tried to hold her and wanted to tell her how much I loved her, but she said we had to get out of the village and find someplace to spend the night before the sun went down. I put her bag over my shoulder and took her hand and together we resumed our trek east. Just a pair of ghosts moving through the afternoon, with just a pair of shadows to prove that we were real. Sensing adventure, a few village dogs followed.

The men standing amongst the rows of brown, rattling corn stalks took no notice. They leaned on their hoes, using their hands only to accentuate their discussions. Occasionally one of them stopped talking long enough to push a little of the dry soil into a mound, or to flatten one out. Every so often a small breeze lifted, and the rustling of cornstalk chatter drowned out their soft voices. Dogs walked the perimeter as far as the shade allowed.

In the next village, women sat at looms with their backs to open doors, weaving history into the flowery red and green swirls that would encircle the neck and hems of their plain white dresses. Their shuttles spun celebration dances in the dusty shafts of light, releasing threads tinted with pink and purple fire sunsets. Gifts from the gods themselves, no doubt. Younger women stood by with their babies draped over their hips as if they were little more than sacks of squash.

Watching them made Dani smile, which made me smile. I kissed her and pulled her along.

The road stretched east like a white snake with no head. We walked without ever stopping to think about its bite. The sun shone fiercely and made heavy shadows in the scrubby undergrowth. A shimmering mass of heated air danced above the concrete, like the breath of the serpent itself.

One of the village dogs followed us at a distance. Its little claws *clickclicked* on the broken surface. When I stopped and turned, it froze in its tracks. "Dog—you're going to be disappointed."

"An animal like this is a very bad sign to the Maya. Worse than a black cat," Dani said. "Especially so close to All Saints."

"Can things get worse?" I squatted and patted the pavement a few times.

"It's a yellow dog that escorts the dead to the underworld." She put her hands on her hips. "Xibalba."

"Then he's lucky I don't know what that even means."

He approached with his head down, then stopped just a foot out of my reach.

"Don't hurt his feelings." I said, "Come here," but he just cocked his head and panted.

"Maybe it knows how mean you are?"

"Way to kill the mood, dog." I stood and brushed the dirt off my knees. "Want me to shoot him?"

"Don't be cruel, Ben. Just make it stop following us."

I took a long drink of water, then offered the bottle to her. "Bet you a thousand bucks he doesn't last a mile. I'm good for it."

"It's easy to gamble with somebody else's luck."

"You being metaphorical?" I took her hand and started walking again.

"You know exactly what I mean. We can't take that money back with us." Somehow, she hadn't broken a sweat. Her wide-brim straw hat let specks of light onto her cheeks and the bridge of her nose. It seemed as if the only thing she feared more than Toussant was getting too much sun.

"Why not? Don't you think the universe owes you something for all you've lost?"

"The universe doesn't owe anybody anything. The last few days should've proven that to you." She turned to see where the dog had gone.

"I don't know, Dani. Seems like the only thing I've demonstrated so far is that I'm too smart for my own goddamn good and too dumb to know it."

"Stop it." She let go of my hand and walked ahead of me. "It's time to forgive yourself, Ben. Your brain is muddled by all the drugs. I begged the pharmacist not to give you anything but then you pulled out that money. You were close to being free—do you even realize what that means? To be free of that poison? I am sorry that you saw what you saw and lost what you lost. But it's over."

"It's never over, Dani." Never." I didn't want to give up my words too easily. They seemed like the only thing I had left at the moment. As long as I talked, I could change the way she saw me. "Maybe I want to go home. Get some real food in my belly. Have a drink with my pap. That'll fix me. Maybe I'm sick of boarding planes and landing in different time zones. Maybe I want to start going to weddings again and see babies being born. I miss my family and I miss my bed. Maybe I get tired of seeing the world through a scope. Watching people in the cross hairs."

"Then it's time to stop." She took my face in her hands. "It's time to find out what the next chapter is. You don't have to forget, Ben. Never, ever forget. But you are not dead. You are here, with me, and I love you. I want to be with you and I want to help you."

Her intensity scared me and I tried to retreat a hair.

"Do you want this to be the dream?" she said. "Or your reality? Because it can't be both. You must choose, so think very carefully before you answer."

"Do I have to?"

"Sadly, you do."

"Do I have to choose right now?"

"No, not right now. But soon."

"Yeah."

But she hadn't finished. She stood in front of me, blocking the way forward. "Who is telling your story? Because you live as if somebody else is writing the narrative and you are only reciting dialogue."

"I don't even know what that means, Dani."

"But you do, Ben. You do." She took my hand. "It's easy for a reader to give a writer too much credit. It depends on schema, I suppose. Can you read a story apart from your own experiences? Can you know which set of values deserves more attention? After a few pages the reader decides whether or not to trust the writer."

"So make a choice?" I said. And as soon as she kissed me and then let go of me, I said, "Do you think it's time for my meds?"

"You really don't understand, do you?"

As she walked on, I tried to think about where I'd gone wrong.

Fortunately, the mutt did last longer than a mile. He stuck to my heel like I owed him money. But no matter how fast we went we could never quite catch up to Dani. It seemed as if she could hear when I quickened my pace and sped her own up to match. So we fell back, the yellow dog and me. Waving at farmers who never waved back. Smiling at women who shooed us away like we were chickens in the corn. The kids were much kinder and every so often a couple of boys would run out and wave and I'd give them some of the candy I requisitioned back in Mérida. Having a reason to smile felt good. It made me realize how I'd angered her.

We found her at a slight dogleg, sitting on an old stone wall in the shade of an older tree—arms folded across her chest. She stared at something in the distance. And she looked good doing it. The air smelled like cucumber. I stepped off the road to take her hand, but Yellow Dog stepped between us and barked. He widened his stance and the hair on its back rose.

I pulled Dani onto the road, away from him.

"I told you I didn't like it…" she'd begun to say as he lunged at the wall.

A velvety blackness stretched out where the stone met the dirt. Yellow Dog retreated a step and danced a half-circle to get behind it. In between the hoarse snap of each bark I heard the dry rattle. I said, "Shit," and went back a few steps to look for a large branch or stick.

Yellow Dog corralled the snake toward the road. The reptile tried to flank him in a lazy S that suggested annoyance more than anything else. The rattler—thick as my forearm and as long as my leg—never let the dog get behind it.

The serpent flashed its pink mouth and doubled back on itself. Yellow Dog put its ears at attention and snapped. Calling him back seemed futile. "C'mon, boy. Leave it." I clapped my hands three times. "Hey."

Yellow Dog inched closer and the snake fell back, still rattling. Jade beads in an empty skull.

As the snake feigned a strike, the dog jumped. While the serpent recoiled from its full extension, Yellow Dog lunged and bit it just behind the head. He growled and shook and shook and shook until the snake fell limp. He loosened his jaw, letting the snake slip a hair, then shook it a few more times. When he finally dropped the snake onto the road he barked twice—more of a high yip—just to make certain the serpent had died.

"What do you think of him now?" I said. "Can we keep him? Huh? Can we?"

She handed me her water without saying a word.

In a show of conquest, Yellow Dog picked up the reptile and brought it to me, its scales dragging on the road. I took a knee, pulled out my new knife and cut the rattles off. They were as long as my index finger. I counted thirty-four beads. *One for each year, just like me.*

I didn't resent it. I knew it was just a snake being a snake. Its blood formed a small puddle that congealed quickly on the hot pavement and I thought a turkey buzzard might swoop down to eat it as soon as we got far enough away. Make the death meaningful.

And after a few minutes, I turned to see if I was right. But the road appeared empty except for the body of the snake. It suddenly seemed like a life wasted. I dropped my trophy into the dust.

Dani rubbed my arm. "Are you okay?"

I nodded. "Just hungry."

"Because you're scaring me a little."

The urge to lie settled into my head, making it hard to see a better option. Finally, in a low voice, I said, "I spent my life trying to get to the next level only to realize I ain't quite got the tool kit for it."

She put her hand on my cheek. When I looked into those amber eyes something in me broke. "Dani, I give up. I just want to go home now."

She kissed me. "You only have to be strong a little longer."

As we resumed walking, I had time to think about my reaction to the stupid snake and forced the sadness back down. I faked a quiet laugh and a smile. "I'm good."

Over the next mile things changed dramatically. Billboards replaced trees. Buses idled in the parking lot of a big Pemex service station. Cheap plaster homes sprang from the earth like rows of well-watered corn. Maya women tended stalls filled with fruit, wood carvings, and plaster statues. Ads for soda and beer and bread made the graffiti seem sincere. Civilization ruining what the conquistadors couldn't.

The tourists came from Cancun and the Riviera Maya. Americans and Germans stumbled into the heat, waving brochures as fans. Thousands of them, sunburnt and hung over. Maya men stood by the bus doors loaded down with t-shirts and silver bracelets and blankets and carvings, proud warriors, hustling. One guide sold beer out of a large cooler and made change from a big wad of cash.

We decided to find a hotel to get out of the sun and ended up at a place called the Piramide Inn. A two-story concrete box with Maya imagery on the rail of each balcony. A covered walkway connected it to a restaurant. I heard splashing on the other side.

I grabbed the office door and kissed her check. "You want to go see if they have a room for us?" I pointed at a group of boys sitting around a big blue cooler. They were tired, dirty, and didn't seem to be having a lot of luck. I liked them immediately. "I'm going to rustle up some intel on a little grub."

As soon as I turned toward the boys they were on their feet. I held up two fingers and said, "*Dos Cocas*."

The tallest flipped the cooler's lid and plunged his hands into the icy water. *Fucking hajis*, I thought, then immediately tried to push it away. *Kids*, I corrected myself. *Fucking kids*.

The tall one didn't necessarily seem to call the shots. He deferred to a kid wearing an old wife-beater who held his baseball cap over his chest and muttered, "*¿Doce?*"

"Twelve?" I laughed. He played an old game. "*¿Habla inglés?*"

The others shouted *sí*, but I only believed the tall one.

"You can take care of my dog? *Mi perro*." In a way, I hoped this meant I'd never have to see him again. Having no ties made me one step closer to getting home. I put my fingers up to my lips and gave the boy a fifty. "*Por todos*."

I hoped the fifty meant I'd never have to see any of them ever again.

"It's okay."

I felt her hand on my arm before I realized she was trying to wake me up. "Ben, it's a bad dream."

My eyes stayed shut even after I realized I'd awoken. Being up was one thing. Being in Mexico, on the run, and strung out on antidepressants felt like another thing altogether. "Yeah."

She said, "Do you want to talk about it?"

"No." I rolled onto my side. Away from her. "I don't want to fucking talk about it."

She sat up, but didn't say anything.

It wasn't my fault I woke up angry.

I said, "If you're going to the bathroom could you please get me some water? I need to take something to get back to sleep."

She padded across the dry tile like a cat. I heard the rattle of pills in a bottle and I knew she read the labels and studied the dosages and precautions. And I knew she'd tell me I had to wait.

"Maybe just a little water?" Her voice lacked the timbre of a fully-awake Danicka. Right now it sounded soft, a whisper with an edge. "And I can talk to you until you fall back to sleep."

My mind phrased my request a hundred different ways. In some versions, I tried to get sympathy. In others I sounded forceful and strong. Confident. As if asking for psych meds authoritatively would diminish her doubt. "Thanks, babe. Just the pills."

She sighed. If I didn't know better, I'd have said she wanted me to hear her exasperation. "Ben," she protested. "Have you been paying close attention to the dosages? I haven't really seen you reading the labels."

"They're in Spanish," I said.

"No…" She set a bottle back onto the counter. "The instructions are in English."

The wheezy air conditioner sparked to life. Musty air blew into the room. The noise masked my reaction. A little laugh because I'd gotten caught. I sat on the edge of the bed, simmering in a quiet anger.

She said, "Please, don't be mad. For a long time I've been thinking—"

I stood and punched the cheap sheetrock wall. The pain cleared my mind. Sharpened my focus like a fucking spear.

She rushed into the bedroom. "Ben?" She lifted a hand to my cheek to soothe me and I pushed it away.

"You and your fucking control. That's what it is, Danicka. You want to be the reason I'm happy or sad and it's fucking working because I am fucking livid." I pointed at her and jabbed my finger. "Livid."

"You're scaring me."

"Yeah, like I'm the scariest fucking thing you've ever…."

She winced and I knew I could never take it back. *Diesel on the fire, that's all.*

"What, Ben? The scariest thing I ever *what*?" Dani paused, looking at me. Studying me. Then the lines around her eyes softened. Instead of getting angrier, she seemed to be moving away from her emotions. Getting colder.

"Go ahead. You got it all figured out, so just go right ahead." Her lack of fight unbalanced me. I heard the thump of pumping blood in my ears.

"If you want to die you can die alone." She took her bag from the closet and set it on the dresser. "I don't think there's anything else I can do for you."

I felt the sting of acid in my belly. Regret and shame cleared my head. And in that instant I saw that I could lose her. I grabbed her arm. Tried to stop her from packing. As soon as she calmed down, I'd tell her how sorry I was.

Dani twisted free of my grip. "A sad quitter in a sad little hotel."

I retreated a few steps.

"Skin and bones with no name, no family, no one to love." She pushed me. "Just a cock and a trigger finger."

"I'm sorry." My words had no heft. She didn't react the way I expected her to.

"Why? Because you want it to stop?" She smiled and faked a pout. "What if I'm the scariest thing you ever fucked? Is that what you wanted to say? You wanted a fight, yes?"

She put her arms around my neck and slid her leg up mine. "Maybe that is why you got into the car with me?"

She kissed my shoulder. I felt her hot breath on my ear. "You figured with me you could just curl up and cry forever."

"Stop."

"What's in there, Ben? Hmmm?" She drew a little heart on my chest with her finger. "Do you even have a soul? Because, Preston—"

"Enough." I backed into the wall and slumped to the floor. My face got hot. I couldn't stop the tears. I needed someplace to put all the rage, but I'd filled that box a long time ago. "When you find somebody you really love, you may as well just fucking kill yourself. It's the same thing in the end."

"It must be, because right now it feels like you are twisting a knife in my back." Dani stood over me, watching. "So sad. Where's this boy's mother?"

"I didn't mean to hurt you or say those things."

"But you said them."

"I know. What kind of man am I?"

"What kind of man are you, Ben? I don't know."

"I don't know."

I reached my hand out and stroked her calf. "I'm sorry, Dani. I am. It's like this blackness gets in me—"

"Stop," she said. "I don't want to hear it from you. How much medicine have you swallowed today? You didn't even try to restrain yourself, did you? Yesterday it was alcohol. As long as you are drunk or waving a gun around you have a way to avoid responsibility for your actions. Live with a little restraint for one day and see how the world looks and then apologize."

"They are prescription...."

"Are you mad? I'm not a doctor but I'm not illiterate. For sertraline, the dose is fifty milligrams a day. For escitalopram it's ten. How many have you taken? I counted six pills, so you're over the proper dosage on at least one prescription, maybe two. How many did you take while my back was turned?"

"Well, you can't quit Klonopin cold turkey—"

"That's why I was tapering you off." She pounded her palm with her fist and fought the urge to raise her voice. "How many chances do you think you get? How many times do you think you can treat somebody this way?"

"I don't know. I said I was sorry."

She wouldn't even look at me.

I sat on the floor for a very long time, empty except for the shame I felt. The only words I could bring myself to say were, "I should have been there."

"I'm not certain I know what you're talking about."

"It's because you don't pay attention. I should been in that fucking poppy field the day X died."

"Do you wish you were dead now? Is that what you want?" She looked through her bag for a pack of cigarettes that she never bought. "You had pneumonia. Nothing could be done, right?"

"Yeah. Nothing could be done." The minutes felt hollow and created a widening gap between the truth and what I wanted to believe. After what seemed like a really long time, I said, "Can I explain? Please, Dani."

She said, "Isn't that what you've been doing? Explaining?"

"This world wasn't made for people like me." I looked at the food I'd knocked onto the floor. The leftovers from our dinner. Red sauce trickled across the cold tile. That moment had been perfect. We laughed and hid under the sheet, talking about what we could eat if we could eat anything in the world at that moment. *Focaccia in Corniglia, udon at that little place in Morgantown, halupki in my grandma's kitchen....*

"The older I get the worse I feel. It's not getting better." I buried my face in my t-shirt. I hated crying in front of her, but couldn't stop. My head ran wild with a cascading series of dark memories and images. I knelt at the edge of the bed to be closer to her. "All I keep thinking about is how these fucking eighteen-year-old privates were looking at me wondering how the fuck I was still walking around when everybody else my age had moved on or out. Tell me that ain't fucked up.

All these fucking kids looking at me like I should be in a body bag. And then I get home and my family can't get over it either. Like they can't figure out how I'm supposed to fit back into their world. They just look at me and wonder when I'm going to disappear."

I slumped back to the floor. Even with the bathroom light on the room seemed very dark. Only a faint glow from a streetlight outside gave any indication that a world existed beyond these walls.

I felt like an empty box. And it hurt to think any more about what I'd done.

From the other side of the bed, Dani broke the silence. Her voice became soft again. "Ben, I've been around. Maybe you can't see things the way that I see them because our experiences were so radically different, but I know what it feels like when brothers and sisters die. I've seen cities burn. I've watched mothers stand at the edge of mass graves, not sure if it was better to believe their sons were dead or alive. Ben, I know the smell of burning flesh." She pounded her heart with her fist.

She paused long enough to take a long sip of water. "Maybe you don't believe me, but I've seen a soul depart the body. I've seen priests lose faith while giving last rites. It all made me wonder how the heart still beat when your parents were gone and your brothers were gone. The only answer I found is that the body knows, even if the soul doesn't. *That* is the world we live in. The body has ways of lasting until the soul is consumed. The body is built to survive. The body knows when a long winter is coming." She extended her hand and I kissed it.

She handed me a t-shirt and I wiped my face. Sweat and tears.

She said, "The soul is built to love and nourish and be part of something bigger, but it knows nothing of what the body does. That is why the soul smiles when the body can't. Tell me the body and the soul are one and I will tell you they are as different as spring and fall. I know they exist in different universes because I have seen the soul go on after the body is dead. I have seen dead eyes and black hearts, Benjamin. You are not dead yet." She stood and went to her bag, as if she were going to pack and unpack it all over again.

Knowing she wouldn't leave me brought me great relief. I could breathe again. But I knew it came at a cost. "So what do I do?"

She crossed her arms, stroked her little amber amulet with her thumb, and leaned against the dresser. "You must see that the sun shines for you alone. You must learn that love is like currency and once you start exchanging it, there will be more of it for you. You must see that your soul neither lives nor dies with the circumstances of your family and friends. Your soul has its own seasons and it moves on according to its own calendar. Do not look at the fallen and think that you belong with them because you shared a uniform. When the universe comes for you, you will know it. Then you can be afraid, but if you want the bright sunlight of a new day to shine on you, then you must understand that things are not going to be as you want or expect. Things are not going to be as Dickens or Hemingway or Hugo have written them. Writers are liars anyway. You can't believe them when you know in your heart that things are very different, indeed."

At some point she'd joined me on the floor. I tried to take her hand and she guided my head into her lap. She said, "Ben, I stood in the breadlines in Stalingrad, ran along sniper alley in Sarajevo. I saw Columbus arrive in the New World with sugarcane and influenza. I saw Paris liberated and Berlin fall."

"But I didn't." Saying it made me feel as if I'd lived one big lie.

"We all did, Ben, but most of us have forgotten. We all cried when Hitler entered Poland and when Stalin entered Prague. We all experienced the trauma of birth and we will all know a last gasp. But who wants so many thoughts like these in our heads like blood clots? I don't. It's too much, Ben. It's really too much."

When I closed my eyes, I felt the edge of sleep creeping toward me, so I jerked myself awake. She put the back of her hand on my cheek and stroked it gently.

In little more than a whisper, she said, "I stood by you when you brought that mountain down on those women in West Virginia. I know what thoughts you held in your head when you did it."

Struggling to keep my eyes open had made them itchy and watery.

She patted down my hair. "I was there on the day you were born. You were there at my birth. It's no secret, Ben. We know these things. These feelings are in our blood. But the years make us forget. Each passing day makes us believe we are different people and makes us forget that we're connected to everybody else. You must remember this. We are all the same person. We wear a billion different faces but we are the same. Of the same mother and father—even our genes say it is true. When we take our first breath we are the same. It's hours, days, and years that convince us that we hate each other. That we are at war. That we are enemies."

The air conditioner wheezed to life.

I said, "Maybe we're all meant to be alone. The idea of any kind of emotional bond we form is just an illusion. We have that moment of being alone together and from that moment on are bound by the shared knowledge. What if our connection is just recognizing the loneliness?"

She said, "Why can't you live with that? Knowing that we are solitary, singular animals and that if we allow ourselves to be together, then we are, in fact, together? Why can't you accept that life is a singular path meant for singular souls and the only respite from the journey is a pair of us working together?"

"Because I can't believe in anything."

"Ben, we are not born by choice. Instead, we are plucked from the womb of the universe by cold hands and dropped into a nest with complete strangers. Whatever soft existence we lived in, that other place was never ours to do with as we pleased. At least here we have the illusion of choice. Whether or not it exists doesn't matter because the illusion is very real. In the end, that is all we need."

"I'm so tired of all this."

The serpent hissed, blowing a gentle breeze through the room. The whooshing drapes sounded like the shuffling of leaves. I held my breath because I didn't want it in my lungs. Deep down, I knew I felt too tired to fight it anymore.

Dani said, "I will help you get back to sleep."

For just an instant, I forgot about the snake. Even though I felt no different, I knew I'd allowed it into me. As soon as I relaxed my jaw it slid down my throat and into my lungs. The snake lay coiled there. Waiting. Wrapped around my trachea.

Changing me.

I tried to pull myself from sleep, but the weight of the dream felt too heavy. The only thing I could do was remind myself over and over that my blood was still mine.

The shushing of leaves from the forest floor quickened. The big cat that waited for me out there in the night sensed I struggled to wake myself. Its black rosettes heaved as it inhaled, trying to learn my taste.

I tried to yell, but my shouts were barely mumbles.

My heart raced and my belly burned from a thousand scorpions tearing their way out of my skin. Their tails stabbed my liver, venom dripped into my veins. No matter how I screamed they wouldn't stop.

My penance.

From my wounded soul, violet blood spilled across the dirty hotel room floor. Rows of rattlesnake beads pushed up through the moisture like spring buds. One by one they unfurled into poppies, black velvet in a crimson skull. Their scent mixed with the sweat and breathy condensation of all who'd died on this rocky soil. The blood came from my fingernails and nose and from my pores. It rose toward the ceiling in a spiral, like a snake coiled to strike.

Dani talked to me, comforting me as she tried to stop the bleeding. But her words turned into smoke that formed a pulsing cloud, a wretched mass that blocked out the sun, turning the sky black. Turning leaves grey. Turning stones white. The smoke sounded like a river raging. In its crimson currents I saw a thousand hands reaching, but not one of them would take mine.

All of my blood pooled at the base of the big oak that grew by the graves in my pap's yard. A deer hung from a limb by its hind legs. It had been gutted. Red footprints went up the tree trunk. They disappeared in the higher branches.

The scorpions left me and followed the blood all the way into the top of the tree, where they ascended into the heavens on the cloud of black smoke. There they drifted, like snowflakes, to the edge of the sky. As they walked across the cosmos their rigid legs left spots, like pinholes in construction paper, which pierced the darkness.

The points of light swirled and gathered in the West like stars rising from the wrong horizon. I heard a hollow thud and saw that the deer had fallen from the tree. It had empty, dead eyes, but did not feel dead. At once it gathered its spindly legs and rose. When it sensed the cat waiting in the dark, it sprang to the East in long arcs across the sky. The spots of light moved in behind the deer, as if pulled along in its wake.

Dani sang to me, trying to coax me out of my sleep.

I resisted. Somehow I knew I had to pay attention.

As the deer faded into the distance, the points of light came together in a new constellation. That grouping of new stars drifted toward me. Toward us. It settled over the hotel and spun, slowly, through the night.

The loud air conditioner blew mostly warm, moist air. From the bathroom light I could see dried blood on my pillowcase. The way it'd spread through the cotton fibers reminded me of a paper chromatography lab from chemistry class. The plasma separated from the red blood cells and seeped out like an orange nebula.

I found solace in the darkness, sanctuary in the final minutes of the day. Like, maybe I was just a ghost, a faint shape moving against a star-filled sky.

The mosquito bites. The maple sheds its leaves. Who am I to rewrite my story? I knew the time to stop fighting had finally arrived.

The river submits to its course. The farmer is bound to his fields. The stars are forever locked into the great nothing. All because they submit to the way things are.

When I realized that Dani had never let go of me, I felt sad and unworthy of her love. I felt like I should cry again, but couldn't.

At that moment, the self-fulfilling prophecy that I had unknowingly instigated when I tried to rewrite my story had been fulfilled.

I had to die to make things right.

Dani said, "And this, Ben, is why I had to get rid of the gun."

FIVE

Ben woke up with a gasp. I had my eyes closed, but did not sleep. He rolled over and put his hand on my arm.

The banging came from a few rooms down. A dog barked nearby. My heart thudded. I went to the window.

"What is it?"

"Somebody going door-to-door." I pulled the curtain back but couldn't see the source of the commotion.

"Who?"

"I don't know yet. But perhaps it means we're checking out early." I squinted into the darkness. "I'd imagine we've been discovered."

I backed away from the window as Ben rose from the bed. When I took the bags from the chair, Ben flipped it onto its side and stepped on a leg, snapping it off. He swung it a few times to get a feel for its heft. After making sure to lock the deadbolt, I returned to the window. "Are you going to fight all of them? With the leg of a chair?"

The knocking grew louder—maybe next door.

"Not going to let them take us without a fight."

"Fighting shouldn't even be part of the conversation at this point." I pulled a dress over my head. The tags were all still on it. I put on my shoes. "Get ready."

I pulled the heavy drapes back and tried again to catch a glimpse of the distraction. When two of the boys from the parking lot this afternoon stepped into view, I opened the door and whispered in Spanish, "Get in here."

They spoke over each other, each practically shouting to be the loudest. The tall one carried a plastic grocery bag filled with sweets and cakes and a bottle of soda. The other wore a white tank that had never been washed. Their words came so fast they barely breathed.

"Slow down," I said in broken Yucatec. I surveyed the exterior corridor that overlooked the parking lot. Yellow Dog stood at the stairs, barking wildly. The youngest boy held it with a frayed pant leg for a leash. I waved him into the room and retreated inside. "Only one of you can speak at a time."

"What are they saying?" Ben pulled on his pants while kicking a shoe toward the bed.

"They said if you don't get dressed and packed, the police are going to be the next ones at our door." I pulled all of Ben's new things out of a drawer and shoved them into his valise.

"How do they know?"

"Get dressed," I said, losing my patience. "They saw Toussant at another hotel only a few blocks over. Finish putting your things in here. As soon as I check the bathroom we can go."

Ben said, "Dog. Be quiet."

"Don't worry about the dog. We should be moving."

As he stood he backed into the nightstand. A drinking glass hit the tile floor and shattered. He zipped his bag, then took mine and said, "Give me a minute to double-check everything. I'm right behind you."

When I stepped into the night, I could see lights on in the other rooms of the hotel. Other guests that had been awakened by the ruckus. An old German man with his linen robe pulled tight stood in the doorway of the room next to ours, waiting to scold somebody. I said, "*Ruhig sein*," before he could get a word out.

Three police pickup trucks slid to a halt in the gravel parking lot behind a shiny black SUV. One of the police officers rushed to the hotel office. He wore a dark blue uniform covered by a flak jacket and a baseball cap with a severely creased brim. Narrow-shouldered and slight of frame, he had deep worry lines around his eyes and stood with arms crossed. I pulled the door shut and watched through the window. The desk clerk couldn't move fast enough for him. The officer's partner lit a cigarette. I checked the door and locked the deadbolt. "Shut out the lights—they're here."

Ben looked through the curtain to verify. "We have to make a break for it."

"In plain view of Toussant? That makes no sense."

"They're at the steps now. So whatever you're going to do...."

I went into the bathroom and tried to force the window open, but it had been painted shut a very long time ago. To the boys, I said, "Can you open it? Then climb down onto the roof below? You must hurry." I spoke in Spanish when I didn't have the correct word in Yucatec.

"They're all out of their trucks now. Setting a perimeter. They're armed. It's a fucking assault."

The pulsing red lights bathed the room in pink and grey. Over the sound of the wheezing air conditioner I could hear the diesel engines and radio chatter. I took the chair leg from Ben.

Then I heard footsteps.

I returned to the bathroom and gave the one wearing the baseball cap the weapon. "You need to hurry. Break it if you have to."

There came a sharp knock on the door and I rushed to Ben's side. The sound of a dog barking followed the shattering of glass in the bathroom and I went in to make sure they were okay.

"Be careful to clear the…allow me." I took the club and ran it along the edges of the window frame to push the remaining shards out. "Now go."

Ben pushed the nightstand against the door. The alarm clock and empty bottles of water fell to the floor. "This ain't good."

The desk clerk's key slid into the lock with a click. Ben grabbed the door knob and moved quickly to the side while hanging on tight.

The clerk gave the door a shove and the police officer ordered her to step aside.

"Ben—"

He dropped to the floor as a line of holes appeared in a flurry of splintered wood. The officer burst through the door and I hit him in the face with the club. He froze, stunned, as blood streamed from a gash on his forehead. He fell backwards to the railing and slumped to the ground.

The desk clerk ran as the downed officers' partner rushed toward the room. Another pair from the lot broke for the steps while the rest shouted from their positions behind the pickup trucks.

I pulled Ben into the bathroom. He locked the door as I went through the window. The tallest boy stood on the roof below, guiding my ascent, while the others scurried around the back of the building. The barking dog gave away their location.

A torrent of gunfire erupted in a flash of yellow light as Ben dropped down to the roof. A cloud of dust and sulfurous smoke drifted through the holes in the hotel's exterior wall. One of the police officers shouted from the window as we ran along the eave to the service area.

We followed the boys onto a dumpster behind the kitchen where a fan blew the scent of old grease into the night. From the other side of the hotel came the sound of trucks shifting into gear. The smallest one clung to the dog's leash, crying. I took his hand.

We bolted like deer, running wildly past the pool. Decorative lights threw our shadows up onto the side of the hotel and the police officers shot at them. The boys crossed the street to someone's yard. Dogs barked as we sprinted past bedroom windows and front doors. Each time, the yellow dog would yip as it ran, as if saying it'd be back for a more vigorous fight later. We followed them through yards of concrete and rubble. Over walls held together by gravity and time.

When one of the trucks entered the street we'd just crossed, Ben turned and fell over a pile of cement blocks. He crashed into the ground with a thud that knocked the wind out of him. A curse came to his lips, but he fought to suppress it. Instead, he let slip a low groan.

The truck's high-powered searchlight probed the night. Ben crawled ahead to stay out of its way. I helped him to his feet and we ran to join the boys together. We found them huddled in a dead end, the older ones helping the youngest over a cement block wall. Somebody yelled in Spanish from the street we'd just crossed.

The older boys pulled themselves up, then grabbed my arms to lift me. The wall had a row of broken glass running down the center, but there remained enough room on either side to shuffle my feet. The youngest boy waved me ahead, but I turned to make sure Ben got up.

The wall separated a larger hacienda-style home from the others. The yellow dog barked from the ground below, then disappeared into the darkness. We worked ahead, in a crouch, to the roof of a garage at the back of the house. I used a cast-iron railing to lower myself onto the hood of an SUV parked in the street, then helped the youngest boy down. As the others took their turn, a burst of gunfire came from the opposite side of the wall. Ben jumped onto the hood, causing the SUV's alarm to squeal. Flood lights clicked on, catching us in the brightness of a temporary noon.

We ran down the next street into an overgrown lot as one of the trucks turned the corner. Somewhere in the night, jasmine bloomed. I blocked my face with my arm and blundered through thorny branches for almost fifty meters. Ben pulled me along behind him and tried to shield me from the worst of it. The boys had no problem twisting and ducking to avoid getting snagged. The spotlight cut through the vegetation, forcing us to chase our shadows. I could hear Toussant coordinating the search through the tinny radio speakers. When we burst onto the next street, the yellow dog waited there for us.

Headlights appeared at both the north and south ends of the road. The boys rushed ahead and disappeared into more thorns. Ben hesitated, then retreated back into the tangle we'd just emerged from. I stood, torn for a moment by indecision. He tugged my arm, yanking me back.

They called from the other side as the trucks sped toward us.

"We're trapped if we stay here," I said.

Somebody fired from the window of the truck to our right, and we lurched ahead. Here the thicket grew a bit more open, but not by much. A stream of light washed over us as the first vehicle turned toward the trees. The passenger shot again as the driver put it into park. Rounds sang in the air as they sailed past us. Together, the police officers chased us on foot as the second truck barreled into the brush. Its headlights bounced as it plowed through saplings and bushes. Thorns scraped the sides with a squeal like fingernails down a blackboard. It hit a rough stone wall with a metallic crash that slowed its forward progress. The driver backed up, put it into gear, and slammed his foot down on the accelerator to race forward again.

But as we pushed deeper the trees got thicker and stone mounds grew from the forest floor at irregular intervals. The pursuing truck stopped and I knew they'd abandoned it to chase us on foot. Gunfire came from two angles now and my immediate goal was to reach the darkness beyond the effects of the headlights. My breath wheezed in my ears and my legs burned. Once we broke through the last bit of light, I realized we'd lost the boys.

"Fuck." Ben squinted into the darkness. "I knew we shouldn't have followed those little bastards."

"It's fine. We just keep going." I tugged his arm, yanking him ahead.

Before we could even get started, a voice called from the darkness. "*Ben.*" In his accent it rhymed with pin.

I put my fingers to my lips to silence Ben.

"Ben," the voice said again.

I said, "I can't see where it's coming from. It should be...."

We dropped into a crouch. I said, "I can't see you."

A commotion came from the grass to our right, about ten yards away. We ran toward the hiss of dry leaves, but still could not see them. In between breathes I could hear Toussant and the police approaching.

The oldest boy rose from a hole in the ground like a corpse back from the dead. I sat on the leaves and slid into the narrow opening, dropping my bag ahead of me and twisting my body when the angled shaft grew too narrow. A cold, moldy breeze blew up from deep within the earth. The other boys and the yellow dog waited where it leveled out. I heard crying and the rustle of the plastic bag.

"You okay?" Ben said in a stage whisper.

I said, "We're here. Everybody is safe."

"I'd rather see two dogs fuck than climb down into that."

"It's safe down here."

He started into the hole. I could hear the scrape of his jeans on the rock. Small pebbles fell as he descended. "What is this? I'm not going to be able to squeeze back through there."

"They keep saying *ts'onot*. I don't know what that means."

Ben grunted as he forced himself through the last few feet. I quickly found his bag and held out my hand to guide him over to us. Then nobody said anything while we tried to catch our breath. And before Ben could protest, the boys pushed ahead into the tunnel.

"Hey…Dani, tell them to hold up. I'm bleeding like a stuck hog."

"Toussant is up there. Listen."

"Dani, I don't like this. If we can't get out…when the sun comes up it won't take them long to figure out where we went."

"Let's have a little faith in the boys. We are alive because of them."

"Yep." He could barely hide the sense of defeat in his voice.

I pushed my bag ahead of me and followed on my hands and knees. Holding my hand up to test the height of the ceiling above me, I found that I had plenty of room to crawl, but no room to crouch. So I pushed ahead.

A layer of putrid slime covered the floor. I tried holding my breath to avoid inhaling it. But the crawl drained me of any strength that remained after the footrace from the hotel, forcing me to yield to the stink. I thought this might have been a storm drain, but the walls and floor were uneven and I could never feel any joints or mortar. Which meant it may be possible they didn't know where we'd emerge.

I very much hoped I was wrong.

If we emerged.

I closed my eyes. Trying to discern movement in the darkness gave me a headache. Instead, I focused on the pattern of *bag, hand, knee, hand, knee, bag, hand, knee, hand* as I crawled along. Maintaining the rhythm required concentration. After a few minutes I could hear the others breathing ahead of me. My shoulders and wrists ached. Sharp stabs of pain coursed down my neck and spine. The skin on my knees grew raw.

I touched a foot and realized we'd caught up to the boys. The youngest whimpered a bit. One of the others tried to soothe him. I shifted position while waiting for them to resume and found the ceiling much lower this time. I tried not to think of the way that made me feel and instead laid down to stretch a bit.

"What is it?" Ben's hand brushed my foot.

"Just resting a moment."

"No…not here," he said. "I can't do this. I can't breathe down here."

"The boys are just ahead. The little one is tired. This is difficult for them too."

"Hey," he said, ignoring my attempts to ameliorate the situation. "Let's go."

One of the boys asked me to translate, although I believed Ben's tone made his feelings clear and remained silent. Or perhaps it was because I knew him and knew what to expect from him. I told the boys, "He said we can rest for a little longer, but then we have to be moving, okay?"

"What'd you tell them?" Ben's voice wavered with his shortness of breath.

"Only what you told me to." The only power I had left was choosing how to reply.

Without any sort of signal, the boys edged forward. Back to the trudging, forced routine, which slowed as the ceiling grew lower. I stayed in a crawl for as long as I could, but soon the cave forced me onto my belly. Water and mud coating my cheek instead of my hands and knees. But I had yet to catch the boys again, so I pushed on.

The adrenaline from the chase had worn off long ago, revealing a new series of aches and pains. My head hurt. My mind drifted with thoughts of being trapped in a wet tunnel in a flat landscape. How a sudden thunderstorm would quickly fill the hole and drain to a place I couldn't even imagine. We were too far from the sea and I saw no rivers or streams on the journey so far. In my life I'd died a thousand different ways and survived them all. I'd been shot and strangled, stabbed. But I could not imagine what drowning would do to me. *Would not.*

The water would fill my lungs, which would scream for wind.

I took a deep breath, to make sure I could.

Because of the mud already on my face I couldn't tell if the water grew deeper or if I'd imagined it. My body felt cold. I shivered.

My thoughts worsened—I could not reel them in. It occurred to me, had we been closer to the sea, a high tide could force the water back up the tunnel. *The dog would warn us, surely.* If the smallest boy had taken the lead, he'd have to convince the others to back up and would have to make that message clear to Ben and me.

Ben.

I realized I hadn't heard him in a while.

"Ben." I stopped.

I couldn't imagine the lights of Place Saint-Michel no matter how hard I tried. I could not imagine the flicker of a film projector or even a single candle. As if the depths of the earth prevented those images from penetrating.

"Ben." My voice sounded weak and ineffective in my ears. I shouted to make sure it wasn't just in my head.

"I'm here."

The reply sounded muffled and distant.

"We are close, okay?" I told him only what I wanted to be true.

I couldn't see the stars, which for so long sat fixed just beyond my fingertips. Arriving in this new land brought them closer than I could've ever imagined. I'd been on the verge of changing them all until this latest turn of events. But now, Cancer and Taurus were not even present as motes of light when I closed my eyes. So in darkness, I pushed on.

When the breeze blew against my back and the tunnel opened up, first growing wider, then taller, I didn't notice. I'd stopped for a moment to stretch my shoulders and the rock no longer pressed down upon me. Resuming the crawl on my hands and knees felt like a morning in bed after so long on my belly. I blinked when I believed I saw shapes moving in the darkness ahead of me. An optical trick. Velvety blackness moving against more of the same. I left my eyes open just to be certain.

"Ben."

"I'm here."

I raised a hand and had to really reach up before I could feel the ceiling again. Still too low to crouch, I could sit with my back straight. I waited with Ben for a moment, holding his hand, then rubbing his shoulders. I tried to smell his skin, but couldn't.

He said, "Where are the boys?"

"Up there somewhere."

"It isn't possible they could've taken a different branch? Is it?"

No, I thought. *Not if it meant we'd gone the wrong way.*

"*K'a'ajale'.*" I asked them to stop.

Not even an echo.

"*Ba'ax ka wa'alik?*" I'd never heard them use a formal greeting, so I asked *What do you say?*

I held my breath and waited for a response.

"*K'a'ajale'.* Can you hear me?"

After a moment I heard noise. One of the boys. "Ben?"

A reply. Then more noise.

"It's the dog? Our lives are in the hands of kids and a dog?"

One of them shouted, "*Beya'.*"

"This way, he says." I patted Ben's knee and crawled ahead. "*Pa'ateni.* We're coming."

After a few more yards, I could hear the boys more clearly. The dog ran back to sniff my face and hair to verify we hadn't been replaced by some strangers in the tunnel. Its claws tapped on the rock floor as it ran ahead. Then, the breeze halted, as if confused, and we fell into a dense blue light, like indigo dye against a background of true black.

I could see shapes slumped against the outside world. I smiled.

We joined the boys on a stone ledge that hovered above a void. As I drifted toward the edge I could see the universe suspended in a hole below us. The cosmos at our feet. *The Milky Way crossed the window in the earth like a fine web of pale silk. Cassiopeia tried to show me Andromeda, even though I couldn't see her without my glasses.*

It suddenly made sense that the heavens rested below us. After all, I had travelled to the far side of the planet. Everything I knew existed five-thousand miles away. The lights of Montmartre and Place Pigalle may as well have been on Venus. For the first time in many years I stared into the sky below me and inventoried all that I'd lost by leaving. The landscape of Monet and good bread. The breath of the Seine in April. The graves of so many old lovers and friends. By leaving all of that, I'd become a new person. I hadn't yet found a reason to love her.

The cosmos at my feet wavered with a splash. Destroyed by a pebble thrown by one of the boys. Ben pulled me close and I tried to forget that I'd meant to make a new life for myself. I felt silly for believing that the reflection of the sky meant my world had been flipped upside down. The boys laughed and threw more pebbles, destroying the universe I'd created in my head.

"We should go before the sun comes up," Ben said, slinging his bag over his shoulder. "We don't stand a chance in broad daylight. They got a noose around us and they're just going to pull it tighter and tighter."

"Ben, it would be okay to let the boys rest for a bit. We are all tired."

Looking at them, he exhaled slowly. The way he regarded the wide-eyed trio said he knew I was right. "The main roads are going to be off limits now. Toussant can set up roadblocks, traffic stops, whatever he wants. We're going to have to go sooner rather than later."

I relayed his suggestion to the boys and they rattled off a thousand reasons why we shouldn't leave. I translated them to Ben, one by one. "This one says there are *wayob* in the forest because there are burials there, but the tall one says they only come out on Día de los Muertos. I don't know the word though. Wayob? Maybe it's a spirit? This one says we aren't safe in the ruins until the sun comes up, but the other one—"

He didn't respond.

"The tall one says they will take the souls of those who have stopped using theirs. We are only safe on sanctified ground."

"Superstition? These boys wouldn't know beans with the sack open."

"What does it matter, Ben?"

The talk of ghosts made the littlest one cry. I told him that they were just stories, meant to scare children. But when the talking stopped, I listened. I'd heard those sounds before. When I was a girl.

In the trees at the edge of the dark forests at the crossroads.

And when I moved to the city, I stopped hearing the noises. As I thought about my childhood, I realized I stayed in the city, in part, so I'd never have to hear them again.

"Ben, let them rest for a bit." I said, "We are safe here, for the moment."

The water in the pool felt warmer than the morning air and tasted like limestone. Here sat the *cenote* the boys had spoken of back in the tunnel. This subterranean pool. This opening between worlds. I floated over the bottomless depths and looked at the fading stars, drinking the wine of the cosmos. I'd wished on them all, once upon a time. But wishing seemed foolish when you no longer celebrated birthdays or looked for animals in the clouds. Wishing reminded me of all the time I'd wasted hoping the universe had a different fate for me.

But that all changed now.

The old woman at Dzibilchaltún gave me a quest when she said, *Bey ti' ka'an, bey ti' lu'um.*

As above, so below.

Meaning I had it in me to change my own stars once and for all. I could liberate myself from the inebriated fugue of twisted agreements and ancient partnerships by seeking an entirely new grail, seeing as my old one had been little more than a receptacle for wine.

I would piece together my new objective from the ancient anecdotes and phonetic scraps held sacred by the priests and storytellers who rode out their last autumns in the dark corners of this land. Like seeds scattered by mice and birds.

I knew if I wanted my own vineyard to flourish, I'd first have to make it rain.

The older boys splashed and laughed by the light of the palest dawn, their voices echoed up through the stone walls, snapping me out of my trance. They ignored

Ben's repeated shushing. Even the dog seemed reborn in the swim to the ledge on the other side. I helped the youngest boy paddle across, wiping mud from his hair and face whenever I could. He smiled as he relaxed. His brown eyes bore a wealth of trust I'd only seen a few times in my life. His innocence gave me strength and hope. I asked him about his mother and he didn't respond. Then the time to depart had arrived.

As we climbed toward the surface, I looked back at the hollow we'd emerged from, but it had disappeared. Devoured by the earth. I knew I'd never see this place again.

The dog sprinted into the dawn and we followed. Away from the lights of town and spying eyes. The stars faded in the oncoming sunrise and the rousing exhalations of the scrubby flora erased the scent of the pool from existence as if the landscape disappeared into our wake.

We edged toward a clearing and I took Ben's hand to slow him down a bit. The canopy of trees fell away—a velvety blue sky dripped into the west. To the east, sunrise rolled in on tattered wings with just a hint of coral. Ahead of us, a shadowy form dominated the horizon. A magnificent mass of matte darkness.

"This is Chichen Itza," I said, looking up at the blocky pyramid. "It's just as I'd hoped it would be."

A forest of alabaster structures appeared beneath the watercolor sky. As my eyes adjusted to the changing light, minor pyramids, platforms, walls, shrines, and temples emerged from the earth. But the giant mass of rigid stone sat alone like an island in a waterless sea. Its presence made me smile.

"So you knew we'd end up here?" Ben dropped my hand and walked ahead. "When did you start planning this? In Mérida, or as soon as we got off the boat?"

"It's no different that the Piazza della Signoria. If you are in Florence long enough, you will see it." The structure pulled me toward it. My own gravity seemed too small.

"No. This ain't a couple of tourists eating a pizza." He shook his head in disbelief. "This feels like you planned this."

"But this is the main route east from Mérida. I didn't choose it. You did. When you refused to go to the bus station as I suggested." I turned and followed the boys.

They ran past a structure that sprawled out in the grass like a crocodile on a riverbank. Beyond the pyramid I saw hundreds of pillars, white and square, rising from the soil like the crocodile's teeth. No wind blew. No insects whirred. Ben put his head down and fell into step behind me.

Finally, he said, "I just want to be able to trust you."

"Then trust me." I let him catch up and forced my hand back into his. "Something wonderful is happening, Ben. It all began last night, even though it seemed painful at the time. Each step takes us farther from everything we are trying to leave behind. There are going to be scary moments, but we are strong together. The world beyond our love is but a dream. That's the only way it makes sense to me."

Swallows emerged to eat the insects that rose from the grass. The boys drifted south toward some thin trees. Heaps of rubble, soft white in the dim light, flanked a crushed gravel path. I asked them to stop while we talked.

"Man never would've looked up if all of the stars were of equal brightness." I placed my palm against his cheek, forcing him to meet my eyes. "Look where we're headed, Ben. That's where we find tomorrow and the next day. With each step, we are writing our future. I have to believe that or else I will fade away like old ink. We have to change our fate, don't you see? It's far too dangerous to leave it in the hands of someone else."

The older boys wrestled in the grass at the edge of the flat, wide plaza. The yellow dog walked back toward us, but only made it halfway before slumping onto the ground itself.

Ben stared off into the distance, as if the right words meant everything to him. The muscles around his mouth softened, but he didn't release his jaw just yet. He put his head down and mumbled, "But how do you know?"

"Hope is the only thing sustaining me. Whether we keep walking or stand still, tomorrow is coming. The stars will dance across the sky no matter what. To reach them, all you have to do is raise your arms. We are not leaves in the wind. We can fly."

He didn't respond. Not even a twitch.

"You have to believe in something, Ben. Going it alone will destroy you."

Ben used the sound of voices from the visitor center as an opportunity to end the discussion. Approaching security guards or groundskeepers. One of them spoke on a cell phone. The other waved his arm, trying to call us over. He said, "They're coming."

The dog rose as we passed and fell into step at our heels.

The boys sat in the grass, feigning exhaustion. They passed around a package of chocolate cookies from the plastic bag that the tall one guarded with his life.

"Let's go," Ben said, walking toward the trees.

The oldest boy said to me, "We are too tired."

"You weren't too tired to wrestle just a few moments ago." I crossed my arms. "Besides, I think you've done a great job of keeping us safe, but now you must go home. Your mothers must be worried."

"It's too early. Look." Avoiding my inquiry, the tall one intervened. He pointed at the few lingering stars. "Wayob. There are people buried in there."

"What's he saying?" Ben asked.

"That we have to wait a bit longer," I translated. "Until the sun comes up."

"Ghosts again?"

"Ben, it's what they believe."

Pointing at the light that fell onto the apex of the big pyramid, the tall boy said, "And the mountain is rising."

I tried to translate for Ben, but he remained focused on the activity near the park entrance. I said, "I'm sorry. I don't know what that means."

Frustrated by his inability to express himself exactly as he'd wanted to, he said, "The mountain…it rises out of the sea."

Looking back at the ruins, I said, "The sunlight on the side of the pyramid?"

He waved his hand across the grass in ever-widening circles. "The sea…."

Ben cut me off. "Time to wrap it up. Class is over."

A cluster of trucks slowed at the gate next to the visitor center. Security guards or park police. Not the trucks from last night. One of the groundskeepers ran over to unlock it. His hat blew off and he hesitated while he considered retrieving it. The lead truck sounded its horn and the man left his hat in the grass.

"I'll take my chances with the ghosts." Ben squeezed my hand and entered the forest.

The oldest boy rose, wiped his mouth on his arms, his hands on his shorts. He dashed into the trees, whooping and yelling. The dog followed. The tall boy pressed his lips together, packed up his wrappers, and followed without so much as a squeak.

The little one reached for my hand.

"What's your name?" I knelt in the grass next to him.

"Zacnal." He scratched at a rash on his belly.

"Stop that." I lifted his shirt—a little girl's t-shirt with a cartoon kitten on it. I *tsked*. "I will get you lotion."

We walked past a smaller version of the big pyramid. This one sat just off the tourist path. And after a few more minutes another large building rose to my left. A platform flanked by wide stairs, topped by a collapsed dome.

"Can you carry me?"

"I don't know. It depends on how old you are."

He shrugged.

The first truck came around a low wall that separated the road from the ruins. Its headlights swept through the dust it created. "Let's walk a bit, then we'll see. Okay?"

I pulled him into the trees as more vehicles approached from behind the visitor center. *Toussant. So much for our head start.*

The canopy overhead thickened, bony fingers squeezing out the light. I couldn't see a clear path through the brush and tried to listen for Ben or the boys. A mosquito buzzed near my ear. In a stage whisper, I said, "Ben."

The architecture changed in the next group of buildings. Gaudy stone knobs and hooks, like ornamental buttons on a coat, pocked their exteriors. Rounded corners and stone lattice and crude faces let this group stand out from the other.

The boy stopped in front of a structure that stood much taller than it was wide. A band of Baroque flourish girdled its midsection. Geometric lattice accents. A hooked nose flanked by two stone eyes had been built into each corner. Zacnal said, "*Chaac.*"

"What is that?"

"Chaac. He makes rain."

After a false start with a blaring siren, the trucks made their way onto the crushed gravel path. We pushed deeper into the trees until we could no longer see any of the ruins. Birds whooped, high squeals that quieted only when we passed beneath them. Some flew ahead, as if leading us. Something that smelled like amber lingered out there somewhere.

I put my head down and quickened my pace.

"Ben," I said. I couldn't hear the trucks anymore over the sound of my breath. I figured they were unable to drive past the heaps of rubble and pursued us now on foot.

Ben had gone. Somewhere in the trees ahead. Zacnal cried, so I picked him up and walked faster. "It's okay."

His head fell onto my shoulder. His little body shook as he sobbed.

"Please, little one," I said. "You must not be afraid."

"There are ghosts," he said, pointing his grubby little finger into the distance. "Wayob."

"No. The boys were playing a game." I turned, but could not hear anything and walked faster. "To scare you."

"I see them. There and there." Zacnal pushed my face to the right, trying to force me to look off into the trees.

"Zacnal." I spun a half turn. "There's nothing, okay. Just us." I watched for movement for the briefest of moments. The forest remained silent and still. The flat landscape spread out in a tangle of thorny bushes and a mixture of small and large trees. Low mounds had been scattered across the ground. Heaps of grey rock that had once been homes, I'd imagined.

Or tombs.

I put Zacnal down and unzipped my bag. He watched as I removed my eyeglasses from their case and tried to take them when I put them on. I said, "Shhh."

But still, I heard nothing.

I took his hand. And then, just as before, he fussed and wanted to be carried.

"Zacnal," I said. "You are too big…."

He watched something. "There. Look," he said.

"It's just a wind." I suppressed the irritation in my voice. "See? Back and forth."

"No," he said. "There."

"Zacnal—I would know if there were ghosts." *Unless I forgot what they looked like.* I tugged, but he wouldn't budge. "There are men following us and they are very real."

He shuffled his feet to match my stride, sniffling. Pouting. When he cried again, I pulled him up into my arms. His shrill words went straight into my head. "No, no, no…."

"Please, stop." My ears rang. My face got warm and I clenched my jaw. "Ben, I need your help."

Zacnal's screams grew. That he even had breath to cry astounded me.

Sunlight poured into a clearing ahead. I focused only on the brightness and ignored the cuts and scrapes I collected as I pushed through the thickest brambles. The boy cried even as I stepped onto the gravel road and put him down.

"Shhh. Please stop." I adjusted my glasses and pushed my hair behind my ear. Sweat formed at my temples. I squinted into the sunlight that fell in a golden strip down the road to the east. I put my hand on my hip and looked the other way. The yellow dog drifted toward us, but stopped and sat in the shade of a thick bush. Morning insects hummed in the rising heat.

I walked west, my long shadow spread out before me. First with my arms crossed, then rubbing my temples. The road went on forever in a straight line, disappearing before it even met the flat horizon. I took off my glasses and put the ear stem to my lips—I needed a cigarette. After a few seconds, I turned. Zacnal sat where I'd left him. "What are the names of the other boys? Can you please tell me?"

He sniffled as he spoke. "Xtaabay."

"Okay. Xtaabay is the oldest one?" I tied my hair up with my scarf. "And the tall one? The boy with the bag—what is his name?"

"Yum Kaax." Something on the other side of the road distracted the boy. He froze. "Ghosts."

"Please, Zacnal. Not now."

Once more I took his hand. I pulled him into the sunrise.

"Yum Kaax, where are you?" He called out in a sing-song tone, half-turning to look over his shoulder.

Beneath the buzz of cicadas I heard something and stopped. *Somebody calling?*

"Ben?"

I walked ahead slowly, thinking if the voice sounded too distant I wouldn't have been able to hear it over the crunch of stone beneath my feet. It felt as if turning my back had allowed a world of motion to exist on the road behind me. But I could never turn in time to catch any of it. Not even a spindrift of dust.

I even held my breath.

"Ben—"

I considered backtracking into the trees, but figured that only increased my chances of coming upon Toussant. Even though we'd not even walked a mile, it seemed as if we could've been separated by much more. I didn't see a clearly marked path and had a hard time believing we could've gotten so spread out in just a few minutes.

Zacnal cried, but I tightened my grip and pulled him along. He dragged his feet and tried to drop into the dust. Unsure of other options, I continued walking into the sunrise.

"Zacnal." A little voice called from the trees much farther up the road. The sound of footsteps running to catch up followed. "You got lost."

Yum Kaax took a knee next to the boy and put his arm around him.

"See? We're okay." Yum Kaax brushed the gravel off his knees when he stood. Turning, he scolded, "Why didn't you answer?"

When I heard more footsteps I put my hand up, shushing him. Ben and Xtaabay ran to catch up from somewhere even farther away. He slowed once he got close enough to talk without shouting.

My hands shook. Anger revealing itself as fear.

"I thought we'd lost you." Embracing me, Ben said, "Couldn't you hear us calling?"

"I couldn't hear anything. I thought you'd left us." I clenched my fists and released them, hoping the feeling would leave as well. After a moment, I regained my composure. "Perhaps they were right. We should've stayed out of the forest."

"Or maybe we're just tired." Ben said, taking Zacnal up in his arms.

"Maybe."

"You okay now?" He began walking east.

"I think so. I'm going to ask Xtaabay if he can lead us away from the main roads."

Ben stopped. "What's his name again?"

I began to write it out in the dirt with my foot. "The *X* is pronounced like *sh*. *Ta*, which rhymes with *voila*. *Bay*, as in—"

Ben nodded to show he tried to understand, but gave up quickly. He cut me off. "Well, let's just leave it at that. If I can't pronounce it I can't remember it."

"But if he's going to help us, you can do him the courtesy of learning his name."

"It won't matter. X marks the spot, right?" Ben turned to Xtaabay and gave him a thumbs up then resumed walking. The boy fell into step beside him. Ben said, "*¿Todos bien?* See, he's good."

The yellow dog ran ahead, staying just a few paces in front of us the way dogs always do.

I lingered, listening to the trees but hearing only birds. The tallest boy—Yum Kaax—waited for me. For the moment I'd been stunned, not because I was afraid of what was in the forest. The sensation was a result of experiencing fear for the first time in many, many years.

We turned east and picked up the pace. As the morning brightened, bird songs increased, drowning out the other noises from the forest. Once we got into a steady, quiet, rhythm, the miles went by like they were falling from the sky.

Dusty sunlight dripped through the gaps where the four-sided thatched roof of an old man's home met low stone walls. The air inside smelled like old, sweet hay. I twisted so that I could watch the street through the door but still remain hidden in shadow. Ben couldn't be permitted to see me here after I suggested he try to buy the boys new clothes and shoes while I tried to find a ride to Cancun. A lie that never needed to be confessed.

"This information is very important to me," I said. Asking for help is difficult because I have very little to offer in return. But what I learn here is about much more than life and death. It's about whatever makes me who I am," I said, my tone hushed. Deferring to Don Trejo's sense of pride came easily. Hiding mine was the challenge.

"The heart of my people. Those three rocks. Not the Holy Trinity." The old man deftly waved off my offer with his straw hat, as if he'd momentarily grown tired of fanning only himself. He didn't seem insulted, which meant he was interested. But instead of making eye contact, he stared at the three hearthstones in the center of the room. He spoke Spanish, not Yucatec. "Those three stones are everything. Once you understand that, you understand the Maya. The fire of our creation burns there."

"The kitchen? It makes sense that the hearth is the center—food nourishes the soul. Bread and wine…." I got lost in my digression and defaulted to Catholicism, which frustrated me. Unzipping my bag, I said, "Perhaps I could make a small donation? For food? Or school supplies?"

"It is a kind gesture, but the children have pencils. They need rain. I don't believe your money can soften the sky." He wiped sweat from his forehead with a red bandana he pulled from the lower pocket of his immaculate white *guayabera*.

"You know that's impossible. Maybe there are still people who can make rain?" After a deliberate hesitation, I opened my bag, slid a few one hundred dollar bills out of their wrapper, and placed them on the small table that sat between us. "I can still help."

"Díos bo'otik." He looked at the money but did not touch it. "There are men who may know how. I am not one of them. I had no one to show me. My father drank himself into the earth at a young age. The attending priest said I could become a man by educating myself with the Servants of the Lord and the Virgin of Matará at Virgen de Izamal in Mérida. The Servants of the Lord certainly educated me, cutting me off from farming and the old gods and making rain. I never bled or cried into this soil, so I never learned how to send *itz* to heaven. I'm not connected to the land, so I can't ask for rain in return. At Virgen de Izamal they taught me to speak to one god only. *Dios te salve, María, llena eres de gracia, el Señor es contigo….*"

Common ground. With a patronizing smile, I thought about my own time with the Monastery of the White Friar nuns in Prague and added, "*Požehnaná ty mezi ženami, a požehnaný plod života tvého, Ježíš.*"

The cadence needed no translation. Don Trejo closed his eyes, waiting for a chance to interject. He pressed his palms together as all Catholic school children are taught and said, "*X cilich María, u Na Dioze payachxnen okal, toon ah-Kebanob, behelac, i, itu kiutzil cimil.*"

"The same in any language, no?" I said, crossing myself.

He shrugged and rolled his eyes up to the heavens. "I took a job in the city once the nuns were through with me. I bought a truck, then two more a year later, and soon lost interest in the *milpa* and growing corn. Sending money back to my mother gave me a sense of pride. But I am *Don* in this village in name only—not a true *x'men*—just the last old man left from those times. I cannot open the doors my father could, but I do my best to help in other ways. Like accepting charity from friends." He stopped fanning himself and gently placed his hat onto the money.

"I am happy to help."

"You will have to travel east to find men who know those ceremonies. Or south. Probably some place far from the road." He poured a little Coke into a juice glass from a one liter plastic bottle. "Before the highway joined Cancun to Tulum you could just go to Cobá. But now you may have to go to Guatemala. I don't know for certain."

"That's so far...."

"Tourists want drums and margaritas. Not mumbling old men. Twenty years ago, maybe it was different. Who knows? The young people from our villages want to work on the beach now and wear American clothes."

My heart sank. "So, there's nothing...."

"The Spaniards burned all the books my people wrote. So many details of our traditions were lost and the Maya can't talk to the gods the way they used to. Spoken words had to be passed on from father to son in secret for fear the church would punish the x'men. My people forgot."

"But written words have survived the Conquest—I saw them. In Chichen Itza and Dzibilchaltún. Carved into stone. I spoke to a woman in a village just south of Progresso—"

"The Conquest was about belief, not blood." His gaze returned to the three hearthstones in the center of the room. Without looking up, he said, "The missionaries whipped the words out of my people. The Servants of the Lord took mine with daily bread. It's difficult to resist on a full stomach. When they took my words, they took my soul."

"I would politely disagree. I think the spirit of the people of Yucatán is very much alive." For a moment, my empathy eclipsed the urgency of my quest and replaced it with a desire to show Don Trejo just how much I appreciated his culture. "In Chablekal and Mérida I felt a genuine hope from the people I spoke to. It's as if the land is breathing after holding its breath for so long."

"You don't know anything about this land or its people." He snatched his hat from the table. The breeze scattered the money. He gnashed his teeth. "Your people sold their souls a long time ago. The church owns them. In return they gave you writing for contracts and rules that you are all too happy to obey. The idea of a soul has been pounded into your heads for two thousand years, but religion is still just a story to you. Two thousand years ago my people built Tikal. My people live out their creation under every starry sky and fight for their souls with every waking breath. They are reborn every time a fire is lit between those three hearthstones. Your people don't know a sip of wine from the blood of Christ."

"Don Trejo, if I offended you I am truly sorry—"

"You came from the north? Through Dzibilchaltún and Mérida?" He stood and slammed his fist into his palm. "How did you arrive in Yucatán? By boat?"

I didn't respond.

"And this is Toussant's money? Would you like to see this village flattened? My nieces and nephews murdered? Because that's what will happen when he follows your trail to me. He will tear the soul right out of these people." He trembled. "I saw the news. I know what they did in Chicxulub Puerto. A massacre."

Without saying another word, I stood, picked up the money, and folded it lengthwise before placing it back on the table. "The money belongs to me. Not Toussant."

He flinched a bit when I said it.

With that reaction—the right one—I composed myself and the anger was gone. I said, "And that wasn't the only thing you were wrong about. My people created literature as a way to fight back against the church. Words are the most powerful weapon this world has ever seen." I shouldered my bag.

Don Trejo held his hat over his heart. He averted his gaze. "This money will help many children."

"It's fine," I said, biting the ear stem of my eyeglasses as I pulled my hair back. "I meant you no harm. When we leave your village we will most certainly take Toussant with us."

"Go to Cobá." His cheeks had reddened and his words came much softer this time. "You may find somebody who can help there. I will pray Toussant does not find you."

"Nobody can take a man's soul. I don't believe that's possible anymore." As I stepped into the sunlight, I said, "I've never been this close and I've been looking for over a hundred years. Long before your time with the Servants of the Lord and the Virgin of Matará."

He hid his reaction by averting his gaze and adjusting his hat. Then, his eyes drifted back up, perhaps to see if I spoke the truth. "What have you learned?"

I remained cold, but softened a bit. "Nobody can take a soul as long as it is tethered to humanity. One just has to be part of the universe. In it and active. Not observing from afar."

The sun shone brightly. No breeze blew. In the sky, I searched for a sign I may have been right and saw none.

"How?" He held his palms up. His voice seemed suddenly small and sincere. "How does one do that?"

"I don't know." His question threw me. I took a moment before answering. I only replied once it felt as if I had found words that truly meant something to me. "Music and art and literature. That's where I'd begin. Music and art and literature are man's way of remembering that he has a soul."

A child screamed. I pulled my bag close and ran toward the church. The hot air dried my tongue and throat. "Ben."

I turned the corner and saw him in the shade of the steeple, holding a plastic bag high above a crowd of children. "Dani," he said, grinning wildly. "Help me. My *chocolotta* mission is in crash and burn mode now."

I slowed when I saw he wasn't bleeding.

"Dani...."

"*Niños. Todos ustedes forman una línea.*" I took off my glasses and wiped the sweat from my forehead. The dog circled, testing me with his nose.

"Hearts and minds, baby. Like Tikrit without the snipers. Look at the chicos." He took candy out of the bag by the handful and the children broke ranks again. Ben twisted and turned to make sure everyone got an equal amount.

"The mama duck feeding her babies."

"I know, right?" He reached over the heads of the taller kids to get to the little ones in the back.

Zacnal split from the crowd when he saw me and ran with his arms open wide. I said, "But you are too big...." as he jumped.

"Look," the boy said, leaning away to flatten wrinkles out of his new shirt—a starched white button-down with a pleated front.

"Are you getting married?" I asked. Hoping for an explanation, I looked at Ben.

"It's great, right?" Ben laughed, proud of the irony. "They didn't have much in his size. I requisitioned what I could. He'll grow into it though."

"Somewhere in Mérida a page boy is naked." I put Zacnal down and rolled up his sleeves. "Where are the others?"

Ben said, "X went to find his *cousin* but I don't believe he's really related to anybody here. He thinks he knows a guy who can give us a lift to Cancun." He turned the bag upside down and shook the remaining candy onto the ground. Kids scattered, filling their pockets with sweets. "Or an island near there. Isla Mujeres? There's a ferry to the island. That's where we could find a boat. I'm not a hundred percent. Anyhow, the lady at the church translated for us, but I'm not sure her work was rock solid."

"I am trying to be a new person, Ben. But these challenges are making it very difficult." I closed my eyes and bit my lip—the only way to make certain I didn't say what I really wanted to. I inhaled deeply. "Don't you think this is something we should've discussed?"

"What's to discuss?" He walked over and kissed me on the cheek. "I'm on a mission to get us home and it feels good. Trying to move past last night and all that. X wants to help however he can. He's growing on me a little, but don't tell him."

"Or he's trying to collect a reward for information leading to our arrest." I crossed my arms. "Is it in our best interest to let this entire village know that we're running from a notorious drug lord and cartel affiliate? Or is this your idea of *laying* low?'"

"It's all good. You're just mad because for ten minutes you weren't in control."

"The man I spoke to had heard about us and our arrival by boat and the murders and fires. It's in the news, Ben. We are federal fugitives. The man refused to help because he didn't want Toussant to unleash vengeance upon his village. He knows Toussant by reputation and wanted to spare his people from the type of horror Toussant is capable of."

"I don't think X—"

"You didn't think at all." I grabbed Zacnal's hand and walked east, past the church. "We should go."

"Dani, just wait. X and the other one will be back in a few minutes." Ben held his ground.

"You can decide for yourself."

"Dani—just wait. We can't leave the chicos."

Zacnal turned and dragged his feet. "Yum Kaax…."

"We're just playing a little game, okay?" I forced a more lilting tone with the boy. "They will find us and we will be on our way."

"Dani—let me find them, okay?" Ben walked backward as he spoke. "I thought I'd done the right thing."

"We'll wait at the edge of town. Thirty minutes. That's it." I turned and faced him. People watched from doorways, from beneath corrugated awnings, and I lowered my voice. "But you must be careful. No more pounding your chest."

He nodded and rubbed the back of his head. I'd hurt him.

"We've put these kids in a dangerous situation." I'd been too harsh. The scars and war stories made it easy to forget he'd built a cage to punish himself, but also to protect himself. If I pushed too hard, he'd lock himself in forever. "They believe we are going to take care of them. So we must, until we can find someone else to do so. Just hurry."

"I will."

Zacnal whimpered, "Where is he going?"

"To gather the others. They will be along soon."

"Yum Kaax and Xtaabay aren't leaving us?" His big brown eyes narrowed a bit while he waited for my answer.

"No." I continued walking. "And even if they did, you can do it by yourself. Do you understand that?"

He didn't respond.

"People aren't always there when we need them. Their absence can help us learn to take care of ourselves. You are strong and smart, do you understand me, Zacnal?"

"Yum Kaax says that we will live with you."

A group of women shucking corn in the shade of a limp blue tarp watched from the corners of their eyes. They stopped speaking only enough to give the appearance that they weren't listening.

"Zacnal...." I pulled him closer to me. "I need you to understand."

He held his hands over his ears and squeezed his eyes shut as he retreated from me. I pulled him back toward me and picked him up.

"I'm sorry." Tucking his head onto my shoulder gave me an excuse to break the stares and move on.

They'd never know this child wasn't the first I'd left behind or how my heart ached for all the children I'd never mothered yet had somehow still lost. To war. To exile. I closed my eyes and shuffled through the dust and loose gravel and I was leaving Paris because I couldn't stand the idea of watching Nazis parade up and down Champs-Élysées. The feeling of Zacnal's warm breath on my shoulder reminded me of the last time I spoke to my sister on the day that I left. She pulled me close and cried. At the time I believed I was being strong.

"Yum Kaax...." Zacnal cupped his hands to his mouth and called out in a sing-song voice. "Yum Kaax."

I *tsked*. "You can't be so loud in my ear," and placed him back on the ground.

He ran back up the street. Ben smiled his relief. A sign that he believed he'd somehow managed to make it all work out.

"Where are we going?" Xtaabay confronted me immediately. His new attire consisted of a black moth-eaten Nike basketball t-shirt and a baseball cap with an embroidered Philadelphia 76ers logo. I suspected the new clothes had something to do with the attitude.

"Cobá."

"What's he squawking about?" Ben said.

Yum Kaax stood between us, silently mediating. I asked Yum Kaax where his new clothes were, since he wore the same shirt he had on this morning, and he patted his backpack—an upgrade from his plastic grocery bag—and smiled. He turned and said, "Look…" showing me the old machete tucked into his thin leather belt.

"You're going to hurt yourself." I slid this machete out and tucked it into one of the straps on his backpack. "Ben, you couldn't have found something better for them to wear? Better shoes?"

"This is what they chose, Dani. It's all beans, bullets, and Band-Aids anyway. "

"No, no, no. Cobá is too far." Xtaabay waved his hands, interrupting. "My cousin can take you to the ocean tonight. One thousand dollars, American. I don't understand—"

"You don't need to understand. We are going to Cobá and you can join us if you cooperate. But if you become difficult, we will have to go our separate ways. Is that fair to Zacnal? To force him to choose?"

"Dani, what is going on?"

"Ben, I will explain it all later." I took Zacnal's hand and walked east, staying near the road's shoulder where the sun's energy fell with less intensity.

Xtaabay stood his ground. Arms crossed. Refusing to budge.

"Stay here if you'd like." I said, "I make my own decisions. Not you—a boy. Not Ben. But if this is what you want, you are forcing them to choose."

"Dani, what did he say?"

"He said the ride fell through. We are walking to the next village."

"Are you sure?' He rushed to fall into step beside me. "He seemed real sure about everything just a minute ago."

Yum Kaax ran to catch up. He held open his backpack and showed Zacnal his new assortment of sweets and cakes. Zacnal tried to get his hand into the bag, but Yum Kaax explained how he'd rationed out the appropriate amount for the rest of the day and that Zacnal had to be patient. The little one whined a bit, but Yum Kaax ignored him and pointed out a large wooden cross that had been adorned with ribbons and bits of metal and broken glass. It resembled the cross outside Dzibilchaltún.

Yum Kaax said, "*Yaxche.*"

I struggled to find the words. "*Green tree?*"

Xtaabay caught up with Ben and the dog while I listened to Yum Kaax.

"Yaxche." Yum Kaax shook his head. With his toe, he drew a cross in the dirt. "To lift up the sky."

"I'm sorry, Yum Kaax. I don't understand."

He ran into the brush at the side of the road and returned with a long, straight branch. After setting his backpack on the ground, he placed one end of the stick beneath it and grunted, acting like he was really straining to lift his things.

"Lever?" When he didn't respond, I tried the Spanish. "*Palanca?*"

A vehicle headed toward us and Ben picked up Zacnal and whisked Xtaabay off the road. Yum Kaax snapped the stick over his knee, threw it back into the scrub in frustration, and ran to join the others in the thick tangle of shrubbery. As the old VW passed, I explained that we couldn't be seen. They knew nothing of Toussant, or of what happened the day we arrived in Yucatán, and I believed it was better if they never found out.

Before heading back onto the road, Ben suggested the traffic would only grow as the day wore on and that it would be much easier to walk deeper in the forest—just out of sight of passing vehicles—where the larger trees grew farther apart.

He gave me a moment to think about it, then added, "And not so many jaggers."

Xtaabay played tour guide, pointing out trees and birds he knew and to make up for our earlier power struggle, I chose not to point out when he was obviously wrong. I was no botanist, but I knew a coconut palm from a *flamboya*. He held his hat over his heart when he talked, just like the old man from the village. He pointed out a line of ants sailing across the forest floor, little chewed off bits of leaves held high to catch little forest floor breezes. He showed us orchids we would not have seen otherwise. Little violet ghosts. Some were in low-hanging branches and Ben held Zacnal up to see. Xtaabay and Yum Kaax debated the presence of balam—jaguars. I told them to find something else to discuss. Iguanas were so plentiful that Xtaabay stopped pointing them out even when he had nothing else to point out. As the soil got rockier we saw the reptiles more frequently. When Xtaabay found his first scorpion under a rock, Ben got nervous and wanted to head back to the highway. Before I could object, Ben warned Xtaabay to be on the lookout for *serpientes*. Yum Kaax spun around holding up four fingers.

He shouted, "*Ka'an*," the Yucatec word for snake.

Zacnal whimpered and demanded Ben pick him up again. Xtaabay charged into the brush with a large stick to look for it.

"No, no, no." Yum Kaax said, "The word is the same—snake, four, sky—ka'an. It means all these things."

"A homophone." Suddenly my inability to communicate as effectively as I would've liked made sense. I did my best to keep my explanation of the word simple. "The words sound alike, but mean different things."

"No, no, no. Same word." He waved his hand emphatically. His eyes got wide, as if to show how exciting this concept should've been to me. "Ka'an is serpent and sky and four. One word means each thing."

"How is the sky the same as a snake?" I tried to provoke him, but he thought the question seemed silly. He used the opportunity to give Xtaabay and Zacnal some Gummi Frogs from his pack. Even as they chewed, they asked about lunch. I did my best to make them forget they were hungry by reminding them about the food already in their bellies. They demanded *real food* and I said for that, we'd need to keep walking.

We didn't get very far before a low stone wall guarding a small cemetery caught the boys' attention. They kept a wide berth and warned us not to approach. The air smelled of incense and dried lavender. Miniature mausoleums, like houses for dolls, had been recently refreshed with bright wreathes and bouquets. Some of the structures had small, ornamental doors of wood or wire. Some had photos of the deceased, in plastic baggies or cellophane, stapled to their doors.

"They are being prepared," Yum Kaax said.

"For what?" I studied the offerings and flowers.

Blue and gold paint flaked off the dry cement. Some had the same square opening as the pyramid at Chichen Itza. A gaping aperture that lead nowhere. A few had crosses or steeples on top, like little churches.

"*Hanal Pixán,*" Yum Kaax said. "When a person dies, the Father-Mother watches the spirit. *Ch'ulel.* They can put its soul into a little baby if they want, but sometimes it doesn't fit and gets lost. Sometimes it can visit us, or visit its ancestors, or it can appear in dreams."

"Like Day of the Dead," I simultaneously listened to Yum Kaax and translated for Ben. "A more…indigenous version, perhaps? Yum Kaax said ...*we can inhabit different houses after we've passed on.*"

"What's that mean?"

"The day is fast approaching. Yum Kaax said that on the night of Hanal Pixán ...*inocentes will knock on the doors.*"

"For what?"

"To wake the wayob. If we're still here, I suppose we'll find out. This is what they were arguing about this morning. Yum Kaax said wayob will emerge from these doll houses."

"You keep saying that word like I know what it means."

"Wayob? It's like a ghost. They used it back at Chichen Itza. My best guess is that it literally means *sleeper.* Or *one who sleeps.* But in this context, perhaps, the intent is more sinister. Like *someone who transforms in his sleep*. But perhaps it is just a ghost. Who knows?"

When Yum Kaax realized I translated for Ben, he listened intently to make sure I got it all right, even if he didn't understand my words.

Ben said, "Well, tell him I don't like it."

"I'm sure he knows." I put my hand on Ben's arm. "Yum Kaax is afraid he might have scared you. He wants me to tell you not to worry, the wayob can only take a person on Hanal Pixán, although Xtaabay doesn't agree."

Not sure whether or not to smile, Ben said, "Ain't that a relief."

Before entering the next village, we passed beneath another large wooden cross. Broken green bottles dangled from the horizontal limbs with bits of twine and wire. Ribbons and strips of faded cloth hung limp in the hot morning air. A group of children ran to defend their turf from the new arrivals. Ben drifted into the gas station for more candy. After placating the locals with sugar, then suffering from the inevitable lack of interest after the depletion of said sugar, Ben showed me a day-old newspaper from Mérida. Our descriptions next to a detailed account of the massacre at Chicxulub Puerto.

Zacnal spied on us from behind the corner of the church. He smiled when I waved. "I don't want to see the paper."

"I figured. But when I get my hands around Toussant's neck again, I don't want you to stop me."

Xtaabay appeared over Zacnal's shoulder and signaled us over.

"Then all will be right in the universe once again." I stood. "I'll see what they want."

Ben watched. Not moving from his spot until he absolutely had to. "What is it?"

"We've been invited to lunch."

A local boy guided us through a narrow maze of buildings. Modern concrete block structures stood shoulder-to-shoulder with ancient, thatched-roofs. At the home of Don Santiago Imán, we ate a thin meal of tortillas and a chicken broth flavored with lime juice under a Doña's very watchful eye. The old man did not speak while we ate. He just sat, rubbing his chin, as if demonstrating deep thought. Over the next ten minutes other old men dropped in, including the village x'men. After lunch we moved into the shade of a *tortillería's* tin awning while the general assembly tried to figure out what to do with us.

When I mentioned we'd be on our way to Cobá and meant them no trouble, Don Santiago Imán loaded us down with a bag containing a small bottle of water that could not be opened under any circumstances, a two-liter Coke bottle half-filled with a strong, clear corn liquor, and a small bundle of tortillas to hand-deliver to Don Alejandro Carrillo Puerto upon arrival in Cobá. And to make sure we got there, they put us onto a truck headed to Tulum. I gave Ben the package to carry and said, "But they are not ours to eat."

"Why not?"

"They are for a ceremony. In Cobá. For rain. I arranged a ride, so it's no trouble," I said. "We have to make a few stops, but are covering a lot of ground."

"And how is this better than what X had arranged?"

"Because I am the one who arranged it."

The next hour disappeared in the bed of an old pickup truck, bouncing south and east—but not always in that order—along heavily rutted back roads. We kicked up magnificent clouds of white dust that hung in the air like a dense fog. The dog skidded from side-to-side until Ben finally wrangled it into a corner. The sun shone like a colorless diamond. Nothing made shelter in this hot, dry place.

Zacnal hid next to me in the shade of a light cotton wrap I'd gotten in Mérida. Unable to relax, Ben watched the road behind us.

Boredom loosened up the boys. Xtaabay taunted Zacnal with a song about the wayob. I asked him to stop.

Xtaabay feigned sadness with an exaggerated pout. Then he exhaled dramatically, closed his eyes, and continued to sing.

"Xtaabay. If I have to tell you again, you'll walk."

Yum Kaax smiled his approval.

Oblivious to anything happening outside his head, Ben said, "What are we supposed to do in Cobá?" He'd been thinking about it since we left. I knew, because he hadn't spoken to me since we got into the truck. "I don't want to get drawn into a situation where I have to smile at people I don't know."

"Why can't you trust me?" When I saw he needed an answer, I said, "Cobá is just inland from Tulum and Cozumel. There will be boats."

"And tourists."

"We'll just have to be smarter than them."

At each village our collection of items to be carried east grew. We received two glass bottles of alcohol and a pickle jar filled with clear water from a cenote at a village called Xkalakdzonot. An hour later, at a village called Chikindzonot we were given more water and a small pouch filled with several balls of fragrant incense. The texture reminded me of the hashish that Ben had found in Toussant's bag. Gummy and dense. The scent remained on my fingers.

Forty minutes later, we stopped at a village that sat within plain view of a major highway running north to Valladolid. A reminder that the real world did exist after all.

While waiting for Don Pakal Pablo—a short man with bristly dark hair peppered with white and silver caps on his front teeth—to collect his peoples' ceremonial offerings, we hid from the passing cars behind a low stone wall. The Doña took our water bottles and disappeared into the darkness of her home, as if swallowed by the smoke from her cook fire. Yum Kaax again tried explaining the homophones to me and kept pointing at the thatched roof, saying, "Ka'an," while Zacnal slept on my lap. Before we could delve any deeper into the phonetic relevance of Yucatecan cosmological terms, the Doña returned with small plastic plates piled high with tortillas and black beans in a thick, dark sauce. Ben laughed with delight. Our water bottles were offered back to us, full, and a small group of children gathered to watch us eat.

I scolded the boys for eating too fast. Ben defended them by saying low blood sugar was a serious medical issue and had to be dealt with accordingly. When a soccer ball appeared from the tangle of legs, Xtaabay and Yum Kaax forced the rest of their food into their mouths and ran headlong into the spontaneous game that took place between the vestibule of a very small church and a pair of steel barrels with a bit of lumber resting across the top. The ever-changing rules allowed for a ball to be played off one of the dogs that ran from end to end with them—the yellow dog did not have the energy to participate—and a goal that went all the way to the church altar counted as two points. The game ended with a debate about the legality of throwing stones at a player on the verge of scoring on a breakaway.

When Don Pakal Pablo returned with a committee—stepping over exhausted children as if they were piles of manure in a pasture—I stood to hear his proposal. The men accompanying Don Pakal mostly wore white guayaberas and several wore straw hats.

They'd dressed up as if they were a formal delegation. When Don Pakal spoke, I realized that asking strangers for help had been a very humbling experience for the village, but they needed the rain. Don Pakal had said *... it seems as if the sea keeps it all for herself.* I told Ben to stand up and he shoved the rest of Zacnal's uneaten tortilla into his mouth as he rose to greet them. I shook hands with the other men as they approached, even though they directed their comments at Ben.

Xtaabay found himself at our side—chest puffed out, muscles flexed, dried beans on his cheek—as if he would receive a fee for mediating the negotiations. The men accompanying Don Pakal Pablo had a lot of questions about who we were and about our commitment to making rain and a long list of demands, how we should conduct ourselves and whatnot. When Xtaabay realized that I'd been planning to go to Cobá to observe the ceremony all along, he relaxed. Once the terms were settled we all shook hands again and I introduced Ben.

When they reached for his hand, he wiped it on his pants. Don Pakal Pablo said, "Soldier."

"Yes," I replied.

I saw Ben's confusion and moved quickly to correct it. "It's very important to get all of this to Cobá by tomorrow night. They trust you because you were in the army."

He seemed a bit stunned and said, "The US Army doesn't even trust me for having been in the army."

Before he could ruin the opportunity, I interjected, "They know about Toussant. Somebody driving down from Valladolid this morning said there were police roadblocks on the highways. A news crew from Mérida arrived in Piste this morning. Toussant burned the hotel down. They say it's safe to assume the police in Playa del Carmen and Cancun are on alert as well."

Ben clenched his fists. I made a move to allay his guilt. "Nobody got hurt."

He nodded and released the air he'd been holding in.

I said, "These men believe we are innocent and that our intentions are good. Or so they say. The small donation I promised seemed to convince them. Either way, it doesn't matter. We can be in Cobá tomorrow."

Ben said, "How are we going to get there? Except for that highway there's a hell of a lot of green between here and the coast. There aren't a lot of ways in, out, or through, and it sounds like they're all fairly well-covered. Toussant isn't going to close his eyes and count to ten."

"Don Pakal Pablo described a shortcut we can take. An ancient road through the forest. It's the preferred route, in fact, for what we're doing. Delivering these items and such."

Ben looked skeptical. "X said we weren't supposed to be in the forest at night?"

"Yum Kaax said they will only take souls on Day of the Dead. Besides, Don Pakal Pablo believes the sacbe will protect us because our journey is important."

"What the hell is a sacbe?"

"Literally, it means *white road.* His ancestors built it and according to Don Pakal Pablo, we should be fine as long as we don't stray into the jungle."

"That's reassuring. And how do we make sure we don't drift off course? So far, ending up where we'd hoped isn't our strong suit."

"Xtaabay volunteered to be our guide."

"This kid doesn't have a clue, Dani. Has he ever been to Cobá?" Ben laughed and looked at Xtaabay, who smiled proudly. "You ever been to Cobá, X? Do you know where the hell you're going?"

"Ben, don't be cruel. When you thought he'd gotten us a ride to the coast he was the best dumpling in the basket. Now he's clueless? It's funny how this is playing out. Besides, Don Pakal Pablo says all Maya know these roads because all Maya know the night sky. And if what Yum Kaax said earlier is true, then the road and the sky are one and the same."

"Dani..." Ben couldn't find the words to express his frustration. He clasped his hands behind his head and stretched while trying to stifle a laugh, an unexpectedly benign reaction. *So this is the real Benjamin Collins.* My heart warmed, but I focused on checking my emotions.

He said, "Star maps? Like this is some mystical portal through space and time—"

"Maybe, Ben." I cut him off to avoid any further embarrassment to our hosts. As I passed his bag to him, I said, "I guess we'll find out tomorrow, now won't we?"

Don Pakal Pablo's last words to us were ...*the sacbe is the universe. It would be easy to get lost.* I couldn't tell if it was advice, a warning, or word play, though the road's flat surface made it appear as if one of their gods had unrolled a blank white scroll all the way to the sea. At first glance, it appeared harmless enough. If sacbe was a homophone for *Milky Way,* then Don Pakal Pablo made it seem as if the road itself—rather than the rigor of walking—should not be trifled with, lest we face a cosmic repercussion.

It's a way to get from here to there. For anything else, it's dangerous.

The forest changed shortly after we stepped onto the path, just before one. The acceleration of trucks on the highway remained with us for the first ten minutes. Once that sound faded no others came to replace it. Birds didn't swoop from branch to branch. Insects didn't buzz.

We advanced into a strange dimming not caused by the passing of a cloud—the sky remained clear like polished glass. The light on the sacbe grew flat and dense, like that created inside a church with many stained glass windows.

But the trees cast no shadows.

Neither did we.

When I pointed this out to Ben, he just dismissed it. "It's more ghost stories, isn't it? When we're on the move, keep moving because it's dangerous to stop. But there are ghosts and jaguars in the forest so stay the hell out of there too. I don't get it."

"What's to get?"

"First of all, it shows this really isn't a place for these chicos," Ben said. He gave Yum Kaax and Zacnal a once over. In his mind, they'd already failed. "Or a dog."

Sensing an insult, Yum Kaax took Zacnal's hand and walked ahead.

"Xtaabay said the dog would keep jaguars away."

"You keep buying into all his shit, Dani. You want something to believe in so you become this illogical fanatic. Like the demons—"

"We are not dealing with the demons, Ben. Just trees and miles."

"So after everything I've experienced since hopping into your little car—the weird voices and memories of places I'd never been—you're telling me that we're not dealing with something otherworldly?"

"Would that make it easier for you? Look, if you see things that aren't there, then it's what's in your head you have to worry about. I just see a road. Nothing more."

"Well, which is scarier? Wild animals and malaria, or demons?" Ben said. "I was learning to live with the demons. As far as I'm concerned, nature's scarier. You know what kind of parasites are out here? At least I can reach out and touch nature. A snake is real. Poisonous plants are real. A bee hive—"

"You were not learning to live with the demons," I said. "That's why we had the incident in the hotel last night. These boys were born here and they raised themselves—they are survivors. I think they are well-prepared to handle whatever happens. Your concern is honorable, but misguided. Or maybe worrying about them keeps you from having to take a look at what's going on in your own head."

"Well, they aren't helping each other with the bogeyman talk. X is going to scare Snacks—"

"Zacnal," I said, subtly correcting him.

"Then we're going to have problems. Everything that goes bump is going to sound like a jaguar to him."

"Are you talking about Zacnal or yourself?"

"Make jokes, but every hunter worth his salt has a cougar story. Henry saw one during all that Lewis shit. My cousin?"

"Yes, a story you've told me many times."

"If they still roam the mountains back home—which are surrounded by people and roads—they are good at what they do. Like ghosts. If there are big cats out here we'll never see them. Maybe that's all the wayob are?"

"See? Nothing to fear then." I smiled, took his hand, and comforted him with my touch.

For the first hour, the walking seemed easy. Rejuvenated by the ride and by the food, we moved quickly. Some of the women from Don Pakal Pablo's village had packed tortillas and salty roasted pork in old newspaper to get us through the night. Xtaabay wanted to carry it, but I gave it to Yum Kaax because I knew he wouldn't eat any. He put it into his plastic grocery bag with the candy and cakes, which he then zipped into his backpack. Each of the boys had a bit of sisal twine knotted around a two liter soda bottle filled with drinking water from the village well. Ben carried mine. Yum Kaax said he'd share his with the dog. I carried the ceremonial items. It seemed unfair to burden Ben with a load that wasn't his own.

Whenever Zacnal or Xtaabay complained about their grumbling bellies, I reminded them they could eat now and go to bed hungry, or eat later and go to bed full. Then I asked them to keep drinking their water. A trick I learned at the orphanage. Lying to children came too easily. Lying to ourselves, not so much.

After the water break, Yum Kaax fell into step beside us. He didn't say anything until I asked how he felt. "Ba'ax ka wa'alik?"

Using a little bit of Spanish mixed with Yucatec, he said, "I can't explain this to you, but I want to. And Don Pakal said I should try."

"It's okay, Yum Kaax. You are doing an excellent job." I put my hand on his shoulder. "Just go slow."

He said, "Don Pakal Pablo wanted me to tell you that the sacbe connects the past and future. Like how a baby gets food from the mother before it's born." He patted his belly. "I don't know this word."

"Umbilical cord?"

He shrugged, illustrating the meaninglessness of my question. With a serpentine wave with his hand, he said, "Sacbe is this road and the Milky Way. It connects the earth to the sky. Like a serpent."

"Which is why *ka'an* is the sky and a serpent? Not just a homophone, but conceptually one and the same? Because the snakes are the umbilical cord between the earth and the sky." I felt a great unburdening with the revelation of that particular linguistic quirk.

"Yes," he said, relieved that I understood.

The realization that our place in time and space was fluid, even if only for a moment, made it seem as if the cosmos would try to say something even more significant to me if I'd just open myself up to it. As if I could turn my palms up and receive whatever message it cared to share.

But fragments of schema slipped in from my subconscious, leaving me unable to distinguish what formed there from any message I'd receive from the sky. I wanted the universe to tell me that this journey east would reveal birth and rebirth in an ancient dream made real by our miles. That I would be like a fire reignited from an ember left to smolder. In the end, I had no choice but to believe what came into my head had come from above. My hands shook with excitement, for if the sky had this much to say to me now, I could only imagine what the stars and Milky Way would share tonight.

From this point forward, my every action needed to be a carefully measured part of who I would become. For the longest time I'd plotted my words as if they were points on an algebraic graph, vertically and horizontally. But this new world forced me to consider other linguistic realms. Now that I knew syllables existed in three dimensions instead of just two, my ideas felt like dark matter in space. Mostly hidden, yet massive.

I needed to figure out how to exist along a new axis.

All I knew was that this road would deliver me to the east where the sun was reborn every morning, where green and blue—the colors which symbolized the freshness of life—resided in thatched roof huts by the sea.

All I knew was that I had no ties to what happened yesterday or the day before that. I had only now, which lived at the bottom of tomorrow. Some would argue that time was relative and while that may have been true for Einstein, I knew that disorder hunted in the past. Only the future held the promise of order. I had to set the terms for tomorrow and for the day after that. The promise of order, like wine straight from the bottle, was not such a bad thing.

Deep down, I knew there would be a price to pay for changing my fate. For seeking alternatives to the agreements I'd made so long ago. For leaving the Old World and seeking answers in the New. Changing parameters and playing fields. Like a domino toppled, I'd set into motion a chain of events that would alter my destiny forever. Deep down I knew that cosmic forces thought nothing of distances measured in mere miles or hours.

And that in the grand scheme of things, my life only meant something to me.

And maybe to Ben as well.

The jungle napped as we moved through the deepest part of the day. Ahead of us waited a crackling fire and new dreams. Behind us were all the lies I told to keep our party advancing.

The boys were tired and said very little as they walked. The time for playing had stopped. It made me sad to see how quickly they became men. Like, once a task had been assigned, they were forced to shed their childish ways and grow up.

Like I once had to do.

If there had been a choice, I'd never seen it. If there had been a way back to the person I'd been before I left home, it hid in plain sight. I resented never being given the opportunity to seek it.

And I wondered what repercussions I'd face for searching for it now. After so much time spent thinking about only myself.

When all was said and done, I figured I didn't need my innocence back. The bad things that happened helped me become the person I was. I understood that my life resulted from a set of variables only I could've created.

But I wanted to be able to laugh again. If nothing else, I wanted to be in on the joke.

When at long last the end of the day poked holes in what remained of the western sky, the world began to look different. Dry clouds that only teased rain draped the land in gold light. We'd walked straight through afternoon to nautical twilight, whose early arrival never failed to amaze me at this latitude. In Yucatán, Venus ruled from an ephemeral throne. While lost in thought, Yum Kaax had taken my hand. The realization made me flinch. He watched my face to make sure I wouldn't change my mind and let go. I let him savor the moment, but my mind screamed, *Please, not you too. I can't break one little heart, let alone three.*

Ben and I took turns carrying Zacnal. From time to time the boy had even napped in his arms. When Xtaabay suggested we stop for the night, Ben encouraged him to give it another twenty minutes. Accepting the challenge, Xtaabay turned looking for *sanctified ground* into a game. And if Ben didn't approve of a spot, I'd kindly translate his veto to *too rocky* or *looks like a good place for snakes*. But after the day we'd had, Xtaabay could take no more of Ben's authority and ran ahead to scout with the dog. Ben carried Zacnal on his shoulders.

A long half-mile later, a dull glow appeared from the depths of the anorexic trees. *Another sign the gods were paying attention to me,* I joked to myself. Without rain, this forest had turned to bone. Emaciated shadows crossed the path at irregular angles that shifted as we got closer. I anticipated katydids and the shrill lullaby of other night insects, but heard none. Xtaabay's dark silhouette passed back and forth in front of the fire as he gathered more limbs for fuel.

He'd set camp up on a rectangle of neatly-placed stone, almost twelve feet by twenty—the golden ratio, of course—that looked like one of the structures at Dzibilchaltún without the gaudy ornamentation. The flat surface was devoid of vegetation except for a small grouping of freshly-placed flowers and clumps of incense ash where the platform joined the sacbe. Ben stepped over the offering and lowered Zacnal to the ground.

Yum Kaax said, "Like a lock on a door."

"It's sanctified ground. This is why we've been seeing the tributes all over Yucatán. These platforms are like spiritual fortresses." I translated for Ben as I rubbed his shoulders. "Nothing can enter from the sacbe while we sleep."

"Such as…."

"Wayob," I said.

"Okay," Ben said, looking right at Xtaabay and Yum Kaax. "No more ghost stories. You all need a good sleep. We'll have plenty of time for talk tomorrow. Tell 'em, Dani."

Xtaabay grumbled as he removed the tortillas from the newspaper. Yum Kaax told him to be quiet, but Xtaabay wouldn't. Yum Kaax tried to calm Zacnal and helped him pick out the fattiest bits for their tortillas. He squeezed a blood orange over their pork. Then Zacnal helped Yum Kaax prepare one for me. Ben was on his own.

"Ghosts and ghost stories are the same thing." I didn't look at Ben when I said it and was content to go back to my meal.

"Which one of them came up with that? Yum Kaax?" Ben chomped on the tough pork and picked his teeth with his fingers. The dog ate what Ben dropped.

"I said it."

The revelation deflated him a bit.

Ignoring him, I stared into the fire. Sparks rose like a multitude of fiery, young planets, so bright and ephemeral that only a god could know their fate in the grand scheme of things. For a moment I thought that I could follow one all the way to the heavens, where the stars were thick like cobwebs. "Yum Kaax, tell us a story. A good one."

"Like what?"

"You choose. I'll listen to anything you have to say."

He stared into the fire. Suddenly he had no words left.

"It's okay," I said. "Maybe tomorrow."

"No." He turned, panicked. "I don't know where to start."

"Anything you say will be fine."

For a moment, he stuttered. As if my question overwhelmed him. Then he reached for a small, straight stick and cleared some pebbles off a patch of sand. Dust rose to my nose. "'Ka'an is snake. Sky. House. A house for stars."

Yum Kaax pointed his stick towards his zenith.

Zacnal and Ben looked up.

Yum Kaax drew parallel lines in the dirt. "The sacbe in the sky," he said, wagging his finger along the length of the cloudy path in the sky over our heads.

"The Milky Way," I said to Ben. "White road. Down here and up there."

Zacnal scooted closer to watch.

"As is the sky, so is the earth." I wanted to make sure Ben understood. "You have to remember that if you're to make sense of this. It's like the world through a stained glass window. The image in the glass and the world beyond exist in the same frame. The presence of the glass doesn't change the scene behind it."

"I don't know if I quite—"

"Think of the Father, the Son, and the Holy Ghost. Three beings in one." I dug through my bag for my pen and notebook. "Right now you don't need to understand. But I do. I've waited a very long time for this. Once I get this down...."

Yum Kaax watched patiently, holding his stick over the sand, waiting to jump back into his tale.

I turned to a fresh page and wrote *Maya Cosmology.* When I gave Yum Kaax the go ahead, he resumed. "The Milky Way is the spine upon which the universe is built...."

A storyteller in the truest form of the word, he pounded the ground with his palm, accenting his cadence with the only drum available, and ended each statement with the swipe of a hand. If he paused to take a breath, I never noticed. If there were details he doubted, he never showed it. His faith remained absolute, his tone authoritative. He strung together concrete details that made me truly want to believe. And for a moment, I did.

Thus began the unraveling of the cosmos.

I continued explaining for Ben. "This is important, because the ecliptic bisects the Milky Way. But Yum Kaax didn't say *ecliptic.* He just drew a line through it, like crossing a *T*." I didn't want to lose Ben because I needed an ally. I needed to not be the only witness to this. As Yum Kaax spoke, I whispered and pointed to the sky. "The ecliptic is the path the planets take. The constellations of the Zodiac—that's why they're important. Together, the Milky Way and ecliptic form a cross. The *Yaxche.* Xtaabay called some of the trees *yaxche* this afternoon on our nature hike, but they are ceiba trees. Kapok. In Asia, kapok seeds are harvested for fiber. Stuffing for pillows. And those crosses we saw outside of the villages today weren't a celebration of Christianity—they represented ceibas. The Yaxche. The cosmos."

I tapped Yum Kaax's star map with my pen. "But Ben, look. It's a crossroads. The Christian cross and the Yaxche represent a crossroads. The place where deals were struck. Don't you see?"

"No."

"The sky—not the earth—is where the power lies. The crossroads just symbolizes this structure. The Milky Way crossed by the ecliptic. I don't need a point on the map as long as the stars are in position above me. Geography never mattered—it just symbolized what happened in the sky."

Without waiting for me to finish my thought, Yum Kaax scratched a zigzag along the ecliptic, then drew legs beneath it. Yum Kaax said, "It's a monster—like a crocodile? But with another head instead of a tail."

Ben said, "A monster at the crossroads? That sounds familiar."

Ignoring him, I drew it in my book. "He said that a figure emerges from each mouth and I'm not sure exactly of my translation. Jaguar Paddler and Stingray Paddler? I don't even know if that sounds right. But they transport a third figure named Wak-Chan-Ahaw—Six-Sky-Lord—across an ancient sea in a canoe. Yum Kaax tried to show me this as we passed through Chichen Itza this morning. The big pyramid surrounded by the wide, grassy area—the mountain rising from the primordial sea. At Dzibilchaltún, the plaza with the cenote played the same part. I don't know if you remember?"

"I don't." The reminder embarrassed him, like it always did. But he dismissed it by shaking his head. "The ruins are maps of the sky?"

"And of Maya Creation. It's all the same, Ben. And look, the mountain is where Wak-Chan-Ahaw places the hearthstones. Don Trejo told me the hearthstones are the heart of his people and I didn't understand until just now." I asked Yum Kaax to show him.

"Orion?" Ben said.

Yum Kaax placed a trio of stones in the dirt—stars in the dust—as he spoke. To populate his sky he drew a line of three equally-sized and spaced dots below the ecliptic where Orion's belt would be.

"Orion," I said.

Yum Kaax drew the dagger hanging from the hunter's belt, confirming it.

The stones he'd placed formed a triangle with the western most star in Orion's belt as its apex. He placed one stone at Orion's right foot and the other at his left. The dagger rested neatly in the center.

I could barely contain my emotions. "Have you ever viewed Orion through a telescope?"

Ben said, "I remember the cloud in the knife hanging from the belt. The nebula? Back home in December you could almost see it without a telescope."

"I think I would like to see that very much." I put my hand on his knee.

Yum Kaax flicked an ember from the fire into the center of the triangle. If it were winter and Orion were in the sky, we'd be able to see the flames of the hearth there too.

"Yes," I said. "Every Maya home has this model of the cosmos at its center. The four-sided roofs—ka'an—the four-sided pyramids. They are all models of creation."

Yum Kaax went on and I continued translating for Ben. "Once Wak-Chan-Ahaw placed the hearthstones, they needed to lift the stars to make room for the people and the animals on the earth. What would you use to raise up something too heavy to lift?"

"A forklift?"

At least he tried.

"Ben—they used a lever. Yum Kaax tried to show me this afternoon. Weren't you paying attention? Wak-Chan-Ahaw and Stingray Paddler and Jaguar Paddler used the Yaxche to lift up the sky. The cross."

Ben remained quiet.

"Every night the story plays out in the sky," I said, writing and talking. "The Milky Way rotates above the horizon as the night wears on. From horizontal to vertical, just like a minute hand on a clock. Every night they look up and see Creation. And if Yum Kaax's ancestors brought this story with them from the Old World fifteen thousand years ago, it could be the purest version of Creation I've ever encountered. The answers are all in here somewhere, Ben. Somewhere."

I put my notebook down and took my glasses off. "The Axis Mundi is a cultural universal. Nearly every group of people on earth has a story or landmark that represents an umbilicus between earth and sky. Mount Fuji and Mount Olympus and the Black Hills and Mount Zion. The Sumerians and Babylonians actually built artificial mountains, just like the Maya. There are other symbols—the Maypole, totems, mandalas and stupas in Tibet, the Bodhi Tree. In Scandinavia, it's Thor's Oak. But the Maya Yaxche is the only Axis Mundi that physically connects the earth to the sky. The Yaxche is concrete, Ben. The Yaxche is the intersection of the cosmos and all creation. The penultimate contract."

"Yeah, but it's a story, like Noah. It doesn't mean anything if you can find a way to make it real."

I dismissed his negativity with a wave of my hand. "Because the earth and sky are connected, the x'men can open temporary doors and send material back and forth. That's why tomorrow is so important. If I can see how it's done...." I took Ben's hand.

"You're shaking," he said. "Just take a minute, okay?"

Yum Kaax waited, watching my eyes as I processed.

I pushed onto my knees and joined him in the dirt by the fire. "Tomorrow, when we reach the end of the sacbe, Don Alejandro will create a door, then open it and ask Itzamna for rain. That's what all this is—the tortillas, the water and the alcohol. An offering. Itz. Blood, sap, water, candle wax. Each village giving up something to get something in return, and tomorrow Don Alejandro Carrillo Puerto will open the door and offer these items, hoping Itzamna will send the rain. It's no different than the Eucharist. The Blood and Body of Christ. Does the priest not open a door? Are the bread and wine not transformed by the Holy Spirit?"

When it had all started to make sense in my head, I said, "Tomorrow is everything. No rain means no maize, means no Maya. *Bey ti'ka'an, bey ti'lu'um.* They die without water. Move to the cities. And all this is gone."

"So that's what this road trip is all about? The epic quest to collect tortillas and moonshine?"

"I think so. Or it means that we are very close." I squeezed Ben's hand. "This is our way, Ben. This is how we free ourselves."

I looked up into the sky and saw it all. Death and rebirth laid out like roads on a map. Silence returned and I refrained from asking more questions for fear of ruining it. Only the steady, low hiss of the fire remained to sing us to sleep. Zacnal nestled up next to Yum Kaax. Xtaabay slept on the other side of Ben, which made them both feel secure.

My head raced with possibilities and I foolishly permitted a spark of a fantasy to take root. I let myself go home with Ben to meet his mother and father and grandparents. I let him propose to me. The fantasy scared me because if any of this became real, I'd again have something to lose.

"I love you, Danicka," he said, pulling me closer.

I could feel his smile. The way he stroked my hair. The way he got as close to me as he could. In a sleepy voice, he said, "Will this work? I mean…"

"Don't think about it now. Go back to sleep."

"I wasn't sleeping. How can I? I can't think about anything else." He rubbed his eyes with his palms. He may have been crying, but I couldn't tell. "If this really means we might be able to go back home, then we have to try it, right?"

"I am afraid you'll only be disappointed." I meant it more for myself than Ben. "Let's not waste energy on hope."

"I disagree. I think we should embrace this, whatever it means."

"I want to, Ben. I really do." I held on to my next words for as long as I could. "But building our own universe won't be easy."

Ben inhaled, like he had something really important to say, and I waited. But as he slowly released it, he only said, "Nothing good ever comes easy," then kissed me goodnight.

SIX

October 28, 2009

Hey Dad,

Not sure where to go with this so I'm just going to come right out and say that I'm not sure I have a place to stay right when I get back. Cora is sharing a studio in Georgetown with another student. It's walking distance to campus and she doesn't want to leave her roommate hanging. I guess there's a little hotel down in Arlington where I can stay when I visit so her roommate isn't put out. We'll work on something more permanent when her lease expires unless I'm deployed again.

Please don't get specific with mom. It's really not a big deal. If it feels dishonest I can stay with a guy in Morgantown. Or if I can get a gig at Seneca Rocks for the summer it won't matter. I'll just throw up a tent at the guide house. I can explain it all to you on the ride home.

Some of this shit is starting to get to me. I miss the green. I need to be home. Need it. I can feel it in my bones. Everything's a hell of a lot more cut and dry back there. I'm starting to see that morality doesn't exist anywhere else in the animal kingdom and I'm starting to think it's a mental illness. A defense we use to protect ourselves from amoral people. It's like water or air—always there, always available—but some people have learned to bottle it and sell it. Governments. Churches. People like me. If you go back in time ten thousand years there was no code of ethics, but I bet somewhere along the line a small group of people invented gods and devils to justify the laws they made to manipulate the rest of us.

And guys like me enforce them.

I'll let you know my flight information as soon as I get it.

Ben

The snap of a twig in the empty forest tore me from my sleepless rest.

Adrenaline forced my heart valves wide open. Made me twenty feet taller. We had no place to hide. No sanctuary could be found on this slab. Made me wonder what I was doing out here with these kids. I wasn't fit to take care of them, let alone lead them.

I put my finger over Dani's lips and listened.

It felt like the kind of silence that wanted you to know something was there. Forced silence. The velvety quiet that existed when something altered the regular pattern of sound. Even the air stilled itself.

I fought to quiet my heart.

Only embers remained in the fire pit, so I knew I hadn't been startled by a sparking bit of ash.

Straining to hear, I slowly rotated my head, but something out there dampened the noise. My breathing still came too loud. I couldn't calm it.

The dog will bark if it gets close.

Then the pattern changed again, more faintly. A shuffle in the dry leaves followed by a forced stillness. All the other noises in my head suddenly stopped.

It came from the edge of the platform.

I stared into the darkness. The lines were blurred, like somebody dragged their fingers through wet oil paint. Dani sat up next to me.

I tried to remain still. *So many stars—if each one were a soldier watching over me I might feel safe.*

Yaxche had gone, replaced by constellations from another season, another time. There went Taurus following the Pleiades by only a few degrees. A nursery for stars.

If it posed a threat, the dog would bark.

Something moved between me and the patch of sky I'd been looking at. Something had eclipsed it. A formless form. A shapeless shape. A patch of darkness grew before me.

Behind the wood smoke I caught a note of musk. A mouth that had recently tasted meat and blood.

This is how they come to take me.

Above, directly at zenith, sat a small star. I didn't know its name, or if it even had one. But when the void moved over me the star disappeared. I could feel the hot breath on my face.

Then it disappeared.

Slowly, the stones beneath me began to whisper. The stars let out a deep sigh.

Then the smell dissipated. All that remained was all that was there before. The sky stayed right where I'd left it. The fire still slept.

I said, "Time to change that."

The remaining wood—five or six large limbs and a piece of hollowed log—joined the embers. I put my cheek against the ground and blew. Before long, sparks drifted skyward to take their rightful place in the sky. Once, as a kid, my old man told me that stars were made this way. I never believed him either.

"I smelled it too," Dani said. She slid beneath my arm, pulling it tightly to her. And she didn't let go until the sun came up.

The morning light dripped through the high branches, scattering angular shadows across the dry ground. Walls of brilliance transformed the airborne dust into a nebulous cathedral buttressed by spindly, dead trees and spired by a razor-sharp sky. Dirt and sweat coated us, an endless baptism. Instead of translucent stained glass to tell the story of our journey east, we had only footprints.

We'd been traveling a half hour before a magnificent wail cut through the stillness. Like a protective father, I stepped in front of Dani. X bolted to the edge of the sacbe. I had to snag him by the arm to keep him from running toward the noise.

"Ben, what is it?"

"It's an animal," I said, stepping toward the noise.

A cat, I thought. *A big one.*

Seeing a predator like this in a zoo is enough to make any man feel small. But seeing it in its natural habitat, struggling to live and breathe, made my own sense of insignificance feel all too real. Like I'd squandered years feeling sorry for myself when I should've been struggling just to keep living and breathing.

The cat's magnificent coat changed from gold to orange when he pulled at the wire snare, blazing like a star against the grainy grey landscape. My other senses faded as I stared, like sight alone was all I'd ever need to feel this alive again. So alive, in fact, I could only assume that I'd stepped out of a dream and into real life.

"Ben, don't get too close."

The hair on Yellow Dog's back rose into spiky tufts. It growled and spit, but kept its distance.

"I got this." I hesitated, trying to buy time. "I got this like…." It looked big, but I had no frame of reference for this and guessing didn't ease my nerves. Could've been the size of a black bear. Maybe smaller. Either way, two-hundred pounds of teeth and claws were nothing to play with.

The cat gasped and choked, suffocating on its own weight. Every pathetic breath, a goodbye. Paws struggled to gain purchase in the dry leaves. The short wire forced it to stay on its feet, exhausted. Choking. The bait, a hindquarter from a deer, hung from a limb attracting flies.

X and Yum Kaax chittered emphatically. I told them to be get back, but they were too wrapped up in their conflict to notice. I pulled my shirt over my head and wiped the sweat out of my eyes. "Tell them to quiet down, please."

"They won't listen, Ben. You need to forget this."

The cord had been tied off to a small, flexible limb as thick as my forearm. Though I tried, I couldn't see an alternative to cutting through the branch.

"It deserves to live."

"So do you," Dani said. "And so do these boys. And so do I."

"I know. Just give me a minute to think this through." I walked nearer to the edge of the snare's radius, eyeballing the limb as I got closer. The acrid smell of urine hit me when I got within ten yards. I looked for blood, or other sign of injury, but couldn't see anything beyond the cable digging into the flesh around its neck.

Yum Kaax ran up and handed me his machete. "Dani, call him back please. Maybe you all should head back to the path?"

"He said he's not leaving you. So you need to lead us away from here."

"I can't—it didn't do anything to deserve this. Just take the boys back to the sacbe. I'll catch up." I pointed at Yum Kaax. "Get on over there now."

He took a few steps back and crossed his arms. Watching stoically as I tucked the blade into my belt and pulled myself into the tree. I paid careful attention to where my fingers went. Made sure my feet wouldn't slip. Tested my weight on the branch before crawling out onto it. Just a foot. Knowing the limb would be thinner farther out, I gave myself another foot and a half.

"Ben," Dani paused to carefully consider her words. "This is careless."

Ignoring her, I settled into a slight crook and hacked at the wood a few times. The cat spun toward the noise. Spitting foam and rage, it pulled on its tether.

"Dani, head back to that clump of shrubs." I wiped the sweat out of my eyes with my shirt then tucked it back into my waistband. "I got this."

The cat let out a chesty cough. It flattened its ears but flailed like a marionette, paws thrashing in the dirt.

"Go on now. Keep them safe." X had his arms around the dog's neck, restraining it.

She looked mad. I couldn't look at her when she was mad. What she didn't understand is that maybe I needed to be right. Maybe I needed to believe I had the capacity to affect positive change in this universe too. I possessed no magic. I didn't have belief and superstition at my beck and call. I just had my hands.

When I struck the branch with the machete again, the cat spun toward me, pulling at its snare. Teeth bared. Eyes narrowed. Terror and survival looked the same when you were in the middle of it. The way it wheezed and gasped when it lunged broke my heart. When it jerked the branch and knocked me off my perch, I never saw it coming.

I gasped when I hit the ground. My diaphragm spasmed. I clawed at the dirt as I struggled to push myself upright. *Drowning.*

The cat spun and pulled at its tether. I kicked to push myself away from it and got caught in a root.

Yum Kaax yelped as he stumbled toward the cat from behind. He swung a stick and hollered. X threw stones from further back. The cat turned, and I pushed myself onto my knees. The branch I'd fallen from had splintered—not a clean break. The green wood held fast. As the cat pulled toward the boys, the limb twisted like a hand at the end of a broken arm.

"Hey." I pounded the dirt. "Look here."

Yum Kaax dove away from the cat, hitting the ground with a thud. But instead of rolling away, he froze.

"X—grab him."

The cat reacted to the new stimulus. Lowering its head. Testing the snare. The branch twisted on a thin axis of fibrous bark as the animal pulled. Every time it jerked, the limb gave a bit more, slowly pulling away from the tendrils that still held it to the tree.

"X—stop. Just wait." I held my hand up and moved toward it, trying to steer it away from Yum Kaax. I waved the shirt at it, but it wouldn't look.

I swatted its tail with a branch. When it turned, a growl came from someplace deep and dark. Guttural, with depth and reverb. For all I knew, it came straight from hell itself.

It twisted, paw raised and full of claws. When it pulled again the branch nearly came down. Leaves wafted through the hot, still air. Dust lingered.

The movement startled the animal. It reared. Eyes wide.

I put the t-shirt on the end of a stick and stepped closer as I circled behind it. When I got within five feet, I tossed it.

It hit the animal in the face, but the animal quickly shook it away. *This shit plan is going to kill me. Not some ghost.*

The jaguar coiled, getting smaller, more compact. When it sprang I'd have nowhere to go but down. I planted my feet and choked up on the stick.

Before the cat could jump, X pulled on the branch at the far end of the snare. Like reeling in a marlin. The cat turned, gasping and choking.

I rushed, tackling it to the ground. Pulled the t-shirt over its face.

It pawed at my hands as it tried to clear its face. Coughing and growling. Wheezing and crying. It twisted, trying to get its back paws into the soil. I fought to keep it on its back. Fought to keep all its sharp things pointed the other direction. I twisted the shirt tight over its eyes with my left hand.

X leapt into the clearing and grabbed Yum Kaax's ankle. He tugged and tugged, pulling the kid through the dirt and free of the clearing. Dani rushed back to help Yum Kaax to his feet.

I push my fingers beneath the wire snare. The raw smell of the cat's musky urine mixed with the smell of my sweat. Its raw flesh bled. Golden fur came out in hunks. It wriggled and bucked. Its cry climbed into my head—shaking me.

"I'm sorry," I said. "I don't want to hurt you."

I shushed it. Did my best to whisper calm affirmations into its ear. Once my fingers found the ferrule that held the snare tight, I worked the cable loose.

A sucking sound accompanied its gasps. I worried about its trachea. Worried about hurting it further than I already had. I apologized a thousand times and worried the apology would be meaningless if it didn't understand.

The animal sagged. Its muscles softened. With the t-shirt held tight in my left hand, I pulled the wire snare over its ears and muzzle.

The animal wheezed and didn't try to stand. It had grown too weak.

I jumped to my feet and backed away.

Dust hung in the air. For all the noise still in my head it may as well have been from an explosion. "I'm sorry," I said to nothing in particular.

Dani took my hand and lead me backwards through the scrub. I couldn't look away. Not until I saw it stagger to its feet and paw the shirt away from its face.

In one glorious moment sunlight fell through the dust onto the jaguar. Its gold coat blazed like a supernova. Its dark rosettes gaped like a thousand black holes in miniature.

When she released my hand and walked back toward the animal, the sound faded with a ringing in my ears. She moved like a person in an old 8mm filmstrip. My heart raced. I couldn't produce spit. I couldn't raise a hand to hold her back. Couldn't say the words to stop her. The haze eddied in her wake, forming loops and whorls in the still air.

She knelt next to the cat and placed a hand on the nape of its neck. Then she bent over and whispered something to it.

As she made her way back to me the ringing in my ears diminished. And the dust sank to the ground. And I asked her what she said.

"This is one of the things we can never discuss. Do you understand?" She picked up her bag.

And I don't know if it was the effect of the trance, or if I'd actually meant it, but I nodded.

"Good," she said. "Now we must go."

Once we hit the sacbe and headed east, the jaguar coughed. The little one covered his ears.

Yum Kaax and X began to run.

I didn't want to believe I'd done the wrong thing, and Dani's actions only confused me further. I wanted to have faith that I'd only done what the universe expected from me. But the way Dani pulled my hand told me I couldn't have faith in anything the universe told me anymore.

We ran too.

The sky appeared suddenly above a lake holding barely enough water to float a dense mat of water lilies. The green leaves and white flowers glowed like Technicolor in the afternoon sun. The dry trees bowed toward the swamp, as if leaning in for a drink. X had said there were five lakes in Cobá, but I only saw one.

Iguana burrows pocked the stony ground. Ancient pottery fragments shimmered in the sunlight. At the far end, sunburned tourists climbed out of a small van and gathered in the shade of a cantina. Fanning themselves with floppy hats and travel brochures. The latest in a long wave of Conquistadors.

None of the boys even noticed that I'd pissed myself.

I changed while they all sat down to eat and washed for a long time. My face looked strange in the mirror. I wanted to tell the person I saw that everything would turn out just fine. And I thought, *Is this what it's going to take? Are you going to have to separate yourself from that coward? Become a new person altogether?*

"Because you can't," I said. The words sounded too loud in my ears. "The only way you're going home is in a body bag."

So I ate without talking. I could never get enough to feel full and kept thinking about Sirianni's back home, and how the mozzarella got a little brown on top. I wondered if I could ever be part of that world. If it was even possible. I couldn't foresee anybody being able to forgive me for the things I'd done. And I couldn't see myself ever being able to talk about them. It'd be a hell of a lot easier just to get a little booze in me and punch out a window. To show that my fear and pain and anger needed to be expressed in something more powerful than words. That my emotions required grand gestures and volume. A demonstration of the pain I felt to give them a glimpse into the world I lived in. And once they were afraid. Or sad. Or disliked the person I'd become, I could retreat, knowing I'd made my point.

Knowing I'd won by losing.

Knowing they'd never ask me any of those same questions ever again, leaving me alone with my own pain, anger, and fear.

I'll never forget the morning I woke up on the FOB to learn I'd been left all alone in this world. That X and Zack had never made it back.

And how I hated myself for just waking up.

All that because I'd been thinking about some pizza.

We'd rented a room at a hotel with a pool. I sent Dani and the boys up while I paid. Before leaving the desk I asked about a pharmacy. I needed Klonopin. Dani wasn't a doctor. She didn't know what would heal me.

The desk clerk said Tulum would be the closest. I bought two tickets for the first bus out in the morning.

I wouldn't tell her, because I didn't want to tell the boys. The way the little one had been clinging to her—I didn't want to have to see his face when we left.

Escaped.

Fled.

But we didn't stay in the room we'd rented. Not after what happened at Chichen Itza. Two gringos and a gaggle of Maya kids attracted a lot of attention, especially from tourists. We showered and changed clothes, then followed the boys past a small hut at the edge of the ruins to look for Don Alejandro Carrillo Puerto. Smoke from a cookfire drifted out of his hut's rectangular door. I waited outside while they presented him with the offerings from all the villages we'd passed through yesterday.

If what the boys said last night was to be believed, the arching thatched roofs the Maya built over their homes represented a handmade cosmology. Four sides, a center, and a hearth. But I didn't believe. Didn't even want to.

I didn't have to leave home to learn the moon looked the same no matter where you hung your hat.

That their stars looked the same as mine.

I couldn't help but feel that I need to see that sky again to provie it to myself.

Women in huipils smiled at us as they patted maize into tortillas. Blood oranges and chilies joined beans in their cooking pots. Children too small to play outside clung to bright white gowns. The oldest among them shucked corn. They called out *Tu'ux ka bin* as we passed.

The goat path twisted toward a magnificent stone structure, taller than it was wide, nestled in the clearing like a sleeping giant. Howler monkeys slept high in a ceiba tree. The hot sun made them sluggish. X hooted and howled to wake them. Yellow Dog ignored them all. Swallows soared in and out of a small temple at the top of a nearby structure that looked more like a stack of river stones held together by the furious heat than a pyramid. Like a hiker's cairn. Fresh flowers, now wilting, stood on an altar amidst bottles of clear and brown liquids and spots of ash where incense had been burned.

Yum Kaax traced the structure's outline with a finger as he spoke.

"A church," Dani said, translating. "Sacred ground. The Catholic priests at Parroquia la Guadalupe in Tulum don't like that the people of Cobá still regard it as such."

Pumpkins and gourds had been stacked on a platform near the edge of its lowest terrace. There were bottles of alcohol and firewood. Bundles of fresh flowers. I said, "Why is it so special?"

In hushed reverence, Dani said, "This is a mountain rising above an ancient sea. Just like their creation story says. They tried to get as close to the stars as possible to trade blood for rain. For life itself."

As we plunged deeper into the forest, the boys sang little songs to pass the time. Tiny white butterflies passed in front of us like smoke. The path twisted and turned around heaps of carved stone, a three dimensional maze of ruined ceremonial platforms. Thick roots reached into the ground, pulling apart a thousand years' worth of construction with little more than patience and time.

When we stopped at the second of the five lakes, caimans scurried into the muck. The boys showed us an ancient mound where clay pots lay undisturbed, their paint intact. Where flakes of flint and obsidian, in various stages of being worked into weapons and tools, lay scattered in the scrub. We went to a place where carved *stelae*—high narrow stones that told stories in pictures and words—were as numerous as trees.

Dani stopped to examine each one. She closed her eyes and repeated the words she read there. Then we climbed another platform, this one well maintained and neatly kept. For the second time today we saw flowers and bottles of alcohol on a stone altar. We ate sour oranges from a tree that grew nearby then swam in a very small cenote. We explored the foundations of ancient homes which still had skeletons buried in the floor. We discovered a path that went south, and X claimed it went all the way to Belize.

"Impossible," I said.

Dani recorded everything in her little book.

On both sides of the path were milpas in various stages of reclamation—the newest ones wore only the thinnest veil of new corn, now dead and withered. Due to the drought, it would grow no higher than my knee. Old stone walls were farmers' last lines of defense against a skeletal forest poised to take over.

No wonder they built pyramids, they had to put all this stone somewhere.

I caught a whiff of silage and thought about how my grandfather fought to keep us fed with his own little rocky piece of earth, and how his ground produced a constant supply of grey conglomerate. Just like back home, the topsoil here was thin, but so much more precious than jade.

Gold couldn't be eaten in drought. The Maya weren't made of gold. They were made of corn.

Life here teetered between heaven and hell on a parchment-thin layer of existence. They planted corn and watched the stars and prayed for rain year after year, and year after year believed the same thing. Rain meant they'd pleased somebody. Drought meant they hadn't.

"Ben," she pulled me out of my trance. I suppose I should've been grateful. She saved me from spiraling, but went on as if she were totally unaware of what was happening. With her, one could never be certain.

She said, "Once you understand how the church complicated things over the last five thousand years, understanding this land becomes very simple. In the earliest parts of history, laws were handed down from the stars themselves. Rituals crawled through prehistory word by word. But in the Old World, these laws have been forgotten. Rewritten by priests and kings. They institutionalized belief."

With a tug of the hand, she brought me to a complete stop. She told the boys not to wander too far ahead.

Then she continued. "Time has radiated out of this place ever since Wak-Chan-Ahaw raised up the sky to make room for the Maya to live." Something in her voice changed. There appeared in it a lightness I'd never heard before. "Like a web over this reality, keeping us all from flying off into the cosmos."

I nodded, but didn't totally buy into it. Maybe I'd just grown too cynical for Sunday school. I smiled like I understood.

"Yum Kaax told us their story, Ben. A very important story. Christianity has one version of creation. Islam tells a slightly different version. Words twisted by priests or imams to suit kings or chiefs. Or Caesar himself. But the words and intent had been defiled many, many times. A single man could change an entire culture by turning a question into a statement." She put her hand on my cheek while she talked. Literally holding my attention. "But the Maya carried these words over with them before Gilgamesh recorded *his* version in written form to be passed on."

She showed me her notebook. Rows of dots and lines with numbers written over them.

I said, "Dates? That's as exciting as a cheese pizza."

"This is the garden from which all Maya time is cultivated. On one of those stela I saw one of the most stupendous numbers humans ever recorded—the universe's date of birth. *Our* universe, Ben. A number that saw the Big Bang bring forth the cosmos in a fiery act of creation. Planets, stars, nebula, and galaxies springing from the loin of the void. The ancestors of the Maya fled the Old World and dared record the date of Creation here, far from those kings and priests. This is the closest humanity has ever come to understanding the infinite."

Keeping up was a challenge, but I remained committed to trying. "So this is good, right? I mean, we can use this?"

"Ben, writing this number down is one of the boldest acts ever committed in the New World." She held up her hand and corrected herself. "The whole world."

She talked faster now. Building toward something bigger still.

"These people live and die by the calendar. Planting, ceremonies, and wars all had their proper moment in the cosmos, and if things went awry, like if Chaac forgot to send rain, people prodded his memory with a ceremony. Like the ceremony we will see tonight."

"So this is a big deal?"

"If you need proof that it's possible to rip a hole in the fabric of the universe and step through, then it is."

We followed the boys to a field where men worked over large pots and choked on the thick smoke they emitted. Farther on, a small stand had been built, four saplings tied together to make a canopy over an altar. Almost like a brush arbor the Pentecostals used sometimes in the wilderness before a proper church could be built, except this one had a small metal pot suspended from the apex of the arch. To the right of the altar a mound of earth bled smoke, as if a fire had been buried. The smell of burnt lime floated beneath the burning wood.

Dani went right over to introduce herself to the old men tending to their ceremonial duties. A lot of people from the village were here, more came through the trees carrying food and drink. Like ghosts emerging from the ether. Because I couldn't interact with any of them, I felt like the son-in-law at his wife's family reunion.

Through the chatter, I heard the crack of a baseball bat followed by whooping and laughter. Finally, a language I understood.

"I thought you might like to see this," Dani said when I told her where I was headed. "You may never get an opportunity to witness something like this again in your life."

"I don't know the words. You'll just have to explain everything to me anyway, which I know you'll do tomorrow. And the next day. And the next day." I smiled.

She looked disappointed, but kissed my cheek anyway. "Be good."

"I will. And don't pay too much attention to the man behind the curtain, okay?"

Teams were uneven. Big kids versus little kids. Unaware of the rules, I'd been watching from the little kids' side and ended up being pushed into the line-up. Somebody handed me an old wooden bat covered with a patina of electrical tape.

Jokingly, I called my shot when I stepped up to the plate and pretended to spit a stream of tobacco juice into the clay. The pitcher called off imaginary signs. With a wide smile, he saw the one he wanted and nodded. He wound up like Doug Drabek and I smashed it into left field. Hoots and whistles filled the air as the ball sailed over a low stone wall at the edge of the milpa. Somebody groaned. In passable English, a kid put his hand on my arm and said, "Don't do that again."

We had to go look for the ball—the price of victory in a land where humility was regarded more highly than skill. Even though it was recovered quickly, nobody seemed to want to play anymore. Something about fairness. One of the older kids passed around a bottle of clear corn liquor he'd stolen from a table. It felt like home when that warm juice hit my throat. I didn't want it to end.

So to keep it going, I offered to pitch.

And that did it. I showed them a really weak knuckleball and a halfway decent curve and they went nuts. I smiled as I kicked pebbles off my makeshift pitcher's mound, wondering how different my life would've been if I'd have played baseball in college like my coaches wanted me to instead of giving it all up for her.

Those are just echoes, man. Clear your head.

All the fielders from both teams lined up to hit.

"I'm not chasing all these balls," I yelled, but they ignored me. "X. Get your ass out there."

He brought out a one-liter Coke bottle less than half-full of hooch. I gave him a fist-bump as he ran into the outfield. Dani would've said that was all he ever wanted. To be on my team. It shouldn't have been so hard for me to have given it to him.

Some of the newer arrivals sat along the foul lines to watch. I waved them out to the field. Within a few minutes two more kids and Yellow Dog joined X.

The next batter had never seen a knuckleball. After expressing some frustration, he demanded I throw only fastballs. Except not so fast. Occasionally I'd throw a curve just to hear the howls of laughter that came as the batter swung himself to the ground. *A man trying to pass himself off as a boy.* I had a good buzz going. *Or maybe I was drunk?* I couldn't tell the difference, but it came on fast.

Soon, a new line formed behind me. Each and every one of them wanted to be the only one to learn my magic. *My magic,* I thought. All I had to do was show them how to put their fingers on the thread and flick their wrists. I didn't need Dani to translate. For once, I wasn't bumbling my way through our cultural differences. More booze appeared at my feet. A large group of older boys and young men came from the direction of the village.

But one of them wanted me off the mound. He looked to be twenty-two or twenty-three. A boy trying to pass himself off as a man. I puffed my chest up and planted my feet. My intent was more playful than malicious, but he didn't see it that way. X ran in to mediate.

"You want it?" He reached for the ball I held over my head and I pushed him back a few feet. "Take it."

Maybe I was drunk.

Nobody else laughed. Trying to end it, X tugged on the tail of my shirt. When I looked down at him, he dropped his shoulders and looked away, stammering something I couldn't understand.

My face got hot and I told myself it was an alcohol problem, not a personal one. I hadn't done anything wrong and had no reason to be embarrassed. Declaring myself the winner, I dropped the ball and spit on the mound. I picked up my hooch.

X didn't follow when I turned.

"You coming?" I said.

He ignored me.

I'd been hit by pitches that hurt less. But I took my coach's advice and just walked it the fuck off.

SEVEN

The morning I left home I attended mass. A feast for the day of St. John the Baptist. After the Recessional I lit an offertory candle and confessed a sin of frivolity, although I'd hardly considered what I'd done worthy of the beating I took from my father.

Then I confessed all the sins I'd yet to commit and described in great detail the sacrifice I'd make to save my mother, and brother, and sister from the same abuse I'd suffered. I'd mistaken Father Radim's unusual silence for approval. Before returning home for the last time, I sat in a pew and cried until the flames looked like stars.

By the time my mother realized that the prophecy of my demise had been as potent as my final words to her, she'd already disowned me. A deceptive action meant to spare her from my father's wrath. But I arrived too late to save my brother and sister. He beat them until he could no longer raise his arm. They crawled into the night together, and I remained forever thankful that they at least had each other.

Had I known then how futile my actions were to have been, I would have stayed and stood up to the monster and perhaps prevented the creation of two new ones.

Had I known I'd come to fear my own siblings more than I ever did my father, I'd have murdered him and had him pulled by the yoke until the earth lapped every last drop of his blood.

The air glowed. Smoke from fires from beyond the trees fluoresced with yellow light. Believers brought homemade candles. Beeswax. They'd been placed around the central altar by the hundreds. Maybe thousands. Non-believers murmured as they ate and drank, neither disruptive nor helpful, like the proletariat that attended

Easter mass every year just to stay right with God. If there was alcohol, Ben had found it, somewhere. That I hadn't seen him told me he'd no doubt blacked out or had sunk at least elbow-deep into a very dark grey.

If the candles surrounding the altar felt like a thousand suns, those other fires may as well have been galaxies.

If Don Alejandro needed somebody like me—a skeptic willing to do almost anything for a chance to change her stars—maybe I wasn't as far gone as I'd believed.

Yum Kaax took my hand. My initial reaction was to let it go. Push him away. Focus on what I needed to make this work for me.

But I couldn't and pulled him closer to me. I didn't possess the structure and strength he so desired. It took almost everything I had in me to muster the illusion of structure and strength. It would kill the boy to find out how much I'd truly bled for the life I'd lived, and that in the end, I desired the very same things he did. Touch and affection. The family we never had. More than those, I needed validation. Human contact that didn't rely on a lie or manipulation. Approval and the chance to prove I was no longer a monster. I needed forgiveness and the hope of the rebirth Yum Kaax offered, even if it was only the illusion of forgiveness and the hope of rebirth.

Don Alejandro circled the altar, his face passed in and out of shadow. He rotated like a planet. Fireflies pulsed in the milpas and at the edge of the forests like lights at Christmas. Layered breads, tortillas, freshly-plucked chickens, and bottles of homemade alcohol covered his table's surface. Two freshly-butchered deer hung from a low branch nearby—the air still smelled of blood. The items we carried were there too, representing the hopes of the villages that couldn't send delegates. Some of the *pom* incense we'd delivered smoked from one half of an aluminum soda can that had been nailed into the hook of a wooden cane. Soot covered the can's surface. The sweetness of the incense clung to my skin. It reminded me of the walnut *koláče* my mother baked for her sister's wedding. I was very young. That may have been the first time I'd ever tasted something so sweet.

Don Alejandro placed a large glass jug near the center of the table. White flower petals fluttered onto us from the naked branches, as if stirred by the faintest of breezes.

"*Zuhuy ha,*" Yum Kaax said. He swirled his finger in the air. "Cenote water from all over Yucatán. Mixed."

Virgin water that lapped the edge of the underworld. Xibalba. Too deep to be corrupted by terrestrial affairs. Some of the water we carried was in that bottle as well.

Four saplings bound by twine arched over the table. Don Alejandro picked up the soda can with the pom in it and waved it between each one. More smoke drifted out from a clay bowl that swung from the saplings, and the x'men pulled some of it into his mouth.

A false ceiling of six vines, knotted together directly above the bowl, floated over the arches. They stretched out to trees and poles beyond the fire.

Yum Kaax said that they were *ixtabi ka'an.*

Umbilical cords connecting the earth to the sky. I said, "Snake-sky."

Below the smoking bowl hung a ring of thirteen gourds knotted together with twine. "*Xpeten ka'an.*"

I said, "A door? Sky-door?"

A single candle sat beneath the gourds, next to the water. A single light to bind the sky to the altar. A single star in a black cosmos to guide the flow of itz through dimensions. *Blood, water, and magic.*

A lonely flame to hold back the night.

Don Alejandro waved his hand.

Four men took their places at their appointed corners of the table.

Small boys formed a line behind Don Alejandro.

"I wanted Zacnal to be a frog," Yum Kaax said. "To be a part of all this. But he was too tired."

"Well, it's been a very long day—" I looked into the darkness, hoping to see Ben had changed his mind. As the night cooled, a wet haze settled onto the trees. The white flower petals fell more slowly now, like a mid-November flurry. The fireflies and stars appeared as if behind a curtain of fine gauze. *If Ben is able to rest,* I thought, *then it's best to let him lie.*

"How else will Zacnal learn this?" Yum Kaax flinched, as if I'd insulted him, then turned to face me. "This isn't written down anywhere."

"Maybe there are books, in Mérida and in…I'm sorry." I blushed when I realized my mistake and offered my hand. "You are just a boy who feels too much, which is okay. You will have plenty of time to be a man and you will be a very good one because you have a big heart. But there is no need to bear the weight of your people. Not yet. I couldn't even bear the weight of my own family. For a young person the burden is infinite, but you must learn to take care of yourself first."

He stared at the fire, pensive and unmoving.

"And I promise I will teach you to write so you can tell this story. You can go to school and read everything that has been written about this and you will know everything there is to know, if that is what you want." I put my arm around him. "But you have to help me understand what Don Alejandro is doing, okay? This is very important to me, Yum Kaax. I've been waiting a very long time for this."

Don Alejandro held the cane over the fire. With a swift scoop he filled the can with hot coals and dropped in a few more bits of incense from his shirt pocket. A dense smoke poured out and sank to the ground where it spread around our ankles. He chanted low verses. I fought to hear his words, but couldn't translate.

Yum Kaax sniffled and quietly whispered, "Okay."

"One day I will be able to repay more than you can imagine."

"It's not Maya," he said stoically, as if the sting of a broken promise was not so far off in his mind. He coughed on the dense, wet smoke, and said, "The words are older than the Maya. Carried over by our ancestors."

Their familiarity had deceived me. "From where then?"

"North?" He shrugged. "Only Don Alejandro knows."

I mentally retraced the route the story may have taken to the New World like I was looking for a set of lost keys. Back up Mexico through the land of the Olmec, to Canyon de Chelly through the words of the Tarahumara and Utes. Into the plains, where ancient Siouan speakers lived and died beneath a great sky, at the very foot of the glacier. Into the clear passage at the south edge of the Laurentide ice sheet through Canada, where the people left behind language like a bird dropped seeds. Algonquian. Yurok. Athabaskan.

Back into the Old World in the footsteps of great, ancient beasts and across the steppe and into the land of the Yakuts, Buryats, and Mongols.

Through the Himalayas, to the land of the Kazakhs and the Persians and Turks.

To the oldest of the Old World. To the cradle of storytelling and culture itself.

To a land where words were invented by the first men to have affairs with the last of the demons that roamed the earth before the flood.

I stopped listening in Yucatec and instead, tried to hear the phonetic forms created by our shared ancestors many millennia ago. Crude, guttural sounds that were only barely pronounceable.

Only when I tried to think in Hebrew and French, Czech and English and German, did I finally began to understand. I considered the languages I didn't know and the indigenous languages long lost to our tongues and a clearer image emerged.

Don Alejandro's chants increased in volume and pitch as he circled the arbor. A wall of haze rose, then spiraled in eddies and looping whirls around tree branches that nourished thousands of new white flower buds.

If the smoke came from an opening door, the blooms were the souls on the Yaxche, somewhere on the other side. Still a universe away, yet almost close enough to touch. Firefly glow pulsed through the cloud, illuminating the nebula. A cosmos, in the trees, just out of reach. For a moment I saw Vincent's *Starry Night* and knew exactly what he'd observed through that little window in the Maison de Santé Saint-Paul de Mausole in Saint-Rémy. Somehow he'd broken through the barriers that connected the earth to the sky and then painted what he saw there.

With rough, gravelly chants, Don Alejandro created ecstasy where none before existed, and the people closed their eyes and raised their palms to the sky. Laughing and joking stopped, and the silent humility of devotion gripped the crowd. The sound of the reformed atheist. The evangelizing agnostic.

Breathing faith.

Breathing creation.

I said, "As is the sky, so is the earth."

Stars on a human scale.

Nuclear fusion dancing at the edge of my eyelashes.

Suns exploding with every beat of my heart.

The heavens crashing onto us like water from an endless cascade.

Stars, which had forever existed only as ghosts in my mind's eye, here, on earth, to sweep us all into their orbits.

A constellation of breath and being created by the light of the fire.

Stars consumed by the pupils of believers hoping for a simple miracle.

A belly that didn't grumble before bed.

A baby well-fed.

A full belly that let a man work.

A full belly that saw the children off to school.

A full belly that let a mother close her eyes and thank the gods above.

A full belly that meant another morning would come, that was all that ever really mattered.

Corn and pork and clear alcohol created the illusion of a full life.

A full life created the illusion of living.

But an illusion was no different than a wish, except for when it fed us. Or kept us from feeling hunger.

An illusion that kept us from dreaming.

From wishing there was a way out.

Only illusion separated the living from the dead.

Don Alejandro transformed this milpa into the center of the universe, if only for a moment. He begged relief from the drought with such focus, even I believed the rain was forthcoming. I listened to the sounds he made and attempted to anticipate the syllables that would follow.

He shook the vines that lead to the hole through which the itz would pass. Men gathered at the corners and clanged sticks against metal pots and pans.

"*Chakob,*" Yum Kaax said.

Thunder. It's coming.

The small boys playing the frogs settled around the feet of the men and let loose a loud peal of bleating. "Reep. Reep."

Yum Kaax strained to hear the old man's words—now beginning to feel familiar to me—a version of the transubstantiation a priest would use to turn bread and wine into the body of blood of Christ. Now I translated for Yum Kaax. "*Use this door to bring sweet life to your people. Bring water with your glory and sweet things we will send you. Four gods are one. Center of four-sky is one. Join two worlds in the wondrous space we have prepared on this altar. Four-gods-one nurture us....*"

With wide eyes, Don Alejandro watched me speak along with him. After recovering from a slight stumble, we said, in unison, "*Gods and God nurture us so we can honor and nurture you.*"

A small man with a crooked back approached the altar, taking Don Alejandro's can and incense. He wore a bandana with a short, arching twig tucked in at his forehead. The leaves drooped down in front of his face, just like the images of the rain god I'd seen all over Yucatán. I said, "Chaac."

"Now Don Alejandro will step onto the road. The white-bone-snake," Yum Kaax said. "We will wait."

"I know. It's the sacbe," I said, leaning forward. "I'm going with him."

Yum Kaax grabbed my arm and covered my mouth with his free hand. But I'd seen the path. After a hundred years of darkness, I found a way to finally emerge in the light.

The table was no longer a table. It became the raised-up-sky, sky-mesa, sky-tree, precious-first-tree. The candle dripped wax, creating an opening here on earth. The light from the flame pierced the xpeten ka'an above it. All I needed now was an offering. I strained to see more, but caught only glimpses of the other side. The door would close without me.

The villagers shut their eyes and swayed to the rhythm of the chants. Don Alejandro chanted as if only he could save them. Smoke left his mouth when he spoke.

If I wanted to follow, I would need an offering of my own. In my head, I prepared an Anaphora from the words of Isaiah and Matthew. Then I bit down hard on the inside of my lip and squeezed my jaw shut. Tears dripped from my eyes. Warm blood filled my mouth. Then I spoke my prayer, "*And one cried unto another....*"

Yum Kaax flinched as Don Alejandro began to shout. The boy sank farther into my embrace and slowly slid a hand up to cover his ear. First the pitch of the shaman's voice grew, then the volume, until a chorus of screamed prayers drowned out all other sound. Candles flickered at the end of his words. Through the smoke I saw some people rocking back and forth with eyes closed, palms held up to the heavens. One old man buried his face in his hands and wept before being consumed by the haze.

My eyes burned, and I tried to blink away the tears. I thought I'd been struck blind until I saw Don Alejandro's dark figure eclipse the fire again. But even that light appeared as a dim orb through the sweet smoke, which itself glowed with a dull radiance, as if illuminated by the light of another star. A sun that emitted at different wavelengths than our own.

When Yum Kaax released my hand to cover his other ear, I lost him.

I called his name again and again, but heard no sound. My throat felt the strain of my cries, but the smoke took my words.

For a few moments, only Don Alejandro's diminishing shouts remained, but it seemed as if he too were walking into the distance. When I finally stopped yelling, only silence remained. No ringing in my ears. No rasp in the sound of my breathing. Not even the beating of my heart. "Ben..." I tried one last time, then surrendered to the solitude.

I tried to stand, but the shackles of a strange gravity kept me bound to the earth. When I waved my hand in front of my face, the fog pushed back. It grew denser against my palm when I applied force.

I held my breath and strained to hear.

When I released my air, tendrils of pressure prodded my face. When I inhaled deeply, my lungs strained from the weight of the new atmosphere. Like trying to inhale underwater. I panicked and forced shallow breaths.

It took a very long time for me to realize I was alone. When I began to cry, it was because I wanted Ben to be okay, and in a way I knew he was.

I wanted Ben to tell me everything would be all right.

I wanted Ben to hold me and block out the outside world, if only for a moment.

I wanted Ben to love me forever.

Until I realized how much I missed him, I didn't feel lonely.

Until I stopped to fixate on a point in the hazy distance, I didn't realize that there were patterns in the smoke. Fractal curves that spiraled toward me, pulling me into something greater.

Fluttering ripples that for the first time gave me a sense of depth.

The feeling of a gentle breeze on my cheek, then a strand of hair blowing across my eyes.

As the cloud dispersed, I fell as if in a dream. The small, white butterflies eddied around me as I passed through them. They felt like warm snowflakes against the bare skin on my arms. I panicked as my momentum increased. Again I called for help. A lonely voice in the dark.

I relaxed when I rose again. My hair blew back, off my face, and it occurred to me that I moved forward. Slowly climbing and falling. Undulating on a wave on a vast sea of nothing. I tried to stand again, but my feet were bound. But the sensation of something solid calmed me. I relaxed and leaned forward and grasped the form. A tree root. A slim trunk, rising from the earth. Cool metal. Smooth. Pierced by a slowly twisting spiral. A canopy of lights pulsated. Fixed, unlike the stars. Still the sensation of motion. Like a Newtonian dance around the center of a galaxy.

Orbiting a central axis in a steady, regular interval. Shapes passing to my right. Alternating patches of darkness and light. Silence and sound. I clung to the cool mass beneath me. Squeezing my legs, wrapping my arms around the shapeless shape. Like carved wood. Not cool, like metal or stone. Its nature familiar to me, if not easily identifiable. I dared not reach down any farther for fear I'd lose my balance and fall into the nether forever. Figures emerged from the darkness all around me. Silhouetted outlines backlit by dim, multi-colored lights. The air smelled like pulled sugar.

I ran my fingers across this thing I'd been bound to, following smooth depressions and folds to a muzzle-like end. The impression of a nose and square teeth. Smoothly carved eyes and brows, topped with finely carved spiral horn. In the time I'd been tethered to it, I'd bonded with it. It remained the only thing in this world that meant anything to me.

There was only one unicorn on the carousel. I refused to let anyone else have it.

The other animals and riders appeared first as dark nebulae against a background of gas lamps and carnival tents that glowed from within like rubies and amber. Through my tears I couldn't easily see the woman, but I knew it was my mother by the way she held herself, cautious and small, arms folded tightly across her chest. I pressed my cheek against the cool wood to hide my face. Even then, I saw her reflected in the mirrors held up by the brightly painted mermaids and dancers that adorned the scenic panels around the center pole. She waved for my attention, her small hand fluttered above the heads of the painted ponies and stoic tigers on the track ahead of me. I turned away again.

The salty groan of the old calliope made it impossible to hear her voice. All around, children laughed and called to their own parents. Some squealed shrill cries that made me anxious and reminded me that when eyes are closed, pleasure and pain sounded very much the same. As the carousel slowed, the volume of the chatter dropped, and the music from the organ spiraled downward ever more slowly, like a dog struggling to stay awake at the end of a very long day. From a nearby tent came the sharp twine of a Romani violin and rhythmic clapping. Earlier, a dark woman with a ring in her nose told me she could see my future—a mysterious stranger and a wild romance followed by a long marriage with many children. I ran from the tent as she laughed.

When the spinning stopped, I climbed down onto the rounding board and ducked through the menagerie to avoid the Bavarian man who operated the carousel because I didn't have another krone to ride again. I kept a close eye on my unicorn—a stargazer and a jumper—to make sure none of the other children claimed her. My sister and brother followed closely, like soldiers, waiting where I told them to, not moving until I signaled and I quite enjoyed this little war. Then, as the other children ran ahead to claim their steeds, we sprang from our hiding place. I ran back to my unicorn.

Summer constellations hung in the sky behind the steeple of St. Cyril and Methodius, an angular copper onion that rose above a red-tiled roof. My sister took a horse just ahead of mine, in the innermost row, after placing my brother on the horse behind hers. A bright golden jaguar stood to her right, a stander with wild green eyes and lips curled in a permanent snarl. A hiss of steam blew through a valve. Then the music sped up. Then once again we were spinning.

I stifled a smile. Pleasure from such motion was surely a sin.

The breeze blew my hair off my cheeks. Something near my belly fluttered. I threw my head back and laughed.

It didn't seem fair that I had to hide the way I felt. That I wanted to read and write and move to the city and visit the libraries and museums. Deep down I believed there had to be more to this world than the farm and the fields. I told myself that I just needed to see Prague and then I'd return to save my mother from a life tied to the soil and sky. But before I could achieve that, I needed to be able to laugh whenever I wanted. Freedom had to be more than a dream to me.

My father appeared next to my mother as we completed a turn and I knew the mere sight of him would be my punishment for enjoying the moment. Every action had a consequence, I'd learned long ago. But learning a lesson seemed no different than memorizing a definition—until practiced, the idea meant nothing. Seeing him there, covered in mud and sweat, was a consequence of my dishonesty. I turned and distracted my brother so he could enjoy these last few moments of pleasure.

But a sudden anger fell upon me, and I gripped the brass pole with tight fists. That he should deprive me of a happiness so many other children were given freely made my face warm. I lifted my chin and met the stare of the man who pushed me away.

The man who turned my brother and sister into monsters by beating any alternative future out of them.

Turned them into demons.

The devil I saw at the crossroads in Mississippi.

My father did that. Not me.

My defiance confused him. His scowl dissolved. He tilted his head and narrowed his eyes.

For the moment, I'd won and took a victory lap.

But as the carousel completed its next revolution, he'd regained his glare. My mother grew even smaller next to his rage.

I need to get off. To help her.

But the spinning continued. A cool wind blew down from the mountains.

I shouted, "Please stop," as I slid my leg across the smooth saddle.

But it moved too fast. The horses kept long strides that felt as if we'd never even touched the ground. I looked for my mother, to show her I wanted to seek her forgiveness, but she'd grown a hunch, as if she'd aged twenty years since I'd seen her last. Silver hair pushed away the black. Her eyes sank into dark, hollow sockets.

"Mother...."

I called to my sister, but her horse pulled ahead. The black steed huffed steam and glistened with sweat. My brother's horse followed hers closely.

I took the reins and kicked my heels, but couldn't gain ground. Even when I stood in the stirrups to ease the load in the saddle, I couldn't pull closer. Autumn constellations appeared in the sky now, stuck halfway between equinox and solstice. My mother could no longer stand on her own. Her knotted, crippled hands reached for help from the people standing nearby.

The music became a blur of noise. The speed felt greater than any I'd ever known. Faster than a real horse. Faster than a sled down an icy hill. We'd spun a thousand times around without ever a hint of slowing down and remained fixed on the track. The wind of a new world blew across my face, and I had a vision of my tomorrow. Instead of years still to come, I saw a future measured in human lives. Faces instead of numbers. I saw blood in cities I'd never heard of—Sarajevo and St. Petersburg. Paris and Warsaw.

I looked for my mother again. She lay on the ground. A priest anointed her with oil.

"No." I screamed and pressed my nails into the palm of my hand. "I will go. Just let my mother live and I will go."

A bright drop of red blood fell onto the unicorn's white flank. I wiped it away, but only managed to spread it into a wide smear. I dabbed it with the hem of my dress.

"Please." I bit my lip and clamped my jaw shut. The pain shot into my head like icicles dropping into the soft spring mud from high cliffs. Tears trickled down my cheeks. Warm blood filled my mouth and dripped down my chin, where the wind caught it and carried it away.

"Mother—" I tried to scream, but a great crack of thunder split the night, silencing my voice and the noise from the steam organ. I turned to catch a glimpse of what had fallen upon us, but saw nothing. The carousel trembled. Wood splintered as the rounding board rippled behind me. The unicorn lurched forward.

I dropped back into the saddle to steady myself. I took the reins and a handful of mane and tried to help her find her rhythm. *Ba-dum, ba-dum, ba-dum, ba-dum....* The beats came more quickly as she sped up. A steady drumming in my ears.

Then all fell silent. Resisting my efforts to steer her, she leapt out of the tent and through the carnival goers. When we landed on the cobbles another thunderclap fell from the sky. St. Cyril's bell rang out from the impact.

We raced through the Romani tents and the menagerie of elephants and lions and bears. I turned and saw my brother and sister and the rest following me through the fair. Once on the straightaway past the main square we rode even faster. I tugged on the reins, but could not slow her down. So I pressed my cheek to her warm flank and gave in to the speed.

Moments after we passed the old town hall, the cobbles gave way to gravel, then mud as we fell onto the countryside. Past the road that lead down to the river and my father's farm, toward the mountaintop in the other direction. Ducking beneath low branches and flying over wide puddles. The village sat far below us, in miniature. And farther in the distance I saw the golden glow of Prague. Floating below the horizon like an apparition. I could just imagine seeing St. Vitus and the castle and the Church of Our Lady before Týn in the Old Town Square if I squinted hard enough.

And from above a light rain fell. It pooled in the grass and in the rutted road. I touched my hair, but it remained dry.

There were no clouds in the sky. No change in the wind.

The closer we got to the top of the mountain the faster it fell. When the unicorn's hooves hit a puddle, the glow splashed in all directions before dripping back to the earth.

It's light. I looked up and laughed. *Starlight.*

At once, moments from a hundred adjacent years in either direction collided, and I realized I had begun pulling the stars down onto me. Riding closer and closer to the heavens lowered the sky bit by bit, and the thought of it filled me with warm joy. This was what I'd searched a hundred years for. I called for my sister and brother as I approached the sacbe.

An empty maw opened directly overhead. A space that neither emitted nor reflected light. The white road that formed at my feet lead right up to it. I felt the wind of creation against my cheeks.

I turned to take my sister's hand, but couldn't see her.

"Evushka," I shouted.

I moved faster now, like water nearing the edge of a cascade. The stars gained speed at the same rate I did. Each hoof beat pulled more of the sky down onto the earth.

"Evushka."

As I entered the road, the rest of the riders approached from the direction of the village, and I slowed a hair. It took my eyes a moment to adjust to the change in brightness. But something had agitated the horses. They reeled in confusion and ran at all the wrong angles. I turned and pushed toward the steepening road. Another thunderclap hit. Then another.

Gunfire.

I lowered my head. No. Not now.

A man called for me. "Danicka."

"Not now. Please."

Riding at a full gallop couldn't get me away from the sound of his voice. One of the horses whinnied and a child screamed. On my lips I could taste gunpowder and burning hair. The downward motion of the stars seemed to slow.

"Not now."

The road grew steeper, and my steed's hooves found little purchase. I lowered my head and leaned forward in the saddle, but the unicorn bucked and twisted just to stay upright.

"Dani...." The voice grew much closer now.

I buried my face in the soft mane. It smelled like roses. Warm tears of sadness formed in the corners of my eyes. My body shook with the violence of an upwelling sob. "No, Ben. Not now."

He grabbed my arm, but I refused to look at him.

"We have to leave. He's coming."

"Says who?" There were other things I wanted to say to him and didn't. He still seemed too fragile, too easily hurt. But not saying them did little to push them from my mind.

I hate you.

"They're going to find us. We have to be out of here before the sun comes up."

You've ruined this for me.

In the distance, I heard the sound of breaking glass.

"Why, Ben? Why now?" I looked up at the sky and saw my door closing. But the stars continued to fall, shattering now as they hit the surface of the earth. Sadness consumed me, and I could no longer suppress my tears. "Why?"

In the light of the fire I saw their faces, standing over me while Ben pulled me off the ground. Yum Kaax collapsed in the dirt next to me, face down, sobbing. He'd wrapped his little hand around my wrist. He said, "You promised."

I tried to speak, but my throat would not let any words pass. Trying to catch my breath made my head light.

"We're intruding here anyway." Ben pulled me to my feet. I could smell the booze on his lips. "How long until you think Toussant would've discovered us on his own?"

The scene had changed. Somehow it had grown brighter. Less yellow. "Stop," I said.

White flower petals tumbled from my hair as I pushed it away from my eyes. They covered the ground all around us, like snow. Other women waved them off their shoulders. Men shook them off their hats.

Ben wavered when he stood and staggered back a step before regaining his balance. He said, "You were shouting."

"Not because I needed help, Ben." I let the flowers fall through my fingers. *Souls that have fallen from the Yaxche.* I said, "It worked."

He pulled me toward the edge of the clearing. Toward the hotel and the village. Yum Kaax wrapped his hands around my waist and screamed my name.

Don Alejandro said, "This one brings the devil with him."

"These souls...." I turned to Don Alejandro and said, "These are the souls I am responsible for?"

"You've opened your own door," the old man said, "Now take them and go."

"But, the boys...."

Ben said, "Yeah, they're safer here. It's time to roll."

"Where? I mean, I don't know where to go."

"We're going home, Dani. I can't keep you safe here. And nothing is going to stop us."

"You can't protect me, Ben. That's an illusion. But I know how to rewrite everything. If it means gouging the original words out of the marble into which they were carved, I will rewrite them."

"This is about human life, Dani. Guns and revenge."

"Says you." I wrestled my hand out of his. "If the edge of the universe is invisible to the naked eye, and the beginning of time has all but been forgotten, then who is to say we don't create our own cosmos every time we wake up or dream? What if I say we stoke the fires of creation every time our minds question the origin of our being?"

"I say this is bigger than guns and revenge." I backed away from him and crossed my arms. I pounded my fist into my palm as I spoke. "If the stars don't rise and fall for me, then they don't rise and fall. That's what I say. If the Big Bang brought forth a universe for someone other than you or me, then it never happened. I say that time is a black hole that devours the minutes as we spend them, and out there, right now, a star that bears my name is emerging from the dust."

"He's going to kill you. More than anything else he wants to watch you bleed." Ben grabbed my wrist.

I said, "Ben, I am trying to be a new woman. With every second I want to be somebody new and forget who I was before all this. But you are making it very difficult."

"I'm not. Please don't say that, Dani." He let go of me and took a step back. "That really cuts me. I'm scared shitless that one of these kids is going to figure out I'm a fake. I'm afraid they're going to see how I never grew up or how I'm only confident because I have to be when the situation calls for it. I'm fuckings scared. I'm doing this because I love you."

"Then it's the way you're doing it that needs work." I twisted free again. "I'm staying."

"He's not going to stop with you. The old man and his wife helped us. And the boys. Toussant isn't going to stop with you." Ben walked into the darkness.

Evushka had begged me to stay and even offered to tell my father a lie to spare me further punishment.

But I'd negotiated my own deal to liberate myself from my family and this way of life. A year of service for eternal freedom seemed too good an arrangement for a girl who'd only previously tasted life in the thin pages of old books.

Evushka wanted to come with me and fell to her knees, begging, even as the head of the caravan left the fairground.

I told her I'd see her in a year.

Evushka said if I left with the Romani, nobody would ever see me alive again.

EIGHT

February 15, 2010

Dad,

 I'm fucking tired of playing this character I created in order to deal with all the patriotic bullshit I fed myself in basic. But until I figure out who to be next it's easier just to keep being this guy.

 And you want to hear the worst part?

 Everybody likes him until he fucks up. He pisses on your mom's carpet or starts a fight with your brother. That's why I'm better off drinking and being hungover and going to bed all alone. Nobody gets hurt.

 I'm sick. There's something deep inside me that eats all the food before it can get to my belly. I never feel full or warm. Booze used to suppress it. Or sex. But she always ended up despising me the next day.

 You ever wonder what it feels like to have a woman tell you she despises *you?*

 Sometimes I can taste it up in my throat, trying to get into my head. Then once I put that bottle to my lips it relaxes and lets me breathe again. But there's no alcohol here. None in a thousand square miles. No way out. I'm stuck with myself for the duration and I hate every fucking minute of it.

 If I could sleep forever, I would, but pneumonia is making the rounds. Everybody has this ragged cough that makes sleeping impossible. Nobody wants to see the doctor because nobody wants to get pulled off duty while the rest of their guys are out in the shit. The Ambien doesn't work anymore, so last night I chased mine with a bottle of children's Benadryl. But I'm telling you—it's coming down. I can sense it. It's all going to hit the fan in a big way.

 We tracked ghosts in the mountains all winter. Treating village gossip like real intelligence. But mark my word, it's coming real soon no matter what and everything's going to go to shit fast.

Just watch the news. That's all I can say. Watch the news. If you're lucky, you might see a ghost.

This place has showed me I won't make it home. Not the way you'd hoped, anyhow. I'll take antibiotics if you can get them.

Ben

P.S. You should see a packet from her attorney in the mail real soon. If you don't mind sending it over here, I'd appreciate it. The sooner I can sign the papers and get that cheating bitch out of my life, the better.

P.P.S. Tell Henry I'm out of Copenhagen. Long cut, please.

I watched her all night long.

A sliver of light from the cloudless sky fell upon her cheek. Her eyes, resting. Her mouth, closed in a natural half-smile that told me nothing about whether or not she'd forgiven me yet.

I tried to read her mind by staring. God knew simple conversation really didn't work with her. Her words—usually a double entendre or homophone or innuendo—made it a challenge to figure out who she really was. What her true motives were. But none of that mattered when I was drunk. Sobriety was my kryptonite. And blacking out was not the same as sleeping.

In this quiet moment of insomnia, with the last traces of alcohol, anti-depressants, serotonin, and whatever the hell else I had in my blood leaving my body, I struggled to keep a lid on my senses and emotions. And I stayed awake to keep the night terrors away. A headache ripped through my skull, and I'd taken a good beating back at the milpa, but I dared not sleep.

On the other hand, my detox resulted in a clarity I hadn't felt since early September 2001. The lucidity itself acted like a drug, and my mind sought answers to questions I hadn't even asked. Under this new spell, my emotions didn't interfere with my curiosity or logic, which made me all too aware of so many things I'd long wanted to forget.

The two conflicting senses danced in loose circles around my head all night long. Fear of night terrors keeping me up to the point of waking exhaustion. Leading my mind to ask strange questions about her. About what really happened to me since my discharge. Since Afghanistan. Since I got into that little silver car of hers.

Dani, I wanted to say, holding her cheek in my hand, staring into those deep amber eyes, *I want to know you better, so I can love you better. I want to feel what you felt, so we never have to be alone in this world again.*

Because it scared me to ask her in the daylight. When she sat awake and alert. And I didn't know why I couldn't ask. But I couldn't. Maybe she was too smart for me. Maybe I didn't want a truth too large to swallow. I didn't want the pain in her heart to be more than I could bear for myself. I didn't want any of the things my dad, or Katy, or Preston, said about her to be true.

I wanted the lie.

I wanted this game. The running. The fighting. The pain.

I wanted her as a checked box on a list of things I needed to get through all this. Another mile on my journey to 'find a way.'

And I was afraid if I knew the truth about her, I'd have to discover some new truths about myself.

And I wasn't ready for that.

When the blue of midnight turned into the pale yellow of early morning I sat up, stroked the back of her hand and whispered, "We have to go."

She pulled away from my touch. She'd gone to bed without changing clothes and still smelled like wood smoke. When we moved from the hotel to the hostel late last night, she didn't even bother to unpack.

"I'm sorry," I said, trying to forget it was my fault she had to break her promise to the boy. But she'd already put on her shoes and glasses, picked up her bag, and headed outside to catch the bus.

She watched the trees beyond the village as we sped away. Waiting for the boys to burst out of the forest and run along beside us for as long as their legs would carry them. Waving and crying. But they never did. And we rode east without speaking.

The bus made no other stops. Picked up no other passengers. The driver just scowled and mumbled. The only other people we saw on the road were headed in the other direction. Trucks and busses loaded with farmers and children. Like refugees fleeing a war zone. In the villages, men loaded luggage and chickens into rusty station wagons. One man appeared from a cloud of smoke to carefully pack his beehives onto the wooden bed of a vintage Ford pickup. Women readied meals and children simultaneously. Dani watched the mass exodus in silence. If she had thoughts, she didn't share them.

In every village we passed, thirsty eyes stole glances at a greying sky.

Dani saw it too. Her mood seemed to lighten as puffy clouds drifted overhead. She hadn't spoken to me all morning, so anything—even this—meant something. As we pulled into the outskirts of Tulum, she finally broke her silence. "It worked," she said, without turning away from the window. Smiling, she added, "It's going to rain. Maybe not this morning, but it's coming."

Tulum felt like everything yesterday wasn't. Plumbing and electricity and paved roads and fast food. Sweltering heat despite the sea breeze. Multi-story buildings that made no shade.

Humidity clung to my skin and dripped down my back. Wide arcs of puffy white clouds bordered by grey blew in from the southeast at regular intervals.

We moved away from the bustle of activity at the bus terminal. Pink tourists heading the other direction formed a line that stretched through the front door and onto the sidewalk. Sunburnt and sweating, they fanned themselves with newspapers and straw hats as they filed into the busses that departed at regular intervals for the international airport in Cancun. Hawkers held up sandwiches, sliced fruit, and ice cold colas. Beyond the terminal parking lot, trucks weighed down with locals and their possessions headed inland in a steady stream, away from the water we'd been chasing for days.

For the first time in as long as I could remember, clouds periodically blocked the sun. Shadows slithered out of the sea and crossed the land like crocodiles. Even though I couldn't see the Caribbean, the moisture felt like a sign that it remained out there somewhere, like fingerprints on a pint glass. Back in Cobá, Don Alejandro would've accepted it as tacit proof of his ceremony's effectiveness. Here, they reinforced Dani's suspicion that some ancient wisdom had indeed worked last night. For once, I didn't have the energy to disagree. To me, the clouds meant somewhere out there, water evaporated. Nothing more, nothing less.

But where there was water, there'd be a boat. A way back home.

As we got our bearings, a small girl in a bright white huipil tugged at Dani's hem. She carried a tray of *dulces*, but hadn't sold any. Ignoring her, I spun to sort out east and west, then poked through the fliers taped to a bodega window.

"I need some of that money." Dani reached into my pack, knelt, and took the girl's hands into her own.

The girl's father watched from a bench beneath a leafy tree in the median from behind a newspaper, a pair of suitcases at his feet.

We locked eyes, and he said, "*Vámanos*, Adelina." He folded his paper and left it, then picked up his bags. Dani continued to talk to the little girl as her father joined a group of people lined up next to a bus to Mérida. Old men in straw hats waited to board. A woman tried to quiet her baby.

The bus driver stood at the door and shouted a last call.

"Dani," I said, squinting at the description of a pair of *narcos norteamericanos* on an *Agencia Federal de Investigación* wanted poster. "Her old man is waiting."

She chose not to hear, brushed the girl's cheek with the back of her hand.

"Adiós, Adelina." Dani watched her shuffle away.

"Look here." I tried to get her to translate because I didn't have any luck. "This is us. They're all still looking for us."

"Everybody's leaving," Dani said, ignoring me. "Why were we the only people on the bus from Cobá this morning? Does that seem odd to you?"

"Well, you said it was going to rain—" I immediately regretted my flippant reply and said, "It's a Sunday, I think. Tourists going home. The people here going to visit their families?"

"So last night was a joke to you? Just where does your boundless wisdom come from, Ben?" She dropped the lightness in her voice and narrowed her eyes. "As if bullying a boy and getting beaten up by his brothers has given you an insight to the cosmos that the rest of us lack? Is that it?"

"No need for all this, Dani. I just meant—" I couldn't look at her, because I didn't want to see how I'd hurt her. My cheeks felt warm, and a little laugh of discomfort slipped through my lips.

"To belittle me? Those people? To dismiss everything that I've been trying to show you since the crossroads? And how do you describe what you saw there in Mississippi? A mass hallucination? A shared delusion?" She made a fist and planted it firmly on her hip. "I can't fight a war on two fronts. I won't do it."

The people on the bus watched the commotion. The driver put it into gear and drifted toward the highway.

"I'm an asshole, okay?" I held up a hand to shush her. "Just don't be mad. I know what I know and I know better than to trust what I see. I know I need to be rational. That's all. I need to think about what's best for me. That's it."

Her lips tried to form words that she didn't want to say. She shook with anger.

The clouds drifted toward us, and I thought about the trip home. It seemed so close now. Like if I played my cards right, I'd be back in my mountains as the winds stripped the last yellows and reds from the trees down in the valley. We could sleep until the Thanksgiving turkey came out of the oven, then sleep again until Christmas Eve. But instead of trying to diffuse the situation, I said, "Go ahead. Say it."

She flinched when the words slipped out, but quickly recovered. Her lips trembled. "That's why you left those boys there. It wasn't what was *best* for you."

I inhaled to form a rebuttal, but she cut me right off with a wave of her hand. In a quiet, restrained tone, she said, "You made me break my promise to Yum Kaax. You made me the face of his heartache. A liar. All because you couldn't be left unattended for a few hours. You're a child, Ben. I thought I'd have met the man by now, but that's my fatal flaw. Seeing good where none existed."

White hot rage flooded my head. So many words came at once. So much anger, like a hurricane of seething fury. In a low voice, I said, "After bleeding and sweating like I do to keep everybody safe? To make sure those boys got to Cobá? And the jaguar—"

"You did that for your ego. A story to tell the guys when you have a can of beer in your hand. Don't act like you did that for us. That was for you, Ben. Only you. The animal couldn't threaten—"

"It would've died, Dani." Tendrils of blackness crawled up my spine. Anger from the pit of my gut tangled with the restraint I struggled to maintain.

The bus to Mérida squealed to a stop at a light. The little girl watched Dani.

"It may have, and we would've continued on our way. It's strange that you should care so much about an animal and so little about those boys. You put them in danger, then showed them that there's no difference between carelessness and bravado. Then you left them. I wanted a goodbye. A chance to reassure them and let them know that there could be more to their lives than they could ever imagine. Bought them a future with this blood money—this is school for all of them. But you stole that opportunity from me. What we did to those boys feels cruel. Mean. And you don't seem to think anything of it."

When the light changed, the bus turned left and accelerated toward Piste and Mérida. In the congestion at the far end of the parking lot I caught a glimpse of the outside world we'd been dodging for so long. Two *hombres* on Ducatis wearing leathers to match the bikes. "Dani—we have to go."

She turned to look. I grabbed her wrist and pulled her into the nearest open door. A big man, breathing heavily through his mouth, placed strips of duct tape across the bodega's plate glass window. He shouted as we ran past the canned chilies to the store room.

In the alley, we turned left and ran ten yards down a corridor that doglegged to the right, then crossed a side street before making a quick right into the lobby of a cheap hotel. Big sheets of plywood covered the windows. I couldn't hold my breath long enough to listen for the sound of motorcycle engines. When I paused to take a knee, Dani pointed to the open door of the luggage storage room.

After a minute in the dark, I finally said, "Fuck, Dani. The gun…" and knew better than to let myself finish.

She said, "A gun against the cartel?"

We sat in the darkness until the buzz of bike engines confirmed our suspicion. The low whine passed slowly from north to south in a nearly imperceptible sweep of volume. At the end of the block one of them turned and came up the street behind us. Dani said, "We aren't safe here."

"Listen." I held up my hand. "It's a grid. Back and forth. Bet Toussant has guys in Cancun and Mérida too."

"He's not going to give up, if that's what you're implying."

"I'm not. But once these guys get behind us we have to make a run for it. Try to get out of town and lay low."

"That's not really a plan, is it?"

"If I can't kill him, it is." I leaned against an empty luggage rack. "You know that's the only way this ends, right? Otherwise it follows us home."

"Like a puppy? Was that what you were going to say?" She stood and put her bag over her shoulder and said, "Things happen, Ben." Then she opened the door to the lobby.

"Where are you going?"

"East." She walked past the front desk. The clerk sat in the office, shouting into the phone.

"What's east?" I stood, and my knees groaned. I peeked around the door. "Dani…."

"The sea. And a boat. A way to prove to you that going home isn't a solution." She said, "Let me lead for a bit. You can take a break from so much thinking."

"I fucked up and I know it. Is that what you need to hear?" I crept into the lobby. "Just stop it, okay?"

She paused at the door before pushing it open. She waved for me to follow as she stepped outside, looked both ways, and then disappeared between the buildings across the street.

I hesitated when it sounded like the bikes were headed back this way and only followed after the noise faded to the west. Somehow, I could find no sign of her.

I stopped, spun, and considered calling her, backtracked a few steps, and thought about walking back to the hotel before she stepped from a narrow space between the bodega and bus station and called my name.

"Ben. Here."

"It's not wide enough." I twisted sideways and pushed myself into the slot. Broken glass crunched beneath my feet.

As soon as I saw I couldn't even turn around my chest tightened. My lungs wouldn't fill completely. I hunched my shoulders and tried to push her all the way through to the other side.

"Just wait." She held a newspaper up to my face, but I couldn't read the Spanish and shook my head. "The picture. Look at the picture."

A white vortex against a field of grey.

"They're evacuating. All these people are leaving. And this is yesterday's paper."

"Bullshit. Let's find a TV." I nudged her toward the main street. "Maybe we can hunker down in a solid structure."

"The storm is too big, Ben. Catastrophic. And it will make landfall right here." She paraphrased the rest of the details for me. "Look. It formed as a tropical depression off Jamaica on October 26."

I said, "The day we left Mérida."

"And here, the paper says it became Tropical Storm Evangelina on October 28 and then turned west on October 29 as a fully-formed hurricane."

"Must've been the day we started east on the sacbe?"

"...as a Category 5 it took a dramatic turn toward the south, with measured, sustained winds of 240 kilometers per hour."

I did the math in my head. "150 miles per hour? Does that even sound right?" I honestly didn't know. Didn't sound good though.

"With reported gusts of 295 kilometers per hour, Evangelina is expected to make landfall late on the evening of October 31, south of Cozumel, between Punta Allen and Akumal—that's here, Ben. Right here."

"Tonight." I scratched the stubble on my chin. "Shelter. We have to find shelter and we should be fine. Look at all this concrete—we'll bust into some place and ride it out."

"Nobody is riding it out. The busses are full. The businesses are closed."

160

I heard the second bike at the top of the alley behind us and pushed Dani farther into the darkness. As we neared the other side, she paused.

"Up the street," she whispered. "Talking to somebody."

"Phone," I said. The man on the black bike had his back to us. "Toussant?"

The other bike came through the alley we'd just left too fast to have spotted us. At the intersection, he hit the gas and zipped over to the next street.

We had nowhere else to run. I had no more great ideas.

"If we can't stay here we're going to need a ride. Once that storm smashes into the coast, none of it will matter anyway."

"It does matter, Ben. That's what I've been trying to tell you."

"Let's go then. Quietly."

Dani crept into the open and took a knee. I stopped right behind her

The man on the black bike stared off at something in the distance. Nodding and saying very little.

"Somebody's getting a talkin' to." I grabbed Dani's hand and lead her to the curb.

"He's telling Toussant that nobody's here."

I heard the other bike behind us. Off to the north. Back and forth.

We sprinted across the road. Four lanes of wide open space. We went east and south at the first place we could safely get off the highway. The streets and alleys were empty and quiet. Even the stray dogs had sense enough to evacuate.

"Somebody's still here," I said. "In town, I mean. There are people staying here, riding out the storm. Has to be, right?"

"Because you want it to be true?"

"Yeah. Something like that."

"I think Hurricane Wilma taught them a lesson."

"You a meteorologist now?"

"That's what the newspaper said." Then, switching gears, she asked, "What makes you think we will be able to find a car? These people don't have the kind of money to just abandon a vehicle."

She seemed to mull over the idea for an exceptionally long time. Her expression gave no indication of her thought process. Finally, she nodded. "There will be resorts along the coast."

Wind whipped off the sea, blowing sand and palm fronds. A warm breeze, tinged with some of the coolest air I'd felt since April. Since that night at the crossroads in Mississippi. The sky billowed like dark sheets on a clothesline. The sea danced in fits of violent tremors. The turbid water looked almost black in places.

We'd been to three resorts and an *eco-park with seaside cabanas*, and stifling my growing frustration had become a challenge. The idea of hurting the kids weighed on me. Leaving broken bodies in my wake. Something had to change, even if I didn't know how or what just yet. The realization that Dani's fragility made her susceptible to fits of explosive anger and rage came from finally seeing that very same thing in myself. People can't hurt you if they hate you.

So I left her in the shelter of the lobby, wrapped in a bathrobe and towels for warmth, while I explored a garage nestled in blowing palm trees between the beach and the pool. As I pushed through the rain, I figured we may have to make a stand here in this fortress by the sea. But when I got to the shed, I smelled gas. And when I beat the padlock off the door, my heart fell.

A pair of Jet Skis on trailers.

Volleyball nets. A half-dozen sea kayaks and paddles. Fifty umbrellas and folding chairs. I dragged everyting into the grass because I knew Dani was right—we had to get inland. But we weren't going anywhere on a riding mower. I pushed it aside and saw a knobby tire peeking out from beneath a mound of tarps and rope.

An ATV with life guard's first aid kit secured to the rack. I put it into my bag.

I turned the key and it rumbled to life. The needle drifted to the right of the E, but slowed just before reaching the halfway point, which was still a long way from the F. I checked the Jet Skis and mowers for gas before heading back.

She waited for me in the porte-cochère. "How far will it take us?"

"I don't know. Half a tank…maybe thirty miles. Or forty."

"Back to Cobá."

Dani had once told me that a story changed depending on the narrator's point of view. That time could alter a tale, allowing us to live simultaneously in our own past and future. That the present existed as a transient state distorted by our perspective and desires. According to her, time was immutable. The universe herself remained powerless to erase it or let it repeat itself. According to her, memory weakened us. Memory could be manipulated by a suggestion or song. Memory could be altered, therefore, we should never trust it. Ultimately, to her, the storyteller imprisoned the listener with her version of the truth.

Point of view let us peer into another dimension. Point of view converted truth into suggestion.

To her, the future was a dream that made the life you've lived feel like an illusion. A trick of the mind. *You can't be in two places at once.*

The purest of moments existed only in the sudden transition from future to past. A breath, for example. Or a smile.

Your childhood friends, if you never saw them again, may as well have never lived at all. The moments that exist only in photographs are no different than the moment that exists in Monet's Woman With A Parasol. *An arrangement of people or objects that have bound themselves to a feeling. When you recall the scene, the emotions manifest as a result of the attachment. But none of it is real.*

"So what is this then? Right now?"

Reality. And like that, it is gone.

"So what is life? What's the point? All the crying, anger, and sadness?"

Life is magic. A gift which you must protect with every ounce of strength your soul possesses. You exist because you want to. The universe exists because of you. And once you lose that desire to participate in what the cosmos has planned, it turns its back on you. You do not want that, Ben. I've been there and have been fighting to get the cosmos's attention ever since.

Any magic I felt happened because of her. I didn't contain the power to be fantastical. I didn't create. Didn't perform, like Katy and Preston.

I only seemed special because I chose to be with her. Because she loved me.

I didn't care if time was an illusion. Or that the universe existed only because I did.

I didn't care because I didn't know how to, or I'd forgotten. Over the last ten or twelve years I'd lost track of who I was and what I was supposed to be. The universe— to continue Dani's analogy—had no place to put me. She said it happened every now and then. Libraries lose books. People forget to pick up their dry-cleaning. Even the US government turns its back on a few soldiers or Marines every now and then. "To the universe," she'd said, smiling just before she kissed me, "…we're all just lost children."

"I thought the universe didn't make mistakes."

"This is not the universe's mistake. You made it."

At the moment, I didn't care. Backtracking through Tulum, skirting Toussant's guns, and retreating into the Yucatán scrub hadn't gotten us any closer to our future together.

The sky darkened, blowing palm fronds and leaves. The steely clouds spit rain and the occasional hail. Once on the highway, I opened the little engine up.

Dani wrapped her arms around me and hid her face against my back. Her skin smelled like roses. When she began to shiver, I went faster, knowing we'd have no chance of getting warm until we stopped and found shelter. She asked me to slow down, over and over, but I needed miles. I needed to get her to someplace safe.

And when I did finally slow, she thanked me. But I didn't do it for her. And I didn't do it because we were almost out of gas.

"Dani." I let the ATV drift to a stop.

She peeked around my shoulder. "Oh, no."

Three boys sprinted toward us, waving their arms and yelling. A small yellow dog followed right on their heels.

"What is it?" I said. "What'd he say?"

"He wants to know if you're angry."

"Christ, Dani. About what? Why would I be mad?" And I knew it was because I hadn't shown them I was capable of compassion and kindness.

X stood there, chest out, chin up, ready to take the hit. Yum Kaax waited close to Dani and refused to look at me.

"Well, this wasn't exactly what I had planned, but I'm not mad at them. So tell them that." I started to push the ATV into the forest. "But why the hell didn't anybody take these kids with them?"

Dani picked up Zacnal. "Because they left to find us."

I knew thinking about it would make it worse. "Tell X to give me a hand."

He helped me push the ATV deeper into the trees, toward a trail Yum Kaax knew. We fumbled through the wet leaves and thick, grey mud for almost forty minutes and didn't get very far.

X wanted us to go back to the village of Cobá, to the hotel, but I said that'd be the first place they'd look.

Yum Kaax had an idea and told us to follow him. He told Dani he knew a place where we would be very safe and headed into the forest, due west.

The rain fell in drenching bands. Residual heat trapped in the ground rose back to the thick sky in vaporous tendrils. I thought it should've been four in the afternoon.

The sky told a different story though. The sky said that this would be a very long night. And that it had already begun.

After another half hour of bushwhacking through scrubby patches of brush and milpas that had been overgrown with the worst kinds of briars and thorns, we reached the edge of a ruin. Manmade trenches and humps in every direction for as far as the eye could see. White and grey rocks spilled out of the earth. Even when darkness and fog consumed the most distant platforms, I got the sense that they went on and on.

"Is this part of where we were yesterday?"

Dani asked, then waited patiently for him to finish. "It's older. Forgotten. His people hid here and waged war on the Spanish after the Conquest."

"War, huh? Is that what it's coming to?"

"Let's hope not."

This world. Pyramids and stars. We weren't supposed to return. That never happened in stories. The protagonists always went forward with purpose. Never back.

A chorus of thunder a hundred miles wide shook the trees. The echo rang through the forest like rock brought down onto rock. A hellish rain pounded us from all directions.

Yum Kaax was right when he said that the roots of these trees hung down into another world—an underworld men didn't want to think about.

I shouted, "Dani—we need to get out of this. Any shelter is better than being out here."

The boy folded his hands when Dani relayed my request. Begging for just the tiniest show of faith. I nodded and waved him on.

Everything from the last few days seemed to come down to this. We only had what we carried and each other. No more magic. No planning. No deliberating. No map. No metaphor. No forgiveness. No dreaming. No nightmares. No fantasy. No promises. Each of these concepts felt like little more than a fallen stone scattered by the storm. Small stones, to be sure, but our lives depended on each and every one.

The sound of crashing hooves charged through the treetops. Limbs and branches snapped at the crest of the stampede. A burst of lightning illuminated our surroundings in green and white. In the flash, I saw raindrops suspended like snowflakes and broken trees dangling like shattered bones in the wind. On the ground, water pooled everywhere, reflecting the dense grey sky. Nature's mean streak. It felt like the entire planet conspired to make sure no serenity came to the unpunished.

Zacnal cried.

"Dani, tell him to go faster." I picked the boy up. "C'mon chicito."

Within the noise rose a deeper static howl. X waved his arms and jumped up and down. Yum Kaax ran past him and disappeared into the storm.

Dani turned. "See? They know what they're doing." She took my hand. Together, we made our way toward the noise.

In the dim light I saw a growing blackness. A darker darkness. A circular void edged by a ruined city and tendrils of water cascading into the earth. A ragged cenote pulling water from the sky. "Stay over here. Away from the edge," I said, pointing to a large platform topped with an immense mound. "Dani, tell them to stay the hell back or we'll never see them again." Even as I said it, I counted heads.

"X—where's Yum Kaax?" I didn't wait for Dani to translate. "Yum Kaax?"

X pointed to the mound and shouted back.

"I don't know what he's saying."

Yum Kaax emerged from the roots and mud near X's head, but didn't fully pull himself out of the hole.

Dani said, "He says it's safe. And dry."

"You first."

X helped Dani and Zacnal up the platform and into the hole, then followed them in. I scanned the horizon, hoping for another option, but saw nowhere else to go.

Inside, the walls were smooth and straight for fifteen yards. But it didn't seem like a room—it felt like a tunnel. A false arch created by a capstone rather than a keystone. It was narrow inside, only a little over three or four feet wide. The other end of the tunnel opened up at the edge of the cenote.

I hunched and gently stepped over everybody to get to the far end, all the while wishing I'd asked for more than just *shelter.*

In the fading daylight it remained difficult to see the water's surface, some forty or fifty feet below. The weather had worn the limestone sides smooth over the years. Like a tombstone exposed to the elements, the names and dates long faded. There'd be no climbing out.

Our temple honored no god, served no purpose save one. This felt like a monument to our health, our safety, to a long life. A prayer for a tomorrow. A sign of how far we'd go just to stay alive.

"Dani, I want you between the boys and the water. Tell them all to sit down here. I want to be closest to the door, just in case."

Then the first drips fell from the ceiling and I wanted to tell them that this wasn't a game. That we had to keep our heads if we wanted to get through this. Keep each other warm. Keep our spirits up.

"Dani," I said, searching for her face in the dim light. "I love you."

"I've always known that," she said, then went back to comforting the boys.

Spiders crept in from dark cracks, pulling dust and bits of web from the ancient joints. Scorpions scuttled across the floor. X smashed them with his tennis shoe and flung them toward the cenote. A horrific gust blasted through the trees, shredding limbs and twisting all but the most limber green trunks. A thousand years of growth destroyed by the exhalations of gods. Zacnal wanted to hold the flashlight from the ATV's first aid kit, but the light dimmed quickly. I asked Dani to tell him we may need it later.

All the while, the roar of water rushing into the cenote grew. Like a vengeful river, straight into the underworld.

"You should try to sleep, Ben," Dani said.

"No. I'll sleep when we're dry." As it was, I fought to keep my eyes open. In every flash of light I saw shadows circling the entrance to the tunnel. An army of claws and limbs thrashing through the torrent.

Yum Kaax edged toward me, trying to say something without saying anything. I put my arm around him and pulled him close to me. X watched. Rejected, he crossed his arms and put his head down.

"*Ven acá*," I said.

And he did.

Together, the three of us watched the storm. Together, we stared into the silver sea that grew in the lee of the ancient temple mounds. As if a temporary moon shined all its light in one magnificent blast before going back to sleep. Through the thunder and wind we listened for the phantoms that had pursued us through the scrub. The ghosts and devils of our own minds. A throaty cough from the static, as if the earth itself had decided to reclaim territory.

In that moment, I felt as if I'd finally sleep. The edges of so many dreams crept into my head. I'd wrestled control of myself back from the drugs. I held my breath.

Yum Kaax jerked to his knees. He pulled away from me and crawled onto the platform.

"What is it?" Dani asked.

"Shit." I'd hit my head when I jerked up. My mouth had gone dry. "Stay here."

I followed Yum Kaax toward the end of the tunnel. "Get back in there now," I said.

And Yum Kaax responded, as if he'd known exactly what I'd meant. But they'd all heard it too, and that made it real.

Staring into the storm revealed nothing. I crept outside, where the rain could wash the sweat and mud out of my eyes. Water pooled in all the low spots now. More ground existed beneath the deluge than above it. I told myself we were high enough. *We'll be safe here.* I lied.

In the distance I saw movement. Shadows coming and going without the aid of lightning. "Dani...."

Broad sweeping beams that barely cut through the rain.

"Dani."

She joined me at the mouth of the tunnel, and the boys jostled to see. Pushing their hair out of their eyes for the best view.

"Toussant found the ATV."

I never saw the light again.

I saw trees uprooted. Water rising to the very edge of the platform. And when the eye of the storm passed overhead, silence consumed the world. Light from familiar stars bathed me in a lonely blue that let me know for a moment what it felt like to be truly by myself. It pulled me out of my body and into the sky. But when I looked down I saw no light.

And then the eyewall slammed into our little temple.

I sat at the edge of the hole for hours. Wind and rain lashed me until I quaked with cold chills. But they were safe inside.

Finally, she called to me from the tunnel. "Come back in, Ben."

I took care crawling over the tangle of arms and legs crammed into the nook.

This time, we sat together. The boys formed clumps on the other side of Dani.

"You should sleep," she said.

"No. I have to be on my toes."

"You will be better off after you've rested a bit. You know I don't sleep, so I can keep an eye on the entrance. I can wake you if I hear anything."

"I have to take care of everybody. It's my job to keep you all safe."

"Ben, when all of this is over I can show you a better side of the world. You know that, right? And you won't have to sleep with one eye open. And you won't have to scan rooftops for snipers. It's hard to believe, I know. But I can show you."

"What will that even feel like? How long will it take for me to believe I'm home again? It's been ten years without a bed."

"We can make a home together, if you want."

"That's all I want." I pulled her close to me. "Can you tell the boys something for me?"

"Let them sleep."

"Tell them I'm sorry? I need you to tell them, please."

"They know, Ben. We shouldn't wake them."

"Can you please just tell them? Tell them if there had been a way to take them with us, I would've found it. And that leaving them here wasn't an easy decision. But I truly thought it was the right thing to do."

"You are so tired. Try to sleep."

"Please...."

"Yum Kaax..." She gently shook his arm and whispered the words I'd said.

"And tell them that I'm not a good role model and I'm not the kind of person who should be responsible for anybody, let alone a bunch of kids. That people who rely on me don't come back. And by leaving the boys the way I did, I thought I'd done them a favor."

I waited as she finished up. But my mind wandered. In the blackness, I travelled. I should've slept earlier, when Dani offered. Should've given in to the exhaustion. But it was too late now. I was up, jerking myself awake every time I dozed off. A wave of dread crept into my heart. Thinking about those nights outside the wire. When X and me would talk for hours.

"Dani, tell them that I went to Philly and talked to his mom, and told her if I could've been there with them that day, I would've. I never meant to abandon her boy."

"Ben." Dani's voice cut through the darkness. "You need to sleep. Your head is a thousand miles away."

When I realized what I'd said, a wave of shame washed over me.

Yum Kaax spoke. Dani waited a moment, patiently listening to the boy like she always did.

"He says this is a doorway to time and space. And that you shouldn't fear saying the wrong thing."

"Yeah. Well, if the universe if so forgiving, why don't I feel it?" I covered my face with my hands and stammered, "Don't tell him I said that."

"I hadn't planned to."

"Thank him for me." With a cold laugh, I said, "I'm not the man they think I am."

"And you don't have to be." She pulled me into a warm embrace and gently stroked my hair. "Everybody feels that way. Alone. Afraid. Don't trust anybody that says otherwise. The loneliness made me a bitter, evil person, and I regret it all. Love becomes something ugly when it's unreturned. Jealousy. Loathing. A passionate hatred is as fulfilling as a passionate love as far as the ego is concerned. So let me take care of you tonight. Then tomorrow, when you are rested, you can get us home. But tonight, let my love protect you."

"But Toussant is out there."

"There will always be demons out there. You can't go on like this. Rest now."

She put my head on her lap and I stretched my legs out as best I could. "Dani..." It felt like a trap.

"Ben. Hush. Isn't that what Katy says? Hush up and go to sleep."

"I'm afraid."

"You're afraid of being alone, but you aren't."

"I don't think I can sleep. My meds...."

"I can help you."

"What if I have nightmares? Sometimes when I have those dreams I don't know what's real even after I wake up."

"You can't ever entirely be sure of what is real and what isn't. If you wake up, and I'm still here, you can be certain I am real." She laid her hand on my chest. "But we can never be sure that we aren't dreaming."

I laid there for a moment, afraid that once I stepped into that blackness I'd never come back. "I can't sleep. I'm afraid I'll never sleep again. It's been three days...."

"Shhh," she said. "Let me tell you a story."

Then she spoke, quietly, in that strange, beautiful language of hers while I tried to remember the stars back home. At some point, just before I drifted off, she whispered, "You need the kind of help that the world cannot give you."

NINE

10 September 1914

Dearest Augustin,

Life in the cafes has taken a decidedly grey turn since you left for the front. Paris is like a convent now. Women console the egos of men who are too infirmed—or too wealthy—to fight. Children run the city. Before I left for Reims, the baker's wife told me her nephew had been promoted to Inspecteur-Générale in Val-de-Marne and has been promised the position of Directeur des Services Actifs just as soon as he can drive.

See? I write to bring you happiness, a reminder of a love like a bright star to guide you in such dark times. When I get too sad, I think of falling asleep in each other's arms on the stairs next to the Monmartre funicular. That night, the sweet, pure moonlight made Le Grand Palais shine like a diamond. After you kissed me and returned to your father's in the 7éme, I watched dawn arrive from the fountain at Place St-Michel because it was the only way to keep the night from ending. That night you showed me that there is no such thing as incurable heartbreak. A very valuable lesson for a naive girl such as myself.

Even my little apartment on rue Herold senses your absence—as if the bed knows it is too big for me alone! But watching you board the train at Gare de L'est that afternoon not so long ago changed me. In that very moment my resolve to see universal justice done stirred something deep within me. A call to action, perhaps? That so many men would never see a return to civility prepared my heart for the horrors we all know are coming. You may not realize, Augustin, that a woman can be just as strong as a man, but in many different ways. Patience, for example. Holding my tongue and waiting for opportunity rather than acting on impulse. My attention to detail is another. Doing the little things that usually go unnoticed. But this is not important now.

Would you sleep better knowing I could be in your thoughts and dreams forever?

That you would never again be able to close your eyes without thinking about the profound ways I've changed your life? Because I have thought about you ever since you left me. That is where my strength comes from. When I returned home after seeing you off at the station I took a vow to do everything in my power to make certain I have enough resolve to see that you get what you deserve from this world.

There have been many nights since then that I'd wanted to go to your father's foundry at Levallois and reveal myself as your true love, but I know the words will sound so much sweeter coming from your own lips when the time is right. Instead, I watch the smelters burn and think about ways to make myself tough as iron.

I have never seen so many mortars and rockets as those coming from your father's furnaces. The process of turning coal and copper into brass makes me believe in magic once again. On evenings when the clouds are low it looks as if the Seine herself is carrying fire instead of water. Still, I am afraid no peace can come from a nation that turns ploughshares into swords. At least you had the foresight (and fortune) to break the contracts with your Prussian mineral suppliers. Almost as if you knew something Poincare himself couldn't have anticipated. (When it was discovered that Mssrs. Bissette maintained relationships with sawmills in Bavaria, they were beaten by a mob in front of the Galeries Lafayette and their warehouse in the Marais burned to the ground. Not even so much as a napkin ring remained in their showrooms. I'd hate to see the same fate befall such a hardworking man as you.)

It saddens me to think France would need so much thunder to defend herself as much as it saddens me to think this war may last through winter. It goes without saying then, the banks are already frozen. As soon as I heard, I converted all my currency into silver and locked up my apartment. Waiting idly for your return sowed too much discontent in my heart. To see justice served, I had to act. But the army has little use for a woman, and I refuse to yield to fate.

So on September 5th, I joined Gallieni's army of taxi drivers!

Augustin, I am close to finding you. After helping shuttle the 6th Army from Paris to Meaux in that old Renault, I organized an impromptu ambulance service (even Jean Cocteau volunteered to drive.) Once the Red Cross assumed operations, I went ahead to Soisson, where I learned that I'd missed your regiment by only a few days.

But I am close and have made a solemn vow to find you by All Saints Day. This yearning in my heart will burn until I see you again.

Fear not, my love. I am coming. Until then, may St. Genevieve protect you.
Daniella

By the spring of 1914, I'd been spending long nights tucked into a dark Latin Quarter alley slumped over a desk. After being dismissed from the Sorbonne for publicly challenging an instructor, translating such projects as the serialization of James Joyce's novel into French and German remained the only education available to a girl like me—a Czech immigrant displaced by a growing Hungarian monarchy with no papers and no birthright. (I'd also become quite adept at producing a fairly passable forgery, hence the sharp increase in the number of signed Victor Hugos to be found in the *bouquinistes* last summer.)

Once I became Daniella Proust instead of Danicka Petráková Prochazka, it became simply a matter of fabricating a story to explain my unlikely lack of Parisian roots. (A wayward Prussian mortar took my father, a war hero, and syphilis my mother (*She had children to feed, after all.*) Perhaps, most tragically, a stampeding circus elephant, in the final days of the Paris exposition killed my one and only brother. (*I just let go of his hand for a moment.*) Explaining my comfortable lifestyle (a late Van Gogh, acquired from a concierge on rue Lepic for a *favor*) required a more delicate form of manipulation.

With those little constructions—simple recipes of syllables and sounds—I bought my way into Paris's most outstanding intellectual circles. Building a new life from the ground up made more sense than trying to patch up the remnants of my old one. For the first time since I left Prague, I had a grip on the tendrils of chaos that consumed me.

That summer began like any other. Blue skies and cool nights followed by grey days that brought drizzle and stifling heat. After Toulouse-Lautrec died, the only Bohemians left in the shadow of Sacre Coeur were wealthy art students from Britain—most of them fourth or fifth-tier royalty, at best—and genuine Bohemians, like myself, that left after the 1867 Compromise. Many Czechs were reluctant to give up the rights they gained by revolting in 1848, and none wanted to add insult to injury by submitting to Hungarian rule. We'd just as soon be ruled by Russia. Or the Prussians.

To bolster my income (and my *fabrications,*) I took a job with a small bookseller just off rue Dauphine. The shop felt old fashioned, but gave me opportunity to meet many of the young intellectuals making the rounds between the various Left Bank cafes.

(These poets and philosophers preferred to drink with the Irish and American authors, all the while despising them for receiving a regular royalty check. *After all,* they rationalized, *somebody had to settle the bill.*)

Before the arrival of The Frivolous Prince, it remained easy for writers with only a handful of published stories to their name to swim with the bigger fish. Augustin Toussant fancied himself a true intellectual, but in reality, he picked the low-hanging cherries. Due to his father's successes, he needed few of his own. Where some saw sleeping on floors and living on absinthe as a way of paying dues, Augustin saw only inconvenience. He knew nothing of the Montmartre heyday (he would have been just a child when Toulouse's *Japanese Diva* was first printed) but made no attempt to understand that the spirit of artistic liberation that emerged from La Belle Époque belied his own attempts to be accepted by his contemporaries on the Left Bank.

The night I met Augustin, I carried the new edition of Kandinsky's *Concerning the Spiritual in Art* (From my own translation!) into Les Deux Magots. Augustin had been telling the group about his recent acquisition of mineral rights for his father's foundry from beneath the nose of a Swiss banker. With my presentation of the new Kandinsky, I'd stolen his thunder. He stood and mumbled a weak goodbye. In that way, he seemed like a dinner guest that left right after the entrée was served. And for that, I pitied him.

The sentiment was short-lived.

A few days later he came into the book shop with enough humility to make me forget he owed me an apology and went home with my translation of Kafka's *Meditation*. Upon returning it, he asked for another recommendation and I reminded him that I was in the business of selling books, not lending them. He spent the afternoon there, listening to my lectures on literary realism and the importance of the American Romantics. Perhaps I saw him as an empty carafe in this regard. A vessel to be filled with my own ideas about meaning and beauty. A mistake I would soon regret.

It didn't bother me that he'd come to recite my opinions on Czech poetry or Freud as if they were his own. Or that his own romantic affectations felt ephemeral and amateurish. I believed he'd free me from having to lie for my supper. All I ever wanted was to be able to live in the light, no matter how dim. I just had to tolerate his flaws and know that being a woman with a strong will in an era of strong-willed men made me a bit more of a challenge to a man like Augustin Toussant.

And so it went....

Reading and picnicking in shady corners of Luxembourg Gardens on Monday afternoons (when he could escape his father's tyranny at the foundry.) On Tuesday mornings we'd take coffee in Galerie Viviene near the Palais Royale. On the first Thursday in June, he took me to a late lunch at Maxime's to celebrate the finalization of his new partnership with the Prussian mineral conglomerate. That afternoon we drank to "… coal from Aachen, iron from Koblenz, and the wealth of the Rhineland for generations to follow…."

Then Gavrilo Princip put down his sandwich and picked up his gun.

In early August, mobilization posters appeared on kiosks from the Grand Boulevards to the Champs-Élysées—by decree of the President of the Republic—that read ... *every Frenchman, subject to military obligation, must, under penalty of being punished with all the rigor of the law, obey the prescriptions of his book of mobilization.*

Augustin visited me in my apartment on rue Herold very early on the morning of his departure. He'd dedicated the previous day to tidying up his affairs at the foundry and napped briefly after his midnight arrival. He wore his dark blue tailcoat, which I hung gently on a brass finial at the foot of my bed. I remember the feel of the embroidery on its collar between my fingertips. His regiment number in red thread that matched his kepi and pants. I knew his goodbye would barely sustain me through the end of summer, let alone the end of the war.

To satisfy my heavy heart, I went to Gare de L'est in the hopes of catching a glimpse of him instead of opening the shop. But the crowds on Boulevard de Magenta were too dense with the mothers and wives whose duty it was to weep as the men filed past. So many tears made the air warm and humid. Very little space remained in the mob for a fiancée who had yet to receive her ring.

I searched for another route to the platform.

On rue la Fayette I ran into a friend, a housekeeper at the George V, who told me the soldiers were being billeted in Villemin Garden before boarding the trains. I raced east, pushing almost all the way to the canal before turning south to the park. Past hay wagons piled high with feed for the cavalry steeds. Past wooden crates filled with tins of sardines and medical supplies. Past racks of rifles that had never been fired. Past ranks of young men who had never taken fire.

I'd searched all morning and had nearly given up hope when I saw Augustin at the edge of the platform. I got as close as I could and called to him.

His eyes met mine, but he would not acknowledge my gesture.

"My love," I said.

He turned, saw me, and disappeared into the sanctuary of the station's hulking glass arches.

My heart sank. I felt like a fool and my face grew warm. I fought back tears.

The woman next to me—an expectant mother, by the look of it—took pity and placed her hand on mine. "Is that your lover?" Her accent sounded throaty and clipped, with a challenging cadence. Grammar school French, but not Parisian at all. She wore a look of fierce concentration when she spoke.

"Yes," I said. *Alsatian?* I thought, trying to place her accent. Still smiling, I added, "And when this is over we will be married."

"Impossible," she said. She grabbed my wrist with her other hand, tightened her lips and squeezed her wedding band into my knuckle. "This man already has a wife."

I shook my head in disbelief. For a moment, I savored the pain of her ring against my bone.

"Not Alsatian," I said. "Bavarian?"

But when she tried to release my hand, I tightened my own grip. She said, "You are hurting me."

"Not Bavarian. *Berlinerisch.*"

Gripped in the throes of panic, she tried to wriggle free of my grip.

"Da," I said, knowing she'd not dare make a sound. I stared into her face and let the rage build. Like an inferno in a dry forest. "Berlinerisch. Why buy the coal when you can get the heiress for free?"

The blood left her face. Wobbling on unsteady legs, she continued to pull away from me.

"Don't worry, Frau Toussant." I released her, and she stumbled back into a brass railing. "Your secret is safe with me, *bengesko niamso. Xas me mulenge kokala.*"

The Romani hex felt just like vinegar on my tongue, but once released, it tasted just like wine.

Cursed German. You will eat the bones of my dead.

After the 5th Army crossed the Aisne at Berry-au-Bac, I stayed on as an intelligence consultant to translate and interpret German radio correspondence. Once we realized the wireless remained more suited to sending false information than receiving poor information, the Germans abandoned it and returned to telephones and dogs as their main means of communication.

Joffre chose to ignore, however, the details of a German plan we'd intercepted. I reported that they intended to take Calais via Ypres in a series of northern flanking maneuvers meant to envelope our defenses. Joffre wanted to dig in instead and ordered the rearguard to requisition shovels and pick-axes from local farmers. By the time I convinced Commander Maunoury to plead my case, the Germans had figured out how to use their siege howitzers to drop shells right into the clusters of men that huddled together in their poorly constructed trenches.

Frustrated by the ineffectiveness of the chain of command, I spent the remainder of my time in Reims helping the Red Cross with their efforts to start an ambulance service there. Once we were up and running, I grew restless and followed the Aisne west to Soisson, where I received word that the British Expeditionary Force would try to outflank the Germans to the north. In an attempt to join up with them, I incorrectly anticipated their next move and overshot them by thirty miles.

After a wayward jaunt to Amiens, I heard that Joffre had ordered the 2nd Army to advance again to slow Germany's fight to the sea. Somehow Papa Joffre's outflanking maneuvers always came a day too late though, as if he were trying to win the race from the back of the peloton. One of my greatest mistakes had been not objecting more strongly to his refusal to look at the wireless transmissions we'd intercepted, but nothing more could be done.

Under darkening skies, I went ahead to Albert and found a regiment of American volunteers that comprised the bulk of the 1st Foreign Regiment in France. Due to a near-constant skirmish with the German rearguard, our going progressed slowly. The Americans—mainly mercenaries and criminals—didn't seem to mind.

But our fortunes soured at a farm south of Bapaume. We came upon two battalions of Germans in a hayfield waving white flags. As we left the road to take their surrender, I cautioned the legionnaires to approach slowly, but they wouldn't listen. They ran ahead to collect their trophies, and I could not stop them. Once they got within twenty yards, a machine gun hidden in a haystack opened fire. I took refuge in a flooded ditch bordered by willows as the remainder of the legion fell back to a defensive position behind the rock wall on the other side of the road. The Americans returned fire for nearly an hour but ran out of ammunition as the Germans advanced. They were all but eliminated, and there was nothing I could do for them.

At nightfall, I went ahead alone.

After reaching Arras, I joined the 10th Army's hasty withdraw to Lens. Low-hanging smoke created an oppressive sky. Flashes of dull light in the fog were a constant reminder of a world on fire. The only way to calm my mind to the danger at large was to imagine the concussive shelling as distant thunder. A storm that would never end. Just north of the main square, we passed a burning church. The men removed their helmets and bowed to a young priest that prayed in the blackened atrium. Each and every soldier slowed to receive his blessing, which the priest gave freely.

That evening, we sheltered in root cellars that had been carved into the chalk along the river. The rats didn't even fear us anymore and crawled through our ranks unopposed. The Germans launched a fusillade of rockets, mortars, and searchlights that lasted until dawn. Unable to advance or retreat, we watched the howitzers destroy the town street by street. At one point, the Germans were close enough that we could see their spiked helmets silhouetted against the glare of a burning building. With no rounds left to spare, we were forced to watch, silently. The men couldn't risk giving up their position without a means to defend themselves. For most of them though, the night remained most memorable because after three days without food, they were finally permitted to eat their emergency rations. Aside from that, nothing else could be done.

The following morning the Germans cheered and sang for hours. From the lyrics, I guessed that Antwerp had finally been taken. While they celebrated, we advanced and encountered a steady stream of weeping refugees on the road to Reninghelst. One man said *We move to higher ground so we don't drown in our own tears.* The weary travelers—even children—carried sacks of valuables and food. Dogs pulled carts with heavier items, such as trunks and bundles of clothing or bedding. We knew that there were spies among them, but could do nothing about it.

The farther north we marched, the greyer the skies grew. A steady rain kept our boots and clothes from drying. What should have been a forest of red and gold had been reduced to bony, blackened fingers that disappeared into a mixture of mist and smoke. Fields of winter wheat and rye had been turned into a muddy, pocked wasteland. The breeze carried the stench of fecal, rotting decay. It truly felt like *la rue d'Enfer*.

When at last we reached Ypres, filth and grime covered me from top to bottom, just like the Wife of Bath from *The Canteburty Tales*. The townspeople greeted us with hot coffee and warm bread. They warned us that the Germans in Antwerp used women and children as a screen, and that by nightfall, they'd be fleeing the town as well. We learned that the most imminent danger waited to the north, where the Germans figured they'd have a clean shot to the sea and Channel ports once they'd pushed through the remainder of the Belgian army. They were so certain of success that they did almost nothing to conceal their plans. German airplanes flew low passes over the ramshackle fortifications and billeted troops, knowing the French possessed no anti-aircraft weapons with which to fire back. The townspeople heard rumors that the Kaiser himself would lead the final attack. By now, Joffre knew that anything less than a decisive victory would be a disaster for France, forcing him to give the general order to ...*drive back the enemy wherever met.*

But Ypres meant the end of the line for me.

Meaning the end of the line for Augustin Toussant as well.

It didn't take long to learn that a group of well-heeled soldiers had bought their way into a rearguard position on the outskirts of Bruges at a place called Sint-Michiels. They occupied an old hunting chateau and had shipments of Bruges Blond delivered fresh from the Straffe Hendrik brewery almost daily. While the men in the trenches lived on bread and beet soup, Augustin Toussant ate fried sole and rack of lamb. The other regiments joked that Michelin would grant the lodge its first star by the end of the year.

Now that I knew where he hid, there remained only one thing in this world that could keep me from exacting my revenge.

And that was the German Army.

"When I heard the British 2nd Division would join our 7th, I tried to connect with them. But the Germans controlled the high ground east of Ypres and attacked our flank relentlessly. As if they knew our every move." I helped Augustin with his shirt, navigating the buttons by touch alone in the near total darkness. "Once again, I believed nothing could be done."

Augustin sat on the edge of the bed. I turned away from the stench of beer on his breath.

I said, "All hope seemed lost. A shell destroyed one of the cable wagons and communications went down. The German 4th Army bombarded Dixmude endlessly. And to worsen matters, the British suppliers were unable to keep up with demand for munitions. That shelling you hear now? All German. The Allies are rationing shells as if they were loaves of bread. Just fifteen rounds per day for the howitzers. Artillery units have been ordered to only fire upon *vulnerable targets*, whatever that means. For the infantry it is worse. So many men dying with nothing but a bayonet with which to defend themselves.

My anger boiled over and I finally vowed to never again say ...*nothing could be done.*"

I helped Augustin to his feet. He placed a hand on my shoulder to steady himself as I buttoned his trousers and fastened his belt. "Too tight," he said.

I said, "You drank too much. Let's walk."

I helped him with his boots and lead him to the door. From the other rooms I heard snoring. Men exhausted from excess, rather than the caress of battle's sweet kiss on their cheek. If I had my way, each of these men would suffer.

"Quiet," I said, taking a coat and hat from a hook on the door. "Don't wake them."

The golden orb of a waning gibbous moon dipped into the western sky. A growing dawn chased away all but the deepest night. Our breath turned to fog in the cold air. The guard at the gate napped beneath a canvas tarp, a sign of exactly how far one had to go to be out of danger. "Now let me help you with your coat."

For almost a mile, I felt content to let the crunch of gravel beneath our feet be the only conversation we needed. In the distance, geese at the edge of a canal honked to greet the morning. I'd waited all night for him to ask me how I'd found him, but my conceit only allowed me to hold my tongue for so long. By now, impatience had bested me. I said, "Don't you want to know how I did it? How I am here, to see you, such a long way from Paris?"

Not impatience, I thought. Pride.

He slowed and released an audible sigh. A sign, perhaps, that he didn't care.

"Once the Germans crossed the Yser, I knew exactly what to do," I said, leading him once again toward the end of the lane. "I could make them *drown in their own tears*, but Joffre wouldn't hear of my plan. As if my success in Reims had fortified his reluctance to trust anybody not wearing a uniform. So I went ahead without his blessing. My parting words to him were, "Prepare to swim.""

For one moment, I wished that Augustin had been just a bit more lucid. In a way, never being able to show anybody what I'd grown truly capable of felt just like the coffin I'd be buried in. As a result, my lies took on a life of their own that grew well beyond this body. I longed for the day when I could just be a strong, good person and nothing more. Just the woman I was born to be. Not the person I'd become. A mask of deceit. A cast-off. A societal reject.

At once a wave of sadness washed over me when I thought of all the friends and lovers I left under cover of darkness, without an explanation. As if I'd burned more bridges than I'd ever cross. I resented the shadows in which I lived. The *little fabrications* I had to create in order to sustain normal human interactions.

Most of all, I felt afraid that after all this, I would not be able to return to Paris for a very long time.

I said, "I forged orders to the British 2nd and to the remaining Belgian defenses north of Ypres. A simple, elegant plan. No wonder Joffre rejected it," and handed Augustin a copy of the letter I'd written.

His hangover kept him from focusing. He squinted at the words and mumbled. Blasts from the French 75s flashed like fireflies in the distance.

"I gave the order to open eight sluices at the Noordvaart, thus flooding the Yser River valley." I took the paper from him, folded it, and waved it as I spoke, like a conductor in front of an orchestra. "I coordinated the efforts of two nations and hundreds of men with little more than these very words."

My voice rose with my emotions. But we were far enough from the chateau that I didn't care. "I did it, Augustin. I orchestrated the innundation of the polders between Dixmude and Nieuport, stopping the German advance. Just one woman—me. Only me. Destroying tons of German supplies and ammunition. The only help I had came from the moon, but if I could've raised the tides myself, I would have."

For the first time since we'd left his bed, Augustin gave a sign that he'd sobered up. I'd counted on his rising anger to make this next part easier.

He grabbed my coat up in his fists and said, "This is treason. You knowingly and purposefully engaged in activity that directly defied the chain of command. You'll get the guillotine for this."

"And still die a hero. Maybe even be granted a sainthood, if the war ends soon enough. But none of that will change the fact that you supplied Germany with arms all summer. Letting them build their stockpiles while France took a holiday. One could probably even make the case that you knew all this was coming." I pulled another piece of paper from my pocket. More words. More destruction. "I know of your relationship with Frau Hannelore Krupp. The young Madame Toussant? I met her at Gare de l'Est."

He smiled and reached for his sidearm.

"Shoot me, Augustin. But first let me finish. Frau Krupp-Toussant is back in Berlin. I stood watch when the gendarmerie deported her. She's fortunate they didn't execute her. Or maybe not. I wrote the arrest order. You can't always rely on luck. Either way, the foundry is now in the government's hands. I worked up the papers myself."

In the distance a bugle sounded. Augustin cocked his ear toward the encampment near the crossroads at the end of the lane. When it faded, he pushed the pistol to my temple.

"'Reveille.' The British troops billeted in Oostkamp are just beginning their day." In my best Cockney, I said, "Unlike you, they been to the front. They know how to react to a hostile act. You might think I'm a bit balmy on the crumpet, but I bet they'd love to hear how you violated a little flower from Manchester, just here doing her part for King and country."

The sudden turn knocked him back a step or two. As if only realizing at that moment that we'd reached a bit of an impasse. That life, as he knew it, had come to a very real end.

I said, "If they don't shoot you for violating Rule 303 first."

He narrowed his eyes, trying to focus long enough to come up with the article I referred to. "303?"

"*303*. Like the rifle. Because that's what they do to foreigners caught wearing a British serviceman's uniform."

He pulled the jacket away like it had been covered with ants. In the dawn's early light he couldn't easily discern French blue from British olive. The lack of a second row of buttons finally sold him on the truth.

He removed the coat and threw it into the trees. "Then I will drag you back to the chateau and kill you there. After what you've done—"

"You won't be welcome." I showed him the last forgery I'd produced. His desertion notification and confession to the crime of supplying an enemy combatant. "Your commanding officer will receive this in the morning mail. Just to be certain, I've sent along copies to Prime Minister Poincaré, Papa Joffre, and *Le Figaro*. It will run in the morning paper."

"What choice have you given me? Is this course of action really proportional to what I've done to you?" He lowered his weapon and fell to his knees. Panic tore away his confidence, exposing the true Augustin Toussant.

"My heart will heal. It always does. But you slaughtered thousands. Maybe more by the time this war ends. Your shells fell into their trenches. Your brass delivered so many men to their death. So if the universe was just, you'd be left to die with the only choice being whether or not to take your own life. But I am in no position to decide for the universe, and will leave you with a few more choices."

"The British or the French? What kind of choice is that? Death by guillotine or death by firing squad. I have a son now."

"Or prison, perhaps. If you are lucky. But you can't always rely on luck." I shivered in the crisp air. For the first time in a very long time, I couldn't be sure of what my day would bring. "Or you can go down to the crossroads. Ask to speak with a being who can provide you with a new set of choices. Choices I don't have the power to offer."

He stood and raised his weapon to strike me.

"You can hit me all you'd like, Augustin. You can't hurt me anymore."

After a moment of careful consideration, he holstered the gun and backed away.

"If I were you," I said as he turned toward the growing dawn. "I'd take my chances with the British or the French. No good can come from a trip to the crossroads."

ALL SAINTS DAY

The crying woke me up. Dani held the little one, rocking him in her arms.

"Is he okay?"

Dani cried too. "Just a dream. Go back to sleep."

"Please tell me." I rolled onto my side and tried to find her eyes in the darkness. "I want to help you."

"Nobody can help me. It's hopeless."

"Let me try."

"Can the universe be changed? I think it may be impossible, but you can change who you are. You can be brave even when you are afraid. You can be strong and fight until the very end, even if you ultimately save only yourself."

"I don't understand where this is coming from, Dani. You're scaring me."

"It's a test, Ben. We act strong and we fight, even when we can't save them all."

"What's the use then? If we can't change anything—"

"I only said perhaps the universe can't be changed. But what if it made a mistake? What if things as they seem are the result of an error? The Big Bang. Evolution. Agriculture. Literature." She grabbed my arm and pulled me closer. She kissed me, then said, "What if you were given one chance to prove the universe wrong? Does everything change? Or just a perspective? A single aspect?"

"You said the universe doesn't make mistakes."

"Then this is a dream. All of it. You need to close your eyes and find a way back to it."

So I tried to find a way back to it...

"Taking fire. Ben—we got a motherfucking contact right there."

"Set. I see him, X. Just stay down."

"I need everybody's eyes on the fire. Zack, where's it coming from?"

"Sir, it's coming from your six. A hundred and fifty meters. Maybe one twenty-five."

"Collins—look at the building with the green trim. That fucking school again."

"Incoming. We got incoming. X—fucking take cover."

"Way too close. Yama, we need eyes. Me and Ben can't see shit over here so you guys have to spot these fuckers."

"Came from the school, X."

"Bullshit it came from the school. You know how I know? Because every time I get eyes on the school somebody takes a fucking shot at us from the trees."

"Uzhmakai."

"Somebody please make this woman shut up."

"Halta wlaarsai, kids. I know you understand me. Your mama's calling. Dinner's ready. Tik ta? Leave the books and get over here."

"Collins—this ain't Red Light, Green Light. You two get your asses out of those fucking poppies."

"Tersha. Yes, you, son. Tersha on over there."

"Sir—where the fuck is he? We can't fall back if we can't see him."

"He's on the roof, X."

"Bullshit, he's on the roof. Got my eyes on the roof but our fucking sniper's still taking shots at us."

"Shit. They're trying to flank to the west. Zack—you need to suppress the whole way up this side. X—you and Ben need to fall back to us."

"Trying, sir. They ain't making it easy. Someone's hitting the road right fucking here."

"Really motherfucker? Ain't that some shit? They're hitting us from two angles—twelve o'clock and—hell if I know. Ten?"

"Listen—we got air support inbound. Fall back and we'll hit them when they scatter. Ben, you hear me?"

"I can't even scratch my dick without those fuckers taking a shot at me, and they're scooting fast. Or there's more of them than we thought."

"Sir, I got eyes on them. They're flanking hard. Trying to wrap us up like…."

"X—fucking fall back, man."

"Yama, I got this."

"Take cover in that fucking ditch then. He's got a fucking bead right on you."

"Well, I thought I had 'em. You ready to move, old man?"

"Just hold up."

"Where do you think you're—shit. Ben, let's just fall back. That's all we got to do now."

"Just cover me, X."

"Shit, Ben. How'd we miss her?"

"I didn't fucking miss her. Just give me a second while…Uzhmakai? Hey, it's okay. I'm not going to hurt you, chiquita. We're the good guys. See?"

"Good guys, huh? We'll see about that in five years."

"Ignore him, chiquita. He gets jealous real easy. Aaraam sha. Real slow. See? Your mama's going to be real happy to see you. Just a little farther now."

"We got to hustle now. Get them creaky joints moving. You're going to have to pick her up."

"She's just scared, man."

"You better hustle, motherfucker. I got your back, but move it."

"Almost there. Shhh. Hush up now. I got you. Listen, sweetie, your mama's right there. Okay? Don't cry."

"Go, Ben, go. Frag out. We need cover here. Yama—"

"Suppress. Suppress."

"Don't cry, little one. Hush up, okay? Just hush up now. Going to be there real soon."

"Shift fire. Shift fire—Ben—you'd better pick it up, man."

"Hush up now. Don't listen, chiquita. Keep your head down. Don't listen, okay? Don't listen."

"Set, sir."

"Reloading."

"Here we go. See? Told you it'd be okay. Hush up now. There's your mama."

"Ben, keep the goodbyes short. These fuckers are boogieing. Suppress."

"Frag out."

"See? Better now. Hasta luego, chiquita."

"Ain't that some shit? You'd sacrifice yourself for the next generation of insurgent?"

"Let's just say I need something to help me sleep at night, right? Where are they?"

"Pushing through that corn right there. Two of them, at least. Follow me."

"Got it."

"Air support inbound."

"I hear 'em."

"You're out of control, Ben. You know that?"

"Tell me about it."

"Look here, the old man has got himself a fan."

"What is it? A poppy? Don't touch it."

"Don't let those emotions in, Ben. You know better."

"It ain't about that at all, X. It's a sign."

"Sign of what? Listen, you need to lay off the NyQuil, okay? You need to stay sharp. I hear at least two of them Taliban motherfuckers out there. They're going to cut us off from the rest of the guys if we don't keep moving."

"Sounds like Yama fell back to the east."

"Yeah, I hear 'em."

"You didn't have to go there, you know. I'm dealing with it."

"Yeah, Ben. I know I didn't. But somebody's got to keep an eye on you. And you sure as hell ain't dealing with it. With pneumonia, maybe you get a medical discharge. Better than a psych discharge any day, in case that's what you were thinking."

"I hadn't been thinking about it, but I am now."

"I'm just saying I know what kind of game you're playing. Back off the Ambien. Get out of the fog."

"Yeah. But if I'm being straight with you...."

"Incoming—incoming."

"Was that Zack?"

"Yama—shit. X, you see where that came from? They're hit."

"RPG from the school, I think."

"X, who is that? Zack? Who's hit? Let's push back to the—"

"Where's your brain, Ben? They got you in a full court press, motherfucker. You pop up like that again and they going to take your head off."

"That ditch, there. I'll cover. Go."

"Motherfuckers—told you they're trying to flank. That came from the fucking corn."

"X, they're everywhere. We stepped right into this shit. Look—I think Zack got nailed from the east. These motherfuckers in the corn are trying to get behind us. If we drift ahead we can hit them as soon as we see them."

"Ben, we just need to hold this shit right here. Just because we think there's two don't mean there's just two."

"X, I'm telling you, something don't smell right. This ain't how it's supposed to happen. We need to regroup."

"Smells like horseshit."

"Frag. Fucking frag. Go, X, go."

"Fuck me, I'm hit."

"You hit? You fucking hit? X—"

"Shit, man. My feet…."

"You're good. Look here."

"Fuck me, Ben. That came fucking close. Look at me again. There's blood…."

"No blood. You are one lucky motherfucker, you know that?"

"Well, fuck you if you're my rabbit's foot."

"I see them. Stay down."

"Let me get up there with you…."

"Stay there, X. Got him. Shhh."

"You got him?"

"Got him. The other one's hiding in the dirt. I see him. Thinks his grenade got you. Well, it didn't, asshole. And there's number two."

"Let me see. Where?"

"Right down that row there."

"We've got to make ourselves scarce now. Them hogs about to be moving in on us any second. We got a lot of ground to cover if we want to hook up with Yama on the backside of this. You ready, old man?"

"They're gone. Where's the LZ?"

"Shit all looks the same to me now. I hear them, I just don't see them."

"Here's our air support. Get behind the wall."

"This wall ain't going to stop those 30 mils."

"Man, I love that fucking sound. You see Yama yet?"

"Naw. It's like he evaporated."

"Like wasps in a tin can. I never get tired of watching those pigs fly."

"Small arms fire. East."

"Stay close. I don't want to get out in that corn only to find we were chasing the wrong ghosts."

"Ben, is that supposed to be funny? Because it ain't."

"Look at all this brass. That's ours. Let's stick to the ditches."

"Listen."

"Yeah. Blooper. On the other side of the AKs. How the fuck we get all the way out here?"

"Fuck if I know."

"When Yama got hit he fell back to Espinoza, I bet."

"Your theory don't come with a set of instructions now do it, Ben?"

"We backtrack to the house and school? Or try to get behind these Taliban fuckers."

"Shit. Not real happy about either of those options. Plan C?"

"Yeah. I don't know. Try to work farther through these ditches. They get deeper ahead. When we get to the river we can work back up to everyone."

"Fuck it. We'll just work all the way up to Kandahar and take a jitney back to the FOB. Pick up a few pizzas, beer. Look. They're bugging out to the north."

"Or they're bearing down on Yama."

"Damn, Ben. If you're going to be the voice of reason then we may as well just keep going."

"You go first. I feel a little better walking through shit you already stepped in."

"Left or straight?"

"Left."

"Looks like shit's winding down over there."

"Well, you'd better hope they make a little noise, X. Once the sun goes down...."

"Yeah. Shouldn't we have looped back by now?"

"That's what I thought too."

"It's all starting to look and smell the same, old man. Are those our birds? Hear them?"

"I hope they ain't because we're a long way from the LZ."

"Shit. I think that's our ride home."

"Talking about it ain't going to get us closer."

"How far you figure we are from the LZ?"

"Mile and a half. Optimistically. Working the ditches is still our best option, I think."

"Yeah, that's how come them birds and the rest of our guys are over there and we're over here."

"X...."

"I know. Let me drive for a while. You can read the fucking map."

And for the longest time we just walked. I followed without saying a word. At a certain point, it hurt to speak, to say the wrong thing. Something exploded in the distance.

Long shadows turned into dusk. Another set of Blackhawks flew over, and we tossed a smoke grenade. We waved our arms, but the birds faded into the horizon.

X took off his helmet. White salt clung to his temples. He wouldn't make eye contact with me. "You're supposed to have shit figured out, old man. I trusted you."

"Why? There's nothing on my sleeve that says you have to do anything I tell you to do. I don't even trust me."

"What are we going to do?"

"We're still alive. So we got that going for us."

"Alive means a lot of different things out here. Alive but not living."

"We'll get back. I promise you."

"How can you make that promise?"

"For one thing, I know I don't die out here."

"How do you know?"

"I just do. You wouldn't believe me if I told you about Mexico and Danicka."

"Well, I ain't about spending the night out here in this motherfucker."

"It's just a camping trip. That's all. Camping with guns."

"All my YMCA camping trips ended with a van coming to pick us up in Jersey in the middle of the night because we either got a hold of some weed, some pussy, or some both." He ripped the cellophane wrapper off some orange cheese and peanut butter crackers from a package his mom had sent.

"Didn't anybody tell you the army was going to be one glorified camping trip?"

He offered me a cracker. "Man, I'd kill for a pizza."

"You got any Snickers?"

"Did you have any Reese's Cups when I asked?"

I laughed.

In the distance, closer to the river, a golden flash brightened the sky. The stars faded and returned as a series of explosions that shook the earth. We climbed out of the trench to get a better look.

"What the fuck is that? Marines?"

"That felt big. Do we know if the Brits have anything going on?"

"What can you see?"

"Shitload of nothing. Come on up."

"Right behind you. Watch your foot."

"Watch your hand. Just hold up a second."

"Want me to go first?"

"It ain't that. I just don't want to pop up like Whack-A-Mole and have some haji bust a cap in my earhole."

"You good now?"

"Yeah. We good."

A barrage of artillery followed along a front line that stretched for miles. A tongue of light burst from each big gun in rapid succession. Like a line of flashbulbs trailing off into the distance. The plains ahead of them exploded without rhythm or reason. Craters pocked the surface. A manmade moonscape.

We moved ahead along the edge of the trench with caution. As the terrain flattened out it became more difficult to see the course of battle. But the nature of the shelling made it easy to see where we wanted to be. A string of fire followed by thunder in the dark. I looked for landmarks in the flashes of brightness but saw only pocked earth and mud. We picked up the pace.

A line of refugees fled the battle on a road on the other side of a fallow field. In the dim light we could only make out shapes. Masses of loose cloth with no real edges.

"Good way for insurgents to blend in. Let's get back in the trench."

My breath rose over my head in a cloud as the air grew colder. The water in the trench deepened. I stayed close to the edges to avoid getting bogged down. Whenever I found a low spot, the mud made a sucking sound as I pulled my boot away. When the shouting on the plain above grew louder, we moved more slowly. Voices in the dark sounded like whatever you needed them to sound like. Every one of them called my name.

As we got closer to the river the brush along the edges of the trench thickened. Scrubby grasses gave way to anemic trees. Fog from the river mingled with the smoke drifting in from the heavy shelling. After having only just appeared, the stars began to disappear all over again.

White and red flares crossed the sky, two or three at a time. Shadows swept past like a watch's second hand as the lights fell to earth. Some of the star shells caught the breeze and swung back and forth from their parachutes. Their light dimmed only as they passed through clouds of smoke or fog. Miniature supernovae existing only for a moment.

"X...."

"Right here."

"Be careful. There's horse shit all over the place."

"Camel shit?"

"No, X. I grew up on a farm. I know horse shit when I smell it and this is horse shit."

"Hear that? That's an old gun there. Sounds like an antique."

"Something the Soviets left behind?" Each slow, methodical shot came with a mechanical click. Like a typewriter key working a typebar.

"I don't know. Maybe. Who knows what the hell they drag out of these hills. I say we stay in the trenches. This mud though…."

Something big hit the ground. The earth shook and my knees wobbled. "Fuck."

I didn't know what we had in our arsenal that made such a horrendous boom. JDAM seemed like a natural explanation, but I didn't hear any planes. My ears rang after that explosion and as my hearing returned, so did the noise of the firefight on the surface. Rifle and artillery fire came from everywhere. Men screamed war cries and shouts of pain in equal measure.

"Ben. Man, this shit is making it hard to breathe. You've got to get me the fuck out of here."

"Calm down, Xavier. I got you, man. I'll get you home." I walked ahead and banged the wooden beams that reinforced the side of the trench. "Getting closer."

"You promise?"

And I knew better than to reply. But I did anyway. "I promise."

Another flare hissed to life above the trench. Another shell exploded nearby. Perhaps within a hundred yards. Dirt fell onto our heads.

"They getting closer."

By now the mud came almost up to my knees. Each step stirred up the foul decay that had settled on the bottom. Every time I lifted my boot I gagged. Rotten eggs, old roadkill, and the ammonia bite of pig manure filled my nose, mouth, and lungs. It stuck to my tongue. When I felt my bile rising, I pushed ahead, knowing that with nothing in my stomach, vomiting would be noisy and painful.

The shouts of the men working the artillery batteries grew, but our path did not parallel their line. It edged toward it, bringing us closer to them with each step. I could hear individual voices, but not individual words.

X and I stopped and covered as another shell hit nearby.

We picked up our pace and it became difficult to stifle the sloshing. I wondered where this trench would end and if we'd ever reach it. If, at a certain point I realized I'd made a mistake, I never once even dwelt on it for fear it would drag me right down to the bottom of all of this.

Mistakes didn't matter when I was alone.

Another shell whistled through the night, this time much closer. Within fifty yards. As I turned to check on X, another fell in the first's wake. The whistle told me it was going to hurt.

"Incom—"

The wall to my right burst open with a wave of splintered wood and debris. The impact pushed me to the other side of the trench, burying me. I clawed my way to the top, but the loosely consolidated fill settled around me like cement.

I shouted for X, but no sound came from my mouth. An inky blackness lingered before my open eyes. Blinking the darkness away only brought more darkness. A dull light flashed periodically, and I didn't know if it was my eyes trying to spark back to life or the sky falling into me.

If X called for me, I wouldn't hear.

I thrashed and twisted, flailing my arms in an attempt to get them above the mess.

"X." I tried calling him again. I knew I made sound, because my throat hurt. The dull light flashed before me whenever I yelled. The ringing in my ears made me dizzy.

I kicked my feet. Pedaling through the stones and wood. Closed my eyes and ignored the pain. Rough ends of wooden beams ripped my pants, snagged my boot. Movement in the darkness below convinced me that X remained down there somewhere, trying to pull himself free by dragging me down with him.

"X." A great static filled my head. And a ringing, like a bell long after it had been struck.

I only knew my face had ended up above the rock and dirt when a flare drifted overhead. The shape of the light sinking through the fog made sense to me, let me orient myself. My hearing returned in small measures. First came rumbles that I felt as much as heard. The snap of a bolt-action rifle. Sniper.

A rhythmic pounding drowned out all other noise. A rapid succession of booms from deep within the earth. From ordinance larger than that which could be fired from any cannon or tank. It came quick *One... two... three... four...* followed by the regular sounds of battle. After a moment, the *One... two... three... four...* started all over again.

When I got my arms free, I twisted. In the dim light of the falling flare I started looking for X. I crawled back to where I thought he had fallen. In the muddy glare of battle, every broken length of wood looked like an ulna or scapula.

"X."

I strained to listen through the din of combat, squinting into the darkness to see movement. When I got myself over to where I thought he'd be, I started to dig.

A pair of flares rose into the sky from behind me. I waited until they started their descent, knowing that the light was my only friend. But when I turned to dig, I saw a dark hand, lifeless, rising from the ruin.

No. X, give me something, man. Fucking give me a twitch.

I attacked the earth, cutting my knuckles on rock and brick, inch by inch exposing the forearm of a man who'd been dead for a very long time. The lifeless limb gave no resistance. I pulled it free of its sleeve. Old graves.

"Shit."

In the growing light I looked for another spot to dig and saw another hand reaching. In the play of shadow and light I saw a boot without a leg, the eye socket and jaw of a bleached white skull. Ribs jutting through a ragged blue uniform. A femur that ended in a jagged edge. The bodies were everywhere. An entire regiment of dead soldiers.

"Ben."

I crawled through the corpses, hearing the clack of bone and rock beneath the weight of my hands and knees. X reached through a tangle of vertebrae, grasping his SOS to the black sky. Pushing away a hip bone and a clavicle exposed his ash and mud-covered face.

"Get me out of here. You've got to get me out of here."

"I'm coming. Right here, man."

"This is a bunch of bullshit, right here. Nobody told you to go back for that little girl."

It stung, but I didn't say anything.

He said, "We ain't going to get out of this."

I held my breath to keep the words from coming out, to hide my anger. To keep the thought that had been rattling around my head since early this morning from becoming words on my lips.

I'd been to his mama's house and saw the flag in its glass case on top of the TV. Saw X's portrait from basic training in a frame next to *The Bible* and *TV Guide*. Saw the *Philadelphia Inquirer* article describing the incident and the hero's welcome he received before they lowered him into the ground.

I visited his grave.

"Halt."

I froze when he chambered a round.

"Who goes there?"

A Brit.

"Specialist Benjamin Collins, US Army, sir. Could you please help me? I lost a man in here somewhere."

Two of them hurried down through the crater and helped me clear the debris while the others watched from the top of the trench. They worked quietly and stoically and didn't stop until X came free. Once he got onto his feet they offered us their canteens.

"Private Jimmy Freeman, at your service. James, when the brass hats are about. You boys blottoed? You Yanks are a long way from the States." The damp wool in their uniforms was a new smell, and I clung to it because it wasn't shit, or smoke, or mud. I strained to see an insignia, but all I got were glimpses in the dark.

I said, "We got hit hard this morning. Our regular patrol, but they were ready for us. Big ambush, had us pinned down. During the action we got separated." I handed back his canteen.

We climbed to the top of the trench. I looked for the mountains or the electric lights of the FOB or Kandahar, but I didn't recognize any of it. The flatness spread for miles. A canopy of smoke and fog. At any given time a thousand different flares or the fire from shelling arriving from either direction filled the sky. In some places, strips of water reflected the light back up to the heavens. In the immediate foreground, a small farmhouse with a tile roof glowed in the glare of its burning barn. Farther off, a narrow steeple stood in sharp silhouette to the town burning behind it.

"That's Fritz's handiwork. A Big Bertha down in Langemarck. That's their sixteen inch gun. They settled in down there after they flattened Antwerp. This strip of land is the only thing between them and Calais, which is all that remains of Belgium at the moment. King Albert's out there somewhere with the last of his army defending the kingdom." He stopped to take a breath, as if he, too, couldn't believe it. "Hey, we heard they hit Paris with a rail-mounted gun from eighty miles out. You know if that's true?"

They both ducked as another shell fell in the vicinity.

"No. I haven't heard...."

"The big ones are ours. The Grand Fleet sitting out there in the Channel just pounding away at the Huns. Doing a fair job of it from the sound. It's not biscuits and jam...." He held a hand up as another sequence of four shells exploded, as if he'd arranged this moment for X and me.

"Damn whizbangs will get you before the big ones do, but they still keep you on your toes? Before we go on, can I take a look at something?" He reached for the poppy in my vest.

"Don't touch it."

195

"Wee bit jumpy, eh? We have orders to be on the lookout for the two of you. The brass hats said to look for a poppy in a lapel, but I guess this counts. Figured you'd come knocking on our back door instead of mucking about in the shite."

"I don't understand."

"The poppy. It's you."

"Why are they looking for us? Because we got separated?"

"I don't rightly know. The Old Contemptibles are just meant to charge into the fray, no questions asked. But if you are in fact the one they're searching for, looks like we're heading up to Dixmuide."

"I don't understand...."

"Me neither. But we've got our orders, okay? If we muck it up we're shit out of luck and jolly well fucked, so put a sock in it. We spent the last three weeks down in *Wipers*, which seemed absolutely regimental and now we're expected to escort the two of you up to Dixmiude. She's been waiting for you?"

"Who has been waiting? I don't understand."

"The Angel of Ypres, that's who. I don't rightly know who she is either, but found out quick enough. Last week, the German XXIII Corps surrounded Dixmiude, and General d'Urbal ordered a half-assed counter-attack. The Krauts drove the French all the way back through our lines to Langemarck. They hit us hard, but the next morning, we retook all the ground we lost. Too bad we didn't have enough left in the tank to sustain an attack. The Jerrys knew it, too." He paused long enough to light a cigarette. The glow when he inhaled showed his eyes watching something far off in the distance. "So we hung on there, low on rounds, nothing but a skeleton crew in the trenches while Jerry reinforcements poured in from Becalaere. We'd been caught out in no-man's-land with our pants down. They had us on three sides and were on the verge of closing in behind us, but the Angel of Ypres swept in from the south and pounded the German flank and saved our asses. Figure she's the only reason I'm here right now. So when I get orders that the Angel of Ypres is looking for a soldier wearing a poppy in his collar, I tend to listen."

"But that was last week. I don't see how...."

"Look, the 7th Division fell back toward Wipers on the 18th. A group of French Marine Fusiliers were to reinforce us after they fell back from Antwerp, but ended up in Dixmiude instead. For three days now we've been promised reinforcements. Then the two of you show up. I'd pretty much forgotten about the poppy. This war is a cruel joke, but none of us are laughing. If you ask me, the bloody universe is taking a piss."

"What's the situation now?"

"The Huns leaving Antwerp are on the verge of pushing through our lines. Every bloody Jerry between here and Bavaria is in West Flanders because the Kaiser expects a breakthrough to Calais at any cost. If it wasn't for our Navy pounding them with their twelve inch guns, we'd be pushing daisies. We have nowhere left to withdraw to. Despite the thrashing the Huns are taking, they still managed to cross the Yser last night. And that, my underinformed friend, is the situation now."

"Yeah, I got it, I think. So how do we get there? Dixmiude?"

He laughed. "You won't believe me if I told you."

"Try me."

"One big push through no-man's land. Heads down. Lot of shooting and screaming."

We followed Jimmy and his boys up a small rise. A rail line that had been built up from the landscape, allowing us to survey the battle.

Storm clouds billowed from the dreadnoughts at sea, releasing yellow lightning. Dull flashes of fire in the fog. Moments later the ground exploded, spitting up earth, barbed wire, and men. The sound followed. A thud accompanied by an immediate crack.

Smaller tongues of flame erupted from everywhere else. From the batteries that resided out in the open, I could see men turning away from the blasts. Some of the batteries were hidden at the edges of villages. The light from those guns made the lace-like brickwork of steeples and town halls glow as if caught in a momentary sunrise. Some of the guns worked at the edge of forests, where trees swallowed up the sharpest parts of the concussive explosions. Only a muffled sickening thud remained. It was as if those guns had given life to the forests themselves, implying that the very land upon which we stood was capable of corruption and violence.

Everything else appeared as a seething mass of glowing embers. Singular bursts of small arms fire covered the soggy plains like moss on a rock. The sparks were in constant motion, ebbing and flowing in the darkness like a tide ruled by many moons.

Flares rose and fell above the tumult. Gold and red and green stars hanging from silk parachutes. Like angels in slow death throes. Like souls trying to escape to heaven, only to be pulled back by the conflict.

And I thought of all the reading I'd done. I thought of all the monsters and murderers and rapists and demons in literature, and how none of them measured up to what I saw before me. The individual horrors of a hundred thousand men. Each heart fighting for another moment. And I knew that those writers were cowards. They invented monsters and demons just to shield themselves from all this.

"At midnight we push through. It's already been arranged." Jimmy handed weapons to X and me. Old Enfield bolt actions with five-round magazines.

He said, "The plan is to get as far into no man's land as possible. The Navy begins shelling the trenches, and we fall in behind the blasts. They will adjust their shelling from south to north in twenty yard intervals for twenty-five minutes, at which time we have to be behind German lines. By then, French reinforcements will have attacked the German left flank, letting us make it to Dixmuide free and clear."

"Just like that?" I looked to X for affirmation, but he gave Jimmy his full attention.

We wound our ways through the maze of trenches and artillery batteries. The bitter powder fumes lingered on my tongue. I couldn't spit them away. We snaked through the rows of men, waiting for the call to go over the top. The moon, which would be full in a few days, reflected in their helmets. Above us, tongues of flame from the cannons shot through the fog.

We got into position at the extreme edge of the British trench, but I could already sense the raging river. A growing blackness with real mass, tugging at me. By the time the kiss of flame touched our cheeks, we were already caught in its current. We surged ahead, using the weight of the flood to drive our bodies deep into their lines. Like a wave pounding the shore. There was no going against it. One cannot fight the sea.

A thousand legs drove the surge, five hundred men screaming and shooting. To stop would be to drown in the mud. Survival became a matter of being a part of the flood.

I watched the big guns fire from their position offshore. Trying to guess where the shells would land. Turning away when they hit. *One... two... three... four....*

The Germans closed in around the craters like ants engulfing a jellybean. Always shooting and pushing ahead. From here their muzzle flash looked harmless. Almost stellar.

We ran ahead. Staying low. Jumping barbed wire. Bodies.

I heard no command to charge. To fall back. To cover. Just running. Bullets ricocheted off the ground all around us. Dust, smoke, blood. I didn't know if the shots were meant for us or not. I didn't know whether or not to take it personally.

Jimmy ducked into a trench that had collapsed into a dead end. He turned and waited for the rest of our group. As the last man fell in, we were back on the plain.

I stopped when the first shell hit. The urge to retreat consumed me. But X pulled my sleeve and I followed right behind him. Flames licked my boots as we ran into the inferno. Heat seared my legs and hand. My gun had grown almost too hot to hold.

The second shell hit just a few yards ahead of us and we ran faster. As if we were meant to reach the impact crater while the worst of the fire still raged. The Germans fell away from our path, twisting and flailing as the flames engulfed them. They screamed as their flesh blistered and burned. Begging for death. Renouncing their Kaiser and country for a quick bullet to the head.

The shouts and cries pushed us farther into the maw. Bolstered by a sequence of tremendous explosions, an exodus of men surged beneath a British flag. Stabbing with bayonets. Shooting into bunkers and foxholes. The French reinforcements flanked from our nine o'clock before falling in behind us. Enemy trenches were mired in the screams of our building victory. We crossed the trembling earth on the heads of the German dead.

More shells came from the dreadnoughts just off the coast. When they hit, men were knocked off their feet. They stumbled and fell, but quickly composed themselves before pushing into the smoke and dust of the overturned ground. I tasted the Belgian soil on my lips. Clay, sand, and salt from the nearby sea. Blood and sweat from men ordered to claim this land for their leaders. I sucked all I could out of it as I ran ahead. For a moment, it made me stronger.

The earth in front of us exploded. A dark heap of soil and blood rose a hundred feet into the air, and still I ran. I felt strong when I took my place in a line like this. I felt no fear when I could look to my left or right and see another man showing the courage I needed to keep moving. We were now a raging torrent, generating a current that fed off its own momentum. And I knew that we would push through the German lines because the force of our forward movement had grown too strong. The flood swelled as men from different regiments fell in behind us. Pushing through trees and farms. Into trenches where the screams of the defeated were drowned out by the screams of the victorious. The screams turned us into a sea that inundated every acre, every foot, every inch of this land.

Another series of blasts shook the ground. My knees trembled, and I wobbled but did not fall. The fields before us burst skyward and turned into smoke. I screamed, stabbing at a man in field-grey with my bayonet. His flesh and tissue had the same consistency as a sack of sand. I twisted the rifle and his flesh melted beneath the steel. And I didn't need to know his name or if his family would forgive me, because I knew at that moment, had the river flowed in the other direction, I would've been on the ground with a blade rising from my chest. I pulled it out and ran on to the next soldier. His hand reached out, a request for mercy from a sky that had none to give. I finished him off with a quick thrust. And I screamed.

Tears fell down my cheeks, and I ran ahead. I knew that I would never win against a raging river, a rising sea, a universe that had other plans for me. I didn't want to be this man. This cold, heartless killing machine. I wanted to weep for those who'd fallen, no matter what color their uniform. I wanted their families to know that in my heart of hearts I truly wanted to be a good man. The kind of man with confidence enough to shrug off insults and misgivings. The kind of man who just wanted to love and be loved in return.

And I wanted to love again. I wanted to abandon the hurt and anger. I wanted to be part of society. A helper, not one who hurts. I wanted to leave my pain on this field. I wanted my family to see my smile and to know it was real and not just a manifestation of booze and sorrow.

I wanted to know if the men who fell here made a difference. If a casualty, no matter how small, turned the tide even just a fraction of a degree. I wanted to know if the number of men I killed equaled the appreciation felt for them by the politicians who signed their orders.

I just wanted to know if I mattered. And if the man dying in the mud mattered.

The only thing I knew at that moment was that the man in the mud was no different than me. I stood on my feet. He didn't. But in the end, we were the same.

At once, there was nothing left to hide from. No bullets whizzing overhead. No shells falling before me. Nobody left to kill.

"I don't understand," I said. And I turned to look at the chaos behind me.

"Nothing to understand." Jimmy took a knee and wiped the mud from his face.

She stood on a crate, smashing her fist into her palm as she spoke. A blur in a tattered fur collar and black beret. Grey mud covered the long dark dress that she wore hiked up over her leather gaiters and riding boots. In the pale light of the campfires she looked like a ghost. Her skin glowed like the paint on a da Vinci canvas. The MADONNA LITTA, perhaps. Her eyes radiated a warmth, as if feeding off the energy and anxiety of the reinforcements.

She turned, sliced the air with her hand, and said, "All of this once belonged to the sea. If not for the canals and sluices, this would be underwater. But the people of this land tamed the Bachten de Kupe, wringing it from Neptune himself, and they would rather die than turn it all over to the Germans. So when the Kaiser crossed the Yser this morning, he forced us to make a decision."

A group of men to my right flinched when a mortar exploded on the other side of a low stone wall, forty yards away. In the seconds that followed, I heard a Frenchman relaying her words to newly arriving poilu.

"They crossed the river without firing a single shot, under cover of darkness. We'll return the favor and push them back to Berlin without firing a single shot, under cover of darkness. If we give up a single yard, Belgium is lost. Then Paris. Then London. Everything hinges on what happens tonight. There is no more land left to yield."

"So what happens tonight?" I said.

"The moon is nearly full." She smiled for the first time and subtly brushed her fingers across a poppy she wore in her own lapel. "We'll blow the sluices. Except for the dunes at Lombardsijde and the Flemish hills to the southwest of Ypres, this is the highest land in the region. The rising tide will wash the Germans all the way back to Roulers."

I waited for some other form of acknowledgement, a glimmer of recognition from her, but saw none. "How can you be so sure?"

She rested a fist on her hip. "With the cosmos on our side, we can't lose."

February 22, 2010

Mom and Dad,

X and Yama and Zack are on their way home, draped in flags. I should've been with them but I'm in a hospital bed. If I'd have been stronger and maybe tried to push through my fever, I could've been out in the shit and maybe things would be different. But a CO in the FOB heard me coughing and ordered me to the infirmary and accused me of being a bad soldier for putting my unit at risk. It had been pneumonia, just like I figured, but I felt better. My fever had dropped. My cough has almost cleared up.

I want to tell you what happened in my own words before you hear it from somebody else. Their version of the truth will be radically different from mine and I can describe my state of mind better than any of them. This decision comes after a lot of long hours in calm, deep thought—not duress.

Now that X and the guys are gone, I wonder if I am truly alone in this universe. I'm the only thing like this in the entire world. A mistake. No person should have to live with this kind of horrible shit in their head. But I'm doing this because I'm weak. I can't fight anymore. I've been propped up by chemicals for so long that when you remove them from the equation there's nothing left. Just zero.

So I swallowed the rest of my Ambien, one by one, and chased them with the Benadryl. And I'm going to send this letter and go to sleep forever to take back all the peace the universe owes me. The dreams are going to stop. Night should be the one chance a man has to not have to fight the world, but they've stolen that from me too. They're going to say I'm a coward but nothing they can say will be worse than the words I have for myself. I absolutely fucking hate myself. But I'm going to try to remember only good things while I fall asleep. And I am not going to pray.

This is happening over here because I don't want you to see the person I've become. It would be better for you to remember me before I had my life twisted into this disgusting mess. If I could just cut that part of me away and burn it, I would. But I never know where to start cutting, or where to end because it's not just one thing, like a tumor. It's all over, like skin, or an infection that flows through my veins. The only people who understand are the ones who are worse off than me. But we all need the kind of help the world can't give.

I am sorry that it's come to this. I am sorry that your boy didn't grow up the way you'd hoped. I know you wanted more from me, and believe me, I did too. I have this image of myself from high school in my tux with Casey at prom. Or on the mound pitching that no hitter versus Preston County. I think I keep those images in my head because I felt happiest then. That seemed like the perfect life. Everything seemed to work out somehow.

You all are so innocent and I feel like I could've been that way too if I'd have just stayed home. Not that my life would've been perfect, by any means. I'm not naïve or stupid. But looking for snipers at the mall or IEDs when I'm at a drive-through isn't how anybody should live. Not just me—anybody. Yeah, I'd love to have my innocence back. I'd love to have a clean slate and no blood on my hands.

I know that this will break your heart, but I'd rather break your heart than let you see the person I've become knowing you'd eventually grow to hate or resent me. But I am not getting any better. This place is making me worse. The idea that I'm doing this for a greater good doesn't help anymore. It's just blood and sadness and a never-ending stream of tears for me now.

I'm free and I'm looking forward to releasing this shit from my head. It'd be different if my dreams were just the product of an overactive imagination, but they're memories. Things I'd seen with my own eyes. My dreams are part of my life story and uglier than anything I ever could've imagined as a kid. This morning I woke up from one about this skinny little kid from the village. He ran up to my Humvee and asked for Gummi-Bears before I could even take it out of gear. I saw him twice a week. Never knew his name or anything, but we interacted and I knew his face. I knew his mother and little sister and that shitty little dog. The kid used an old pant leg for a leash. In other words, he wasn't a stranger. Anyway, I told him to back away from the vehicle as a sniper put a hole through my side view mirror. I jammed it into reverse and I remember the dog barking and chasing us as I backed down the street. That night I found one of the kid's shoes in the bumper.

That's why I have to do this. If nothing else, be happy knowing that I won't suffer anymore. I am a horrible person and I'm doing the world a favor. I don't deserve to live.

Please tell Grandma and Pap, Levon, Henry, Jane, Rachael, Katy, Chloey, and everybody else I forgot how sorry I am. You can tell them the pneumonia killed me if that helps.

I love you both. This will be the last time I hurt anybody ever again and I'm sorry that it's you who will be hurt the most. I love you guys so much and know you did your best. You gave me a happy childhood, with everything I could ever want. I never felt hungry, never jealous, and never sad. The kid you raised had been pretty happy with himself. This was all just a sick mistake he made. His decision. If he could take it all back and make it right somehow, he would.

But he closed his eyes and it disappeared. Everything he'd worked for wiped out in an instant. Everybody he loved, dead and buried. Every laugh, an echo. Instead of silence, his head is filled with a never-ending wave of noise. Like the sound of a star exploding.

In his head, an ocean of static. His ears never stop ringing.

He wonders if he'll even hear his last breath.

He loves his mother and father very much. His last thoughts are of them.

"The water rose, destroying everything. The monsters fled into the mountains, taking their evil ways with them. When the seas finally receded, the monsters and the men met at a crossroads, agreements were made, and they established an institution to mediate relations between them. After the floods, the world had become a place where magic no longer happened. Common man could no longer cast spells or worship the gods as he pleased. Miracles fell under the purview of the church as part of the agreement. Magic became the realm of women willing to forgo marriage to endure stigma and scrutiny and eventually death by drowning or burning. The early church wrote new myths and legends and all the old ones faded into oral tradition. Telling the old stories resulted in punishment or death, as per the agreement at the crossroads. After many years passed, only children repeated those old tales. Forests filled with dread wolves and old witches sounded silly to ears raised on water into wine." She held my head to her chest and wiped tears away from my eyes.

"In the churches of Abraham, as in the Maya cosmos, a new world emerged from the flood. In the chaos that followed, men offered themselves positions of power that had never before been available to them. Creating titles like *czar*, *emperor*, and *king* out of dust and water, statuses that could be inherited by firstborn sons for millennia to follow. But to maintain those titles, secret arrangements were made. The monsters came down from the mountains to offer wealth and strength in exchange for just a little blood and a commitment. Nothing more. A little blood to prove one's intent. A covenant, if you will. By being pushed into shadow, the scale had become unbalanced, the monsters became more powerful than ever. Fighting out in the open became the surest way to lose. But in the darkness, a play could always be made."

I hadn't opened my eyes. Of all the dreams I'd had, the dream of her voice whispering softly in my ear sounded the sweetest. My sleep had always been filled with places I'd never been. Of highways that followed wide rivers and rolling mountain curves all the way to the sea. Superhighways that turned into dirt roads before ending in a wild wilderness or fiery desert. Lonely places where the only thing left to do would've been to get out of the car and walk until the gravel gave way to a path that had no end, or at least no end that I could ever reach.

But I'd arrived at the end, I felt it. At the end of a very long road that had been very rough on me.

I didn't want to be alone anymore. Her voice proved to me that I wasn't.

I began to believe her.

Dull grey light filtered in through the openings at each end of the stone arch, letting me know I had lived to see another day. Lightning cut through the bands of rain like a flashbulb supernova. The boys sat inside the mouth of our shelter, squealing and laughing at the thunder. Yellow Dog sat back a bit farther from the edge.

Below the hiss of a storm, a mechanical drone at the limit of audibility broke through the weather. I closed my eyes to try to decipher the sound.

"Toussant," Dani said. "There were spotlights an hour ago. Cobá is not very far from here. He's waiting out there with his men. Offering me *surrender terms* as he puts it. That's what you hear."

I sat up and stretched. "Do you think the boys are a little too close to the edge over there? I mean if Toussant's out there...."

"Go and see for yourself."

I'd forgotten how real sleep reset the body. The aches and pains that had been growing over the last few days made it difficult to stand, let alone shuffle to the end of the tunnel in a half-stoop. Yum Kaax chittered some sort of greeting, waving a stick as he spoke.

Beyond the edge of the tunnel I could see only water in the faint glow of early dawn. Enough light remained to discern shapes and fog, but not much else. A grey sea that reflected nothing but the dull grey sky. The clouds on the pool looked like so many bodies in grey uniforms, face down and bloated by the flood. Wind whipped bands of ripples across the surface. Leaves and branches floated in a current that circled endlessly in the water that ponded in the space between the ruins.

Maybe it's just a reflection of the clouds.

X taunted a snake with a small branch. The reptile swam toward our stone platform to escape the deluge. I saw another coiled around a small tree. Off to the right, a bloated brown viper maneuvered gracefully through a tangle of roots. Its head hovered just above the surface, like a submarine periscope.

"What are we going to do?" Dani said. She used her hand to shield her sleepy eyes from the light that trickled in.

"Maybe we should wait? Lay low and see if Toussant moves on. I honestly don't know."

She took my hand and lowered herself to the ground. She patted the floor next to her. As I sat, she leaned forward, an invitation to put my arm around her. She shivered.

"Toussant ain't moving on, I'll tell you that much. That son of a bitch is here to stay." I dug through my bag for the button-down work shirt I'd bought back in Mérida, eased it over her shoulders, then pulled her over to me.

She said, "For many years I never felt a chill. Or heat exhaustion. Or too sad, or too happy. Or hungry. After that night in Mississippi, I felt all these at once. But mostly anger. And hunger. And cold. The worst of the feelings. My hope is that little by little, happiness will push away some of those raw sensations. But I'm not optimistic." She rested her head on my lap.

"It's okay to be optimistic." I pushed the hair away from her face and watched her eyes study the boys playing at the end of the arch. "What happened that night?"

"Not now. Once we are safe I will tell you everything you want to know."

"It might help me right now. To be honest, I'm a little lost. I just want to be found."

"I know where you are."

"You always do. Maybe that's why I'm asking. Like, did you know I would get into your car this spring?"

"I did."

"How?"

"It wasn't the first time we'd met. But please don't ask me to say anymore."

"I won't. At least not until we get home."

"It's not my home."

"It could be."

"Listen to you," she said. Once she seemed satisfied that the boys would be safe while she rested, she closed her eyes. "Who is this person, so full of light and hope?"

"Hell if I know." But it was a feeling, not a sensation. I'm not sure that I ever knew the difference before. "Why don't you rest? Try to nap?"

"If I could, I would."

"Then let's just be together for a while."

The wind and rain slowed, as it always did. Thunder faded into the distance and the sound of water dripping off leaves and stones grew. Grey and yellow birds emerged from dry hollows and flicked through the moist air. The sun rose, even though we couldn't see it. Most of the blackness of night had left the clouds. Only shades of deep grey remained.

As the air warmed, tendrils of mist rose from the pools of water that covered the land. The fog amplified the chirps of tree frogs and other insects. Black shapes ascended the sturdier trees and growled into the fog. Their calls sounded throaty and wild. Only after Zacnal dropped his head and called back with a distinctive *ooh ooh ooh* did I realized the animals in the trees were monkeys. The other boys laughed, then in a moment of adolescent one-upmanship, tried to show him how their calls were better.

Zacnal giggled and pointed. To my ears, the rock walls only seemed to amplify the noise. I ran my hands through my hair.

"Dani."

She watched them with a slight smile and didn't look away when I said her name.

"You all need to stop that. Shhh." I tried to maintain a soft tone and gestured for them to keep it down. "Dani, please tell them. I hate being the bad guy all the time."

Yellow Dog joined the chorus.

"Yum Kaax," she said, pointing to the dog.

More monkeys called from the trees around us. Behind us, and possibly to the east. Fairly close, but still out of sight. Separate groups competing for sonic dominance. A call and response of scraping yelps. Inhalations and exhalations of the most horrific kind. The dense fog made it all sound very loud. And very close. The boys laughed and craned their necks to see.

"That's enough. You guys need to cut it out." My chest tightened with anger. "Why should I even have to say it? Everybody knows we can't be fucking around, yet there they are fucking around. So when I tell them to shut up I'm the bad guy asshole and everybody can hate me."

Before they could comply, the clap of an automatic weapon penetrated the haze.

Dani sat up and scrambled toward the mouth of the tunnel. I grabbed the bags and followed.

"From the east, I think." *Between the road and here.*

X grabbed Dani's hand and frantically gestured toward something in the distance. The monkeys ramped up their cries.

"He says he can show us the way to Cobá. But we have to go deeper into the forest to find the path that goes back to the village."

A large crack of thunder boomed nearby. I flinched.

"Deeper doesn't sound better. These kids are going to need to eat. And it's dangerous. I don't want to run the risk of engaging these guys either, but…if the boys weren't involved, maybe." I pulled a section of root from a crack in the wall and twisted it until it broke in two. "Fucking Toussant's not playing around anymore. If they rode out the storm in their trucks, they're going to look in Cobá. They're going to find us."

The howls from the treetops grew as the monkeys became more agitated. Zacnal rounded his lips to return the call and I grabbed his arm. "Don't."

He yanked his arm out of my grasp and folded his arms across his chest. Yum Kaax slid between us and clenched his jaw.

"Look," I said. "We can't stay here. And you guys have to get your shit together. It's my job to keep you safe. Do you understand? Mine. That man out there wants to kill us. That's why I left you back there. It had nothing to do with whether or not I liked you. Okay? It was to keep you safe. To get you as far away from us as possible."

"Ben...." Dani started. "They understand. But now is not the time—"

"It is the time. There's never been a better time."

Another crack of thunder rolled through the fog. In the silence that followed, a jaguar coughed. I smelled its musk in the dense air and dismissed it as a deceptive memory.

Dani said, "I heard it."

The howlers worked themselves into a frenzy, climbing through the snapped limbs to the very top of the trees, flexing their throats and bellowing with all their might. The noise cut right through the rock of our little shelter. Hoots and barks escalated as the monkeys shook themselves against the limbs like prisoners trying to break through the bars of their cages.

I eased myself past the boys, out of the tunnel, into the water. It rose to my knees and came up to my waist at its deepest point. From a tree not twenty yards away, I saw the second group of primates, taunting the first. Yellow Dog tested the water, determined it was too deep, and retreated to the sanctuary of the arch before resuming his verbal attacks.

In a momentary break in the noise I heard the cat again. Coughing its territory call. "You hear that? Behind us. We have to go."

X hit the water like a wounded duck, splashing and flailing to find his footing.

I grabbed his arm and pulled him to his feet. "Dani, tell him I need him to man up. No more little boy stuff. This is real."

Dani tried to find the right words. And X nodded as she explained in slow, stern sentences. When she finished, she stood and waited for X to acknowledge me.

"*¿Comprende?*" I held out my hand. When he took it and shook it, I said, "*Gracias.*"

Another round of gunfire ripped through the fog. The snap of an AK. Much closer this time. As I spun to look for the flash, one of the howlers slid from its perch, its weak grip kept it upright while it fell. It tumbled and hit the water at the base of the tree with a pronounced splash.

The monkeys on both sides of the pool paused in stunned silence. The stillness caught me off guard and I lost my train of thought. The howlers from behind the arch raced through the naked trees, closing the distance between the two groups in a matter of seconds. Once the second group fixed on the new intruders, they joined the first group in a new round of shouts.

"That way." I patted X on the shoulder and nudged him ahead.

Another gunshot brought down another monkey. And another. In between shots I heard the static of radio chatter.

"Go," I said, pulling Dani into the pool behind me. I found a tree at the edge of the fog in the direction X had pointed and focused on nothing else. Dani took X's hand. X grabbed Yum Kaax's hand. I carried Zacnal.

The cat coughed another stanza of territory calls—a throaty sawing followed by a rich hiss—but at the moment it remained the lesser of two evils. Zacnal shook every time a shot was fired. One by one the howlers fell, and the boy grew hysterical. I tried to turn him away from the trees, but he twisted and fidgeted so that he could see. He extended his hand and screamed, "*Tuucha….*"

X splashed ahead to take point with Yellow Dog on his heels. They immediately exited the pool and began the short climb up a small ruined mound. He swatted at the snakes with a stick, clearing a path for Dani. Yum Kaax took Dani's bag while she climbed. I passed Zacnal up to her and told them to keep moving. Yum Kaax stayed back with me, pausing every so often to make sure we weren't being followed.

"C'mon, buddy," I said, patting his shoulder to keep him ahead of me.

From the depth of the fog at our backs, I heard a distinctive hiss and turned as a red flare rose through the mist. It burned brightly, like a falling star in reverse, before disappearing into the vapor. A voice, thick with German accent, followed. I heard only emphatic ramblings, punctuated with Dani's name. He spit it as much as said it.

"Don't look back, baby. Just keep going."

Climbing through the thorns and downed trees, loose rocks and deep pools made the going slow. Whenever sweat fell into my eyes, I turned my face toward the light rain that fell. It masked the noise we made as we marched ahead.

All around, shapes emerged and disappeared behind the veil of fog. Trees that had been stripped of their leaves stood like old bones rising from an open grave. Swallows came and went from secret recesses, sussing out the insects that rose from the wet earth. The landscape that we'd escaped into less than a day ago had been mostly flattened. The smell of water returning to the sky filled my head.

I didn't know what to make of this light, this dawn struggling to become day. After so much darkness these last few weeks, a metaphor of stepping into the light never felt more appropriate than it did now. These black hours stretched back for as far as I could remember. When I closed my eyes to process the last few days, only an afterglow remained, like the ghost image from a flashbulb. The illusion almost made me believe we were some of the few survivors in this new world. All we had to do to get home was outlast the only other men to have survived out here.

After an hour it seemed like we had barely gone a hundred yards, although when I looked back I couldn't tell where we'd started. We were still waist-deep in water, and the sun had yet to burn through. I knew we were moving. I just couldn't prove it.

This path, this trail through the jungle, felt like the only road I'd ever known. It lead from the mountains of my birth to a sea that separated me from everything I loved to a forest that told thousand-year-old secrets in whispered voices. This road punished those who backtracked or tried to change course. It ran in a straight line, as far as I could tell, but not the shortest distance between two points. It grew by a mile for every step I took. It stole away a year of my life for every moment I stopped to breathe.

Somewhere out there waited my promised land. A painted, plastic promised land. This one thing remained true. One way or another, the promise of going home felt real.

And as I built up this idea of home and an end to this long journey in my head, I realized I'd never see either. The universe showed me I was not meant for such things. The miles had taken their toll and I knew I had to fulfill the promise I made to my parents in that letter. I'd become unsalvageable, like a ship upon a reef. The miles and experiences hadn't changed the man I'd become. Neither had love.

So I made a promise, right then and there, that when the time came, I'd sacrifice myself to let Dani and the boys reach safety.

And because I was doing it for them, and not for me, I felt okay.

In all directions, silver water in wide pools reflected the sky. The rain came in gentle bands that kept us wet, but not cool. The air thickened, making breathing difficult. Insects established a food chain hierarchy in the new world that emerged after the storm. We swatted with branches and our hands, but were still the easiest prey in a thousand square miles.

Dani negotiated a brief rest for the boys on top of a wide, flat ruin. Trees that blew over in the storm ripped carved stones from the hollows they'd rested in for over a thousand years. Snakes continued to seek high ground, and I stayed awake to push them back into the water when they got too close. Iguanas, on the other hand, bobbed their heads like it was any other day on the beach.

"Let's get a move on."

But the boys refused to stand up and continued to nurse the small cuts and insect bites that ravaged their legs and hands. The gentlest of mutinies. They all had a look I'd seen plenty of times before.

"They want to eat," Dani said. "They haven't eaten since yesterday."

"Tell them I'll order General Tso's and lo mein as soon as they get me to a phone." I took Dani's hand and gently helped her onto her feet. "Sorry. That's just how it is."

With that, they were moving. I watched them creep back into the jungle. *La selva,* they called it. A word I'd come to appreciate because this didn't feel like any kind of forest I could've ever imagined. The closest was the old growth of my West Virginia home. When Henry and I rode the rails down Blackwater Canyon it felt as if we straddled a thin line between reality and a hallucination. But at least back there, I wasn't so far from home and family.

A new chorus of raspy howls sank through the fog. The monkeys remained hidden this time. Thinking about the dead ones made me sad.

I tried to shake the image away as I followed. My foot caught a root that had been uplifted. I fumbled to catch myself as soon as I realized I'd tripped, but it was too late. I hit the mud and loose rocks in the small pool on top of the platform.

"Fucking—"

Yum Kaax heard the commotion and called for Dani. X laughed.

Dani made her way back through the tangle she'd just crossed even as I shouted for her to keep going.

"I'm okay."

"Are you certain?" she asked. The concern on her lips faded into a slight smile when she heard the tone of embarrassment in my voice. "Xtaabay says he will make you a stretcher if you are unable to walk."

The cries of the howlers compounded my embarrassment.

I pushed myself onto my knees. Blood dripped from my elbows into the cloudy grey water. "That won't be necessary."

She watched me and pouted her maternal concern.

I waved her ahead. "Move on out. I'm right behind you."

I pushed some of the loose gravel aside to form a small pool, bent low, and splashed water onto the cuts. The blood cleared, but my anger didn't. My breathing deepened and quickened, and I tried to control it.

As I stood I heard a rush in the brush behind me, almost like a gust of wind before a storm. Bushes exploded in a flurry of snapping sticks and spinning leaves. A flash of dull yellow light hit me with a thud, knocking the air out of me. Black spots crossed my vision. The unseen weight drove me into the ground, forcing my face in the gravel and mud.

Its jaw clamped down at an awkward angle on my bag. The canvas twisted in its teeth, confusing it. When it tossed its head from side-to-side the strap pulled tight and I fought to steady myself. He'd gone for my spine and missed.

"Dani." I turned and swatted the side of its face with a loose fist. "Dani...."

The cat reared and I scrambled to my knees. It retreated a step but did not release, pulling me backward onto my ass. It loosened its jaw to get a better grip.

I lurched ahead, pushing myself back through the mud in an attempt to get my feet beneath me, but the cat refused to let go. With flattened ears and narrowed green eyes, it jerked its head—the move meant to snap my neck. I grabbed up a handful of gravel and lunged at its face, shoving the loose sand and rock into its nose. It bared its teeth as it shook away the sting.

I rolled forward, pushed myself onto my feet, and sprinted. My heart thumped. My chest burned. I stooped to grab a thick branch from the ground as I pushed through thorns and branches. "Go. Run."

Dani turned.

"Go. Just go. "

Without a word she picked up the pace, pulling the little one through the brush. Zacnal screamed a terrible scream and X yelled a war cry while swinging a club of his own. Yellow Dog retreated as it barked, torn between rushing to meet the attack and staying to defend the boys.

"Don't stop."

I raised my hands in front of my face and bolted over a mound into a pond. The water slowed me as it rose over my knees. When it got to my waist, I threw myself onto the next mound and pulled myself up, using roots as a ladder.

The cat didn't follow. The dark rosettes on its bright golden hide pulsed as it recovered from my counter. It lowered its head and snorted grit out of its nose, a moment of distraction as it sought an alternate route through the water. It shook a paw, then crept down to the pool after us.

Dani kept the boys well ahead of me, demanding they keep moving. But we couldn't keep this pace up for long. Toussant moved too quickly, and we were famished.

The jaguar worked slowly, like a sparking flame along a trail of gunpowder. Deliberately stepping over fallen trees and brush piles that I crashed through in my haste to gain ground. The tiny spots that dimpled his face were as clear to me as my own pupils in a mirror, it was so close. The glow penetrated the midday dusk that fell on the lowest level of the jungle. Its shoulder blades slide back and forth like twin pistons. Its tail up. Its head down, low to the ground to stay on my trail.

Surely there were easier meals than this, I thought. *There has to be a deer trapped in a pool somewhere. The monkeys....*

I did everything in my power to shake it. I aimed for the rockiest areas, hoping to slow it down. I went for the thickest patches of brush, then doubled back toward Dani and the boys at a full sprint, trying to lose it. I laid logs across my path, or tried to block it with branches of thorny limbs. But the cat always appeared after a few moments like a phantom in the mist. Its head swiveling from side to side like a slow burning metronome. Sniffing out our trail. And the snail's pace chase would resume.

As I climbed out of yet another pool, I looked for Dani and the boys. I whistled for the dog and heard no reply. The dead fog just stared back at me. I pushed ahead, figuring I'd drifted just out of their range of hearing and panicked when I realized I couldn't remember the last time I'd actually seen them.

"Dani."

The howlers called in the distance. The cat trailed not so far behind.

"Tu'ux ka bin."

Nothing.

I ran ahead, sweat fell into my eyes. Despite so much water my tongue stuck to the roof of my mouth like a peanut butter and jelly sandwich with no jelly.

"Dani." I cupped my hands around my lips, as if that'd help. "Danicka."

I put my head down and blindly pushed into the fog. Over my heavy breathing, I heard my name—the shrill tone belong to Zacnal—and changed course. The sound moved at odd angles. Elevated and abject. I got disoriented. "Hey...."

"Ben. We're here."

A strange form materialized from the void. A hulking blank mass. Angles and textures foreign to this forest. Its presence made me feel a little woozy. The sensation that the universe had bent back on itself to bring two distinct points in time together, if only for a moment, made me tremble.

Even when I touched the smooth surface, it didn't alleviate my disorientation. I ran my finger along sharp white lines designed to cut through the roughest of seas. I banged the fiberglass with my fist. Until I saw it spelled out in plain text, I couldn't confirm whether or not I'd left this plane of existence and tumbled into another.

Remedios the Beauty.

The boat sat high on top of a stone platform, held fast by the angle of the wall and a large cluster of tree roots. I ran my fingers along a bullet hole in the bow.

"Ben." Dani leaned over the rail. And I swore if I would've waited long enough she would've tossed a life preserver out to me.

"Dani, this doesn't make sense."

"It doesn't," she said. "Now come up here. Quickly. Our bags are up here. Our passports."

And it felt just like the day Toussant caught up to us in the Gulf. A moment from the past that shouldn't have existed, yet did. "How is this possible?" I said.

"Don't ask, Ben," she said. "This is a gift. And we must use it as it best suits us."

X stood in the bow and pointed into the water. The jaguar padded through the swamp, a clumsy mix of walking and swimming.

I backstepped and scanned the ground for a weapon. The animal hesitated, as if encountering me face to face had not been what it'd expected.

"Dani. I'm going to stay here. You need to take the boys and go." I planted my feet and held the bag out in front of me like a shield.

"Ben, just get up here."

"Dani, this is a chance for me to redeem myself." I tried to let the moments wash over me.

I held my breath, but it still felt like drowning. And I didn't know how to save myself anymore.

Every bit of air I released felt like a minute from my past. I wasn't just fighting an invisible current. I swam against years of my own life. With every breath I battled a year of high school, an ex-girlfriend. My discharge.

A burst of light tumbled past my head. A sharp hiss made me flinch.

I looked up in time to see Dani preparing to strike another road flare. "Move, Ben."

The cat reared from the glow and raised a paw, torn between its desire to eat and its fear of the unknown. The sulfur and magnesium smoke instigated a series of sharp sneezes. It slapped at the flare with its paw, then backed away.

I grabbed the rope ladder and pulled myself up. The cat coughed and jumped past the light, hitting the water below the stern with a splash. I scrambled over the rail and landed on the deck with a solid thud. Yum Kaax pulled the ladder up behind me.

Dani and the boys gathered and stared. I sat up and tried to orient myself. "Reynard?"

"No." She looked at the hatch, riddled with holes, and I knew.

A loud bang rocked the hull, and I moved to look over the side. The cat jumped again, missing the rail by mere inches. Its claws scraped the fiberglass.

Now agitated, its tail flicked from side to side. Its whiskers drooped. Its pink tongue slipped between its teeth as it watched, appearing no more dangerous or threatening than a housecat watching birds from an open window.

Dani tossed another flare at the ground between its paws. The light bounced into its chest, and the cat arched its back. Perhaps sensing the battle had come to a draw, it turned, then retreated into the scrub in a low crouch.

"I need something to drink. Or my meds." I sat up and reached for my bag. My heart popped in my chest. Anxiety and anticipation collided into a blur of excitement.

She exhaled slowly. "They seem to be gone."

"What's that mean?"

She rolled the bottle to me. "I found it in Reynard's console. He could've taken them. I don't know."

I slammed my fist onto the deck.

"Ben," she said. "I have no reason to lie to you."

"I know." I threw the bottle over the rail and tried to focus my energy into controlling my emotions. But my hands trembled. My face got hot. "I know, I know, I fucking know. If it didn't feel like there was a rat in my gut trying to chew its way out—because that's what it feels like. There's something down there nagging me. Constantly picking away at my insides."

She said, "I know."

"I'm so tired. I need to sleep. I need eight hours without nightmares or any kind of thinking at all." I wanted to be carried home and tucked into bed. And I felt like if I had that, I could wake up and be the person I used to be. Not a new man, but the man I'd been before the drugs and blood and mud. "I need help."

She kissed my hand.

"Then we will find the help you need." She said, "For far too long you've been a man living without a future. I think that needs to change."

"I don't even know what that means."

"You don't have to make any promises, Ben. Don't you understand? Nobody can make promises about tomorrow. Just worry about right now. Do your best to control this moment, because the rest doesn't matter yet."

For the first time in a very long time, she made me believe I could pull the two halves of who I used to be back together. "So what do I have to do?"

"You have to get us back to Cobá before it gets dark. We survived last night because we knew what we were up against."

"And tonight?"

"Tonight, we don't know."

We ran when X heard voices.

The fog amplified the sound of Toussant and his men thrashing through the forest and their radio squelch. They snapped branches and shouted at each other. By now I knew their ranks had swelled to include contractors, the policía, and locals hoping to make a quick buck. X bolted ahead with Yellow Dog, cutting a path through the pools and ruined temple mounds. Yum Kaax stayed with us, helping Dani with Zacnal if she needed a break from carrying him for too long. When we first met the boys, I thought Zacnal was six or seven years old. But after spending a few days with them, and seeing how he clung to Dani, I started to think he was more like four or five.

Our heightened fatigue meant we were stumbling over toppled slabs and hidden roots more frequently. We ignored all but the worst of the cuts and bruises. *A trail of blood....* Below the knees, we were raw and mud-splattered. But the increasing density of temple mounds changed our perspective. One by one, they emerged from the fog like strip malls at the edge of a city. As they grew taller and more ornate, I felt as if I were shrinking and would soon disappear from this world altogether into a labyrinth of tombstones.

Dani put Zacnal down while waiting for me to catch up. The growing chorus of frogs meant I had to get closer before speaking. She said, "I don't see Xtaabay."

"Just wait. He'll realize we aren't behind him and turn around. How you doing?"

"Okay. You?"

"Yeah." I tried to smile at her to show her I'd meant it. "Going to be dark soon."

A light splash came from the fog ahead of us. I pushed the boys and Dani behind me. "X," I said, afraid to say it too loud. "That you?"

Dani pulled me into the scrub that clung to the side of the mound to our left.

"X?" I held my breath while I waited for a response. "What the hell is he thinking?"

Yellow Dog emerged from the fog and yipped. I relaxed a little, but then realized the noise was a bad idea. "Dani, tell Yum Kaax to grab him."

Before Dani could say it, Yum Kaax shouted and tugged at my shirttail. I turned and saw the cat crouched in the water about thirty yards behind us. "Let's go."

We ran on. The dog stood its ground. Hairs on its back raised. Ears low. Teeth bared. Its legs splayed for solid footing on the slippery stone.

"Leave him, Yum Kaax. Let's go." I picked up a softball-sized rock. Without taking the time to aim, I hurled it. The asymmetrical limestone hunk splashed in the water a few yards off-target.

The cat closed in.

Yum Kaax handed me another, not quite the size of a baseball. I pushed him toward Dani and Zacnal and turned for another go.

Leading with my left foot, I held the rock behind my back. Feeling for laces. Seeing the pitch all the way through to the plate. I went into my wind-up. When I released it, I flicked my wrist down.

It spun and dropped before hitting the animal just behind its shoulder. A slow, but otherwise perfect fucking sinker.

The cat flattened its ears and recoiled and tried to paw at its flank. It craned its neck to lick the wound, which didn't bleed.

"Go," I said, pushing Dani ahead of me. As I grabbed Yum Kaax's wrist, I said, "Forget the dog."

But he fell into step behind us. Barking as he ran.

Without a real destination in mind, we pushed north with an eastbound course correction thrown in for good measure. The trees and shrubs grew thicker here, and after thirty or forty yards, I stopped to throw another rock. Before I could release, the cat went into a low crouch and slunk behind a wall.

When I turned to run again, I nearly knocked Dani over.

"Why'd you stop?"

"Listen. X is heading that way."

A wave of bats dropped from the trees. Backlit by sunlight filtered through thinning clouds, they swooped through the fog, gulping the mosquitos that rose from the moisture. Tiny squeals and squeaks penetrated the dusk.

X called again. He'd climbed halfway up a heap of rock and stood, waving his arms. As soon as he saw us, he climbed onto the steps of a small platform with a low building on top. It looked a bit like the one at Dzibilchaltún.

"C'mon down from there." I waved at him to join us. "Dani, ask him to come on down, please."

But X shook his head and gestured.

I went up the steps to get him.

"Ben, be gentle."

"Who says I won't, Dani?"

She followed me up, with Yum Kaax and Zacnal in tow.

Before I could yank X back to reality, he waved a hand, drawing my attention to the vast complex of ruins spread out before us. Lanes and alleys interlocked between platforms, lined up row after row like vast city blocks. High terraces and steeply angled walls.

X crossed his arms. "Cobá," he said, as if he had planned to deliver me to this very spot all along.

"Then why don't I recognize anything?"

She set Zacnal down and joined me at the edge of the platform. The way she shielded her eyes from the sunlight that forced its way through the clouds seemed kind of triumphant and symbolic. She said, "I think these are the outskirts."

"So the village is close?"

"Relatively. But he says we should stay here. There's one way up and it would be easy to keep *balam* away." Before finishing her thought, Dani bent over and scratched a small thorn from her calf. She tapped the blood with her finger and rubbed it against her thumb. For the moment, she seemed somewhere far away. She dipped her hand into a puddle to rinse it. With her jaw held firm, she said, "He thinks we will be safe from the spirits here too."

"What do you think?"

"Do you really want to know what I think?"

"I do. I want to believe what you believe, Dani."

She narrowed her eyes and thought for a moment. Then she touched the cut on her calf and showed me the blood. "When Jesus said *take this cup* and drink he didn't know he was repeating words from a ritual that had been forgotten for ten thousand years. Everything up there is part of Creation. But the Maya fled the Old World and brought those ceremonies with them. Just like the dinosaurs in Conan Doyle's lost world. Time has rediscovered a lost idea. Ben, this is where the earth and the sky meet. Right here."

"So you think Christianity evolved from the same thing this Maya stuff did?"

"The crossroads are in the sky all summer long, right in front of us all. It's why Christ had been crucified on a cross. It's why people look to the sky when they pray. They are searching for answers in the stars. Ancient memories remind them that the story of creation is up there for all to see, but over the years we lost the ability to open those doors for ourselves. But I can do it, Ben. I can open this door again."

"Again?"

"I'd have to be certain, but I think that's what happened at the crossroads. I thought I'd tricked Preston into calling him for me. But now I wonder if Scorpius and the Yaxche were rising just before sunrise that day. If it's true, I am forcing the universe to see me as one of its own."

"What about me? Do I get to be a part of all this?"

"Yes, Ben. We all are. Whether we like it or not." Frogs called from the edges of the quiet pools, much louder now.

"Well, if somebody asked me to rank threats, I'd still put *Día de los Muertos ghosts* third, behind *savage predator* and *narco mercenaries*. But if the ground does open up and spit out its dead tonight I won't be too surprised." After last night and everything that lead up to it, I wondered if that sensation in my gut had been caused by an unrealized fear of what could happen if we found ourselves stuck out here after dark. I said, "What do you think we should do?"

The gesture phased her, and she hesitated before speaking. "All Saints is more important than Christmas or Easter because it is birth and rebirth in one. But the meaning is not the same throughout Mexico. Don Alejandro said that in some regions they just play at visiting the dead. Like how in the Old World it's just another feast day where the dead are bound by contracts that have existed for two thousand years. But here, the people arrived ten or fifteen thousand years earlier. Long before Enheduanna used words to give us power over the monsters. Old World contracts are void here. That's why I believed I was able to do what I did in Mississippi. At the crossroads. I believed if I'd stayed in France or Sarajevo, where the old contracts are still valid, that never would've worked."

Owls hooted as they flew from the uppermost branches to join the bats and mosquitos in the shadowy sky. Casting an apologetic glance at X, she said, "We should try to reach the village."

We ran through the ancient lanes. A maze of old foundations. Blind alleys and dead ends. To the east, howlers began their nighttime calls. Yellow Dog responded with drawn-out howls of his own. Toussant shouted orders to his men, who fell onto us from two sides now from about sixty yards out. As the air cooled, it drew up the moisture that covered the earth. A haze formed, casting the land in a dull yellow pallor.

A series of crashes came from the scrub on the platform above us and from our left. So I pulled Dani north. Tree branches splintered and rock flakes flew when errant rounds hit them. Dani fell to the ground and pushed the boys into the water. Toussant's men couldn't get an angle on us and would have to drop into the maze if they really wanted to finish this.

Toussant tried to stay on the perimeter, firing at us from odd angles. Bits of limestone hit my back and I shielded my eyes with my arm. But that was as close as he got. Two of the federal agents that had stuck by him all day ran west in an attempt to flank. A third directed two more of Toussant's men through the pools behind us.

Somewhere ahead of us, the cat released a territory call. I grabbed Dani's hand. She took Zacnal's. We changed directions and ran back from the edge the maze.

But every time we veered off our original course, an alley ended or an old wall had collapsed and we'd have to backtrack. I'd have to stop and find the sun to reorient myself before moving on. And I knew that wouldn't work after dark.

X shouted and grabbed my shirt to get my attention. A hundred yards back, the cat blocked our exit. It dropped its head and advanced.

Yum Kaax scurried up the wall toward a collapsed structure, a cube that had half-fallen in on itself. I pushed, lifting him toward a root he could use to pull himself up. The cat approached cautiously as Yum Kaax reached down to help X and Zacnal into the crack at the top of the wall. And as Dani began to climb, I let her use my shoulder as a step. From the trees beyond the city, a strange glow rose from the forest floor. Like a flame on a gas stove. The lights made faint halos in the mist. I said, "You see that? Fairy lights. I saw them in the swamp back in Alabama."

"I do. But there's no time."

I held the dog up, and both X and Yum Kaax grabbed him by the scruff of his neck to get him into the chamber without hurting him. Yellow Dog growled and spit, proud and brave even as his legs dangled helplessly beneath him.

The cat picked up its pace. No longer hunting, it trotted ahead in a quick sprint. I jumped and caught the lowest roots on the first attempt. As I tried running up the wall, the foundation crumbled and my handhold pulled free of the rock.

I slipped, gashing my cheek on the stone as I tumbled to the ground. I stood and jumped again, jamming my fingers into a high crack. But my toes couldn't find holds, and I shuffled as I slipped back to the ground.

X grabbed my wrist when I jumped again, giving me a little more leverage. Rocks fell free of the wall and rolled to the ground as I climbed. I jammed my fingers into a nook. The stone ripped the skin away from my knuckles, but the hold allowed me to wedge my toes into a small depression. At the top, I pushed my bag through the narrow crack, then followed. My shirt ripped, and I cut my shoulders and elbows. As I caught my breath, I heard water rushing somewhere below the partial floor. As my eyes adjusted to the semi-darkness, I realized we'd run out of room to maneuver. "Is that the only way in or out?"

"The floor has collapsed in the corner there. We can squeeze through to the back of the wall, but it's a very long fall if we slip. Still, it might be a way out," Dani said. "And there's a window which leads out onto the terrace, but it's too narrow for you."

"Shit." I stood on tiptoes to peek through a gap in the stone and get a bearing on the cat, but my field of view felt too shallow. In the lanes beyond I could see the flashlight and headlamp beams of Toussant and his men. They paralleled each other in adjacent rows. Some edged along the top of the walls farther back. Two appeared at the end of the alley we'd just passed through, walking shoulder-to-shoulder. I said, "They're tightening their perimeter. We can't stay here."

I got onto my knees to get a better vantage and eased toward the crack we'd crawled in through. "The coast looks clear. Maybe Toussant scared it off. We don't want to get trapped in here, so if we—"

The jaguar leapt at the hole from the hollow beneath me, snapping its jaw shut inches from my face. It scratched its way into the chamber. I could smell the old meat on its breath.

I jerked back. Dani stepped in front of me and kicked it square in the nose with her heel. The cat fell back to the ground with a thud.

It twisted itself onto its feet in one reflexive motion. Its skin tensed—a match lighting a thousand fires. With a twitch of its whiskers, it reared and catapulted itself back up the wall toward the crack.

"Ben—" Dani said, tugging my elbow. "It's coming through. Help me."

I held a rock out, ready to smash it in the face, but its eyes drifted to its left. Distracted by something out of frame farther down the ruin. It relaxed and slumped back to the ground.

Yum Kaax shouted. Angry bursts at full volume.

"No," Dani cried. "Get back here."

I pushed myself onto my knees. X struggled through the small hole in the far wall. Yum Kaax had him by the ankle, but X kicked and twisted until he wriggled free. I leapt across the room to squeeze myself through, but my shoulders were too broad. Once outside, X exploded ahead along the thick, high terrace, straight and fast like a shooting star. The cat chased him from the ground below, running parallel to the boy.

Its claws tore at the soil and leaves. Yellow Dog barked and followed X down the wall.

I rushed over to the bigger opening beyond the collapsed floor to climb over the rubble outside. "X," I shouted as I climbed out of the chamber. "Get back here. Dani—tell him."

The cat flew fast to the end of the fortification, barely straining to change direction. Instead, he flicked his tail and twisted, his muscles shimmered and flexed like a batter swinging hard at strike three. The animal left X without any room to run. The boy waved at us to go on.

I got up to my knees and fired a rock at the cat. It missed wide left. The angle was too shallow. Yum Kaax handed me another. It connected with the ledge just shy of the jaguar and ricocheted into the weeds.

A bullet hit the rocks near my feet, and I pushed Yum Kaax toward the trees behind the ruin. A second hit just inches from the first, spraying chips of limestone. Blood flowed over my eyelid to my cheek. I put my sleeve to my forehead and tried to open my eye.

"Ben...." Dani grabbed my ankle and tried to pull me down the back of the ruin. Yum Kaax stood on the ground helping Zacnal.

"I have to get him." I gently blinked the blood out of my eye. "Yum Kaax—you and Dani and Zacnal need to go now."

Toussant dropped into the end of the long alley and approached the platform in a deliberate crouch. I slid back to keep more of the rubble between us and searched for a way to get out to X.

A miracle.

Yellow Dog growled and barked. It stood its ground between X and the jaguar, feigning short charges then retreating.

"X...."

But the cat stopped pacing back and forth, as if tethered by an invisible rope. It calculated and inhaled, and I swear I felt a warm breeze blow past my face. The animal's spring-like spine coiled as it reared, judging the distance between itself and the boy. It backed up and flexed, hesitating just a moment before taking a magnificent leap at the corner of the ledge. It swatted as it landed, knocking the dog down into the scrub on the backside of the ruin. X tried to grab it, lost his balance, and fell down after it.

"No. Jesus, no." I scrambled onto the fortification over the scree. A flurry of gunfire erupted from the ground below.

Zacnal let out a cry. A small trickle of blood appeared at his hairline.

Dani patted his scalp. "He slipped and hit his head."

"He's not hit?"

"No. But we can't stay."

Another round of shots hit the rock inches from my hand. I retreated farther down the backside of the barrier. "X," I shouted.

"Ben, you have to come down here." Dani helped Yum Kaax traverse the bottom talus at the edge of some dense thorns. Zacnal clung to Dani's shirt, crying. "You have to help me, do you understand? I need you."

Toussant and his men rushed toward the terrace. Some shouted in Spanish, some in English. Charging corners in a tight formation. One threw a smoke grenade toward the cat, but the animal remained focused on its prey. The men halved the distance between us in a matter of minutes, their shadows danced in the vapor. *Twenty-five yards.*

"Ben, I need you." Dani released Yum Kaax and held Zacnal against her chest. Yum Kaax scrambled along the ledge, trying to coax the little one to join him.

A burst of light followed by a loud crack broke the stillness. *Flashbang.*

And there sat the jaguar, on top of the wall, its eyes narrowed. Nothing at all like a housecat at the door. White whiskers drooped over a limp pink tongue. I caught only a glimpse of the teeth.

His fire comes from an earlier creation, a time when there were no men to interfere with the doings of the gods. And no roads, or walls.

When animals like this were created, the stars rested flat on the earth's surface. Men sent the animals and stars away. Now we looked at them both and wished that we had them back.

I turned toward the cat and threw another rock. It ignored the miss and peered down at X. Its tail rose as it gently lowered itself to the forest floor. Without a sound.

"Run, X." I turned and tried to find a foothold on the wall below me. Rocks fell beneath my heel. The wall decomposed in larger sections now. Big stones rolled onto me from the wall above. Dani called for me. I pushed her cries away. "Get out of there now."

The cat crouched in the brush.

"Move it."

Its front, right paw raised mid-stride. Silence belied its presence. The vastness of this ancient city echoed distant birds and passing breezes, but made no effort at all to record the sound of the cat's movement. No snapping twigs. Each paw lightly tested the earth before putting any weight on it. Each step followed a pause to give the impression of stillness. Waiting felt like watching a fire burn down, only colder.

I threw another stone.

"Ben," she said, helping Zacnal press a wadded shirt to his head. "I need you to help me."

Toussant and his men shouted to each other from the other side of the wall. Part of the group tried to find a way around. The rest were coming over. A metal clank rattled in the room we'd just vacated. Smoke poured out of the openings. *Tear gas.*

Dani took my hand and pulled me toward the trees.

"Dani...."

"You have to trust me, Ben. Trust something." She said, "This time is different."

I picked up Zacnal and carried him down through the roots, over the pitted limestone. Once we hit the wet earth, we sprinted like tomorrow was a departing plane. Yellow Dog ran alongside us, with its head down. In the low light, I couldn't tell if mud or blood covered its fur.

Toussant stood on the wall and fired two rounds. "I'm going to hang each one of you from a tree and let the vultures pick you apart. Then I'm going to burn every village from here to Houston."

I slowed.

"Don't stop, Ben. Soon it will be too late."

Hanno said, "Then I'm going to West Virginia."

Dani shook her head. "Don't listen."

The old mounds funneled us to the north and to the east, away from dead ends and blind alleys. Toward wide plazas that had been cleared of old growth. Last year's milpa. As the sun dipped below the horizon the sky grew deep blue. Venus appeared in the glow of dusk. A bright pinpoint of luminous hope. The milpa where I'd hit my last home run sat off to the left.

From the dark recesses of the forest I caught more of the faint glow in my periphery. It always hid in the darkest brambles. Secret hollows where even the brightest noon light never penetrated. A ghost image. Like the passing of a shooting star or the fading light trail a firefly emits before sinking into the grass.

Dani said, "Candles."

A volley of gunfire came from the ruined wall. A muzzle flashed. Toussant shouted, and his men opened fire at something behind them.

Dani said, "It's starting."

Some of the mercenaries broke from the group and ran. They called to each other frantically, searching for a way over the wall and out of the forest.

I said, "Don't stop," but she released my hand and turned.

"Hanno, you must listen to me. Go back to the platform with the flowers and incense. You will be safe there. The night will take you if you try to follow." She repeated her words in Spanish for the Federales.

"Dani, we have to go."

"Hanno. This is the only way to save yourself."

"That was what you said to me in Sarajevo right before I was arrested." Toussant waved the contractors to advance. They regrouped and crashed through the brush to the left.

In a voice nearly low enough to be a whisper, she said, "I saved your life there too."

"He's made up his mind, Dani. You did all you could."

She wanted to stay. She wanted to make him believe.

"Dani, we have to go."

Yum Kaax beat a straight trail through the heart of the old city. Leading with confidence. He set the pace and looked over his shoulder to make sure we kept up. None of us wanted to be the one that needed a break. Especially as the dim flames in the forest multiplied and brightened. The moist air created small halos around the lights. *Las luciérnagas*. Shadows ebbed and disappeared as they encircled us. Small white flower petals stuck to the moisture on my arms and face.

One of the mercenaries opened fire into the trees.

Toussant ordered his men to stand their ground, but muffled shouts quickly drowned out his voice. A volley of sustained gunfire from the ruined platform filtered through the haze. Then for a moment, the air remained still, except for a distant knocking sound from deep within the forest.

One of the men threw another flashbang. Temporary daylight showed us a clear path toward the big pyramids and village. Another grenade—either smoke or teargas—popped and hissed. Followed by two more. One of the Federales released about thirty rounds from an AK, shouting and cursing. Once he emptied the clip, he never reloaded.

"Fall back," Toussant shouted, and they chased after us. The beams from their headlamps fell onto our backs, our shadows wobbled on the ground ahead of us as we ran. More smoke grenades were thrown. Fireflies pulsed silently in the trees.

If my legs burned I didn't know it. If my lungs screamed for relief I didn't feel that either. It seemed that the only real sensation was her hand in mine, or I knew I'd lose her forever. If not to Toussant and his revenge, then to the golden glow of whatever crawled through the forest.

If it was going to be death at the end of Toussant's knife, I could imagine the consequences. But I still preferred it to the other.

A signal flare rose overhead with a hiss, darkness slithered around trees and through ruins to escape the falling light. Gunfire cut through the night. Much closer now than before. Leaves and branches hit by bullets spun slow spirals down to earth.

I said, "Dani, if I ever get a chance to do this again, I think I'll get it right. But I'm afraid...." I couldn't say it.

Yum Kaax hollered and pointed toward an island of dull luminance floating in the fog ahead of us. Zacnal ran back and grabbed Dani's free hand.

Villagers crowded onto La Iglesia's wide ceremonial platform. They shouted encouragement once they saw the boys. Haze from cookfires and incense clung to the moist air. At the back, a bonfire burned, a beacon for these lost souls. Thousands of candles had been placed on the stone ledges that encircled the platform. Sugar skulls and marigolds covered the ground around it for a hundred square feet, at least. Platters piled with cut mangoes and pineapples. Gourds and pumpkins. Some of the plates had laminated family photos on them. Men stood at the edge of the platform, clanging pots and yelling into the forest. Dimming flashlight beams cut through the thickening smoke and fog behind us.

There were pillows and blankets, freshly laundered and folded. There were new toys on the pillows. Dolls and picture books. Most of the people had their suitcases with them, as if their exile had been cut short by today's date.

The shots came more deliberately now. Toussant's men opened fire without regard for their targets. They weren't taking anything home with them. Flashbangs and tear gas grenades popped at more frequent intervals. The light reflected off the stones before us.

Dani turned to me and said, "We're close."

Yum Kaax and Zacnal ran ahead, carefully picking a path through the offerings.

"Go with the boys and I'll lead Toussant away." I slowed and ducked behind an old mound. Sweat and blood burned my eyes. I wiped it away with my sleeve, then splashed water onto my arms to cool down.

"You don't have to save anybody but yourself. If you want to live, then you will live. It's that simple." She stood, pulling me to my feet. "It's time to demand something of the universe for all the blood you've given it."

Up ahead, the villagers helped Yum Kaax and Zacnal up through the candles that dripped cascades of beeswax down the sides of the platform. I watched until their tiny silhouettes disappeared into the crowd. A light chant grew from the shadows of the forest, spurring us on. A chorus with real dissonance and depth. The light from the candles wavered between verses. With it, the knocking sound increased.

Dark figures appeared in the dense smoke from behind the platform. Short and thin, limbs distorted by the light. The villagers grew silent as these young girls wearing white huipils passed through the wet smoke. Their faces were smeared with crackled white lime, except for their eye sockets, which were covered with black ash.

I pulled Dani close to me. She said, "In Poland, they pray out loud as they walk through the forests so that the souls of the dead might find comfort."

The song changed as the girls grew closer. It reminded me of the one the X sang on the sacbe. Distorted by the haze, the soundwaves flickered. For fleeting moments, the refrain sounded like trumpets and violins. They ignored us as they trailed past and filled the space behind us, like honey falling from a comb.

"The Innocents," Dani said. She knelt and reached out a hand. "They will make it safe for the dead to return. They are going to the dollhouses, knocking on doors."

Some of them sucked on the sugar skulls. Some of the smaller girls held the hands of some of the taller ones. Some touched Dani as they went by, running fingers gently over her hand or leg. Dani bent low when one tugged on the hem of her dress and into her ear.

When the girl released Dani, she pulled me toward a platform.

I turned to watch them disappear into the dark haze. "What did she say?"

"If we stay out here too long they will think we are dead as well."

We wove our way through the pumpkins and gourds and when we reached La Iglesia's large stone foundation, the men from the village reached down to pull us into the safety of the incense and smoke. Other men drank clear liquor. Some older girls sang the same song the little ones out in the trees did, as if recalling their own time waking the dead. Yellow Dog barked a welcome.

Alters filled with incense offerings of flowers and alcohol sat on each corner of the platform. The people had brought enough food to get through three more nights like this one. Sweet pastries and breads. Boxes of dulces from Mérida or Cancun.

And behind me, muzzles flashed. Grenades exploded. Quiet lightning across a dark sea. Toussant's men fighting for their lives. But the sound never reached me. And because of that, I detached myself from their pain and fear. Dull yellow light pulsed from deep within the cloud, telling a story without exposition. When a smaller spark broke off from the group, I knew it was because one of the men had tried to run.

"It's him." Dani slowed to watch. "Toussant."

And when the light fell to the ground like the most timid of shooting stars, I knew it was because he hadn't succeeded.

There were no words for what happened here. But for once, it wasn't my dream. This one belonged to somebody else.

On the ground below, more of the girls emerged from the forest, a hundred or more by now. Their song grew louder as their ranks swelled.

Dani had remained quiet through it all. I asked if she was okay.

"Nothing could be done," she said. Her eyes looked at something even farther away. "There was no other way."

Zacnal tugged my wrist, pulling me from a deep sleep. The waning stars were foreign to me, but I didn't care now that they faded. The sun had yet to rise, but an inferno grew over the ocean, a signal to all of us here that we must recreate that fire if our souls were to be nourished. At that moment I understood why red represented rebirth— *chaak*. Like the blood that flowed back and forth through the universe.

The crow of a rooster made the new day real. Speaking quickly, almost ranting, Zacnal pointed at the trees and said, "Xtaabay."

Dani sat awake, stoic. Maintaining hope had finally worn her out. She ran her hand over the boy's smooth black hair and sang a quiet lullaby.

I watched her face because I needed a cue from her to know how to respond.

I tried to place my hand on Zacnal's shoulder, but he twisted away. He saw me as a monster. But instead of giving up, I tried again, pushing myself up onto one knee and putting my arm around him.

The gesture made him nervous. His muscles stiffened.

I pulled him toward me gently and said, "I'm sorry."

His hands hung limp at his side.

I held him. "I'm so sorry."

But he didn't understand. He twisted away and said, "Xtaabay."

Warm tears fell down my cheeks, and Zacnal ignored me. He stood at the edge of the platform, up on his toes, and cupped his hands over his mouth. "Xtaabay."

Yum Kaax glared, jaw clenched. He grabbed Zacnal's wrist and gently pulled him back from the edge.

Some of the villagers stirred from their sleep. Propped up on elbows, still wrapped in blankets, watching. The last of the candles dimmed. No birds called in the forest.

Zacnal called out again. I stood next to him and stared into the trees. The morning grew from the shrinking haze of night. I owed him my attention, at least, but didn't know what else to do. So I called for Xtaabay too.

I yelled with my heart. With my soul. I yelled with my tears and my words, with my skin and bones. I cupped my hands to my lips and shouted with everything I had in me.

Dani joined us. Don Alejandro stood at her side. Watching the boys, saying nothing. Old men and women who knew more about loss than I did gathered on the steps.

Yum Kaax stared down at his feet, his idea of what it meant to be a man conflicted with his boyish feelings. I extended my hand.

And when he finally came over, I put my other arm around him. And when he started to cry I hid his face from the others so they wouldn't see. Dani went to him and kissed his forehead. Yum Kaax held onto me even tighter.

I said, "I'm sorry."

Zacnal's voice grew weak and he asked Dani to pick him up. The sudden silence made it seem as if we were back on the boat in a calm sea. I didn't know what else to do.

"I'm so sorry."

A low cough came from the trees to the west. Don Alejandro squinted into the darkness. "Balam."

Some of the men shook their sons from their dreams. One woman helped her mother to her feet. They all gently pushed each other toward the edge of the terrace.

"I see it," Dani said.

Then the cat emerged from the trees to the west of the clearing and repeated the call. Dusky beams of early morning light fell onto its hide. Gold rippled like light on a rushing river. Murmurs and prayers flowed through the crowd. *The congregation.*

But the boys had to finish telling their own stories. Together, they shouted a stream of curses at the animal. Pointing and stomping their feet on the rock. Some of the villagers shushed them. But they had to finish their own stories.

Yum Kaax ground his fist into his palm like he'd seen Dani do a hundred times since we left Chichen Itza. The cat called again, drowning out the boys and their anger. The forest even rumbled. There was no mistaking it.

Yum Kaax threw a rock and then a bottle. Zacnal beat his fist against his knees and shouted curses. Don Alejandro tried to quiet them, but they'd have their say.

The cat lowered its head and shuffled ahead a few steps. Tenuously padding the mud at the edge of the trees. I wanted the act to be an acknowledgement that this era had come to an end. A symbol that we'd have to run no farther. But interpreting signs had never been my strong suit.

As it sniffed the air, a second call came, much closer this time. From the east. Don Alejandro rubbed his jaw. "Xtaabay."

Some of the villagers repeated the word.

Dani said, "It's a homophone."

"What does it mean?"

She wiped a few tears away with the back of her hand, then looked up at me and said, "It means this is true. All of it."

From the eastern edge of the clearing the second cat emerged. Covered in darkness, even as it left the shadows. Its coat, all black, as if the rosettes had grown large enough to consume each other. Only by comparison did I realize how much older the other cat was. When it walked, it treaded softly upon the ground, making barely a mark. This new one moved the earth with each step.

Zacnal pointed, smiling. "Xtaabay."

Dani watched, but the words didn't come so easily to her. She hadn't ever counted on such a moment. With a sudden inhalation, she composed herself and put her glasses on. Without any sort of ceremony or theatrics, she said, "It means that you can go home."

I nodded because I did believe her. And the reality of it all scared me.

She sensed my fear. She took my hands and said, "And I am coming with you."

ELEVEN

February 26, 2010

Hey Dad,

Looks like I'm coming back early. But not home. I have to spend some time at the VA, but you both should be able to visit soon.

But if anybody asks, could you please tell them it was a medical discharge? I hate to have to ask you to lie for me, but I think a medical discharge will be easier to explain than a psychiatric discharge. No matter what my DD-214 says.

See you soon,

Ben

It didn't feel like home until we reached the Outer Banks. The Wright Brothers National Memorial in Kitty Hawk. But the Gulf Stream didn't seem to want to let us go. Then as we tacked toward the Chesapeake, I saw some of the hotels along Virginia Beach. No high-rises. Most were family-run, five stories or less. One summer we vacationed there and I saw a fisherman catch a shark in the surf. He buried it in the sand instead of releasing it back to the ocean because he didn't want anybody to get bitten.

That was the first place I ever saw the ocean. I remember sitting on the beach and looking due east, wondering what waited on the other side.

Because I now know what's over there, I can never get back. That person is gone. Knowing came with consequences. One of them was being changed by the knowledge.

Then I saw the old Cape Henry lighthouse. The clear blue sky turned grey. The wind blew whitecaps across the bay. When one of the crew said we'd crossed into the muddy waters of the Potomac my chest got tight. That water carried a bit of my home with it.

Upstream to Arlington where some of them were buried. To Georgetown where I realized my marriage had failed. Harpers Ferry where Virginia becomes something different. Past Sharpsburg and Antietam. Then a whole lot of nothing up to Cumberland and Westernport. Then even less as the river was reduced to a trickling spring off the backside of Backbone Mountain, just a little north and a little west of my home outside of Davis.

But the stream that ran past my house went west and north to Pittsburgh and Louisville. Less than ten miles from the source of the Potomac by road. The Blackwater flowed into the Cheat, which flowed into the Monongahela, and then the Ohio. Off to St. Louis. New Orleans. That the waters should meet so far from where they were born told me that a life lived linearly is also a life lived rigidly. There wasn't a lot of room to maneuver in the shortest distance between two points.

The trees dozing along the banks clung to the last of their yellows and reds. There were no ruins here. No monkeys or yellow dogs. Just the building glow of dusk-to-dawn lights in the early dark of late fall. Football season, Thanksgiving, and then the first day of hunting season, and wondering how to explain to my pap that I didn't need to shoot a buck this year. Or ever.

Dani said, "The first few days will be the hardest."

"Yeah. Could probably use a few more days to adjust though. Maybe just to get my feet back under me. I feel like I'm waking up from anesthesia."

"You will always need a few more days."

Then the wide Potomac turned into a river I didn't know, and the banks closed in on the boat really fast. *The Occoquan.* I didn't want to go back home. Thinking of the two hour drive down to the Louis A. Johnson VA Medical Center in Clarksburg, West Virginia to wait two more hours just to get Taco Bell or Cracker Barrel before driving two hours back up the mountain. I said, "When all is said and done, what will be different? When I wake up tomorrow—"

"Maybe the universe won't be changed by what we did. Does it only matter if we moved stars?"

"Did we?"

"I suppose that depends on how you see it. Which version do you prefer? The one where you are only a little less sad? Where you are a still a victim of forces beyond your control? Or the one where you challenged the universe and won back your right to live as you pleased?"

232

"I don't know." And I really did have to think about it for a moment. "Whichever is true, I guess."

"You have to see things differently. I can't do it for you."

"Don't be like that."

She crossed her arms and leaned over the rail. We idled slowly in the loose current, drifting toward a slip at the dark edge of the marina. "If you can quiet your mind for a bit you may just see constellations that were once hidden from you. The space between the stars is as important as the stars themselves. Story happens in that space."

I nodded.

"The world is a better place with you in it." She stood and pulled her coat tighter.

"I will try, Dani. I'm going to listen to the doctors and ask for help when I need it."

"I believe you are sincere."

"It's just a lot to take in. It's hard to know what's real. I mean, how am I supposed to explain what happened?"

"You don't. Ever. You can talk about it with me, but you can't ever tell anyone else. Do you understand?"

"I do."

"Good. Because our ride is here."

"What did he say when you called him?"

"Who?"

"My old man."

"I didn't call your father."

"Katy? Which is fine. Not really in the mood for Preston though."

She waved to a man on the dock. Wrapped in a puffy down jacket, face in shadow. As we moored, he pulled back his hood. I saw the black Sixers cap. On his feet, old school Jordans.

"Collins," he said. His voice told me it was true. "How you doing, old man?"

"X...."

ACKNOWLEDGEMENTS

The world was a different place for me back in 1998. Heidi and I had just gotten married and we decided to let a coin toss determine what our life together would look like once we had those rings on our fingers. If it were heads, we'd go to grad school and study Maya archaeology. If it were tails, we'd go to Orlando and work for The Mouse.

This book was born in the fall of that year, in our little apartment just off International Drive, less than five miles from Disney property. Saying goodbye to the Appalachians, whitewater rafting, and my identity had been harder than I ever could've imagined. When I traded my mountains for beaches, I felt like I'd given the best part of myself away.

Then I started typing.

The first version of this book involved a young Henry Collins wandering the mean streets of Orlando, distraught and depressed after a pair of drownings he wrongfully took responsibility for made him a pariah back home. After a rough night on a beach near Mosquito Lagoon on the Canaveral National Seashore, he decided to end it all and fled to Yucatán where he met a pair of boys named Trejo and Paco, their little yellow dog, and a surly jaguar. And instead of a shallow grave he found the will to live. Except the wild, ancient land had other ideas and refused to let him return home without a fight.

Heidi was the only other person to have seen that version of the book.

Before beginning grad school at Seton Hill I gave it another unsuccessful go. Then I took Henry and put him in my thesis, the novel that would eventually become *Hellbender,* and this book went away for a very long time.

It was only after meeting the amazing Jennifer Barnes and John Edward Lawson at Raw Dog Screaming Press and completing *Revelations* that I realized there was something special in here, and decided to revisit this beautiful little idea I'd once had. As always, I owe a tremendous debt of gratitude to Mike Rega Jr. for his subtle advice and guidance. (By now you should know I am always paying attention.) What I didn't know when I decided to reopen this old file was how hard it would be to tease something true out of what I'd written so long ago, and the process took more out of me than anything I'd ever attempted up to this point. It made me quit. It made me angry. It made me wonder if I really wanted to write anymore.

When I finished it the first time, I dedicated it to Heidi with the words you'll see below. And each time I thought I'd truly finished it, I added the date.

But this is the last time. Some 5329 days after the first draft, which was some 1250 days after that weird Florida afternoon when I sat down at that old typewriter with an idea to turn my whitewater rafting stories into a book. But my feelings are as true now as they were then, and I am happy to see that I got this bit right the first time.

For Heidi,
who inspired me to pick up a pen
and inspired me to do something worth writing about
04.21.2002
04.28.2005
03.05.2015

ABOUT THE AUTHOR

Jason Jack Miller knows it's silly to hold onto the Bohemian ideals of literature, music, and love above all else. But he doesn't care.

His own adventures paddling wild mountain rivers and playing Pearl Jam covers for less-than-enthusiastic crowds inspired his Murder Ballads and Whiskey Series. He wrote Hellbender as a student in Seton Hill University's prestigious Writing Popular Fiction program, where he is now a mentor and adjunct instructor. The novel won the Arthur J. Rooney Award for Fiction, the MacLaughlin Scholarship, and was a finalist for the Appalachian Writers Association Book of the Year Award.

When Jason isn't writing, he's with Heidi, his wife, either in Paris, perusing the bouquuinestes or in the Cinque Terre trying to taste ALL of the focaccia. And for the rest of the year he plays the role of Mr. Miller, mild-mannered science teacher at Uniontown Area High School. Follow him on Twitter and Instagram @jasonjackmiller or email him at jasonjackmiller@gmail.com.